D0247189

Life is sweet with

Jenny

COLGAN

NEWHAM LIBRARIES

90800100248418

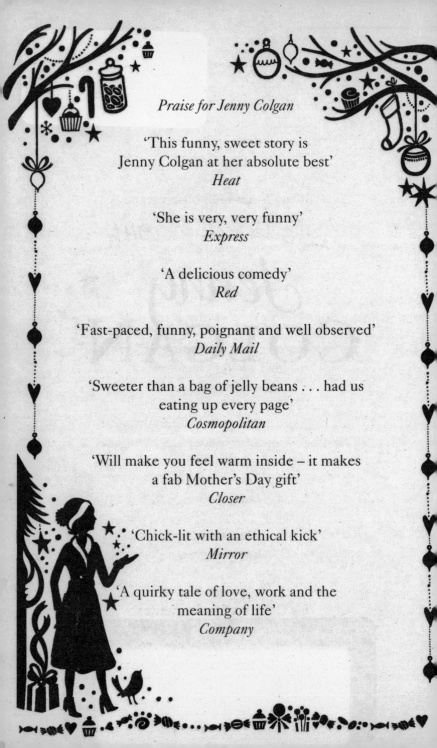

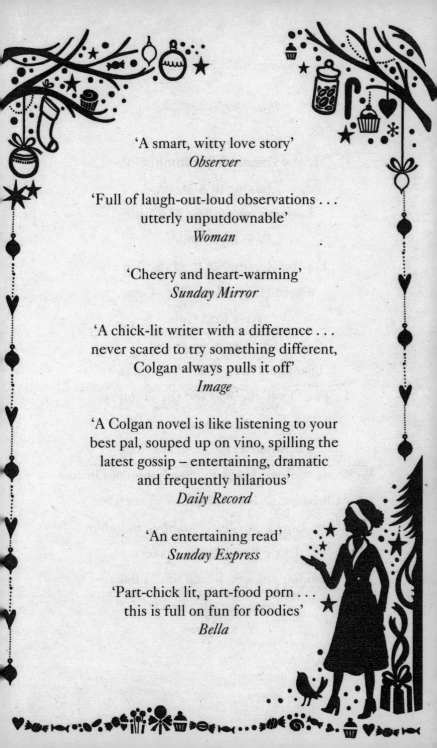

'A smart, witty love story'
Observer

'Full of laugh-out-loud observations . . .
utterly unputdownable'
Woman

'Cheery and heart-warming'
Sunday Mirror

'A chick-lit writer with a difference . . .
never scared to try something different,
Colgan always pulls it off'
Image

'A Colgan novel is like listening to your
best pal, souped up on vino, spilling the
latest gossip – entertaining, dramatic
and frequently hilarious'
Daily Record

'An entertaining read'
Sunday Express

'Part-chick lit, part-food porn . . .
this is full on fun for foodies'
Bella

Also by Jenny Colgan

Amanda's Wedding

Talking to Addison

Looking for Andrew McCarthy

Working Wonders

Do You Remember the First Time?

Where Have All the Boys Gone?

West End Girls

Operation Sunshine

Diamonds Are a Girl's Best Friend

The Good, the Bad and the Dumped

Meet Me at the Cupcake Café

Christmas at the Cupcake Café

Welcome to Rosie Hopkins' Sweetshop of Dreams

Christmas at Rosie Hopkins' Sweetshop

The Loveliest Chocolate Shop in Paris

Little Beach Street Bakery

Summer at Little Beach Street Bakery

Jenny COLGAN

the Christmas Surprise

sphere

SPHERE

First published in Great Britain in 2014 by Sphere
This edition published in 2015 by Sphere

1 3 5 7 9 10 8 6 4 2

A CIP catalogue record for this book
is available from the British Library.

ISBN 978-0-7515-5397-0

Typeset in Caslon by M Rules
Printed and bound in Great Britain by
Clays Ltd, St Ives plc

Papers used by Sphere are from well-managed forests
and other responsible sources.

MIX
Paper from
responsible sources
FSC
www.fsc.org FSC® C104740

Sphere
An imprint of
Little, Brown Book Group
Carmelite House
50 Victoria Embankment
London EC4Y 0DZ

An Hachette UK Company
www.hachette.co.uk

www.littlebrown.co.uk

Dedicated to the memory of Ali Gunn,
1968–2014

Introduction

Okay, so normally I think, oh, introductions, these things are FULL of spoilers, and generally skip them.

But whether you are a complete newbie to the world of Rosie Hopkins, or read the last one a year ago, I would say, honestly, read this bit. I won't spoil a thing, and it might well be really useful.

Now, I love a series of books as much as the next person. I grew up slavishly devoted to Malory Towers, the Chalet School, the Dark is Rising and the Chronicles of Narnia, and as an adult I am equally enamoured of Shopaholic, Game of Thrones, Rebus and so on.

BUT. There is a problem writing books in a series. First of all, can people come straight in without having read the earlier ones? (For example, you're always going to have a good time with *In the Fifth at Malory Towers*, whereas I'd really really recommend you start with the very first of the Gormenghast trilogy, and even after that concentrate quite hard.)

And secondly, how do you quickly catch up when you *have* read the others? (Actually, Jen, believe it or not we do actually have other things to do in our lives apart from memorise the names and whereabouts of every single character in your novels. Seriously? You do? ☺)

So, aha! Here is something I really hope will help: my as-yet-unpatented Colgan OmniSequeliser. Glance down the bold headings, and all your questions will be, hopefully, anticipated and answered, whether you're a total newbie or you've read one or both of the previous novels (if you're reading all three over a big weekend splurge, I grant you permission to skip this bit).

SO. There is a summary of important bits, a full character list, a family tree, a map, and everything else I can think of so that I don't spoil your enjoyment of the book by having a character walk by and casually dump tons of exposition on you like a dog having a spew. You know the kind of thing I mean: 'Hi, Stephen, how are you?' 'Well I'm fine, thanks, after my terrible flashbacks to my landmine accident in Africa, triggered by that lorry crash at the school that gravely injured nine-year-old Edison, who's also making a good recovery, thank you so much. How are you?' I'm going to try very hard not to do that.

Then I am off to market the Colgan OmniSequeliser to *Dragons' Den*. Except that my favourite was sexy stern American Doug with the glasses, and he doesn't do it any more. I don't like Duncan, he's creepy.

Okay, time to put on my deep, dooming voice: PREVIOUSLY, in the world of ROSIE HOPKINS . . .

Who are Rosie and Stephen?

Rosie Hopkins was an auxiliary nurse working in London and living with her boyfriend Gerard when she had to move to a tiny village in Derbyshire to look after her ageing great-aunt Lilian.

She was dreading it to begin with and thought she'd stay for five minutes, but she fell in love with the little town – and with Stephen, the son of the local posh family. He was shut up in the desolate Peak House, nursing a wound he'd received when he'd been working as a teacher in Africa for Médecins Sans Frontières (his father had wanted him to join the army, but he wouldn't). He'd been blown up by a landmine that killed the two small boys he was with. The guilt had haunted him ever since. Meeting Rosie helped to lift him out of this, but it is still, sometimes, a struggle.

His mother, Lady Lipton, has never quite forgiven him

for following his vocation into teaching. His father died whilst Stephen was in hospital overseas; she knows she shouldn't blame Stephen for this, but she does, a little.

Rosie, on the other hand, has flourished in Lipton. She has revitalised the sweetshop and turned it into a magnet for town gossip and treats, and met many good and true friends in the little community (she has also made one or two enemies, including Roy Blaine, the evil town dentist). She still cannot get used to country ways, but she loves Stephen and Lilian so much, she reckons this probably won't matter.

Rosie and Stephen got engaged at Christmas – yay!

What's Lilian's story?

Lilian was born in the little cottage in Lipton that Rosie now lives in, and spent all her life there until very recently, when she moved to a really nice and very expensive old people's home.

When she was a teenager in the war, she fell madly in love with a local boy, Henry Carr. Their short but serious romance was blighted when they found out he'd accidentally got another girl – Ida Delia, Lilian's erstwhile best friend – pregnant before he and Lilian got together. Being Henry, he did the right thing and married Ida Delia, a marriage that was not happy, before he was lost in the war. Lilian mourned him all her life. That marriage produced a daughter, Dorothy Isitt, who still lives in the village.

Amazingly, last year, Henry was found: he had suffered head injuries and amnesia, and had started a new life on the other side of the dales. He and Lilian were reunited at the very end of his life, which Lilian mostly thinks is better than nothing.

Who lives where?

Lady Lipton lives in the huge crumbling Lipton Hall, which costs a fortune and is falling down. Stephen used to live in a tied house, Peak House, which belongs to his mother's estate and is a formidable and draughty place on top of the downs. Now, however, he has moved in with Rosie. Rosie lives in Lilian's tiny but cosy cottage, right next door to the sweetshop, and Lilian has moved to the old folk's home.

Who else is in their families?

Well I'm glad you asked. There's Angie, Rosie's warmhearted, flirty mother, who brought Rosie and her brother Pip up single-handedly. She now lives with Pip and his wife Desleigh and their three children, Shane, Kelly and Meridian, in sunny Australia, and wishes Rosie lived there too.

Stephen's mother is Lady Lipton, feared doyenne of the town, who lives alone at Lipton Hall. She is snobby, difficult and looks down on Rosie. She does love Stephen really, but their relationship can be fractious. Stephen also has an elder sister called Pamela, who lives in America.

And who are their friends?

Rosie's best friend in Lipton – and occasional colleague – is Moray, the handsome GP, who is still keeping his boyfriend under wraps, fearing village gossip more than is actually necessary. Moray and Stephen fell out when Moray didn't want to go to Africa to work with him. They are (occasionally grudging) friends again because they both care about Rosie. Rosie sometimes uses her nursing experience to help Moray out in a crisis.

Tina works in the sweetshop with Rosie, and is engaged to the lovely local farmhand, Jake. They are getting married this year too, and Tina is wildly overexcited about it. She has twins, Kent and Emily, from a previous relationship. Then there is Edison, a very literal nine-year-old who lives with his New Age parents and baby sister Marie in a cottage in the woods. Last year he was involved in a terrible accident, but he is healing well.

How much time has passed?

Rosie moved to Lipton two years ago, and this book opens after Christmas, when Stephen proposed to her. She has been pretty much on cloud nine ever since.

So, now you are ready for *The Christmas Surprise*! But if there is anything you feel I haven't covered, tweet me right now on @jennycolgan and I'll endeavour to get back to you at full speed.

My very very warmest wishes to you and yours over this festive season.

Jenny xxx

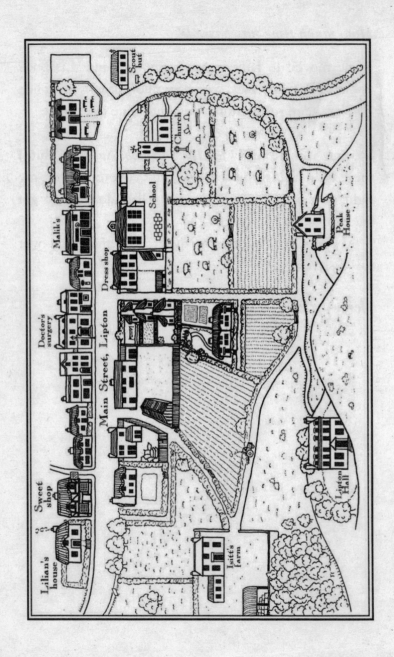

Scout hut

Church

School

Malik's

Dress shop

Doctor's surgery

Main Street, Lipton

Peak House

Sweet shop

Lilian's house

Isitt's farm

Lipton Hall

The Hopkins Family

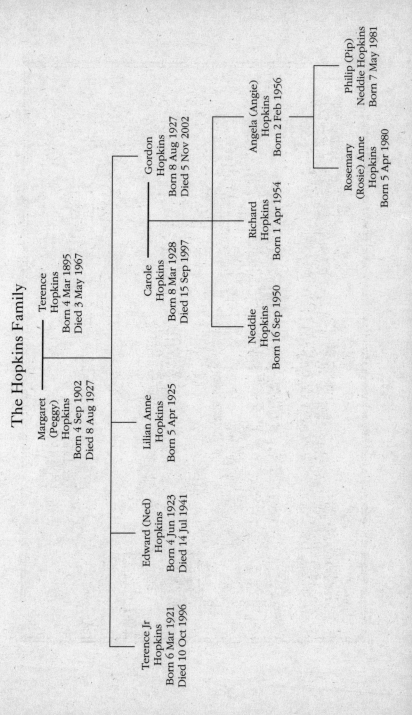

1   *To everything there is a season, and a time to*
    every purpose under the heaven:
2   *a time to be born, and a time to die; a time to*
    plant, and a time to pluck up that which is
    planted;
3   *a time to kill, and a time to heal; a time to*
    break down, and a time to build up;
4   *a time to weep, and a time to laugh; a time to*
    mourn, and a time to dance;
5   *a time to cast away stones, and a time to*
    gather stones together; a time to embrace, and a
    time to refrain from embracing;
6   *a time to get, and a time to lose; a time to keep,*
    and a time to cast away;
7   *a time to rend, and a time to sew; a time to*
    keep silence, and a time to speak;
8   *a time to love, and a time to hate; a time of*
    war, and a time of peace.

Ecclesiastes 1-8, King James

I will honour Christmas in my heart, and try
to keep it all the year.

Charles Dickens, *A Christmas Carol*

Chapter One

Christmas was over. The baubles had been carefully wrapped, the tinsel packed up, the great tree that stood in the middle of the little village of Lipton, nestled amongst the rolling Derbyshire hills, taken down, its hundreds of white lights coiled away and stored in the old timbered attic of the Red Lion pub.

The snow was still there; a cold Christmas had given way to an even colder January. At the Rosebury home where eighty-seven-year-old Lilian Hopkins lived, the snow made all outdoor walks and activities moot. Most of the residents played chess, knitted furiously, arthritis allowing, or watched television. Since the death of her erstwhile boyfriend Henry Carr on Christmas Eve, Lilian mostly looked out of the window, a small smile occasionally passing across her face. Henry had been the love of her life, her childhood sweetheart from the war years, who had comforted her when her brother Neddie had been killed at the Front; who had held her hand and made plans for the future after he was called up, who had kissed her fiercely down behind the churchyard where the wild roses grew. He had been her first and only love; her old, neat face and tidy bobbed hair never betrayed the depth of feeling that had once burned there.

Meeting Henry again had been bittersweet: astonishing, wonderful and a strong reminder of time passed that could not be found again. But she had held his hand and been with him to the very end, and that was more, she knew, than many could say of the love of their life.

Further down in the village, the little mullioned windows of the sweetshop were cheerily lit up against the dark and cold, the boiled sweets in the window display glinting and glowing, the bell above the shop tinging every time someone else gave up on their New Year's resolution and slipped inside for some warming peppermint creams, or marshmallows to float in hot chocolate.

And in the tiny back room of the little sweetshop, in the little sink installed there for washing hands and making tea, Rosie Hopkins was being violently sick.

It had been, at least for Rosie and her boyfriend Stephen, the most wonderful Christmas ever. Stephen had proposed on Christmas Day. There had been tearful goodbyes to Rosie's family, who were visiting from Australia, all promising to be back for the wedding, or at the very least insisting that their honeymoon should take place in Oz, which had made Rosie smile. It was hard to imagine Stephen lying on a beach taking it easy with a beer. Stephen was more of a striding about the moors with a stick type person, Mr Dog lolloping ridiculously by his side (he was a tiny mongrel who always seemed to make people laugh. Rosie and Stephen were both very sensitive about people making fun of him).

They had gone back to work, Rosie to the sweetshop of course, which rang with the cheerful noise of children with Christmas money to spend, and Stephen back to teaching at the local primary school, which had two classes in its nicely restored building.

The year was bright and crisp in their hands, freshly minted, and they were too, everyone so excited by their news and enquiring into their plans for the wedding and the future.

Tina, Rosie's colleague at the shop, who was also engaged, was delighted at their news. Rosie apologised for upstaging her, and Tina said, don't be ridiculous, they were going for a hotel wedding, whereas presumably Rosie would be after the full massive affair in the big house,

Stephen being gentry and everything, and Rosie had shivered slightly and thought that Stephen would hate that. His mother was something of a snob and very concerned about lineage, and she would want to invite everyone in the surrounding counties who was in Debrett's. Rosie found the whole thing madly intimidating, being particularly concerned that they'd make her wear family jewels that she would lose or break or something. The idea of that many people looking at her filled her with nerves anyway. She and Tina were very different.

Stephen hadn't really mentioned the wedding itself, beyond referring to her as 'the wife' – not that she had ever thought he was the type of guy who would have a lot of input into invitation design and all that – and she occasionally fantasised about them just slipping off somewhere really quiet and doing it, just the two of them, at Gretna Green or a little room somewhere.

Then she thought of her mother's face – and, worse, her great-aunt Lilian's – if they tried to slope off somewhere, and how her nieces would react to her retraction of the fiercely extracted promise that they could be bridesmaids (although Meridian, who was three and something of a tomboy, had made her agree that she could be a boy bridesmaid, and Rosie had decided to attempt something along the lines of kilts). Well, they would have to put on some sort of a do. But for now she was revelling in the very sense of it, of being newly affianced, of waking up every day next to the man she loved so much and still couldn't quite believe was hers. Let the snow fall, she thought. Everything in its own time.

That, of course, was before she started throwing up in the sink.

Tina, on the other hand, was having so much fun selecting stationery, choosing flowers and colour schemes and favours, and censoring speeches. Her wedding would be held at the Hyacinth, the local fancy golf hotel that served overpriced non-ironic prawn cocktail and usually had groups of loud red-faced men propping up the corner of the bar and complaining about foreigners. She was having a sit-down dinner for a hundred in the main banqueting hall, with a black and white theme for the guests, a choreographed first dance (Rosie couldn't imagine what her charming but straightforward fiancé Jake would think of that) and just about every girl in the village as a bridesmaid.

But Rosie did love twirling the beautiful ring around her finger (they'd had it resized to fit; it was extremely old and belonged to the slenderer fingers of an earlier age, or, Rosie imagined Stephen's mother thought, a more refined breeding) and caressing the dull patina on the gold, which could not dim the deep shine of the four stones, so fashionable in their day, that went with the colour of her eyes. It was by far and away the most valuable thing she had ever owned, and she was terrified of losing it. Stephen laughed when he saw her constantly fiddling with it.

'It's like you've never had any jewellery,' he said, and Rosie had looked at him and blinked and said, well, no, she hadn't, nurses weren't really allowed to wear it, and he'd pulled her close and said he wanted to buy her all the jewellery in the world, and she reminded him that they didn't have any money and he'd laughed and said, oh no, they didn't, would fish and chips do for now, and she'd said, yes that would be fine.

So even despite the odd spewing moment, it took Rosie a couple of months to notice that she was feeling a little peculiar most of the time. She assumed it was just excitement at the way their lives were going, and even then she was busy in the shop and assumed it was nothing, and she couldn't possibly go to Malik's shop – the local Spar, which sold everything – and buy a pregnancy test because it would be round the village at the speed of light and everyone already had more than enough interest in their lives together, thank you very much, so she'd have to wait to drive into Carningford, the nearest large town, AND she hadn't mentioned it to Stephen in case he got unnecessarily worked up (proposing to her was, she sensed, probably enough of a gigantic upheaval in his life for one year).

It was late February when she snuck away one Monday morning, telling Tina she was going to check out some new Parma violets, and drove to Carningford at top speed. Then when she left the chemist's, with shaking hands, she realised that she couldn't wait after all and had to go to the horrible toilets in the shopping centre that were full of teenage girls shouting. She wondered how many people before her had done exactly the same thing, how many people had had their lives changed in this exact space simply because it was close to the chemist, and she looked at it and didn't understand what it meant, and read the instructions again and still didn't understand, and then finally accepted that there were two lines, clear as day, one straight, one a little wobbly; one was her and one was Stephen, and together they meant . . .

'Oh my God,' Rosie said, dropping down onto the loo seat. 'Oh my God.'

In the next booth over, a couple of teenage girls were talking loudly in a strange accent that was half local, half an attempt at a kind of London slang.

'So I says to him, awriight . . . '

Rosie fumbled for her phone and thought she was going to drop it straight down the loo. She wanted to wash her hands, but oh, she was here now, and what was she going to do anyway, she couldn't call outside.

7

'So I says to her, you backs off RAGHT NOW, innit . . .'

Stephen didn't keep his phone on in class; she'd have to call the office. She tried to keep her voice steady when Carmel, the school secretary, answered, although it was considered very odd to call a teacher in the middle of the day.

'You want Stephen? Is everything all right?'

Rosie thought again how, even though she didn't miss London very often, she had rather enjoyed its anonymity.

'Fine!' she trilled. 'All fine! Great, in fact! Just a little thing . . .'

'Because you know it's choir and he's a bit busy . . .'

'I'll be two seconds,' lied Rosie.

'I'sa gonna duff you up,' said the voice loudly from the next cubicle.

There was a silence.

'I'll just get him,' said Carmel.

Rosie rolled her eyes, her heart hammering in her chest.

'What's up?' said Stephen, when he finally got to the phone. 'Carmel says you're being duffed up!'

'She NEVAH,' came the voice.

'Uh, no,' said Rosie. A mucky toilet in a horrible going-downhill shopping centre with two screeching fifteen-year-olds – a reminder of what awaited them one day – wasn't exactly how she'd dreamt of this moment.

'Um, it's something else.'

'Good.'

'So AH says, YOU UP THE DUFF?'

'Who are you with?' said Stephen.

Rosie closed her eyes.

'Nobody. But listen . . .'

'An' SHE says, SO WHAT IF I AM, an I'm like, SLAG . . .'

'I'm up the duff,' said Rosie.

'Wha'?' said the girls next door.

'Mr Lakeman, I need go toilet, please,' came a small voice from Stephen's end.

'What?' said Stephen, who thought that saying 'pardon' was common.

'Um. Uh.' Rosie realised she was about to burst into tears.

'Um, yes,' said Stephen desperately.

'Yes?'

'No, I'm talking to Clover Lumb. I mean, yes?'

'UH,' said Rosie. Her hand was shaking as she held up the little stick. 'Yes. I mean. I think so. No. Definitely. Yes. YES.'

There was a long pause.

'Oh my goodness,' said Stephen. 'Miss Hopkins, you do not mess about.'

Rosie choked, half laughing, half crying.

'Plus, I was rather under the impression that I'd already sealed the deal.'

'That's right, I did it all by myself.'

Stephen let out a short. barking laugh.

'Oh Lord, I guess it was always going to happen sooner or later.'

'I did tell you we should get central heating.'

'This really is quite a lot sooner, though, isn't it?'

For a moment Rosie forgot all about the horrible toilet, the fact that it was freezing, the obviously earwigging girls next door, the whole new world that had suddenly flung itself open in her face. Despite everything to come, it was, as it so often was, just her and Stephen, in their little bubble, just the two of them, while the rest of the world faded away to white noise.

'BAD sooner?'

She could hear the warm smile in his voice, and everything around her suddenly became warmer too.

'Lord, yes. Awful. You can tell my bloody mother.'

'Well you can tell Lilian.'

They both thought for a second about Rosie's beloved great-aunt.

'No, we can tell her together,' said Stephen eventually. 'Anyway, order a lemonade in the Red Lion and it'll be common knowledge all over town in about fifteen seconds.'

The two girls were pretending to do their make-up at the counter when Rosie emerged from the cubicle, purple in the face. They looked at her shyly.

'Uh, congratulations,' said the first one, who had been the loudest. Her normal voice was back. Rosie couldn't help smiling.

'You guys are the only people who know,' she said. 'Whoa, that's the weirdest thing.'

She breezed home again, hugging the secret close to her all day, letting it keep her warm in the cold. Stephen called again at lunchtime, reporting that he had done absolutely nothing useful with fractions but in the end had just got the children to practise their number bonds.

'Are you all right?' he said. 'How far gone are you? Do you need to sit down? Are you feeling sick?'

'No,' Rosie said, having vanished into the tiny back room of the sweetshop. It was little more than a sink and a kettle, and she never shut the door, but today she did. If Tina thought there was anything odd about that, she didn't mention it. 'I feel completely fine. Except, you know ... OH MY GOD! OH MY GOD!'

At the other end of the phone, Stephen nodded.

'Also,' he said cheerfully, 'your knockers are probably going to get huge.'

Actually, they were feeling a bit swollen, Rosie realised. She'd put it down to post-Christmas over-indulgence, which, she realised, probably also explained a couple of nights when they weren't as careful as they might have been.

'Seriously, is that all you're thinking about?'

'That is the only thing I can think about that isn't absolutely terrifying.'

'Well you didn't want Mr Dog ... Oh my God, how are we going to break it to Mr Dog?'

'I think *your dog*...' Stephen hated the name Mr Dog and thought he should be called something sensible, like Archie or Rex, 'could do with being reminded once in a while that he's just an animal. I don't think it will be bad for him at all.'

'Hmm,' said Rosie. 'Oh Lord. The timing is awful. Goodness, this is all going to be awful.'

There was a pause. Stephen wanted to pull her into his arms and bury his face in her hair. He resisted the urge to run straight out of school and up the road.

'Oh darling, do you really think that?' he said instead.

'No,' said Rosie. 'I'm just panicking.'

'Well it isn't going to be awful. It's going to be ours, and it will be wonderful, and full of love. And dental cavities.'

'Ha,' said Rosie. Then, quietly, 'I love you.'

'I love you too,' said Stephen. 'Right, I have to go, there's some kind of spilled milk catastrophe. Little buggers...' he paused, 'with whom I am soon going to have masses of tolerance and patience.'

Rosie smiled and put the phone down, then burst

into tears. Come to think about it, she had been very emotional recently, but everyone had put that down to the engagement.

Okay. They would talk about it tonight, but the most important thing was not to tell people. When was it, twelve weeks you could mention it? Right. Well, she couldn't be more than five or six, not really. She'd have to get online and check it out. But that meant they had lots of time to get used to it and calm down and start to prepare themselves and ... Oh, to have Stephen's baby! If it were a boy, would it be tall and handsome? And a bit moody? And if it was a girl, would his heart turn over? Would he collapse with joy and be madly in love with her and spoil her to bits?

Tina knocked on the door to come and wash up teacups and Rosie tried to pull herself together. Right. She was going to be calm, collected, professional. No one would suspect a thing, not until they'd got everything sorted out. It would be cool.

'Hey,' said Tina pleasantly. 'You okay?'

'I'M HAVING A BABY!!!!!!!!!!!!!'

In the end, Tina decided to shut up shop for twenty minutes, given that the post-lunch crowd had dropped and it wouldn't really kick off again till the school came out, when it went crazy. She put up the ancient 'Back in

Ten Minutes' sign, which reminded Rosie that it was a Wednesday and Lilian still grumbled that they didn't have half-day closing. She refused to visit the shop on Wednesday afternoons, even when Rosie pointed out that if they didn't open six full days, they'd all starve.

The cottage was right next door to the shop. The rooms were small and the ceilings were low, but it was cosy, cluttered with Lilian's old floral coverings and her horse brasses polished to a high shine. On the wooden mantelpiece were the silver-framed photographs of Lilian as the beautiful young woman she'd been, and a picture of her young man, Henry Carr, whom she had loved as a teenager and believed killed in the war until he had re-entered their lives the year before. Having been blown up and suffered brain damage, he had built another life for himself until fate had thrown him in the way of the sweetshop. His family in Harrogate had very kindly made up a box of snapshots for Lilian, who treasured it above all other things. A particularly handsome shot of him laughing at someone off camera in his khaki uniform, marked 'Africa 1942', had pride of place.

Downstairs there was Lilian's bedroom, which she still used when she stayed over from the nursing home; a tiny doll's-house kitchen with exquisite china hanging from hooks; and a bathroom. Upstairs, in a loft conversion that could only be reached by pulling down a set of steps from the ceiling, was the beautiful, austere white-painted bedroom Rosie and Stephen shared, with its views both ways: to the rolling hills on the north side of Lipton; and across Lilian's lovingly tended kitchen garden, and the bower gate at the end with its rose trellis, to the fields beyond.

Rosie loved this tiny house – they both did, otherwise they would have lived in Stephen's chilly Georgian stone house at the top of the hills, a place Rosie always associated with freezing winds and the lonely state she had found Stephen in the first time she'd ever met him. Plus, it wasn't technically theirs: it belonged to the estate, which belonged to Stephen's mother, and neither of them liked the idea of living under her thumb like that.

But the cottage, she thought, wasn't very practical now. Goodness knows how Lilian – however comfortably ensconced at her very nice old people's home – would react to her bedroom being turned into a nursery, and as for when the little one started crawling up the stairs ... Rosie blinked as Tina brought her a cup of tea.

'It's rosehip,' said Tina. 'I guess you're off the caffeine now.'

'Oh yes,' said Rosie. 'Oh my God, I hadn't even got round to all that stuff. No shellfish ... no more visiting the great sushi bars of Lipton.'

This went straight over Tina's head; she had been born and raised in the village and had relatively little interest in what went on elsewhere.

'No booze … hmm.' Rosie thought with some guilt about the fizz they'd consumed at New Year. 'I have had a bit, though.'

'Don't be daft,' said Tina. 'So has about a hundred per cent of everyone. Half the babies on earth wouldn't have been conceived if their parents hadn't got off their box.'

'Yes, I suppose,' said Rosie. 'Cor.'

Tina shook her head.

'It's lovely news, but I'm so sorry.'

'Why?'

Tina's head took on a pitying tilt.

'Well, you know … you'll have to postpone the wedding.'

Rosie blinked twice.

'That hadn't even occurred to me,' she said, thinking about all the fretting she'd been doing about the seating plan, getting her relatives over, coping with Stephen's horrid posh friends, dealing with her new mother-in-law. 'Yay!' she added.

She texted this news to Stephen. *WOO HOO!* came a text back about thirty seconds later. She giggled.

'I think he's happier putting off the marriage than he is about the baby,' she said to Tina, who looked totally scandalised. 'And it will give me loads of time to dedicate to yours,' she went on quickly. 'I can help you out more.'

Tina brightened immediately. 'Oh yes,' she said. 'And everyone will think mine was the best.'

'Yours was always going to be the best,' said Rosie. 'Crumbs, believe me, I'd got about as far as bridesmaids in kilts.'

They reopened for the post-school rush, Rosie slightly calmed down by Tina's good sense about babies – and she should know, she'd had twins at twenty-five, had had to raise them on her own, and they were turning out fantastic.

'Of course, the actual having of them isn't that nice,' said Tina, but Rosie made a dismissive gesture. That was at least eight months away. Plenty of time to worry about it later.

The sweetshop filled up with little faces beaming cheerfully as they made their choice from the vast array on the shelves that covered the walls of the shop, with its mullioned windows, its large glass jars, its golden bell, and the old adverts on the walls for Cadbury's and Fry's.

Today Ethan wanted flying saucers, and as he was the toughest kid in the school, everyone else immediately started to clamour for those too. The girls, including Tina's daughter Emily, were going through a candy necklace phase, which made Tina grimace, as it

17

left red and orange saliva marks on absolutely everything, plus there was an odd thing going on amongst the elder girls where they would all buy one and then compete to be the last to eat it. Rosie made a mental note to stop stocking them; it wasn't good for them. Maud the doctor's receptionist popped in for chocolates, and when Rosie looked enquiringly at her – normally she bought them at the weekend so she could watch her reality voting shows with a box by her side – she made a face and said, 'Don't look at me like that. It's February and still full of snow. I'm sick of it. Chocolate will help. I'm hibernating until the sun comes out again. It's like Narnia: always winter and never Christmas.'

Oddly, Rosie had got so used to the weather that she had barely noticed that snow had been falling for three months. She didn't really expect it to finish before April anyway.

'Oh Maud,' she said.

'It's all right for you,' said Maud. 'All exciting, newly engaged, second winter in the countryside. Try your forty-eighth. All I want is to be on a yacht in the Caribbean. Is that seriously too much to ask?'

'You could try asking Hye.'

There was a pause, then they both laughed uproariously at the idea of getting the greedy, selfish head of the practice to do anything as generous as that, even though the rural GPs all made a good living.

'Thanks, Rosie,' said Maud. 'You've cheered me up already. I might even try and keep these till the weekend.' She looked at them sadly. 'Probably not, though.'

The freezing February air blew into the cosy shop as Maud left, and Rosie found herself counting up … September, maybe? She'd need to do the sums. But a lovely autumn baby, the leaves red and gold on the trees, the harvest sun beautiful, huge and heavy in the sky … She was lost in a reverie when she saw the small, thin figure standing in front of her, eyes blinking behind his glasses.

'Ahem,' said Edison. He was one of her steadiest customers, an extremely literal child with a hippy mother, Hester, who made him wear hand-stitched items and thus ensured his unpopularity at school. Hester's New Age beliefs and dislike of refined sugar didn't stop her from constantly asking Rosie to babysit. Rosie had also helped deliver Hester's new baby, Marie, at Christmas.

Edison was walking by himself again, after spending time in a wheelchair following a dreadful accident before Christmas. Stephen had saved his life, but he had still been injured. All the attention during his recovery – particularly now, when he was walking, carefully, with a large and ornate stick – had done wonders for his confidence.

'Hello, sir,' said Rosie. 'Have they stopped spoiling you to bits at school yet?'

Edison frowned. He wasn't very good at being teased.

'I don't think I am tebbly spoiled,' he said, pushing up his glasses. 'I am most likely not to have tantrums mostly.'

Rosie couldn't imagine Edison crying about anything.

'I was only teasing,' she said. 'Are they being nice to you?'

Edison frowned.

'They mostly say, "Edison, you can play football with us." But I don't play football now. And I didn't play football before. Hester says ball games are just male greshun.'

'Does she?' said Rosie blandly. Her thoughts on Edison's mother's contemporary parenting style were always best kept to herself. 'Well, maybe when you get rid of the stick you can play.'

Edison looked terrified.

'But what if the ball hits me, Rosie, and breaks my glasses?'

'You could just say "Ha ha, I don't mind" and play on.'

'But if I was hurt and there was blood?'

'It's only a ball, Edison.'

'I'm scared of balls,' said Edison gloomily. 'Can I have some Edinburgh rock?'

Rosie pulled down the jar.

'Are you sure,' she asked, as she always did, 'you don't want to try something else?'

Edison looked confused.

'But I know I like Edinburgh rock.'

'Yes, but you might like something else even more.'

'But that would be A RISK.'

Rosie smiled and shook him out his little bag.

'Here you are. How's Marie?'

His baby sister had been born on Christmas morning. Edison could not be talked out of calling her Marie, after Marie Curie, and now Rosie rather liked it. With a thrill of half panic, half excitement, she realised that Marie and her baby were going to be close in age.

'Noisy,' said Edison shortly. 'And I wanted to play Lego with her, and everyone said, "OH EDISON, NO."' His face looked pinched and sad. 'You know she can hold things! I thought she could hold my Lego Chima!'

Rosie smiled.

'But what does she do with the things?'

Edison thought about it.

'She puts them in her mouth.'

'There you are,' said Rosie. 'You can see that might be a problem.'

'But Lego isn't nice in your mouth.'

'Well you know that,' said Rosie. 'She doesn't, she's only a baby, she doesn't know anything. That's why she

21

needs a big brother to show her that Lego is bad.'

'Oh,' said Edison. 'I could teach her all of that stuff.'

He wandered thoughtfully out of the shop as Rosie moved over to serve some of the more indecisive children. She yelled after him, 'But don't give her any Edinburgh rock!'

Edison rolled his eyes at her. He was definitely growing up, she thought.

After they'd shut up shop, Rosie couldn't settle till Stephen came home. Often he was in before her, with huge stacks of marking, but he had some gruesome Ofsted meeting tonight he couldn't miss. She made a chicken pie, but couldn't concentrate and put weird ingredients in it. Mr Dog hopped around and she didn't tell him to stop jumping up. She lit the fire, but her hands were shaking. She spent a lot of time examining herself in the mirror in the bathroom. How could she not have noticed the swelling in her breasts, the new blue veins that had appeared under her pale skin? Her stomach was the same as ever – i.e. not quite as flat as she would like it to be – but her thick dark curly hair seemed to have extra bounce in it for some reason, and wasn't growing as quickly as it usually did, and she realised that that was because her body was diverting all its resources to nourishing the life within her.

She was still in the bathroom, slightly stunned, when Stephen turned up, with his heavy, slightly uneven tread – a result of being blown up by a landmine in Africa while working for Médecins Sans Frontières – and his emphatic greeting for Mr Dog.

'Does having a baby make you burn food?' he called. 'I had no idea. Where ARE you?'

'I'm in here,' she managed weakly. Stephen banged open the bathroom door.

'Have you spent all day in dodgy bathrooms?'

As soon as they saw each other, though, all banter and bravado was gone, and they simply stared at one another.

'Crumbs,' said Stephen, looking at her in the mirror, a hint of wickedness about his normally serious steely blue eyes.

'Innit,' said Rosie, looking back at him.

'You know, we couldn't even name a dog,' said Stephen.

'Lord, I hadn't even thought of that.'

And laughing with their secret, the special thing of their very own, in the little cosy cottage under the big frosted sky, they fell into one another's arms.

Chapter Two

Lilian Hopkins was sitting smugly in the day room, with a petition. The petition was to stop the football being shown on the TV downstairs. The four men in the old people's home were displeased.

Her frenemy, Ida Delia, who had been married to Lilian's first love before he had been presumed lost in the war, stood behind her, for once on the same side. Both women had made an enormous point of being in mourning for Henry Carr, wearing black every day. Rosie teased Lilian and said it was turning her into a Spanish *condesa*, which troubled Lilian not at all. Continuing with her conversion to Catholicism, she had added a mantilla, which Rosie was quite shocked at. But she had to admit it was rather dashing, with Lilian's slash of red lipstick and pale face.

'Also, I might take up smoking,' Lilian said, at which Rosie really got annoyed. 'I'm just trying to hasten being back with my Henry again, and I've heard it's nice.'

'It's not nice, it's foul,' said Rosie.

'Well, all right, perhaps just some heroin.'

'If all the sugar you exist on hasn't killed you' – Rosie obviously approved wholeheartedly of sweets as a treat, but Lilian's commitment to them as a full-time diet caused some tension between them – 'then I can't imagine a bit of heroin is going to do it.'

'Excellent,' said Lilian. 'Get me some heroin. Ask Moray.'

'Moray doesn't know how to get *heroin*.'

Lilian looked at her over the tops of her glasses, as if disappointed at Rosie's naivety.

'He's a doctor!' she said. 'When I was a girl, all you could get was morphine. When Ebidiah Lumb got his arm chopped off in the thresher . . .'

Rosie looked at her.

'Yes, well things are very different now.'

'I doubt that,' said Lilian. 'That old miser Hye never throws anything away.'

Rosie thought of the dispensary at the surgery, which she'd had cause to visit once or twice, and figured there was probably something in that.

'Well anyway. I'm still not getting you any heroin.'

'After all I've done for you,' said Lilian.

'Lilian, I have something to tell you …'

They had hugged their secret to themselves for weeks like fairy treasure, bedazzled by what they had created with their love. However many people had done so before them (about nineteen billion, Stephen reckoned), it could not diminish their private joy by an iota. The outside world, on the other hand …

'Do you think Lilian will guess?' Rosie had asked.

'Yup,' said Stephen. 'Though it doesn't matter if she guesses or not, because like everybody else, she asks us every ten seconds anyway. Oooh, when are you getting married, are you going to take on your title, when are you going to have a baby, she's not getting any younger.'

'They actually say "she's not getting any younger"?' said Rosie, stung. She was thirty-three.

'Never,' said Stephen quickly. 'They never say that.'

'Hmm,' said Rosie, who was on her way up to see her great-aunt with a little black bomber jacket, very Mary Berry, that she'd been unable to resist for her in the January sales.

'The problem is—'

Stephen was there before her.

'If you tell Lilian before you tell your mother, you'll be in a heap of trouble.'

Rosie shivered.

'Can you IMAGINE?'

Angie, Rosie's mother, was fiercely protective of Rosie, even all the way from Australia, where she lived looking after Rosie's brother Pip's children, whom Rosie adored.

'In my head,' said Stephen, 'they would both rise up into the sky and have a great fight.'

'Then your mother would grow to the size of Godzilla . . .'

'Let's not tell my mother till it's here,' pleaded Stephen, stroking Rosie's soft curls. 'And maybe not even then. She'll barely notice. Hide it every time she comes round. If she finds out, tell her we sent it to boarding school in the womb.'

'That'll totally work,' said Rosie. Her eyes widened. 'Oh my God, does it matter whether it's a girl or a boy?'

Stephen looked away.

'Seriously? Screw that.'

Stephen was set to inherit the huge, unprofitable, crumbling estate currently being run by his mother. His elder sister Pamela had quite a lot to say about that.

'Yes, but . . .'

'Oh God, if it's a boy, Pamela is going to do her nut.'

They looked at each other and started giggling.

'So,' said Stephen. 'Is there anyone who isn't totally going to do their nut about this poor baby?'

Angie first. If this had been a cartoon, Rosie thought, there would have been heavy hairdryer lines coming out of the phone. All Angie's doubts over Stephen's suitability as husband material for her only daughter were blown away in an instant.

'Oh moi Gawd?' she shrieked, in her hybrid English/Aussie accent, even though she'd only been in Australia for two and a half years. 'A boybee!!!'

'Speak English, Mum,' said Rosie, pink with pleasure.

'WANNA SPEAK TO ROSIE.'

Rosie could hear Meridian, her favourite niece, on the other end of the line, and a bit of fumbling as she grabbed the phone.

'HEYYO, AUNTIE ROSIE. WHEN ARE YOU COMING FOR SLEEPOVER?'

'Soon,' promised Rosie. 'Hello, my darling Meridian.'

'I JAMES BONG.'

'Hello, James Bond. Listen up, James. You know I am going to have a little baby for you to play with! She'll be your cousin and you'll be the biggest.'

There was a very long pause. If Rosie hadn't been able to hear Meridian's noisy breathing down the phone, she'd have thought she'd hung up or wandered off.

'James Bong?'

'DOAN HAVE BABY, AUNTIE ROSIE,' came the voice very clearly. 'BABIES ARE PIG'S ARSE.'

'Meridian!' Angie said sternly.

'Okay,' said Rosie. 'Well, you know I'll still like you very much.'

More noisy breathing, then Angie grabbed the phone back.

'I'll tell her it's not coming for ages. It's not, is it? I mean, darling, you were looking quite well-rounded at Christmas ...'

Rosie rolled her eyes. Anything larger than a size 8 her mother made a fuss about. She was, and always had been, quite a bit larger than a size 8.

'No, Mum.'

'Oh, okay, good! Right, Meridian, don't worry about the baby.'

'I WILL KILL THE PIG'S ARSE BABY WITH MY ROCKET CAR.'

'She's thrilled,' said Angie. 'And so am I, my love. How are you feeling? Are you sick? Have you told that old dingbat yet?'

She meant Stephen's mother. Rosie had called her worse.

'Not yet.'

'Oh man, don't let her get her claws into the baby. She'll be sending it out chasing horses and trying to make friends with Prince George and whatever posh people do.'

There was a pause.

'Can it make friends with Prince George?'

'No, Mum.'

'Ooh, I'll have to come over. Or you guys come to us!'

'You want me to fly to Australia with a newborn baby?'

'You've got the ticket!'

Her family had given her a ticket to Australia for Christmas.

'Anyway, babies are easy. Just coat the dummy in sugar water and you can basically pop to the shops.'

'Thanks, Mum,' said Rosie, rolling her eyes.

'Also, on the flight, you give them a little bit of valium ...'

'Mu-um!!!!!!'

'Oh my Rosie-Posie, this is so amazing.'

'Well, Pip's got kids.'

'Yes, I know.' Her voice softened, and she sounded English again. 'But when it's your daughter, it's something else. Something a bit special ... PI-IP!!!! YOUR SISTER'S EXPECTING!'

'Bonzer!' shouted Pip from what sounded like a long way away.

'Are you out in the garden splashing in the pool this early in the morning?' asked Rosie suspiciously.

'Yip,' said Angie proudly. 'You'd love it here, Rosie.'

Rosie looked out of the window at the frost-spattered trees and the sparkling garden.

'Maybe,' she said. 'But here is pretty good too.'

'Is it as cold as it was at Christmas?'

'It is FAR worse than it was at Christmas. And there's not even any Christmas!'

Rosie moved to the front, where Farmer Isitt was walking his old horse. On her back were two of the village children, screaming and laughing, their breath visible on the dark air.

'Brr,' said Angie.

'No, it's all right,' said Rosie, smiling. The fire was crackling invitingly down below. 'And I'm fine. Hungry.'

'You're always hungry.'

'Yes, thanks for that. And my bosoms … Uh, never mind.'

'I never will know where those came from,' said Angie wonderingly. 'Lilian and I are flat as pancakes.'

There was a pause while they both wondered, briefly, about Rosie's father, a travelling man Rosie had never known.

'That child is going to have plenty of family,' said Angie fiercely, putting Rosie's thoughts into words. 'Too much probably. You don't have to worry about that.'

'No,' said Rosie.

She rang off promising to send a picture of her bump week by week, though the idea that she would even have a bump seemed very odd to Rosie, some kind of medical miracle that she couldn't imagine happening.

She went back downstairs. Stephen didn't quite look up; he was gazing at his laptop, as usual cursing the ridiculous slowness of their rural internet connection. It never really bothered Rosie. Angie posted pictures of the children on Facebook every single day, along with inspirational messages about guardian angels and things you had to 'like' if you loved your daughter or your niece or stuff like that, and Rosie normally let it load at its own speed then crawled through it later. It was nice keeping up with her old friends – Mike and Giuseppe both changed their relationship status about once every two days – and she ordered supplies for the shop, but apart from that it wasn't something she was crazy about. Stephen, on the other hand, liked to read the papers and keep up with rugby teams and so on, and was always grousing about how long it took.

'So, you know,' she said, 'we'll have to move to Peak House. We'll freeze our bums off.'

Stephen looked up.

'I didn't think of that,' he said and bit his lip thoughtfully.

When Rosie had arrived in Lipton, he had been living in Peak House, the draughty Georgian pile that belonged to the big house. It was right at the top of the hill, open to the wind and rain, but the views were staggering. Stephen's memories of it were not, however. He associated Peak House with cold and loneliness; and

Lilian's little cottage, where they now lived, with cosiness and warmth and coming home, and being happier than he'd ever known.

'Are you sure?' he said. 'Babies are only little.'

'I'll be sure until the first time it crawls straight into the road and gets run over by Isitt driving his sheep to market.'

'Well Lilian and her brothers all grew up here.'

'Yes, and they slept four to a room and had an outhouse in the garden.'

'Sounds cosy enough.'

Rosie looked at him.

'Seriously?' he said.

'Seriously. Talk to your mother.' She smiled tentatively. 'If we're going to be a family ...'

'Oh, pulling that one, are you?' said Stephen, smiling, and dragged her over to sit on his lap. 'You've got this all figured out, haven't you?'

Rosie shrugged.

'It *does* have a lovely big garden,' she said. 'And maybe ... maybe we could put double glazing in.'

'No, it's good for children to grow up totally freezing in a haunted house,' said Stephen airily, and she knew she'd won him over.

'And,' she pointed out, 'we should sell this place anyway. Lilian's home is getting so expensive, and if I'm going to be taking some time off ...'

Stephen winced.

'I hate being skint sometimes, it sucks.'

He turned and kissed her.

'Would you have preferred it if I'd gone off to London to become one of those banker boys after all?'

She grinned.

'No! Anyway, you'd have been rubbish. Always staring out the window and thinking about the hills and reciting poetry.'

'Rubbish doesn't matter if you're a banker. They give you millions of pounds anyway. And if you *don't* make millions of pounds, they get the taxpayers to give it to you.'

'Oh yes,' said Rosie. 'Maybe we should all do that.'

Then they both looked cosily into the fire together and smiled at the same time.

'Neh,' they both said, as Mr Dog came up and lapped at their hands.

'I am the smuggest witch in the entire world,' said Rosie, getting up to put the kettle on, already feeling pleasantly drowsy although it was only early in the evening. Stephen went back to his computer. She heard him from the kitchen.

'Hmm,' he said suddenly.

Rosie popped her head round the door.

'Hmm,' he said again, and Mr Dog scampered over in case 'hmm' meant 'I appear to be holding some unwanted treats.'

Stephen was staring at the computer screen.

'Do you want to tell me, or is it just going to be a mystery?' said Rosie. 'Have some aliens landed? Prince William is a woman? A sheep is a bit poorly over in Carningford? They're introducing a new baby tax and the government is going to want forty per cent of our income?'

'Sssh,' said Stephen, not taking his eyes off the computer. 'My French is rusty.'

'Ooh, my French is rusty,' mimicked Rosie. She often teased him about it, but she envied his wonderful education really, even if his own mother thought it had been wasted. He spoke excellent French, had good Latin – though it wasn't much use – and even though (against his father's wishes) he'd studied English at university, he had a knowledge of geography, physics and history that Rosie couldn't remember them even touching on at her school. 'Dear me. Perhaps I shall first translate it into Mandarin and then work it out from there. Also, don't shush a pregnant lady! I am not to be shushed! I am extremely special!'

'Hush,' he said. Then he looked up. The expression on his face was completely unreadable. 'Um,' he said. 'Would you like to ...'

'I can't read French,' said Rosie.

'I'll translate.'

'What IS it?' she said, completely confused. She didn't like his face at all; the colour had drained out of it and his eyes had taken on a fixed, distant look. 'What is it? Is something wrong?'

Stephen didn't answer, merely blinked, which made her even more curious and worried. She nudged a protesting Mr Dog out of the way, then crawled up next to Stephen on the sofa and peered over his shoulder at an official-looking email. All she could make out was the Médecins Sans Frontières logo.

Before Rosie had fallen in love with Stephen, she had nursed him back to health after his accident in Africa. Her greatest fear was that he would want to go back there again when he was well, but he had sworn that he didn't; that he had never been happier than he was here in Lipton with her, teaching at the little local school, the pair of them lunching in the Red Lion, taking long, chilly walks across the moors at the weekends, which Rosie normally would have hated, but because she was walking next to him as he brandished his stick and told her old stories about the hills, with Mr Dog running about like mad, and because it always ended up in the nice tea room two villages over that did great cream teas and Eccles cakes, she actually loved.

But he was still having treatment for his PTSD; still on occasion had nightmares, the terrible sweating dreams that left him pinned to the bed, staring wildly, the sheets screwed up in his fingers, Rosie by him, holding him close, bringing him back home, back to normality.

She was not thrilled when he got emails from Africa. 'What is it?'

'Someone else is pregnant,' said Stephen heavily. He shook his head. 'Wow. Weird.'

'Who? What? Stop being cryptic.'

'Jabo . . . and Akibo . . .' He still found it very difficult to say the boys' names, even after all this time, though Rosie knew it was good for him to do so. 'Jabo and Akibo. They had a big sister.' He frowned. 'Not that big. She didn't go to school.'

He glanced warningly at Rosie, in case she had something to say about this, but she kept silent.

'She's having a baby too. The family wanted me to know. In fact I think . . . ' He half smiled, then his voice went rather wobbly. 'I think they want me to be god-father.' His hand went to his mouth.

Rosie was by his side immediately.

'Sssh,' she said. 'Ssh. I think this is amazing. They're showing you . . . they're showing you they don't blame you. That it wasn't your fault. Which it *wasn't*.'

Stephen nodded slowly.

'She can't be more than fourteen. Oh goodness. I think we'd better send them some money.'

'I think so too,' said Rosie, full of relief. She had been absolutely terrified for a moment that he was going to say 'I think I have to go out there.'

Stephen shook his head.

'When's she due?' said Rosie. 'Is there a pic?'

But there wasn't, just the bare facts relayed by someone called Faustine.

'What a terrifying name,' said Rosie.

'She is terrifying,' said Stephen. 'But in the best possible way.'

He noticed Rosie getting up and picking up her coat.

'Where are you going? Don't go out in this. Stay home, please.'

'I have to,' said Rosie. 'I have to go to the home before Lilian finds out and has me flayed.'

Stephen nodded and got carefully to his feet, glancing briefly back at his laptop.

'I'll drive you,' he said. 'My most precious cargo.'

'Bit less of the cargo,' said Rosie. 'Though I'll be the size of a tugboat by the time this thing's finished.'

She was surprised, truly, at how happy the news made Lilian. She was expecting sarcastic remarks and jibes, the normal way her great-aunt showed her affection without ever really letting down her guard; a carapace against a harsh world she had worn her entire life. But her face was wreathed in smiles, and for once she was short of a snappy answer and simply said, 'A baby.'

'Looks like it,' said Rosie, enjoying the huge fire, even if it was gas, in the residents' posh lounge, football free as insisted on, even though the men of the institution had protested furiously, pointing out that they were hopelessly outnumbered as it was, whereupon the old women had pointed out that that meant they were spoiled all the time and the nurses gave them extra cake and they always had someone to dance with at the tea dances and it really wasn't fair, and the whole thing had turned into a gigantic stand-off until Cathryn, who ran the home kindly but with absolute authority, told them all to behave themselves or no blackjack, which calmed things down quickly enough. Lilian had had the temerity to add, 'So it's settled, then. No football on the big TV,' and Cathryn had sighed and said fine, and the men had all kicked off again until Lilian and Ida Delia had quelled them by turning round and – in unison – announcing that they were recent widows.

Now, Lilian was unusually speechless.

'A baby,' she said, and her clear, very pale china-blue eyes watered, very slightly. Then she glanced down. 'Well. Well it will be nice to have a baby.'

'If I'd known you'd enjoy it this much, I'd have had one before,' said Rosie, delighted.

'Yes, who with?' said Lilian. 'Could have been anyone really.'

'Yeah, all right.'

But Lilian smiled again.

'Well. It is wonderful to have a baby around the place.'

Rosie nodded. She was beaming, glowing with happiness and excitement. She looked into the fire and dreamed of showing Lilian the little bundle, with Stephen's blue eyes and her black hair, pink of cheek and round and warm as a loaf of new bread; she dreamed of watching her grow, going to the little village school with her father in the morning, him pointing out the animals and the trees and . . .

The two women sat companionably together, both lost in reveries.

It was the last peaceful moment Rosie was to know for a long time, for the tinsel was gone, the joyful lights had been put away and the Christmas bells had ceased to chime. A dark door had somewhere slammed open, and a cold, desolate wind was beginning to blow.

Chapter Three

For the days they are gone and the night soon must fall
No longer will oxen stand warm in the stall
But surrounded by darkness his power glows bright
His love heals and guides us through cold endless night
The prince of compassion concealed in a byre
Watches the rafters above him resplendent with fire

'The Nurses' carol'

Moray's kindness and gentleness oddly enough made it worse.

Rosie and Moray were best friends really. She was used to them sharing a bottle of wine, slagging each other off, making stupid jokes. As he was the local GP and she an ex-nurse, she often helped him out with certain patients here and there when they were short-handed – it was very hard to get full community coverage out in the wilds of Derbyshire, where farmers lived few and far between, and disliked being treated by outsiders. So she and Moray were good muckers, ever since her arrival in Lipton two years before, all alone and a complete stranger to country life.

So it was hard to see the sadness in his shrewd blue eyes, and to hear the tenderness with which he'd said, 'Oh Rosie, I am so sorry' when she came back after the awful trip to the hospital in Carningford, after the awful, awful ultrasound, Stephen standing there gripping her hand tightly as they both looked at the little screen, Rosie with blue gel on her tummy, both of them staring quietly, endlessly at the grey, fuzzy, indefinable space where they'd expected to see a baby.

Rosie had swallowed hard.

'It's just our first shot,' she had said, bravely echoing words she'd heard other people use over the years. 'We weren't even trying for a baby, were we? It's just one of those things.'

The radiographer had politely retreated from the room to find a doctor.

'Stop it, love,' said Stephen, his throat tight, holding her close.

'What?'

'Stop doing that Rosie thing and trying to make everything all right. Okay?'

Rosie swallowed.

'I . . . I don't know how. I mean, we have to just pick ourselves up and . . . It happens all the time and . . .'

'Ssssh,' said Stephen, gathering her fully up in his arms. There was blue gel all over his jumper, but he didn't notice. 'Ssssh.'

'But we can try again . . . Some things just aren't meant to . . .'

'Ssssh,' he said, again, burying her dark curly head in his shoulder.

'It was so little,' she said, her voice choking up. 'Just a—'

'It was our baby,' said Stephen fiercely. 'And don't you dare say it happens all the time. I don't give a toss about how often it happens. It happened to us. To us, Rosie. And you can't pretend otherwise.'

'I don't want to . . .'

Rosie tried to speak through the lump in her throat, but found she couldn't get it out, not at all. Stephen stroked her hair, gently.

'Oh Lord,' she said. Then it poured out in a flood, and she cried and cried and cried all down his back.

The hospital staff led them kindly to another room. Walking out, barely able to stand, covered in tears and red of nose, both of them limping, Rosie barely noticed the horrified looks of the women with their bumps proudly displayed in the waiting room. Stephen did, but ignored them.

They were counselled up and sent home and told simply to wait for the worst. And when it came, it was just as bad as they had been promised.

Rosie couldn't look at another woman's bump for a long time.

Rosie's mother Angie was sensible and pragmatic; she mentioned how many more times they could try, what a good chap Stephen was, how many pregnancies ended this way just because something wasn't right (and never, ever mentioned – and Rosie would have been astonished to learn of them – her own nights of sobbing for the pain of her only daughter, who was far too far away).

Lilian simply nodded as if, as ever, she expected life's disappointments to fall into her lap, and merely stroked her niece's hand and came up with the most meaningless platitudes she could manage, in case she accidentally burst into floods of tears. And Rosie knew: she KNEW. One in four, Moray said. One in four. One in four tiny little specks of life weren't meant to be, couldn't hang on. One in four women had been through this; laughed, lived, carried on, made other babies, lots of babies.

But as Stephen pointed out, it wasn't one in four for them, it was one in one.

Later, as she had quietened down, and Stephen was in the process of dozing off, they managed to make it up the narrow staircase to bed, holding each other up.

'At least we don't need to move to Peak House yet,' said Stephen, as Mr Dog snuffled down in front of the dying embers of the downstairs fire, after making his usual unsuccessful assault on the upstairs bedroom.

Rosie gave her best shot at a smile.

'And we don't have to buy all that plastic crap,' she said.

'There we go,' said Stephen, climbing into bed.

They paused and looked at one another.

'But one day we will,' he promised. 'One day we will.'

Another month passed, and Rosie was back in that damned Carningford Hospital trying not to glance at the ugly shopping centre, visible through the window, where she'd done that test so many weeks before. It had been such a long spring, she thought. The weather felt like it was going to stay with her mood for ever; that she was a new, low Rosie who would never unfurl again. She was keeping her head down, working hard, but she couldn't help feeling that something was wrong. She couldn't explain it any better than that, but she knew as a nurse that these feelings should get checked out sooner rather than later.

So here she was, visiting the specialist. Meeting with Moray to fix it up (Hye would have been unsympathetic and quite possibly unhelpful) had been unbearable. Moray had been kind, telling her it hadn't been long, and not to worry, whilst, she knew, sharing her pain.

'Don't get all panicky,' he'd warned. 'Nothing worse for getting pregnant. You're only thirty-four.'

'I know,' said Rosie. 'I know, I know. But I don't think it is that. When I . . .'

She didn't want to talk about what had happened after the scan, that awful time she wanted scoured from her memory for ever. She tried again.

'There was definitely . . . I definitely have pain . . . more on one side than the other, it's definitely . . .'

'Ssh,' said Moray. 'Not to worry. I'll send you to get checked out, okay?'

There was a pause.

'Or I could do it.'

He winked at her, and despite herself she found herself smiling.

'Oh Moray, you hate fannies.'

'I'm not crazy about old men's ears either, but I seem to spend enough time peering into those.'

'Oh GOD, and you'd have to get Maeve in to supervise. No no no no no no.'

'It's a waste of resources,' said Moray.

'No it's not,' said Rosie. 'I count as a family member, practically. You're not allowed to look up my fanny.'

'But I so want to,' said Moray.

'Shut up.'

It was exactly the right way to cheer her up, and she stood up gratefully.

'Any time.'

'I'm going to report you to the GMC.'

Moray rolled his eyes and handed over the referral letter he'd printed out.

'That's right – I want to complain about that doctor who, instead of assaulting me, sent me off to some woman to check out my bits.'

He reflected.

'They might be pleased to get something to balance up all my fan mail.'

It was true, Moray was beloved for miles around for his good looks, good doctoring, and being just about the last doctor on earth to actually do house calls.

Rosie smiled and kissed him. He winced to see the worry in her eyes.

'Don't,' he said. 'You're young, fit and healthy. It'll work out. It's why you'd want Stephen's grumpy babies that's the real mystery here.'

She smiled.

'Thanks.'

She turned round before she left, hoping to catch him in a moment of weakness.

'So, are you and Moshe coming to dinner, then?' Moshe was Moray's boyfriend.

'Are you trying to catch me in a moment of weakness?'

Rosie nodded.

'Yes.'

Moray's reluctance to come out to the village had surprised the more metropolitan Rosie for a long time, and nothing seemed to be changing any time soon. Rosie thought he was worrying unnecessarily. Moray thought people who weren't him seemed to have all sorts of very clear ideas of what it was like to be him that he didn't necessarily share. But they didn't let it stand in the way of their friendship.

'Have we or have we not just had a long conversation about keeping our relationship professional?'

'Yes,' said Rosie. 'And we decided not to, remember?'

She shook the envelope at him, and for a moment both their faces became pensive once more.

'Soon,' said Moray, kissing her gently and waving her off with a worried look. 'Soon. And call me . . .'

Rosie nodded and swallowed hard.

'I will,' she said. 'I will.'

And now here she was in the clinic. It was full of bored, unhappy-looking women, many, she noticed, a great deal older than herself. The clinic dealt with a mix of private and NHS clients, but Rosie was simply there to see a gynaecologist. On the walls were arty black and white pictures of babies. Bit tasteless, she thought. Or maybe it was focusing the mind. Either way, she tried not to look at them, and listlessly leafed through an old magazine.

'Miss Hopkins?'

Rosie couldn't believe what a throwback she felt, but she did slightly wish they were married already. She flashed the vintage ring perhaps more obviously than she might have done otherwise.

Dr Chang was incredibly glamorous, the type of very slender thirty-something woman Rosie had once upon a time emulated. She had a put-together look, together with matching shoes and a bag, and properly blow-dried hair. Rosie felt an odd urge to impress her, but wasn't sure how. It certainly wasn't with this X-ray of her Fallopian tubes, which Dr Chang was examining now on the light box on the wall.

'You see,' said Dr Chang in a loud, quite posh voice, as if Rosie were peculiarly stupid, 'there is evidence of growth here, and here, and bad blocking here and here. You were very lucky to get pregnant at all.'

This made Rosie bristle. There had been nothing lucky about it ... Then she thought back over the sweet joy of those two special months, and thought she was going to tear up again. Noticing, Dr Chang slid a box of tissues over her desk in a brusque movement. Rosie wondered how many women had cried in her office. All of them, probably.

There was much more in a technical vein, but basically the message was pretty clear: it had taken the miscarriage to show what Rosie now knew. Now she thought about it, she'd never – in her twenties with her then-boyfriend Gerard, or even before – had a pregnancy crisis, or anything to worry about. She thought she'd just been lucky. Obviously not.

Dr Chang discussed options: a fairly full-on IVF procedure which apparently they should have started a couple of years before they'd actually met; surrogacy and other words that made Rosie want to be ill; and adoption.

'I'm sorry it's not better news,' said Dr Chang finally. 'You've just been unlucky, I'm afraid. If you desperately want a baby, there are routes you can take, but I have to warn you, they are expensive and sometimes heartbreaking.'

Rosie swallowed. She hadn't wanted to tell Stephen about the appointment today; she didn't want to bother him, particularly when they'd agreed not to try again for another year, agreed to relax, put it out of their heads.

But next year the odds would be even worse than this year, and so on and so on. And if she'd ever wondered whether or not she wanted a baby – although she was crazy about her nephew and nieces – knowing she was pregnant had made it very clear to her that she did.

She let the tears run down her face.

'Is your other half here?' said Dr Chang, her expression becoming slightly more sympathetic.

Rosie shook her head.

'I didn't want to worry him,' she whispered.

'Well,' said Dr Chang, 'if you want to tackle this, you're going to need to be able to talk about it. Talk about everything. This kind of thing can challenge even the strongest relationship, you know.'

Rosie nodded. She thought they were strong ... but were they strong enough for this?

Stephen wasn't used to Rosie not being there when he got home, and he missed her. But it gave him a chance to call his PTSD therapist. He didn't like doing it when Rosie was around; felt it was selfish to impinge on her misery, and he wasn't even sure she wouldn't be angry that he was discussing it with an outside party. But he was upset too, and he found himself worrying all the time. If Rosie couldn't carry a baby properly in a wealthy country with good medical care, what chance would Célestine have in a country that wasn't yet developed; that had proper hospitals only if you could afford to pay?

He thought back to his time there. He had loved Africa from the second he had set foot on its soil; smelled its smells: the bright colours everywhere, the blazing sun, the optimistic lives being lived in the most difficult of circumstances, contrasting so strongly with his spoiled, discontented friends from university. He was young, fit and full of the desire to do some good. And although a certain level of disillusionment was necessary – essential from the point of view of the charity who'd hired him – nonetheless he took satisfaction from small victories when large ones were hard to find. He worked hard on anything practical he could do, and put his teacher training into use in the most unusual situation possible: a school with anything between thirty and seventy students, depending on the harvest and the rains, of varying ages, who spoke a mixture of English learned from Nigerian television, French, and the local language.

It is hard to tell who will make a good teacher until they are tested. The most unlikely characters thrive in front of a room full of pupils. In his private life, Stephen was reticent and distant, a hangover from a lonely, awkward childhood of feeling different from the other Lipton children but not being able to quite understand why, as well as a strict father who wanted his son to be a mirror image of himself, and found a quiet, sensitive, poetry-loving boy rather than a hearty, hunting-shooting-fishing type bound for Sandhurst very difficult to deal with.

But with a class, he came alive. He was funny, patient, kind. His group leader, Faustine, who had thought of him as a drifting posh boy wandering through gap years for want of direction, instead found him committed, engaging and devoted to his charges, as he took on everything from teaching them how to use sterilising tablets, singing funny songs, attempting to give them a notion of world geography from an atlas published in 1957, to fearlessly killing a snake that crept into the toilet hole one day, a feat that, had Stephen told him about it, would have given his father much pleasure.

Everywhere he went in the village, he was accompanied by Jabo and his little brother Akibo, who were both absolutely devoted to him, so when Stephen planned the field trip to see the rarely flowering cactus one of the other aid workers had mentioned, they were of course right up the front, carrying the water bottles proudly, touching Stephen's shirt from time to time to show the rest of the class that they were with him.

Civil war had supposedly ended there six years before; the region was supposed to be cleared, and safe from landmines.

People make mistakes.

Waking up in the military hospital to which he'd been evacuated was the single worst moment of Stephen's life. The noise, then the deafening quiet; the evisceration; the sight of his own blood pumping away into the sand – so much of it: that only came back during his dreams, on the nights when Rosie held him so closely he could forget where he stopped and she began; could draw the strength he needed from her warm body to bring him back to life.

But waking up miles away, his leg a ragged mess, unable to move, knowing he had not saved the boys: that was with him always. He did not like to receive emails from his old employers. He wished Rosie was home.

Stephen picked up the phone. His therapist was a thin, whip-smart, very quiet older woman who let him get away with nothing. Moray had recommended her and he had been absolutely right to do so; Stephen would have turned frosty under too much empathy, or combative against too much intellect, but Diane had the right mix of sharpness and a calm kindness – so sharp, in fact, that he never once suspected that although she returned home every night to her immaculately tidy apartment, ate a healthy dinner with her incredibly clever and intellectual husband as they discussed the serious issues of the day, went often to the theatre and smart restaurants with their equally clever and intellectual friends, she spent all night dreaming that she was instead in the unforgiving arms of a taciturn man with a limp.

She was based in Harley Street in London, and they often had phone consultations.

Stephen told her everything that had happened, and how painful it was, particularly at school, where they were doing a project on Africa and starting a charity to add money to the fund he was putting together. Rosie also had a tin in the sweetshop. Their first object was to fund Célestine to get to the mission hospital to have her baby. After that, Faustine, Stephen's ex-colleague from Médecins Sans Frontières, had suggested that rather than just give money to the family, which could provoke resentment, they should attempt to help improve the school, which at the moment was still the large, boiling shed Stephen had known so well. Stephen had agreed with this.

'But it's just … ever since … I mean, it was interesting to begin with, with the two babies growing, but now … now it's all fallen apart and I can't help thinking about it. And I keep replaying Africa in my head over and over, and it isn't helping me and it sure as hell isn't helping Rosie.'

He swallowed hard. There was a long pause. Finally Diane, in her cool tones, suggested something she believed could work extraordinarily well: facing up to your worst fears, if it could be done, seeing them and taking away their power, had had spectacular success with PTSD, phobias, all sorts of trauma.

'Well,' she said. 'You could visit.'

Stephen had about a million reasons immediately as to why he couldn't possibly: school term, the cost of getting out there, which would take away from the fund-raising, leaving Rosie.

'Would you need to leave her?' said Diane. 'You could take her with you. A trip somewhere else, away from all her memories and routines.'

'To see a pregnant woman,' said Stephen.

'The world is full of pregnant women,' said Diane gently. 'That's something she'll have to get used to on her own. And you can always have another baby. Might be a good idea to take the trip before it's too late.'

'I don't think so,' said Stephen. 'But thank you. As ever, it's good to talk to you.'

Diane smiled ruefully to herself as she replaced the phone.

Chapter Four

'So, we're having black napkins for the men, and white for the girls, and mixed black and white almonds . . .'

Tina was blathering on. Rosie wasn't listening. Instead she was wondering. She knew, she knew, everyone said, that she should probably be over it by now. She was otherwise well, if worried about the future, but oh, she was still so sad.

Every baby she saw, every advert, every television show seemed to be there to taunt her. Stephen had mentioned Célestine from time to time, and she couldn't bear to hear about that either. She wasn't sleeping well, absolutely anything made her cry and she still hadn't told Stephen about the awful news from the check-up. She had to get a grip, she had to. Lilian was worried about her, which wasn't good for Lilian; and she knew she was no fun any more, that it was rubbish for Stephen to get home every night to a tired, washed-out, miserable fiancée.

'How about,' he had said the previous weekend, 'how about we get together and go through wedding plans? Mother wants to know.'

She had been so grateful to him for making an effort; it was so kind of him, and thoughtful, even if the very idea filled her with horror at the moment. She had gone with him, though, up to the big house.

'So,' Lady Lipton had sniffed. Tall and broad, she was dressed, as usual, in numerous layers of clothes of obvious quality but dubious age. 'I think we'll use the same seating plan from my wedding. So we'll keep all the Yorkshire families apart from the Lancashire ones, *obviously*, then we'll put one bishop per table; they get terribly dull unless you space them out.'

Rosie had smiled weakly, doing her best. This wasn't like her at all, but sometimes with Lady Lipton it was easier just to kind of lean back and let her roll all over you.

'So *how* many do you think your people will have to have?' said Lady Lipton, as if everyone in Rosie's family was a burden that had to be accommodated. Which was, Rosie thought, exactly how Lady Lipton *did* see the Hopkinses, apart from Lilian, whom she adored.

'Um, twenty?' said Rosie tentatively, not really

having thought it through. Her mum and that lot, if they could get over … Michael and Giuseppe and her London friends, even though she'd been neglecting them terribly lately. She assumed all her village friends would already be included.

'*Twenty?*'

Stephen squeezed her hand under the table, as Rosie wondered if this was a lot or a little, and cursed himself. They were both so caught up in themselves these days, he should have taken her somewhere nice or fun, not to sit in his mother's back kitchen, which was neither.

'So you don't want your family there? Or don't you have many friends?'

Rosie swallowed.

'Um, is that … I mean, you're already inviting people from the village, aren't you?'

Lady Lipton looked over the top of the reading glasses she despised, and discarded around the village at regular intervals.

'The *village*? No, of course not.'

'Oh, okay. More, then.'

Lady Lipton had sniffed and said that was all very well, but where were they going to get staff for the event? They couldn't invite Mrs Laird – her loyal daily – when she'd be needed in the kitchen. Stephen said hotly that not only was he inviting Mrs Laird but she'd be sitting at the top table with him, seeing as she was just about the only person who'd ever been kind to him as a child, and Lady Lipton had rolled her eyes and said it seemed a bit rich to talk about unkindness when they were going to move into one of her houses. After that, they made their excuses and left, before they'd even agreed on a date.

'Oh dear,' said Rosie, as Mr Dog barked a cheerful goodbye to all his pure-bred cousins he'd had to leave behind in the courtyard at the back of the house.

'Oh I don't know,' said Stephen. 'I thought that went all right.'

They looked at each other and Rosie smiled, reluctantly.

'You know there's no rush,' said Stephen, as they drove a little further up the hill and parked at Peak House to take a look at it. The early evening sunlight illuminated its stern windows; it was a chilly house, but a beautiful one too. As usual, it was unlocked. Rosie thought again about the fact that her period, once more, had come exactly on time. She might dream of a lovely miracle, but as Dr Chang had warned her, there wouldn't be a miracle. Just a choice.

They had wandered through Peak House hand in hand. The ceilings were high, and the floors original oak and parquet.

'You could make this place really nice,' said Stephen doubtfully.

'With a mere jillion dollars,' smiled Rosie, and they had kissed one another and stolen upstairs to the bed where they had spent the first, extraordinary few months of their courtship, mostly without leaving it, and as the evening sun poured through the dirty windows overlooking the crags and the astonishing valley on the other side of the house, they both felt better, if only for a while.

Rosie hadn't mentioned the wedding again.

Tina went off to pick up the children and finalise the stationery patterns, even though the wedding wasn't going to be till Christmas, seven months away, when the farming work was quieter. She was clearly enjoying being prepared. As she left, she leaned over to give her friend a kiss on the cheek.

'I'm sorry for babbling on,' she said.

Rosie shook her head.

'No,' she said truthfully. 'I like it.'

The shop bell tinged. Edison's mother Hester didn't often come into the sweetshop. She was opposed to sugar on the whole, and was what Rosie's mother would have called a 'knit your own yoga' type. Sometimes it wound Rosie up – particularly when she made Edison wear hand-made clothes and denied him television, plastic toys and basically the chance to fit in with his peer group. But other times she admired the entire ethos. Hester and her university lecturer husband were living it, not just talking about it: they lived out in the middle of nowhere without an internet connection, grew their own vegetables and made their own clothes. Terrible, terrible clothes, but the spirit was there.

Edison was allowed to pop in to the shop from time to time because Rosie basically provided free babysitting, as Edison had latched on to her when she had moved there, and she liked him. But today it was Hester who came in, carrying Marie, now five months, who was as round and flaxen and rosy of cheek as Edison was pale and thin. Rosie swallowed heavily.

'Hello!' she said, trying to look anywhere other than at the baby. 'So good to see you!'

Hester looked, as ever, slightly harassed, as though she'd got lots of better things to be doing elsewhere. Marie was wrapped up against her in a complicated ethnic-looking shawl thing that seemed designed to roll the baby out at any opportunity. Rosie had developed over the last two months a sort of eye slip with other people's babies; as if they were something that she didn't really want to look at, like a snake. She let her eyes slide away and plastered on a smile and tried to pretend they weren't there, just in case she couldn't handle it.

'Yes, well,' said Hester, harrumphing. 'God, you don't know what work is till you've got two children.'

'Right,' said Rosie carefully.

'Listen, I have to run in and see Moray. Can you hold on to Marie for a minute?'

'Um, not really,' said Rosie, flinching. She absolutely was not ready to touch a baby. Hester knew what had happened; how could she be so insensitive? 'I'm not qualified.'

'Oh for goodness' sake, I thought you were a nurse,' said Hester.

'Well, yes, okay, I'm technically qualified,' said Rosie. 'But—'

'Well, fine. Perfect. Moray is giving me a VAGINAL EXAMINATION.'

Two nine-year-old boys who'd been examining the chewing gum shot looks at each other and started backing out of the shop.

'To check the stitches on my ANAL TEAR.'

She was holding the baby out now, with a look on her face that said she would simply plop her down if Rosie didn't take her in the next couple of seconds. Rosie felt her heart pounding through her chest.

'Okay, okay, hand her over,' she said, finally, anxious not to make a scene. 'Okay. Fine. Two minutes.'

Hester undid the complicated scarf carrier, and Rosie tried to follow the procedure but couldn't.

'Here's some EXPRESSED BREAST MILK,' said Hester. 'Put it in the fridge then heat it up in a bain-marie.'

Rosie gave her a look.

'And if she needs her nappy changed, wash it out, it's hemp. Reusable.'

'Don't be long,' said Rosie, through clenched teeth.

'Now don't give her any sweets. I know your tricks!'

Hester handed over the heavy, warm bundle and dinged her way out of the shop.

The boys had gone and the shop was empty for once. Rosie sat down in the back, where there was a kettle for making tea, and an armchair they brought out for Lilian, and gave her attention to the little thing in her arms. She tried to stop shaking. She was terrified. What if she wanted to keep it? What if she couldn't hold it properly? What was bloody Hester thinking? How thoughtless could she get? Thrusting a baby in someone's face when they'd just lost one was completely cruel and selfish.

There was a little mewling noise from her arms. Nothing grizzly, just a tiny, curious sound. She looked down.

There was no doubt about it, Marie was a beautiful baby. Her eyes were grey blue and, like all babies, she looked wise beyond her years, as if she had spent infinity staring at the stars and had only just landed on earth. Her skin was peaches and cream, not the angry red of some little mites; she had a fine covering of soft blonde curls, which were currently hidden by a knitted red bobble hat. Her lips were like little pillows, making an 'O', and she gazed at Rosie with calm, fixed curiosity.

'Well hello there,' said Rosie, stroking the little chest tentatively. She swallowed. There was something about her smell, that mix of warm bread and soft sweet milk and cosiness. It was so powerful, she didn't even realise she was crying until a tear dropped on to Marie's forehead.

'Our baby would have been nothing like you,' she choked, rocking her a little. 'He would have had dark hair and been noisy and clenched his little fists ...'

Marie's little fists *were* clenched, she saw. She put her finger inside one of them, and immediately Marie grabbed it and clung on for dear life, trying to draw it to her mouth to suck on it.

'Oh no you don't,' said Rosie, attempting to smile down at her. Marie grinned back, a big gummy beam right across her face.

Rosie pulled the baby close and wept all the tears she had left to cry. No more avoiding other people's babies, she thought. It would be all right. Surely.

Marie nuzzled into her neck, then started ferreting about for a breast.

'Ha,' said Rosie. 'No, I don't think so. Not … not yet.'

She stroked the beautiful little forehead and felt calmer, and stronger, and Marie smiled at her once more.

Hester arrived back half an hour later, as usual not mincing her words about her various gynaecological difficulties, and failing to notice, helpfully, that Rosie had given Marie her bottle stone-cold, having no idea what a bain-marie was, and that the baby hadn't minded a bit. She had also done a huge poo just as Hester walked in, so Rosie was very pleased to hand her back before the smell spread around the shop.

'Enjoy that?' said Hester with the same confident belief she always had that looking after her children was the biggest treat Rosie could conceive of.

'She's lovely,' said Rosie, honestly. She felt as if she'd somehow been cleansed. 'Now, can I get you anything?'

'Oh God, no,' said Hester. 'It's poison, this shop, you know. Pure poison.'

That night, Rosie dressed up, and put on a full face of make-up for the first time in months, and presented herself to Stephen when he walked through the door, and the look on his face as she greeted him with a glass of wine and a smile was such a mixture of joy and happy relief that she grinned back at him hugely. He picked her up and twirled her round and kissed her happily and deeply as Mr Dog whipped round their ankles, leaping up and down in delight.

'Did it work?' said Moray.

'Well she didn't steal the baby, if that's what you mean.'

'Thanks,' said Moray, heartfelt. 'Thank you. It was just a hunch.'

'Fine,' said Hester. 'And thanks for the antibiotics. Can it be our little secret? I don't actually believe in them.'

'Always,' said Moray.

'Excellent,' said Stephen, when they came up for air. He didn't know what had brought about the change – he expected it had a little to do with the afternoon at Peak House, and to be fair, it was that too. Regardless, he just saw it was there, and that was good enough for him, and it made him feel better too. 'Let's go to the Red Lion tonight and get pissed.'

Rosie laughed.

'Seriously, that's all you can think of for getting the most out of our lives?'

'You, me, you enjoying a glass of wine again on a Saturday night' – Rosie had stopped drinking since the pregnancy – 'the fire lit in the pub, all our friends coming in and saying hello, some farmer gossip, then fish and chips on the way home. I absolutely cannot think of anything I could possibly enjoy more.'

'Well, when you put it like that . . . ' said Rosie.

'Quite!' said Stephen.

A few quick calls and Tina and Jake were both in the pub when they got there, along with Moray, whose face split into a secret grin when he saw them both.

'Well, hello,' he said. 'I thought you two had gone full hermit. I blamed him, obviously.'

Rosie smiled back.

'Well, we're out now.'

'Would you like . . . ' Moray indicated the bar area generally, not wanting to ask Rosie outright if she wanted a drink.

'Glass of white wine, please,' said Rosie. 'Large.'

Moray and Stephen exchanged looks.

'Okay, when we carry her home, I want the bottom end,' said Moray. 'Not the spewing end.'

'Oi,' said Rosie, who could not handle her drink in the slightest.

'It's all right,' said Stephen. 'We'll do what we always do, and pretend in the morning that you were really charming and amusing whilst pissed.'

Rosie's brow furrowed.

'Okay, lime and soda, please.'

'Ssssh, we're only teasing,' said Moray, going to the bar. He came back with a bottle of the pub's very indifferent wine for Rosie and Tina, and pints of Derbyshire Gold for himself and Stephen and Jake.

Rosie hadn't been out for so long, she had forgotten how jolly it could be. Everyone came over to say hello, pleased to see them out and about. It was time, she decided. Time to embrace what lay ahead.

There was the thought running at the back of her head that she still hadn't told Stephen about her other health problems.

Later, she told herself fiercely, taking another sip of the wine.

Later, they were staggering up the road when Stephen stopped suddenly and pointed out a star overhead.

'I see two stars,' said Rosie.

'Ssssh,' said Stephen, as they both started laughing. 'Put one hand over your eye.'

She did so, falling about with the giggles.

'That's Polaris,' said Stephen. 'You can see it from Africa. It feels about a billion times closer, like you could touch it.'

He pulled her to him.

'I'd love to show you Africa.'

'Would you?' Rosie was under his coat to keep warm, and her voice came out slightly muffled, but still doubtful. 'I thought you never wanted to go back.'

'Well Diane thinks it would be good for me.'

'That's because *Diane* secretly wants to do kissy kissy with you. It's totally obvious. She'll want to come with you and be all like, "Oh, here I am in Africa, KISSY KISSY, it's totally therapeutic."'

'Don't be ridiculous.'

'I am not being ridiculous, I can always tell.'

Rosie popped her head out and looked up at the sky. 'We can't afford it.'

'I know.'

She looked at him.

'Except . . .'

'What?'

It shot across her: what could be better than getting away, having a trip, taking some time out? This was just what she needed. To do something a bit different for a bit.

'We could use my plane ticket to Australia.'

Stephen had forgotten all about that. Rosie's mother and brother had given it to her for Christmas.

'It's open, it cost a fortune. I bet we could change it.'

'I thought you needed to keep it for when you wanted to run away from your evil fiancé,' teased Stephen.

'There is that,' said Rosie. 'But wow. It would be . . .'

it would be an adventure, wouldn't it? And we could take lots of pictures and show the village kids where the fund-raising is going, and ... '

She looked at Stephen looking at her.

'What? What is it?'

'You are some woman, Rosie Hopkins.'

Rosie woke up with a groan and a headache.

'Tell me I didn't just agree to go halfway across the world with you to somewhere without any luxury swimming pools.'

'Nooo,' said Stephen, rolling over and taking her in his arms.

'Oh good,' she said, snuggling down again under the covers.

There was a pause.

'Shit, I did.'

'You can go back on your word,' said Stephen sleepily.

'I don't want to go to Africa! What about all the lions and tigers?'

'Well, there's no tigers for starters. They don't live in Africa.'

'Not even if they marry lions?'

Stephen cleared his throat.

'I release you from your promise.'

'See, this is exactly what will get me eaten in Africa.'

Chapter Five

Lully, lullay, Thou little tiny Child,
Bye, bye, lully, lullay.
Lullay, thou little tiny Child,
Bye, bye, lully, lullay.

'I still can't believe you're going,' said Lilian, stirring her tea crossly.

Rosie felt a bit annoyed at this. Lilian had been to London three times in her life, and Cherbourg once (which she had absolutely adored, talking about the French ever since as the ultimate arbiters of taste and style), with her younger brother Gordon. Rosie wanted her to say 'Wow, that's amazing, how wonderful,' rather than 'You're completely crazy, what are you thinking?'

'What about when you're being held hostage?'

'Lilian, stop being racist.'

'I'm not being racist. There's loads of places where people get held hostage – Cumbria, for instance – and I don't want you going to any of them.'

'People don't get held hostage in Cumbria!'

Lilian furrowed her brow.

'A lot of mysterious things happen in Cumbria.'

'Well anyway. The charity is going to let us ride along with them, we'll be perfectly safe.'

Lilian sighed.

'It all sounds very fishy to me. Are you *sure* you can't just send them a postal order?'

Rosie shook her head.

'Stephen wants to go. He feels committed, from before. It's his duty to the family to make sure the girl is well taken care of.'

Lilian pouted.

'That's a given, if he's taking you.'

'I think they've got plenty of medical staff there,' said Rosie. It hadn't actually occurred to her that her skills might be needed.

'And where does it end?' said Lilian. 'Are you sure you won't make things worse rather than better?'

'You can never be sure,' said Rosie. 'About anything.'

'Hmph, I suppose that's true,' said Lilian. 'Well, come back safe and never leave the village again. That's all I ask.'

Planning the trip had been, in retrospect, wonderful for Rosie. She couldn't forget what had happened, of course, not entirely, but there were vaccinations to arrange, routes to plot. They'd booked their flights – Angie had not been exactly happy to know they weren't coming out to Australia, but had heard the spark of life back in her daughter's voice and that had been almost enough – and Faustine was going to let them camp with them, so all their money could pay for Célestine's trip to the mission hospital. They'd also sent vitamins, supplements, nappies and baby clothes on ahead.

Moray poked his head round the door, having been in to see one of the other residents. He'd heard Rosie's voice.

'Hello!' he said. 'Give me some gin!'

Rosie looked up.

'It's a bit early for gin.'

'Not when you've been doing what I've been doing,' said Moray. 'Are you joining me or shall I tell you in great detail? It involves use of the word "weeping".'

Rosie fled to get the gin bottle and the tonic from Lilian's mini fridge, and grabbed a lemon and some ice from the kitchen, and they sat round the fire, a convivial threesome.

'So you've heard of her nutty plan,' said Lilian.

Moray gave a half-smile.

'Rather you than me,' he said. But in fact, after the hard time Rosie had had so far this year, he absolutely approved. A change of scene, some sunshine, and other people to focus on rather than turning inwards. He was the only person aware of her fertility issues, and he hated her carrying the burden alone, even though he understood her reasons.

'Actually,' he said, 'I think you'll fall in love with it and go all Meryl Streep and come back saying "I hed a ferm in Efrika" and start talking about the moon over the savannah and the smell of the dust.'

'I don't see what's wrong with Lipton,' said Lilian.

'I'm only going for a trip,' said Rosie. 'Don't listen to Moray.'

'Until Robert Redford turns up with a big gun and sweeps you off your feet,' said Moray, and they both swooned a little, and Lilian said what on earth were they talking about, and Rosie was shocked when she realised Lilian had never seen the film, so she found it in the library and put it on, and they had more gin and tonics and watched it and all three of them swooned over Robert Redford, and Stephen was entirely confused when Rosie turned up at home late and slightly tipsy, talking about how much she couldn't wait for their trip.

It had been a good, busy summer season and now it was late October, with fewer daytrippers and hikers coming through. Célestine's baby was due in two weeks, so they probably wouldn't be there to see it born, but they would visit the capital, spend a night in the village and make sure everything was all right there, then travel on to a backpackers' hostel in a beach resort and have a little holiday too.

Rosie clutched Stephen's hand very tightly as they shut up the little cottage, and turned the sweetshop sign to 'Closed'. In the three years they'd known each other, they'd never had a holiday.

'Well, it's not really a holiday,' said Stephen, smiling apologetically as he sat trying to apportion out their holiday money, while Rosie puzzled over the packing. 'A new start. A healing process. Will you throw a humbug at me if I use the word "closure"?'

Rosie swallowed. He was so happy about this trip, so hyped up and enthusiastic. And she was too, of course. But she couldn't forget that she hadn't yet come clean with him; hadn't shared everything about what had happened at the hospital.

'Then we can come home,' said Stephen, 'and make a baby of our own, and then we can forget about ever having had a holiday or a second's free time ever again.'

76

He came up behind her and kissed her.

Rosie stiffened.

'What?' said Stephen. 'Sorry. Sorry, love, was that insensitive?'

'No,' said Rosie, shaking her head. 'But there's something I have to tell you ...'

It wasn't, she knew, the fact of it – or if it was, he didn't touch on it. It was the months and months she had gone without mentioning it; it was such a huge part of their future, and she had selfishly kept it to herself, assumed he wouldn't be able to cope, thought she could deal with it all herself.

And all she could say, numbly, was that she didn't know why she hadn't told him; that she'd thought it was already bad enough (and there was a tiny part of her that had wondered if, possibly, the immaculate Dr Chang might after all have been completely wrong; that maybe, in the intervening months, it might happen of its own accord, prove them all completely wrong and they would never have to face up to it and deal with it). And Stephen had accused her of wanting to control everything, to keep that knowledge for herself, and she could only agree.

'Did you think I was going to jilt you?' Stephen had said furiously. 'Is that what you think of me? Hmm? Just dump you the second you stopped being breeding material?'

Rosie's head had drooped.

'You always bloody do this,' he said. 'Something goes wrong and you bottle it up and screw everything up. How can we work like this, Rosie? How? You think if you live in a pretend sweetie dreamland, bad things will go away. But they don't, do they? They don't. They get worse.'

Neither of them got much sleep that night.

Jake drove them the two hours to the airport in his old Peugeot, chatting amiably with Stephen about the price of cattle most of the way, seemingly not noticing that they weren't speaking to one another. Rosie stared out of the window, but saw nothing. Autumn was bright across the country, brown and red and orange displays of leaves framing harvested fields with their great rolls of straw. Huge grey clouds loomed across the sky; rainfall was visible on distant, shaded hills.

Rosie rubbed her arm reflexively where she'd had her injections, and tried to remember where her malaria tablets were. All she could think about was how Moray had tried to make her laugh by pretending to give her the injections without looking, and then had had to ask if she was pregnant, and of course she'd had to say she wasn't. And at this rate, she never would be.

They were carefully polite to one another. Stephen slept for most of the flight; Rosie, edgy and upset, failed to concentrate on the films she'd been so looking forward to seeing (the nearest cinema to Lipton was forty-five minutes away). Stephen's hair had flopped over his forehead as he slept. She wanted to stroke it, but didn't dare.

Our first holiday, she thought bleakly. You're returning to the scene of the worst day of your life; I'm an infertile old cow you're almost certainly going to have second thoughts about marrying. Happy holidays.

The airport was the first shock: a massive roof, no air conditioning, boiling hot, everybody shouting it seemed at once. People approached them from all angles, speaking loudly in French, asking if they needed taxis, hotels, bags carried ... Rosie, who had only ever been to Spain before, on a package trip, looked around her in bewilderment. Stephen strode past it all, looking, Rosie thought, in his khakis and collarless cotton shirt, very much like he belonged here. She, on the other hand, was already regretting wearing jeans; they were hot and felt thick and uncomfortably creased against her skin.

'ETIENNE!'

A voice was calling insistently in their direction, and Stephen turned towards it. Standing waving furiously was a tiny, strong-looking girl with short dark hair, a light tan, and a pair of khakis exactly like Stephen's. Her face was animated, her teeth very white.

Stephen's face broke into a smile.

'FAUSTINE!'

The two of them jumped into a massive embrace, then they started speaking rapidly in French, of which Rosie understood not a word. She coughed, gently.

'Sorry, sorry,' said Stephen, his face still energised and excited-looking. 'I haven't seen Faust since … well, since everything.'

'He was very naughty boy,' said Faustine in the most charming French accent. 'We write, we call, we send all the message, *tu sais*? And he does not answer us, he has forgotten us, he does not like us any more.'

Stephen shook his head.

'Oh it wasn't quite like that.'

Faustine smiled.

'But now you are home, yes?'

'No,' said Stephen. 'I'm back.'

Rosie was glad he said this.

'This is Rosie. My …' he paused for a second, which caught at Rosie's heart, 'my fiancée.'

Faustine made a face.

'*Oui? Alors*, my goodness, congratulations,' she said, but she did not exactly smile. 'You work in Africa too?'

'It's my first time,' said Rosie. 'But I can't wait to see it.'

Faustine simply raised her eyebrows.

'*Alors*, follow me.'

If the inside of the airport had been hot and stuffy, outside it was like stepping into an oven. Immediately Rosie pawed through her luggage looking for her sunglasses. She couldn't remember feeling the heat of the sun so strongly before. Everywhere people in bright clothing were getting into cars, piling luggage on to scooters and bicycles, selling small boxes of bits and pieces, newspapers, SIM cards, bottles of water.

As if reading her mind, Faustine took out a large, dirty-looking plastic bottle and passed it round.

'Drink,' she said. 'You'll get thirsty.'

Rosie wanted to pour the entire thing over her head, but took a few mouthfuls and passed it on to Stephen, who winked at her conspiratorially as Faustine barked a few commands in French into her phone. About five minutes later, just as Rosie was hoping they were staying in a nice hotel somewhere with air conditioning, a rickety old van with the organisation's logo on the side bounced up, the driver, also in khakis – Rosie was beginning to curse the flowery dresses she'd packed – waving to them brightly.

There was no suspension in the van, and they bounced uncomfortably in the back seat. There was air conditioning, of a sort, that puffed out occasional huffs of lukewarm air, as if in a bad mood, but it was pretty tricky to catch them.

Even so, the city was such a stunning sight that Rosie forgot everything: she just wanted to lean her head out and catch all of it.

Cars in varying conditions of terrible cluttered up the roads, with things attached to the top, mismatched wheels, men hanging off the back. There were some traffic lights, most of which were systematically ignored. Their driver spent a lot of time leaning on the horn, as did everybody else. Stephen and Faustine talked about all the people they had in common – none of whom Rosie knew – but she found she didn't mind, as she stared at the colourful, chaotic, brightly lit scene in front of her eyes. Little children charged about – some, she noticed, carrying baguettes under their arms – men shouted angrily into their phones; there were animals everywhere; terrifyingly small mopeds laden with people and parcels weaving in and out of the slow-moving traffic; music wailing from car stereos.

Rosie forgot she was uncomfortably hot and thirsty and would really like a long hot bath; she forgot that she was slightly jealous that Stephen was so animated speaking to this funny-looking little French firecracker. Instead, she simply breathed in the sights and the smells: the women in their bright prints; the boys, by contrast, in Western clothes; the children wearing incongruous outfits that she guessed must come through charitable giving: One Direction T-shirts, Justin Bieber, lots and lots of Manchester United. A little girl, her hair pinned up, sitting peeling corn by the side of the road, looked up as they passed and gave her a smile and a tentative wave, and Rosie waved back, wanting to stop the van and jump out and give her some of the large assortment of sweets she'd insisted on packing.

She tried to take some pictures, but they were picking up speed; she wanted to remember it all for Liilan, who had insisted that she tell her everything. Despite Rosie's rather weak exhortations to the contrary, Lilian would never travel again now; her old bones simply weren't up to it. So she needed to see it through Rosie's eyes.

As they left the city behind, Rosie wiped her face with the back of her hand; both were covered in a fine light mist of red dust. Out in the countryside, the wind blew sand across harsh landscapes of dried-up fields. In a corner, she saw a large group of huts, huddled together as the sand scoured them. It must get into every nook and cranny. On the other side ran a single railway line.

'Why is there just one?' she asked, interested.

Faustine laughed, which Rosie thought was unnecessary.

'There's only one train,' said Stephen over his shoulder.

'One train?'

'Yes. In the whole country. It goes from one side to the other, once every few days. So they don't really need another line.'

'They DO,' interjected Faustine fiercely.

'Well, yes. They do. But it's not on the priority list right now.'

As the hours passed, and her bum grew increasingly numb, and the roads became harsher and worse, Rosie lapsed into a kind of passive dream state, taking in the unchanging landscape. Eventually they stopped at a kind of roadside inn, built roughly of wood in a pentagon shape.

Faustine jumped down.

'She's gone to put a rocket up their arse about not undercooking supper,' said Stephen. 'For your all-new African stomach.'

He looked at her carefully. There was an element of truce in his expression.

'I'll be fine,' said Rosie crossly.

'Tell me that on the squat loo at four a.m.,' said Stephen.

Rosie got out to stretch her legs, whereupon she was immediately divebombed by nine thousand mosquitoes, so she got back in the van and covered up with DEET and a long-sleeved shirt and a big hat that she had been vastly opposed to packing but now was delighted with; likewise the scarf.

'They really are bastards,' she said.

'They are,' said Stephen, batting them away. 'But look.'

Over the flat plains in the distance, the bright orange-gold sun was sinking at a rate faster than Rosie would have believed possible. As it did so, the sky took on a fierce flat line of bright purple. The sun dipped quickly behind the mountain range in the distance, the purple flared brightly then turned speedily to black and, like diamonds popping out of a necklace, suddenly there was one star, then another, then another, and within minutes the entire sky was raining on them, great crystal stars so close Rosie felt she could put out her hand and simply pluck them down.

'Oh my,' she breathed.

Stephen came across from behind the van to the rock by the side of the road she was standing on.

'I know,' said Stephen. He touched her shoulder and, meeting no resistance, moved his arm around her. It felt like they were the only two human beings on the face of the earth. She had never felt further away from home, nor more in touch with the planet she'd been born on. She turned her face to his.

'I should have told you,' she said.

'You should have.'

'I'm sorry. Everything felt so—'

'You do this all the time, Rosie. You're worried I'm too fragile for bad news.'

Rosie nodded.

'I know. I know. I don't mean to, but—'

'You don't need to protect me. But you do need to let me protect you when it matters.'

Rosie shook her head, and he took her in his arms.

'Aren't we a team?'

Rosie nodded again.

'Are we going to get through this together?'

'I was hoping I'd think up a really good way how.' Stephen smiled.

'And stun me with your amazing genius?'

'Something like that.'

He shook his head.

'There is only one way, Rosie. Together. That's the only way. Whatever happens.'

She looked up into his face, almost more handsome for being unshaven.

'All right,' she breathed. 'Okay.'

'Good.' Stephen turned her to face the sky. 'Because together, we're amazing. Look where we are!'

Rosie took in a great breath of the warm, scented air.

'What can't we get through together?'

'Nothing,' said Rosie.

'Apart from that squat toilet,' said Stephen. 'There, you're on your own. Come on.'

He took her hand, batted the bugs out of the way and led her over to a low stone wall. Apart from the odd wooden structure behind them, there wasn't a light to be seen anywhere, but the moon that was starting to rise was absolutely huge, the largest Rosie had ever seen, and the stars lit up the landscape so it didn't feel dark, not really, not like down in the Lipton valley in the depths of winter when the clouds rolled off the dales and you could barely see the icy breath in front of your face.

'You never know who's going to like it and who's going to hate it,' Stephen said. 'Sometimes the most unlikely kids come out here and just get stuck in and have a marvellous time.'

'Like Prince Harry,' said Rosie promptly.

'Ha. Well I don't know about that. But then other people who really want to be here and do good, they can't bear it. Can't bear seeing people suffering, and living in hardship.'

'And getting their faces eaten,' pointed out Rosie, flailing at another mosquito.

'And that. Can't live without eyelash extensions, that kind of thing.'

'Well you always knew how high-maintenance I was.'

She looked up. One star was glittering more brightly than the rest. 'It's beautiful here. And I'm getting in the mood to think about our wedding again. Can't you propose to me? Just one more time.'

'No! I did it already! And my knee isn't up to it.'

'It's so dry and warm here,' said Rosie. 'Ideal conditions, I'd have said.'

'You've got a big insect bite on your face.'

'So you DO want to take it back?'

Rosie was pretending to take her ring off, and Stephen was observing that she couldn't seem to get it over her finger and had she started putting loads of weight on already, and was he too going to let himself go and grow man-boobs, when Faustine appeared with two plates of food.

'I got them to make it specially,' she said, watching unsmilingly as they horsed around. They followed her to an outside table. Two men sitting there shook Stephen's hand but looked at Rosie suspiciously. She fiddled again with her ring, then sat down.

The food wasn't at all bad: grain, tomatoes and stringy chicken.

'You got meat?' said Stephen cheerfully. 'You're good.'

'You're paying for it,' said Faustine.

Once they had eaten, Rosie began to feel incredibly sleepy. They had had a very long day.

The wigwam-shaped building with bunks round the walls was cooled by a wheezing, anaemic fan, though Rosie was so exhausted she hardly noticed it. She did what she could in the toilet area, which was not much, brushed her teeth, kissed Stephen good night – he was sitting outside by the campfire, drinking some kind of tea and speaking in French again – and fell asleep in minutes, listening to the scuffling noises of animals, the quiet murmur of voices and the buzz of the mosquitoes in the room (she was under a net Stephen had bought her, and she thought fuzzily that she might just wear it all the time). The glimpse of the bright stars through the little hole at the top of the wigwam was the final thing she registered before dropping off into a surprisingly deep sleep.

Chapter Six

O Little Town of Bethlehem
How still we see thee lie
Above thy deep and dreamless sleep
The silent stars go by
Yet in thy dark streets shineth
The everlasting light
The hopes and fears of all the years
Are met in thee tonight

Rosie woke, hot, thirsty and disorientated, with bright sunlight heating up the structure from outside. There was no one in there with her, but the other bunks had been slept in. She got up, stretching and cursing her hair, which had now frizzed out about a metre either side of her head. She thought of the chic scarf tying back

Faustine's hair. She needed one of those.

Outside she smelled coffee and headed towards it cheerfully. Faustine was busying herself over the camp-fire with a coffee pot whilst their driver cooked some eggs.

'Hey!' said Stephen. 'Hello, sleepyhead! Now this is why you want to be with the Frenchiest aid organisa-tions. They care about their coffee.'

He handed her a cup, loading it with sugar even though she didn't normally take the stuff. It was dark, strong and delicious. Rosie blinked in the bright sun-light, looking at the pale, barren landscape.

'It is better when you get up earlier and you do not miss the cool of the morning,' pointed out Faustine. Rosie looked at her suspiciously.

'Thanks, I'll bear that in mind,' she said.

There was a little stream for washing – Stephen warned her not to drink the water – then they were on their way again, bumping along endless potholed roads, occasionally seeing old, overstuffed vans, crammed with thin cattle or large groups of men or sacks of flour, rum-bling up the road towards them, often on the wrong side or straight down the middle. The roads got worse, and it was hot, and Rosie started to feel herself getting a bit tired, then told herself not to, but to keep her spirits up. Stephen was looking distant and faraway, which could be good or bad, she knew. She squeezed his hand and was reassured when he squeezed back.

'Are you ready?' she whispered.

'As I'll ever be,' he said, his hand moving instinctively towards his injured leg, his jaw set.

Eventually the minivan turned down a smaller road, cutting through a forest, then a smaller one again, and finally, at least three hours since they'd seen anything that looked anything like a town, they came to a clearing at the end of a sandy sort of path.

All the way, Rosie had tried not to have preconceptions about what it would be like; but here, undeniably, there were huts with straw tops in a circle around an open area, and a fire with a huge old metal tin hanging over the top of it.

As soon as the van drove in, there was a roar, and a huge heap of children, yelling and shouting enthusiastically, ran towards them, seemingly unbothered by their own safety.

For the first time Rosie saw Faustine smile, as she stepped down from the vehicle. Earlier, Rosie had mentioned the sweets she had brought, and the Frenchwoman had frowned and demanded them, saying, 'You'll cause a riot handing those out. Give them to me and I'll use them as vaccination bribes.'

At the time Rosie thought she was being bossy. Now she could see exactly what Faustine had meant. There were so many of them, all of them excited and delirious just to see the car. Handing out sweets would have been awful.

'*Bonjour, bonjour,*' said Rosie as she got down, and the boldest of the children flocked around her, chattering like birds and touching her hair. One little girl who must have been the same age as her niece Meridian clambered up on to her hip. Rosie looked at Faustine, who already had a child in each arm, and the Frenchwoman motioned that it was fine.

The children followed them across the open space. There were, Rosie noticed, children everywhere, and women wearing long skirts and headbands (she desperately wanted to tie back her own hair, but all she had was a spare pair of knickers and she didn't feel it was quite the time or place). Some women had babies tied to their backs, not wearing nappies, just with a cloth between them and their mothers. The babies looked incredibly comfortable, Rosie couldn't help noticing. And there were old men, with sticks and white hair and bare chests, wizened and bent over by the sun. But there were no young men. There were no fathers, no chaps to help with the work that was obviously going on – wood chopping, water carrying and fetching. Stephen had said they had all gone, to join the army, or to look for work in Dakar or Mali or Nigeria, but Rosie didn't realise what that meant until she saw it: a place devoid of men. The women looked tough and strong. She imagined you had to be.

One old man came up to Stephen, looked at him for

a long time, then burst out into conversation. Stephen nodded, and more came over to join in. It reminded Rosie of the Red Lion.

Eventually they were beckoned towards one of the huts. They passed one building, relatively modern, that Faustine indicated had been built by the charity. Inside, a heavy-set woman with extremely short hair was standing in front of a class of at least fifty children sharing a few slates in an airless, scorching room. The boys sat at the front and the girls were behind them, despite being much smaller. Faustine rolled her eyes but nonetheless waved cheerily at the teacher, who waved back.

A few feet from the hut they were heading for, the children stood back, looking anxious. Faustine was deep in conversation with the woman who had brought them there. Rosie couldn't follow the language but could tell by the increasingly exuberant gesticulations that something was displeasing her.

'What is it?' she asked Stephen.

'Ssssh,' he said, face strained. 'They're saying she's not well ... Célestine.'

'Not well how?' said Rosie. 'She's only eight months along.'

'They're not sure about that.'

'Faustine's a doctor though, right?'

Stephen shook his head.

'She's had first-aid training, we all did, but no, she's

a regional manager. She's got administrative skills.'

'But it's called Médecins Sans Frontières.'

'Yes, that's right. But you wouldn't waste a doctor on managing everybody else, would you?'

Rosie's brow furrowed as Faustine disappeared into the hut.

'Well, I should go in,' she said.

'You haven't been invited,' pointed out Stephen.

'No, but I want to take a look at her anyway.'

'I suppose you could, though I'm sure she's fine.'

'I'm not,' said Rosie. 'How old is she?'

Faustine came hurrying back out of the hut, pulling out her phone. She was swearing.

'What's up?' said Stephen.

'There's something wrong,' said Faustine. 'It's been wrong for a while. And the nearest team is eight hours away. I'm only meant to be here to hand over money and sign some paperwork ...'

'Can I see her?' said Rosie.

'Are you a doctor?' said Faustine rudely.

'I'm an emergency nurse,' said Rosie, forcefully rather than apologetically as she usually did. 'But if that's no use ...'

Faustine backed down.

'Please,' she said.

Inside the hut it was incredibly dark and hot, with a warm, sinister scent: smoke, with something underlying it. There were very few possessions – a couple of tin plates – and an older man and woman sat looking frightened by a small fire, which made the room suffocating. They looked up at Rosie with fear in their eyes.

Rosie moved towards the bed. On it was a young girl – very young. She was barely developed, not fully grown, and her frightened eyes were enormous in her heart-shaped face, her stomach painfully distended but not huge.

'Célestine?' Rosie said, quietly and calmly, and knelt down next to her. The girl nodded. Rosie cursed and wished she hadn't spent all her French lessons up the back of the class with her great mate Trix making 'hee haw hee haw' noises.

Faustine was there behind her, however.

'Can you say I'm here to help her?' said Rosie, and Faustine translated immediately. Rosie felt Célestine's forehead. She was burning up.

'Oh Lord,' said Rosie and felt down between the girl's legs. As she'd suspected, there was a moist patch on the sheet.

'Have you got a medical kit in the car?' she said. 'Also, I have to scrub up.'

Faustine brought in a large box that had been under

the front seat, and Rosie did the best she could with the disinfectant wipes and boiled water on offer.

'I think she's got puerperal fever,' she said urgently. 'I've seen it before. She needs to be in hospital. Her waters have broken but her labour hasn't started and she's got an infection. How pregnant is she really?'

Faustine asked the older couple – Célestine's parents – who indicated various measures.

'Ask the girl,' said Rosie crossly. 'And tell her we need to know; we absolutely need to know exactly. It's going to make all the difference.'

Faustine spoke to Célestine gravely, then counted back on her fingers, checking quickly with the parents.

'Oh, that explains it,' she said finally.

'What?' said Rosie, who was palpating Célestine's stomach, trying to feel the baby move.

'She told her parents it was when her betrothed came home in the winter time, but it wasn't. It was the festival when the warriors arrived in the village. This baby is very late, not early.'

'Crap,' said Rosie. 'Right. Okay. OKAY!' For she had felt a flutter under her hand, a tiny movement that told her what she needed to know: this baby was alive.

She looked at Célestine's face.

'How long has she felt so bad?'

'Three days,' translated back Faustine, and Rosie swallowed in disbelief.

'Where's the nearest hospital? This baby needs to come out now. Every second we delay, we're increasing the risks – these are real risks. Is there a helicopter?'

Faustine snorted.

'No.'

'Well we need to drive her somewhere, then. Where's the nearest hospital?'

'She will be in far more danger in the hospital,' said Faustine. 'It's a haven of infection. It's not safe. We were going to take her to the mission hospital, but it's an overnight drive back towards the city.'

'But she needs drugs, monitoring ...' Rosie pulled back the sheet on the girl's narrow hips. 'I don't think she can even give birth. She needs a Caesarean.'

Faustine looked and nodded.

'I'll radio in to our nearest field team. They're work-ing in a refugee camp ...'

'Well they need to be here,' said Rosie.

She took out a cool disinfected towel and rubbed it on Célestine's head, then went outside to think.

'What is it?' said Stephen, who was pacing in the shade, the children making passes at his stick.

'She needs to give birth,' said Rosie. 'She's got an infection, and if we don't get the baby out it will kill them both.'

'Can you do it?'

'I can try and induce it.' She looked at Stephen. 'But

she's far too young to have a baby, you know. It's going to be a difficult birth. She really needs a section, and I definitely couldn't do that. Or not without killing her; there's no anaesthetic. CHRIST.'

Stephen looked at her.

'Oh God,' he said. 'Oh God, I can't believe I brought you out to this.'

Rosie shrugged and shook her head.

'Well let's just try and think that it would be even worse if I wasn't here ...'

Faustine came running out. Her face was calm, but very pale.

'She's fitting.'

'Oh crap,' said Rosie. 'This baby can't wait. It can't. How far away are the field team?'

'Eight hours,' said Faustine.

Rosie swore.

'She hasn't got eight hours. I've seen this before.'

Both the others nodded.

'Unpack me a pair of gloves,' said Rosie. 'Faustine, I'll need you.'

Célestine's parents, who had already lost both their sons, sat looking carefully ahead, too numbed by fate to do anything else. Rosie pulled on the gloves and got Faustine to try and cool the girl with stream water –

Stephen fetched it – though it was not as clean as she would have liked. She set a pot to boil on the fire, then, very carefully, gave the girl a 'sweep': a gentle stimulation of the ovaries to try and bring on labour. Now that her waters had gone, the baby really needed to be delivered or risk even more infection. And round here, everything you touched was infection.

Célestine moaned and clutched at the thin cotton covering her. Faustine murmured to her comfortingly in French and mopped her brow. Rosie had found a stethoscope in the medical bag but could tell too from touch that the baby was alive. For now.

Suddenly a great wrench went through the girl and she cried out.

'Yes,' said Rosie. 'Yes. That's labour starting.' She looked at the girl's face in pity. 'And it's not messing about.'

All through the day and on into the night, Célestine laboured in the boiling heat, her cries faint as Rosie did her best to hold on to her. The group doctor was talking her through it on the radio, but she remembered most of it from her training, and from delivering Edison's sister at Christmas time, although that seemed now incredibly far away; a different era, almost, in a clean room, with a doctor present and a healthy, motivated mother. Célestine on the other hand was unresisting, her eyes cloudy.

As they went on through the night, still with no sign of the back-up team – their jeep had broken down on the way and there was no prospect of replacement parts, it seemed – everyone dozed in broken jerks here and there whilst Stephen brewed tea and more villagers arrived, their faces grave, with offerings of food.

By three o'clock, Rosie felt incredibly filthy and delirious with tiredness; she couldn't imagine what Célestine was going through. Célestine's eyes flickered occasionally; she was in a strange world of her own, a world of animal noises and deep disconnection. She could not answer a basic question. And she was not dilating, not properly.

The group doctor was asking Rosie with some urgency if she could possibly perform a section, and she was telling him with absolute clarity that she could not, practically, morally, ethically or without some risk of killing both mother and child. The group doctor pointed out that she was likely to do that by doing nothing, and Rosie squeezed her eyes tight shut and wiped her grimy forehead and looked at Stephen, who looked back, neither of them knowing what was right and what they should do.

Eventually, twenty-four hours after Célestine had gone into labour, they heard the most welcome noise ever: the sound of a heavy four-wheel-drive car turning into the village. Rosie jumped up as the team thundered towards the hut, her heart pounding with relief, but as the three sober-looking people came in – two men, one local, one French, and a woman – one look at their faces told her everything she needed to know.

She offered to leave, let them perform their duties, but as she did so, Célestine roused briefly, made a little noise, and grasped Rosie's sleeve with weak fingers. The doctor nodded and Rosie sat back down.

'Hush,' she said to the girl, mopping her brow gently, trying to bring her temperature down. The truck had ice, which she tried to feed Célestine, stroking her, cooing to her, using words that weren't of any language but the international sound of one human being attempting to comfort another.

The team prepped as quickly as they were able, and one of the men approached with a gas mask, ready to administer a general anaesthetic. Célestine turned her face away, and Rosie, with gentle coaxing, attempted to get the mask on her. There was a bit of a muddle – a strangulated yell, an arm flailing out briefly, the French doctor swearing – then, suddenly, Célestine turned towards Rosie, looked at her once – a sharp, entirely clear, direct look that Rosie would never forget – and said huskily, very slowly, '*Bébé . . . vive.*'

Then slowly, almost happily, her eyes drooped and then closed, so that she looked for all the world like a baby going to sleep. She exhaled once, a long, ragged sound, and then, as they all froze watching, her grip on Rosie's hand unfurled and she lay still.

Her mother, in the corner of the hut, sank to the floor with a howl. Faustine immediately went to take her out. As Rosie stood there, numb, the doctors continued as if nothing had happened.

'You're going to . . .'

They looked at her.

'You can clear out now if you like; this will have to be quick,' said one of them in broken English.

Rosie stumbled out of the hut, into the arms of an anxious, waiting Stephen.

'What?' he said, but she could only shake her head, too shocked to speak.

One of the children led them down a long path towards a waterfall, where the water tipped and spilled over boulders, frothing at the bottom. Neither of them said a word as they stripped down to their underwear and got into the water.

The swift current blasted off the sweat and the muck

and woke Rosie out of her stupor. She let herself be completely consumed by the flow and the cleanliness. Finally, feeling cool for the first time since she'd arrived, she stood upright on two stones. Then she burst into tears.

'Ssssh,' he said, taking her in his arms, his chest glistening with spray. 'You were magnificent! You did brilliantly!'

'I couldn't help her,' said Rosie. 'I couldn't help her.'

'Of course you did,' he said in surprise. 'You did everything right, Rosie. Everything. You kept her going until the medics got here.'

'I shouldn't have started labour,' said Rosie. 'I should have just waited.'

Stephen shook his head.

'Don't be ridiculous, she was already very sick,' he said. 'There's no way she'd have lasted that long. No way. They would have been too late, Rosie.'

Rosie choked back tears.

'She was only a child.'

'It's different here,' said Stephen. 'And I don't mean different because it's Africa. I mean because it's deep bush. Deep in the country. You help where you can, you comfort where you can, and you don't panic. And you

104

didn't panic. When the time came, you did everything right.'

Rosie was still coming to terms with what had happened. She had seen people die before, of course, in A&E. From horrible, pointless things. But not from something so preventable.

Stephen held her tightly close to him.

'Come on,' he said. 'We'll go and get some sleep. You did your best darling. That's all you can do. I was very proud of you.'

She looked up at him and swallowed.

'I just want . . .'

'I know,' said Stephen. 'I know. You want everything to be fixed, you want everything to be fine. But that's the first lesson you learn out here: you do what you can.'

He swallowed.

'I learned the hard way too.'

They picked their way back up the path to the little cluster of huts in the sandy clearing. As they grew closer, they heard it. At first Rosie thought it wasn't possible. Or that it was somebody else's; the village was full of children. But as they approached the dingy little hut, it became clear from the huge crowd of people outside it that the mewling noise was coming from within.

Faustine beckoned them over. Her face, with its clear skin and fine dark brows, was an exhausted mask. Rosie noticed the smell of blood immediately and looked up, full of foreboding.

Faustine shrugged.

'Without you they would both have died.'

Rosie gasped. Already Célestine's body had been removed. Sand was being swept across the floor. Sitting in the corner was a woman Rosie had not seen before; a heavy-set older woman who nonetheless was breast-feeding a tiny infant. And there too, with the same numb look of shock they had worn for the last two days, were Célestine's parents: stoic, resigned, as if a life in which your children died before you was absolutely normal. Rosie felt her heart begin to break.

She approached the child. It was a little boy. He had been cleaned up and had finished feeding; the woman happily handed him over for Rosie to have a look. She put him up on the bed to check him over. He responded well to stimulus; his pupils contracted well; there was no jaundice. But she noticed that his right arm did not shoot up when he was dropped gently backwards, as she would expect. She tried it again and again, and looked more closely at the arm. The tiny fingers, with their perfect little nails, did not grasp on to hers as the left hand did without any trouble at all. The hand – he was a very pale coffee colour – was lighter than the other, with a bluish tinge all the way up to the elbow.

'Faustine!' called Rosie. Outside, the doctors were

smoking and chatting to a middle-aged man who had appeared and was gesticulating with some importance. 'Can you send one of the doctors over?'

The local doctor came over and followed her in. She showed him what she'd noticed and he screwed up his face and gathered the others.

'They were about to check the baby again,' said Faustine defensively. 'They were clearing up after the mother.'

'I realise that,' said Rosie patiently. 'I just want everyone to take a look.'

Now there were the first stirrings of life in the grandparents. The man came over to examine the baby with them. His face looked concerned. A loud debate started that Rosie could not follow, but at one point the baby started crying again. The wet nurse took him back and someone brought her a plate of food, which she ate with her free hand. Stephen ushered Rosie out of the hut and over to where a canvas tent had been set up for them. Inside, four comfortable-looking camp beds had been unpacked. Suddenly all Rosie wanted to do was lie down and sleep.

Stephen sat next to her on one of the beds.

'What's wrong with the baby?' he said, straight out, holding her gaze intently. Rosie thought he must be very tired too.

'Um, it's hard to tell,' she said. 'His neurological

impulses all seem fine; his pupils are responding, his grasp, all of that; he seems very smart and alert. But his right arm is a problem. It's possible he was lying badly in the womb, that it's got damaged in some way. It may have developed that way, or they may have been in such a rush to get him out they damaged him somehow. But his arm is limp and I don't think ... I don't think it's a temporary thing. I don't think it's ever going to work.'

Stephen swallowed. She still didn't understand, not in the slightest, the intense look on his face.

'I mean, he'll probably be all right with one arm ... It's a shame it's his right, if he's right-handed, but people can compensate a lot.'

'Not here,' said Stephen shortly.

A small child came in and offered them two cups of tea, which they took with thanks, even though it tasted very odd to Rosie. But just to drink something warm and wet was very comforting. Her eyelids were starting to droop.

'Oh,' she said, wearily. In her head, she had an idea that the MSF people would take him, would know what to do with him, or, he would be subsumed into village life, raised collectively with the other children, playing joyfully in the sand, sitting in long rows at lessons ...

'So—'

They were interrupted by the middle-aged man Rosie had noticed before, the one with the air of self-importance. He wore a very smart robe over a business-man's shirt with a white collar and beckoned them to come.

Stephen glanced at Rosie and they followed the man back to the hut. Outside, Faustine was hovering, look-ing worried. Célestine's parents were standing stiffly, the baby fast asleep in his grandfather's arms.

'Now here's the thing,' said Faustine, slightly nervously. The entire village was watching them.

'What's going on?' asked Rosie suspiciously. Stephen looked at her just as the man holding the baby stepped forward.

'It's to do with the concept of being godparents . . . '

'You are KIDDING me,' said Rosie.

Stephen had led her to one side very quickly.

'You see, what godparents do—'

'Is send presents at odd times of year because they can't remember birthdays!' said Rosie. 'I should know, I've got three. You buy them a nice christening present, then put them up in their gap year! THAT'S what god-parents do.'

Stephen ignored her and went on. 'There's another element to the whole concept . . . '

'FINANCIAL,' said Rosie quickly. 'We agreed to support the family. With money! So they can feed the baby.'

'It's slightly more than that . . . '

'I realise that,' said Rosie. 'Except, obviously, you're not serious.' She realised she was babbling. 'Because of course he has his grandparents here, who can—'

Stephen was shaking his head.

'They don't . . . they can't . . . ' He took a deep breath. 'You have to realise, Rosie. This baby – he can't work in the fields. Not with one arm. He can't be a fighter or a hunter, he just can't. They can't look after him.'

'We can help them.'

'That's not the kind of help—'

Rosie looked at him.

'We can't just *take* a baby.'

Stephen bit his lip.

'"Will you care for them, and help them to take their place within the life and worship of Christ's Church?"' he quoted.

'Yes, but that's just something you say, like renouncing the devil and all his evil works.'

Stephen held her hands.

'Remember how happy we were at Christmas?'

Rosie nodded, painfully. So much had happened since.

'I always remember someone saying how ironic it is that Christmas is celebrated in the home but we're celebrating the birth of a homeless child.'

She just looked at him. In the trees, strange birds

called, insects made noises. The crackle of the fire and the chattering of the villagers could be heard. Somewhere a woman was crying. The bush was never quiet. She held his gaze for a long, long time, until finally Stephen spoke softly.

'They can get the local official. For a fee, he can handle the paperwork.'

'This is RIDICULOUS. It's off its head! Don't be daft, we can't have a baby.'

There was another long pause in the chattering dusk. Somewhere far away an animal howled. Rosie found tears coursing down her cheeks.

'We can't have a baby,' she said, for the second time in three days. The words were stones in her mouth.

'Nobody wanted this,' said Stephen. 'But . . .'

They looked at each other for a long time. Everything else seemed a long way away.

'This is going to be . . . you know, this is a big deal,' said Rosie softly, shaking all over.

'Parenting,' said Stephen. 'But you know, we were—'

'Yes. All parenting. And this might be more complicated than most. Adoption can be very difficult.'

'So can having your own kids,' said Stephen. 'Look at those awful Mountford brats.'

With a sudden wobbly smile, Rosie thought of the Mountford family, the richest in Lipton. The father ran a car dealership in Carningford, and the children always had the newest toys, the most up-to-date technology, and as many sweets as they could cram into their gobs. Rosie never liked to say anything about them at home, partly because they were children, and partly because they were splendid customers, but the way they ordered everyone else about, and made all the other children of the village dance to their whims in order to win an invitation to one of their infamous birthday parties, which had in the past featured circus animals, chocolate fountains and carousels (Edison had never been invited), was absolutely cringe-inducing.

'It's true,' she said, her mood lightening a tiny bit. 'We couldn't possibly do a worse job than the Mountfords.' Her heart started to beat incredibly fast.

'We could,' Stephen began slowly. 'We could . . .' He stared straight into her eyes.

'I think,' said Rosie, 'I need to meet him properly.'

Rosie approached carefully, her heart beating like a drum. She thought back over the months of emptiness, the terrible gap in her heart, the dreadful sense of her potential wasted. She had never been one of those people who cooed over babies, never believed that all she needed to fulfil her in life was a little bundle wrapped in Baby Gap. But the knowledge that she wasn't having Stephen's baby had broken her heart, totally and surely, and she knew that deep down she hadn't begun to come to terms with it.

The grandfather did not say a word; simply held out the child. The entire village was watching, and Rosie sensed that they were all holding their breath as much as she was.

She took the warm bundle into her arms. His little face screwed up, snuffled a little, then, even though he was already sleeping, his mouth opened into a tiny tiger yawn. Rosie propped him up, her hand strong on the back of his neck, and laid his tiny head against her shoulder. The baby moved a little, nestled, found a perfect hollow in her shoulder Rosie had not even known was there, and curled his head straight into it.

The man was talking to her, but Rosie couldn't hear him. She leant in closer, but she still couldn't hear his voice or make out what he was saying.

'Apostil,' said Faustine, then she said it again, louder, when Rosie clearly didn't understand. 'His name is Apostil. Ah-pos-teel.'

'Like Apostle?'

'No, like Apostil.'

Even through the flood of emotion, Rosie's first, ridiculous thought was that they were going to be having a lot of conversations like that in the days and years to come.

The villagers melted away, seemingly satisfied that the matter had been settled, except for the wet nurse, who lingered at a distance. Rosie was incredibly grateful to be left alone with the baby.

She walked up carefully to Stephen, holding the tiny form in her shaking arms. He gazed at them both.

'Do you want to hold him?' she whispered.

Stephen stared at the bundle for a long time.

'Here's the thing,' he said, swallowing. He rested a little more heavily on his stick, as he did when he was nervous. 'The thing is ... you have to be sure, Rosie. You have to be sure, right now. Because if you ... if you hand him to me ... if you hand him to me now ...'

He looked her straight in the eye.

'There's no going back. He'll be ours.'

She stared at him intently.

'Did you think this might happen?'

Stephen shook his head.

'I only ever wanted the same for Célestine as you would have had.'

His face twisted into a smile that contained a trace of the old Stephen.

'Also, I may be wrong, but I suspect this is really going to screw with our holiday.'

She held his gaze.

114

'You want me to give him to you?'

Carefully, Rosie handed over the tiny, precious bundle. Somewhere a soft voice started to sing something that sounded like a lullaby.

Salay salay chinkama
Tulay salay wawama
Chinka lolo wink wa salay.

More voices took up the quiet refrain on the still air. Stephen held the baby tentatively, supporting his head as Rosie showed him. He looked straight into the child's face, and as he did so, Apostil woke up. To Rosie's surprise, he didn't cry, but instead met Stephen's gaze with a calm, measured look of his own. She crept closer, unwilling to interrupt this moment. Man and boy stared at one another.

'He recognises you,' she whispered.

'I think he's older than me,' said Stephen wonderingly. 'Look at him, Rosie. Look at that child and tell me he doesn't know everything in the universe.'

Rosie glanced up at the huge stars that were appearing overhead.

'Well he did just get here from there.'

'I think maybe he's a genius,' said Stephen, unable to tear his eyes away. 'We'll probably have to make special provision for him.'

Rosie grinned as there was a sudden loud noise.

'The genius just pooed all over your shoes.'

'And I don't even mind,' said Stephen, still trans-fixed. 'Look at me, standing here, all not minding.'

Apostil blinked his huge eyes twice, slowly.

'I agree,' said Stephen. 'You must feel better.'

Rosie smiled.

'Hang on, the van brought nappies. Not many, though. Give me a minute.'

She went off to find them – Faustine had kindly put them by their tent – but paused and turned back to look. Father and son, she thought, frozen in time, both utterly absorbed in one another; and she snapped a quick picture on her phone. Her first baby pic.

It hit her then like a ton of bricks. Oh my goodness. Oh my goodness. A family. I have a family. Everything I wasn't sure I would be able to have. Sometimes, even, knowing Stephen's fear of tradition and being tied down, she had had the tiniest suspicion in the base of her mind that he wouldn't be that fussed if they couldn't have children, even though that was ridiculous; he wanted her to be happy. But now ... look ... in the most unlikely of settings ... here they were. My mum, she thought. Oh my God, I have to phone my mum. Then she stifled a giggle at the thought: and Stephen's mum. Nobody here, of course, could possibly have any idea that the future Lord of Lipton had just been born.

She was still giggling, a little hysterically, as they changed the baby. The wet nurse looked covetously at the towelling nappies, so of course they gave her half. Apostil was, apart from his little arm, the most beautiful infant, Rosie thought. A pale coffee colour, which she knew would darken with time; great dark grey eyes with heavy lids and thick black lashes; a perfect round bow of a mouth and a little button of a nose, and soft black hair whorled on his head. He was utterly exquisite. Even though they were both exhausted – and the other members of the team were trying to sleep across the way in another canvas tent – they lay awake, looking at each other and occasionally tearing up a little, unable to believe the little miracle that was lying between them. When he woke, the wet nurse came and fed him. The medical team had brought powdered milk, but they didn't want to use it quite yet; they would make sure the wet nurse had plenty of extra food and nutrients.

'What are we going to tell people?' said Rosie, twirling his tiny hairs around her finger, planting kisses up and down his shoulder blades.

'We shall tell them precisely the truth,' said Stephen, kissing them both gently. 'That out of the worst of things, sometimes the best things can come.'

Chapter Seven

Myrrh is mine, its bitter perfume
Breathes a life of gathering gloom
Sorrowing, sighing, bleeding, dying
Sealed in the stone-cold tomb

They buried Célestine in the morning. There was wailing, and singing, and food brought from all around, and Rosie and Stephen stood frozen in the middle, witnesses to the pain, even as friends and relatives came and blessed the baby and wished them well.

Rosie wished she had thought to take a photograph of Célestine, but of course it would hardly have been appropriate. She stood next to the girl's parents, with the uncomfortable realisation that they were barely older than herself. The father was strong and proud. The mother could not hold the baby, could not bear the pain, and Rosie understood.

'One day,' she said, as Stephen translated, 'may we bring him back to meet his grandparents?'

The woman nodded fiercely.

'You are the least crazy grandparents Apostil has,' said Stephen.

They did have two photographs, both taken by Stephen on his previous trip: of the two boys, Jabo and Akibo, grinning fiercely and nervously, and peeping out from behind them, Célestine. Rosie snapped images of the photos to take with them, crying all the while.

'She was only a child,' she said.

'Ssssh,' said Stephen, his face serious. 'I know. And now we owe it to her to raise her boy the best we can. He's our boy now.'

The way he said 'our boy,' made Rosie's heart burst.

The village sang, and a white missionary priest with a strong South African accent came by, looking harassed and tired out, his eyes tinged a notable yellow from repeated bouts of malaria. He said a Mass in a hurry, barely stopped for a cup of tea and was on the point of dashing off again when Stephen asked him if he would baptise the baby.

'The baby lived,' the priest said gruffly. 'I heard. And what, you're here to buy it?'

'No,' said Stephen. 'Not quite. I owed this family a debt.'

The priest pulled down his glasses and peered at Stephen aggressively.

'Oh yes? And now you want me to sign all your paperwork and give you certificates and make things easy for you to take away a baby and leave behind a mess.'

'No, Father,' said Stephen simply. 'I just wanted you to bless this beautiful baby. But it is up to you.'

The man peered crossly at Apostil, who was snoozing, waking up, looking around him, making little purring noises, then dropping off to sleep again.

'What's wrong with this child's arm?' he said.

'We don't know,' said Stephen. 'But if there's anything we can do for it, we will.'

The priest harrumphed.

'Africa is not your shopping ground,' he said.

'I realise that, Padre,' said Stephen quietly. Rosie looked at him, impressed by how hard he was struggling to keep his temper. 'It is not why we came.'

The priest looked them up and down more closely.

'Don't I know you?' he said shortly.

'Yes,' said Stephen reluctantly.

'I do know you. You were here before. You're that boy who got blown up.'

'Yes.'

The priest shook his head.

'Idiot you were.'

Stephen stared straight ahead, his gaze stony. There was a pause.

'But you were a good teacher, hey? I remember you now. You were good. Good with the boys. Is this a boy?'

Stephen nodded.

'What's his name?'

'It's Apostil … apparently.'

'Apostil. Is that it?'

'Um …' Stephen looked at Rosie for inspiration.

'Oh goodness, names!' said Rosie, her hand flying to her mouth. 'I hadn't thought … My goodness. Well. We should have Stephen in there too.'

'I've never liked it.'

'I like it. Stephen. Stevie. Steve-Steve.'

'Stop it! No.'

Rosie smiled.

'Okay. Akibo, then.'

Stephen nodded. 'Yup. Good. Anything else?'

Rosie thought about it.

'Do you know what would be nice? For Lilian?'

'Henry?' guessed Stephen immediately.

'No,' said Rosie. 'I think she'd be a bit annoyed about that. She likes to have dibs on the only Henry on earth. She gets really cross when the Fonz is on TV.'

'Seriously? She hates Fonzie? Oh. Okay.'

121

The priest cleared his throat and looked pointedly at his watch.

'I was thinking Edward,' said Rosie. 'Neddie. After her brother who died in the war.'

Stephen thought about it.

'Yes. Okay. Yes. Do that, it's lovely.'

And immediately following the funeral of his mother, with Faustine and the local doctor as godparents, they christened Apostil Akibo Edward Lakeman, and without their even asking, the missionary priest drove four hours back along the dreadful dirt road through the woods later that day with a birth certificate signed and stamped, naming them both as parents. When she saw it, Faustine's eyes widened and she told him he had just saved them a quite insane amount of paperwork. Rosie went to the van and gave him her emergency bag of sweets, minus the chocolate, which she'd smuggled to the wet nurse. He was touchingly pleased.

After that, everything changed more rapidly than they could have dreamed of. The holiday company very kindly let them cancel their reservation, which was useful, as they needed to book a hotel room in the capital and sort out the rest of the paperwork. And, of course, fill everyone in back at home.

The next few days were a blur of hotel rooms, bad

phone connections and long days spent in stifling buildings in the capital. After the quiet and calm of the bush, the city was more familiar, with its traffic and bars and mobile phone shops and policemen and general sense of business. But there was work to be done. And some of it Rosie could absolutely savour.

'Mum?'

'G'day! I thought you were on that safari holiday!'

'Ah,' said Rosie.

'Did you see any tigers?'

'Mum, this is Africa, they don't have tigers.'

'Oh. Elephants.'

'No. No elephants. We heard lots of hyenas.'

'Oh.'

'And parrots. We saw a lot of parrots.'

'We got parrots! Sydney's full of parakeets! I wish you'd come here instead.'

'Mum, shut up a minute. Look. This is costing me a fortune to phone that I don't have, so you have to listen.'

'GRAMMA! WANNA TALK AUNTIE ROSIE.'

'She's busy talking to me.'

'SHE ALWAYS TALK TO ME!!!'

'Uh, hi, Meridian,' said Rosie, resigning herself to a long conversation about Spider-Man.

'I IS IRON MAN,' said Meridian self-importantly, settling herself down for a chat. Rosie could hear her shifting around down the telephone.

'HERE ARE THE BRAVE FINGS WHICH I DOES DO. ONE. I DOES FLYING. FREE. I IS IRON MAN! '

'Mum!' shouted Rosie. 'This is important.'

There was a bit of wrestling and yelling at the other end. Rosie looked down fondly at Ap, who was dozing gently on her lap. She had expected yelling and crying and the exhausted world of some of her friends who had had babies then not got dressed again for about four years, but Apostil so far seemed to be a placid, easy-going little fellow, with a curiosity about the world (which Stephen was convinced was a sign of scientific excellence) rather than an instinctive fury at it. When hungry he would make a hungry mouth and his good arm would thrash up and down a little, but that was about it. He would need a full medical inspection when they got back to the UK, but if Rosie could go on her instincts, he seemed to be in fine fettle. She felt aston-ishingly grateful.

It wasn't that, though, that ran through her thoughts every waking second, and every dreaming second too. It was the incredible fact that while she had thought that falling in love with Stephen had been the biggest adven-ture of her life – all-enthralling, all-encompassing in every way – now she had fallen in love again, completely and utterly, and the feeling was oddly the same. She just wanted to look at his beautiful tiny face; his strong, compact little body that nestled so perfectly in her arms. She wanted to kiss him over and over; breathe in his delicate milky smell; gaze at him. Stephen teased her.

'You know, you are going to make things very difficult for Mr Dog.'

'Mr Dog will manage,' said Rosie confidently. 'He's a very affectionate animal.'

'That's because you've spoilt him rotten. You're not doing the same to Apostil.'

'You're right,' said Rosie. 'Do you want to send him to boarding school now, or shall we wait till he's out of nappies?'

He grinned.

'Give him here.'

He put Apostil down on the bed. Apostil wriggled a bit and then spent some time trying to get the fingers of his good hand into his mouth.

'I'm your dad,' said Stephen, smiling. 'And you have to listen to me all the time. Because my wife-to-be doesn't.'

'That's me,' chimed in Rosie. 'Your mummy.'

They grinned at each other with the amazing novelty of saying these phrases.

'I run a sweetshop. Excellent, huh?'

'But you have to listen to me,' said Stephen. 'Okay?'

Apostil continued to fixate on his fingers, then gazed right past them both.

'Great,' said Rosie. 'He's not listening to either of us.'

'He's looking over our shoulders like he's checking for someone more interesting to talk to at a party.'

🍬

Finally, Rosie could tell Angie was alone.

'Did you lock yourself in that cupboard again?'

'Hush, you,' said Angie. 'What is it? I've got supper on.'

'Right,' said Rosie. 'Okay. Well. Um. You know the "more grandkids" thing?'

'What?'

This wasn't working, Rosie could tell.

'Well, anyway, we came to visit a family here that Stephen knew.'

'A family where? On safari?'

Finally Stephen shouted out from across the room, 'Tell her to get on her computer.'

Sure enough, he'd managed to upload a picture of Rosie cradling Apostil in her arms, grinning like an idiot (Rosie thought), looking beautiful (Stephen thought).

'OH MY GAWD!' screamed Angie down the phone. 'You bought a baby!!!'

'We did not buy a baby,' said Rosie. 'Don't say that, it's completely offensive. We're his godparents. It's our job to take him on.'

'Oh my GAWD, you've got a baby!' said Angie,

backtracking completely. 'Oh my GOD. Tell me every-thing. EVERYTHING. Boy? Girl?'

'WAS GOAN ON, GRAMMA?'

'You've got a new cousin!' Rosie could hear the tears in her mother's voice.

'DOAN WANNA NEW COUSIN! IRON MAN SHOOT THEM WITH MY HAND POW POW POW.'

And Rosie did her best to choke out the entire story, sad and happy, again and again as Pip came in to hear it, then Desleigh, his wife.

'He's a cracker,' said Pip finally. 'Well done, Rose. Wow. You are a very unpredictable sister.'

'I know,' said Rosie, her lip wobbling. She looked round their basic hotel room with its stained basin and faded bedstead. Outside, the noise and the heat came barrelling up all night long, and bugs scuttled across the floor at all hours, as they waited day after day at the British Embassy for the case to be processed. She had never been happier in her entire life.

'You've done WHAT?'

Rosie squeezed Stephen's hand, and they each cov-ered one of Apostil's tiny, perfect shell-like ears. Rosie had heard Lady Lipton – Henrietta – cross plenty of times, but this was something else, a whole new level of fury, whereby she was basically talking at a level only dogs could hear.

'Listen, Mother.'

She was nowhere near listening.

'The family trust isn't going to like this, Stephen. Not one little bit. '

'Well fuck the family trust,' said Stephen. 'His name can be Lakeman, I don't give a shit.' Lipton was the estate name; Stephen used the old family name, Lakeman.

Rosie smiled and squeezed his hand.

'Well, Pamela will LOVE this.'

Stephen's elder sister liked to argue about primogeniture.

'I said she could have it,' said Stephen. 'I don't care.'

'Well, we'll see,' said Henrietta, sniffing. 'So, God, tell me the worst ... is this baby *brown*?'

Rosie and Stephen looked at each other, and Rosie had the most terrible desire to burst into fits of laughter.

'No, Mother,' said Stephen carefully. 'He's green, like all babies born in West Africa.'

There was a long pause.

'You think this is funny?' said Lady Lipton.

'No, Mother,' said Stephen. 'I think it's wonderful.'

There was another long silence and Rosie thought Henrietta was going to slam down the telephone. Then she sniffed so loudly they could hear it two thousand miles away.

'So. Ahem. You say you've sent pictures via The Email?'

'Yes,' said Stephen.

'I don't know how to work The Email.'

'Maybe Moray or Mrs Laird could help you,' said Stephen.

'Lilian could probably manage,' said Rosie, as Stephen shushed her.

'But ... but you have absolutely no idea what it takes to raise a baby. Especially not a different type of baby! Especially one where you can't predict how he'll turn out, who he'll be like – do you even know anything about his family? About his breeding? Oh, you're very smug now, but you just wait and see, it's no walk in the park, this lark ...'

Stephen put the phone down on the bedside table, and moved over to where Apostil was waking from his nap. The baby gave a loud enquiring mewl.

'Hey there, little fella,' said Stephen, as Rosie leapt in to kiss him and take him for a feed.

'Is that ... is that him?'

Stephen picked the phone up again. Lady Lipton's voice had a definite tremble.

'Well,' said Stephen, looking down at Rosie on the bed. 'It's a baby and it's green, so I guess ...'

'Stop it, Stephen,' said Henrietta. 'We'll discuss this more when you get home. Assuming you're coming home.'

In fact Stephen was leaving the following day because he had to get back to school. Rosie would just have to wait it out. This was going to cost them every cent they had. Good training for parenting, Stephen suggested.

'What have you called him? Please let it be something sensible. Stephen would be absolutely fine.'

'Um, he already has a name,' said Stephen.

Henrietta let out a sigh.

'Let's hear it.'

'He's called Apostil.'

There was a long pause.

'That is the most Catholic name I've ever heard,' said Lady Lipton eventually. 'Lilian is going to love it.'

Chapter Eight

In the bleak midwinter
Frosty wind made moan
Earth was hard as iron, water like a stone
Snow was falling, snow on snow, snow on snow
In the bleak midwinter, long ago

It was the oddest thing, after the weeks of paperwork, the waiting, the worrying, the learning how to be a parent, to come back from the boiling hot sunshine, the colours, the exhilarating rush of noise and smells, the juxtaposition of all the signs of modernity – smartly dressed commuters, mobile phones, new cars – with goats in the road, people living anywhere. Rosie loved the colour, the bustle; understood immediately why Stephen had loved it too.

It wasn't just her who felt new. Something about this baby, from this family, seemed to have healed Stephen too. He hadn't had a nightmare the entire time they'd been away.

She'd missed him terribly when he left for home. But now it was time for her to go too.

There had been many, many meetings – and more to come – and Rosie was worrying terribly about the shop. Tina had held it just about together, but she'd been away for so long. They'd hired a fantastic young woman called Memento, who had got her through all the interviews and the paperwork, and the embassy had been incredibly helpful, and now here she was, flying for the first time with a baby.

She'd packed ridiculously early, nervous about the flight. She needn't have worried. Faustine was in the capital and not only gave her a lift to the airport but helped her through the time-consuming business of paperwork and stamps, speaking imperiously to the customs officers and guards, waving sheafs of paper menacingly and displaying her MSF badge at every opportunity. Rosie couldn't believe how lucky she was to have met her, and how that slightly prickly exterior hid someone extraordinary at getting things done.

They didn't hug, but Rosie touched her on the arm as they took their leave at the gate.

'Thank you,' she said. 'Thank you.'

Faustine shook her head.

'Thank *you*.' She kissed Apostil's little head, and a flicker of something that looked almost like envy crossed her face. 'Take him home,' she said. 'Raise him well.'

'I'll try,' said Rosie, and watched from the safety of the other side of the gate as Faustine turned smartly and walked away into the colourful, noisy hurly-burly, off to save the next, and the next, and the next.

And now here she was. Apostil had lain in his bassinet and gurgled, intrigued by the lights and lulled to sleep by the motion of the plane. Rosie had been unable to sleep, unable to believe everything that had happened. It felt like a dream, but one that became more real by the second, as she watched sitcoms on the flight TV system; looked at adverts for watches and perfumes.

Stephen came to pick them up from the airport, pointing out that he had had to fight off half the village to do so. Appy had been happy in his bassinet all the way, but Rosie had been too keyed up to sleep, too nervous about seeing everyone, about settling in. They'd led her to a special room at immigration at Heathrow, which had also made her very nervous, but in fact the staff had been incredibly kind, just going through their paperwork until they could confirm that Apostil really had been adopted and really was a British child now. Rosie appreciated that they couldn't be too careful, but it was wearying, especially as he woke up and, unusually for him, decided to start bawling his head off at everything, making her look like the worst fraud of a mother ever, and wildly unsuited to raising a caterpillar, never mind a baby.

Apostil's tantrum ultimately proved timely, however, as the customs staff couldn't wait to be rid of them and pushed them though as quickly as they legally could.

Stephen was beside himself, desperate to see them.

'How can you miss someone so much when you've only known them a week?' he said, charging forward to scoop them up at Arrivals. When Rosie saw him standing there, she suddenly burst into tears. The emotions of the last few weeks had been so overwhelming, with everything coming thick and fast, her life changing in such a rush from someone who could not be a mother to someone who was, and always would be, that she hadn't realised until she saw him how pent up she'd been. It was as if her shoulders had been up around her ears and were finally relaxing.

'What's the matter?' said Stephen, genuinely surprised. 'You've got him, we're all together . . .'

'I know,' said Rosie.

Stephen drew her to him.

'I'm sorry I had to leave you in Africa alone,' he said. 'I couldn't stay any longer.'

'I know, I know,' said Rosie, burying her head in his strong shoulder. It wasn't a good look, having a total nervous breakdown at the airport.

Stephen reached into the sling and tried to dislodge Apostil, which was easier said than done, given how good Rosie had got at tying him round her. Eventually she did a pirouette so they could unwind him and Stephen could set about hugging his son, whilst Rosie tried to clean the make-up from underneath her eyes.

'I was worried they wouldn't let you in,' said Stephen. 'So I called my old mate Biff at the Foreign Office.'

'You didn't!' said Rosie indignantly.

'Certainly bloody did. Did you get a passport in five days or what?'

'I did find it all wonderfully efficient,' said Rosie. 'Yuck, you disgusting privileged types.'

'Yes,' said Stephen, nuzzling Apostil's head. Apostil was looking about somewhat warily. 'Oh, I have missed that smell. Anyway, yes, I apologise for making things easier for us all.'

She smiled at him. 'Sometimes it is very useful you being a hideously overprivileged snotbag.'

'Only sometimes?'

He kept hold of Apostil and tried to take Rosie's bags too, realised this was impossible, gave it up as a bad job, handed Apostil back reluctantly and hauled up the bags.

As soon as they hit the freezing cold air outside – there was frost on the tarmac, and people waiting for taxis were blowing out smoke as they huddled into their coats – Apostil's head jerked upwards as if someone had prodded him. Stephen and Rosie looked at him grinning.

'Yes,' said Stephen. 'Welcome to the world you must now live in!'

Rosie pulled a woolly hat from her hand luggage – she had worn it to the airport on their way out, a million years ago – and tried to arrange it on Apostil's tiny head, but it fell over his eyes and he started waving his hand about madly, whilst Rosie and Stephen fell about laughing and Stephen tried to take a picture.

'We are terrible, terrible parents,' said Rosie, noticing someone looking at them curiously.

'I think this is the last time he's going to feel warm and cosy until the spring,' said Stephen. 'And we haven't even moved into Peak House yet.'

Inside the car, Stephen had fitted a brand new baby seat. Rosie frowned.

'How much . . . '

'Ssssh,' said Stephen. 'Don't start me. There's four more at home. People have been showering us.'

'What do you mean?'

'SHOWERING US. Everybody knows about

136

Apostil, everybody is totally fascinated, and all those nosy parkers have been getting their kicks by coming round and passing on their old shiz to us. We've got three buggies, too.'

'Or,' said Rosie, getting in the back as Stephen turned up the heating in the old Land Rover, which didn't go very far. She hoped Apostil had enough blankets on. 'OR they're being kind and generous from the bottom of their hearts.'

'Whilst being unbelievable nosy parkers,' said Stephen. He looked at the heating gauge again and frowned.

'This won't do, will it?'

Rosie winced.

'Well ...'

'I never noticed it being this chilly before.'

'It's got a hole in the floor.'

'I thought that was, you know, atmospheric.'

'It is,' said Rosie. 'Atmospheric, like the South Pole.'

'Hmm.' He looked at her. 'Look at us! Bringing our baby home!'

Rosie beamed, a smile of pure joy.

'I know! Drive slower!'

'I can't drive slower, we'll freeze him to death.'

'Oh yeah,' said Rosie. 'Man, we have a lot to learn.'

Even though it was only November, the lights had already gone up around the little village. Nothing too fancy – just plain bulbs, the same ones strung every year from lamp post to lamp post, but there were plenty of them, and they were beautiful, and against the glittering diamonds of frost snow, they turned the main street into a fairyland.

Stephen had left the fire crackling in the grate, and the embers were still warm when they returned (fireguard, Rosie found herself immediately thinking: fireguard). Mr Dog gave a mighty hop and a small yip when Rosie appeared. She let Stephen hold Apostil, and opened her arms to the little white dog, who looked a bit like a mop but was as sweet, lazy and gentle as the day was long.

'Hello, DOG THING!'

Mr Dog's little pink tongue licked her enthusiastically on the face, his tail going nineteen to the dozen.

'He'll be glad you're home,' said Stephen. 'Back to being spoiled.'

'Nooo!' said Rosie in agony. 'I can't spoil him any more in case he smothers Apostil!'

'Divided loyalties,' said Stephen.

'Not divided,' said Rosie. 'He's not smothering my son.'

She sat down on the sofa, grateful to be close to the fire. Apostil's eyes opened; he was hungry, and she gave him a quick bottle. He was normally swaddled tight and fast asleep by now. Memento, the girl at the embassy, who had four children of her own, had shown her how to do it, and how not to jump up every time he made a tiny noise. If it had been up to Rosie, she would have been jiggling and kissing him awake every five minutes. It was absolutely thanks to Memento that Apostil was good at sleeping at night-time rather than appallingly over-fussed in the manner of Mr Dog. Although Rosie never met Memento again, she never forgot her for that invaluable advice, and when new mothers came and went in the shop, complaining bitterly about having had no sleep, she would diplomatically pass on the simple wisdom that had made a time of such extraordinary upheaval so very much easier.

But now he was utterly transfixed by two things, could barely contain his delight: the fire flickering in front of him, to which he held out his good hand in awe, and the scruffy white bundle beside him, that Stephen had by the rear end in case Mr Dog licked him to death.

Both Rosie and Stephen kept a close eye on the baby as he turned from one thing to another. Finally he turned and looked straight into Stephen's face, and for the very first time gave a huge, gummy, unmistakable grin, that went to his eyes and lit up his entire face.

'OH MY GOD!'

'He smiled! He smiled!'

Rosie ran around looking for her phone to take a picture, but there was no rush; as soon as Apostil realised the effect his grin had elicited from his overwhelmed parents, he repeated the trick immediately. Then, just as Stephen was satisfyingly proclaiming that the child was patently a genius, he'd always known it, smiling at five weeks was a clear sign, Apostil went too far and threw up all over Lilian's treasured faded Victorian Persian rug. Mr Dog immediately started licking it up. Rosie and Stephen just looked at one another, frozen. Rosie started to giggle.

'We're brilliant parents,' she laughed.

'Made for this,' said Stephen. 'Oh Christ, I think there's some on my shoes.'

Rosie knew the shop would be busy the next day, but she had to open up, she absolutely had to. Tina was only just holding it together between the shop, the children and the wedding stress. Plus they needed a busy day, and she knew for a fact she would get one. It had been hard to figure out exactly where to put Apostil – she didn't want him in their bed, even though she'd read a million online threads about the benefits of co-sleeping, until Stephen had threatened to unplug the wireless router if she didn't stop obsessing over every tiny detail. Upstairs out of the bed was, as usual, absolutely freezing.

Downstairs close to the fire was too unnerving in case a spark jumped out (of the closed stove? enquired Stephen, but Rosie couldn't leave anything to chance). And Mr Dog would need to be shut in the tiny kitchen, which was tricky, as it didn't have a door and was full of food. The Moses basket Rosie had brought with her from Africa was put down in Lilian's room, which was cosy from the sitting room and had the benefit of a closing door. After checking the baby monitor forty or fifty times, they agreed that this should be Apostil's room.

'For now,' said Rosie. 'It's Lilian's room really.' She and Stephen shared a look. They couldn't do it tonight, with everything so new, but the time was undoubtedly coming when they would have to discuss their finances, and moving. Soon.

It was Rosie's first night sleeping without Apostil, and she found it difficult to get comfortable, till Stephen moved closer and held her and she turned in for a kiss. She grinned at him in the dark.

'What?'

'This feels naughty,' said Rosie.

'What, because we're parents?'

'Yup.'

'I don't think he's going to march in.'

'Not yet . . .'

Rosie listened to the monitor.

'What if he wakes?'

'We could be quick,' said Stephen with a glint in his eye.

Rosie thought about everything they had on their plates – the new baby, the shop, money, the house, the challenge of Apostil's arm, the total change in absolutely everything that was going on in their lives – and decided that he was right. If there was one place where she could forget her worries, be in the moment, stop making lists and fussing and worrying about everybody else, it was here, right here, with Stephen's hard body next to her in the bed, his muscular arms around her, his stubbly face against hers.

'No need,' she said, returning his kiss.

'Um, there is need,' said Stephen, his voice a low rumble. 'You've been away for AGES . . .'

Chapter Nine

First through the door the next morning was, to absolutely nobody's surprise, Hester, with Edison in tow, and baby Marie, now a stout, lively eleven-month-old, tied up in an ethnic sling not unlike Rosie's. Rosie couldn't have known when she had delivered Marie last Christmas how much help this would prove months later and thousands of miles away. She wanted to hug them both. Hester would undoubtedly have had something to say about that.

Rosie had decided just to take Apostil with her to the shop. She had the car seat on the floor where she could put him if he wanted to look about, but for now he seemed very happy trussed tightly to her back. Stephen had popped his head round the bathroom door earlier and grinned at the sight: Rosie was in her beloved bath, Apostil lying on her stomach happily kicking water in the air.

'I can't believe you've already got him into your interminable bath habits.'

'Bath habits are good habits!'

'Not the way you do it.'

Rosie stuck her tongue out at him.

'Right, don't drown the baby. I'll see you later. Have a good day.'

He knelt down and kissed them both.

'My two favourite people.'

Rosie reflected as she heard the cottage door close downstairs how funny Stephen was. When there was nothing to worry about, he could become introverted and difficult, turning his worries inside. When they had a million things to do, some of them incredibly tricky, he seemed to take it all in his stride. She was much less confident than he was about the social workers who were due to visit, not least because it was entirely within his power to be incredibly rude to people he thought were busybodies.

She dressed Apostil in some of the clothes Tina had thoughtfully left for her. They were Kent's, who was nine now, and therefore a bit dated and heavily biased towards *Cars* and *Ben 10*, but that didn't matter. She topped it all off with a brand-new cable-knit jumper and cardigan set – slightly too big, but that didn't matter – and a pair of knitted bootees. There would have been knitted trousers too if she hadn't thought it was a bit much and made him look like a dolly.

Lilian had obviously been making her new status of great-great-aunt very clear at the home, because the old ladies had been knitting like there was an Olympic medal in it for them. Not only that, but everything was absolutely perfectly done. Rosie had her suspicions that Lilian herself would have patrolled the lines, pointing out mistakes and demanding that people start over.

The shop was, as usual when Tina had been in, immaculate. Tina couldn't bear a speck of dust, or a glass jar even slightly out of place. She had also put the Christmas decorations up, and it was lovely to see the little snow train again, running happily through a forest of lollipop trees and candy-cane avenues in the front window, cotton wool strewn about with the kind of abandon that implied that the twins and Edison had had a hand in it.

Fairy lights were strung up amongst the shelves, on little hooks that Jake had screwed in so they didn't knock them over every time they went to fetch some liquorice torpedos (top shelf, rare buy, boys only). The lights worked very nicely, reflecting off the sweets in their original glass jars, making the boiled sweets look like stained glass and the rainbow pips shine brightly. There was tinsel too, reflecting the light again, and the shop was cosy (until you went out into the little back room, which was perishing). Rosie looked at her lovely apron that she normally wore, then realised she wouldn't be able to get it on, so washed her hands and prepared herself for what was clearly going to be less a working day and more a full-on interrogation.

'ROSIE!' shouted Edison as the bell tinged. He ran towards her, then frowned.

'What's round you?'

Smiling, Rosie turned round.

'OHHH.'

'Didn't Hester' – Edison didn't call his mum Mum, although Marie seemed to have learned 'Mama' and used it all the time, however much Hester tried to hush her – 'didn't Hester tell you?'

'She said there was CLONAL PRIVILEGE,' said Edison loudly. Rosie was trying to work out what cloning had to do with anything when she realised what Hester had actually said and raised her eyebrows.

'Did she?' she said merrily.

'Hello!' said Hester, totally unembarrassable, as always. 'Oh, is that how you tie your sling? I prefer the more traditional way.'

Rosie wanted to say 'More traditional than being taught in a village in the African bush?' but had sworn absolutely blind that she wasn't going to get into a pissing competition with Hester of all people, so she held her tongue.

'Hello!' she said instead. 'Hello, Marie.'

'She can't talk,' said Edison, his eyes narrowing. 'Hester says she can, but she can't really.'

'Actually she's developing her own language,' said Hester. 'It's a sign of unusual intelligence.'

'Ga ba bla BLAH ga dah!' said Marie triumphantly. Rosie winked at Edison.

'So let's have a look then,' said Hester in a sing-song voice. Rosie turned round again. Marie instantly put out a fat hand and tried to whack Apostil on the face.

'I need a mirror in here,' said Rosie.

'Oh look,' said Hester. 'She's communicating with him. Amazing.'

'Stop whacking him,' commanded Rosie.

'What's his name?'

'Apostil,' said Rosie promptly.

'Oh,' said Hester. 'It's a shame you didn't go with something more traditional and African.'

Rosie was glad they were facing different ways.

'That's the name his birth family gave him,' she said. 'We thought we'd respect their wishes.'

Hester was unconcerned.

'What's wrong with his arm? Is it a tribal thing?'

'No!' said Rosie. 'It's just a birth defect. He'll do perfectly well without it,' she added fiercely, hoping as she said it that it was true.

'Of course,' said Hester soothingly. 'And you'll be teaching him to speak his own language, I expect.'

147

'French,' said Rosie.

'You know,' said Hester, sounding testy, 'you have a very grave responsibility to his heritage. He will need to grow up knowing who he is.'

'He will,' said Rosie. 'He's our son, but he has a family in Africa that he'll see as often as we can manage. I don't know what else we can do.'

'Lots!' said Hester. 'For a start, he won't be able to digest bread.'

'Right,' said Rosie.

'He won't! Evolution! You'll need to get special meal in for him.'

'He's not a dog.'

'M-E-A-L. It's a grain they use—'

'We'll see how he goes,' said Rosie, finally running out of patience. Also Marie had one finger up her nose and the other hand reaching out for the bubble gum. 'One step at a time.'

'Becoming a parent is the most amazing step you'll ever take,' said Hester. Rosie, who had only just accepted the concept that she would never have children of her own, absolutely bristled at this.

'Don't be daft, there's loads of amazing things people can do.'

Fortunately at that point the bell rang again; it was cheery Maeve Skritcherd, the receptionist at the medical practice.

'AHHH!' she shrieked, rushing forward. 'Where is he? Where is he? Let me see him!!! Let me get my hands on him!!!!'

Rosie remembered that Maeve had been waiting for years now for her lunkish adult sons to move out, find good jobs and nice girls and settle down and give her grandchildren. She was far too nice; the boys didn't want to go anywhere. Rosie made a mental note not to make the same mistake.

Maeve was now basically wrestling her for control of Apostil, and Rosie laughed and happily gave him up; it was time for him to wake from his morning nap, and he did so, blinking sleepily around.

'He's GORGEOUS!' shrieked Maeve. 'He's beautiful! Come here, you lovely yummy yummy gorgeous boy!!!'

She covered his head in kisses and Rosie relaxed. This was more the reaction she'd been hoping for. Hester sniffed loudly.

'Sugar-free mints, please.'

Edison looked disappointed.

'Hello, Edison,' said Maeve. 'Are we seeing you later?'

'No, he's fine,' said Hester swiftly. Despite Edison benefiting massively from wonderful medical care during his recovery, from both the hospital and the local team, Hester made a big fuss about how she was mostly treating him homeopathically.

149

'Well that's good.'

Edison pushed up his glasses.

'Will you be needing some babysitting?' he asked Rosie seriously. She couldn't stop herself laughing.

'Edison, you're NINE.'

He looked sad.

'Yes, but I'm very sponsible.'

'I have no doubt,' said Rosie. 'But Apostil is very little and needs his mummy. Maybe when you're both a bit older, okay?'

'Only I need money to buy Edinburgh rock.'

He looked imploringly at everyone. Maeve rolled her eyes and gave in.

'And a small bag of Edinburgh rock, please.'

'You don't have to,' said Hester, but made no move to stop her.

'Not at all,' said Maeve. 'This is a happy day.'

And after that, the deluge. Everyone from Malik down at the general store, who brought her a pack of nappies – a surprisingly kind and useful gift – to Mrs Manly from the boutique, who reminded her that Baby, as she called Apostil, would need to come in for his full layette, whatever that was, everyone had a few words to say. Even Roy Blaine, the nasty dentist, could be seen peering in through the window. And Rosie was so happy and her heart so full of everyone admiring her lovely baby – and so sleep-deprived, to be honest – that she waved at him, but he stalked on.

Moray came after morning surgery. Tina had arrived for her shift, declaring Apostil a treasure, then launching into a very long story about wedding favours that Rosie could only barely follow. She took Moray next door for a cup of tea.

'He's lovely,' said Moray cheerily. 'Hello there, little chap. Look at you!'

Rosie beamed.

'That's a lot of wool,' Moray remarked.

'Lilian's army has been going totally bonkers.'

'Oh yes, have you seen her yet?'

'We're going this afternoon, we only got in last night.'

'She'll be beside herself.'

'I know.' Rosie imitated Lilian's acid tones. 'Did anyone in YOUR family go all the way to Africa for a baby, Agnes? Or did they just squeeze them out like the common people?'

Moray laughed, and lifted Apostil with an easy familiarity.

'I should wait for Stephen to ask you this . . . ' began Rosie.

Moray flashed her a look.

'Don't tell me . . . you need a dashing gay godparent. Everyone else has got one.'

Rosie winced.

'I know. But you're our favourite.'

She paused.

'How many godchildren have you got?'

'Seven. I'm warning you, I'm shit at it. I won't remember his birthday or go to his school play, because I really don't give a fuck.'

'That's okay,' said Rosie. 'I don't care. I was only trying to save you the embarrassment of having to explain that you're NOT Apostil's dashing gay godparent and have everyone think you've done something horribly wrong.'

'Oh God, I didn't think of it like that.'

'Yes, quite. Everyone will ask, "Are you having Moray for DGG?" and I'll pause and look sadly into the middle distance so they won't ask me any more about it.'

'You wouldn't do that.'

Rosie looked into the middle distance and made her face sad.

'Okay, okay,' said Moray. He narrowed his eyes. 'But I LIKE the devil and all his evil works.'

'His birthday is the twenty-eighth of October,' said Rosie. 'We'll probably have the blessing at the Christmas Day service. Please bring Moshe this time.'

'HA,' said Moray. 'You're not serious. Mind you, our wonderfully inclusive vicar would get a massive—'

'DON'T be disgusting in front of my baby.' She covered Apostil's ears. The happy-clappy vicar, never known to turn down an invitation that might include free food, managed to please neither the traditional churchgoers nor the new generation of Liptonites. Lilian in fact had become a Catholic after Henry's death, finding much comfort in its more rigorous certainties and approving mightily of the new Pope, who, she had noted loudly on more than one occasion, probably wouldn't eat quite as many custard creams after Sunday service.

Moray turned his attention to Apostil's bad arm. The baby lay looking up at him from his layers of wool, blinking steadily.

'Come on then, let's take a look.'

He bent it backwards and forwards without Apostil seeming to notice. Moray made hmming noises.

'Can't the nerves grow back?' said Rosie.

Moray gave her a look.

'He's not Doctor Who, Rosie,' he said.

'You can be anything you want to be,' whispered Rosie in Apostil's ear, as Moray continued to look serious.

'No, the problem is more that the message from the brain to tell the nerves to work simply never got through.'

They both looked at the little arm, curled in, the fingers bent into a permanent curve.

'So what's best?' said Rosie, her throat dry all of a sudden. 'It's weird, because we think he's perfect.'

Moray put his arm around her.

'He IS perfect. He's a smart and alert and perfectly healthy-looking bouncing baby boy. But when he starts to want to use it, to develop, then you'll want to consider a prosthesis.'

'A what?' said Rosie. Her heart was suddenly in her mouth, even though she had known this would need to be discussed.

'A prosthesis. A false arm. They're amazing these days. It's not like he's going to be Captain Hook.'

Rosie tried to swallow but couldn't.

'Will it . . . will it fit over what he has?'

Moray looked her straight in the face, clear-eyed but sympathetic.

'No, Rosie-Posie.'

There was a long silence. Apostil started to fuss, and Rosie picked him up and settled him against her chest, where he immediately nuzzled in.

'They're not . . . ' She tried to shake the wobble in her voice. 'They're not chopping bits off him.'

Moray patted her on the shoulder.

'Look,' he said. 'You have a little time to think about it. You're a parent. It's a big adjustment. And when the time comes, you'll want to do what's best. For now, please, Rosie, talk it over with the big man, then just enjoy your baby.'

Rosie nodded, numb. She looked down at the little

head, with its whorls of perfect black hair, and kissed it. The idea of the tiny form on a big hospital bed … giving him a general anaesthetic … Apostil not having the faintest idea what was happening to him, waking up without his arm …

She choked slightly. Moray's phone beeper went off. He glanced at it and cursed.

'Another tinsel accident,' he said. Quickly he pulled Rosie and Apostil to him. 'Look, I have to go,' he said. 'But Rosie. Think. Think where you were in the summer, so numb and bleak. Think how far beyond what you ever expected to happen this is; how much better. It's amazing. You've done so well, you're so lucky. Don't you see?'

'Yes,' said Rosie in a trembling voice.

'Well focus on that, then. Everything else in its own time, capisce?'

She nodded.

'I know. I know we're lucky.'

'You're INSANELY lucky,' said Moray. 'Your beautiful healthy baby is going to be fine. And by the way, he's lucky too. And so's that stupid man of yours who absolutely does not deserve this.'

Rosie smiled.

'Yes. Yes, I know.'

'Fine. Good. Right, I'll see you later. Get as much sleep as you can manage. And a solid sense of perspective.'

155

Rosie stuck her tongue out at him.

'And go and make Lilian happy.'

'I'm not sure about that,' said Rosie. 'I was counting on her being all for the baby when the rest of the village disapproved. But everyone else in Lipton has been absolutely amazing, so she'll have to go the other way. You know Lilian.'

Moray grinned.

'I do. Tell her Hye's a big fat racist and thinks you're ruining the entire white look of the village.'

'He SAID that?'

'No!' said Moray. 'I'm just helping you with the gossip.'

'That's actually slander.'

'I know,' said Moray. 'But he's a terrible, terrible man.'

Moray's boss Hye, head of the GP practice, made Moray do all the work, took a huge salary, spent half his life on holiday, never made a house call and expected special favours from everyone in town because he over-prescribed antibiotics.

'But he's not a racist,' said Rosie.

'He's chairman of the golf club!' said Moray. 'That is probably basically the exact same thing.'

Rosie worked for the rest of the day, leaving Apostil napping in the sitting room, the baby monitor turned on to full, accepting gifts and good wishes and selling large amounts of selection boxes and a quick run on chocolate buttons, which she put down to people subliminally thinking about babies. Then she let Tina cash up and nipped off up to the care home, driving incredibly carefully on the icy roads.

She took a deep breath as she locked the car, hugging Apostil close. She was looking forward to this.

Lilian tried to pretend she wasn't peering out of the window of the front hall, which had a lovely fire going and decorations all along the mantel, as well as a large tree filling the entire house with its beautiful pine scent. As soon as she saw the craggy old Land Rover pull up (Rosie worrying all the way how on earth they were going to afford a more suitable car), she made herself scarce as quickly as she could, which wasn't very. She still walked without a stick, but not very far. Cathryn had suggested a walker, at which Lilian had harrumphed so loudly she'd woken Archie Geffel.

She checked her lipstick, which had an infuriating tendency to lose itself in the cracks around her mouth these days, and made sure that her dress was nicely ironed, which it was, not that Rosie would notice. Her great-niece normally dressed like she'd got up with her eyes shut and had never heard of an iron; what on earth would she be like now she was a mother and had an excuse?

The big, sonorous bell rang, and one of the nice strong young orderlies went to answer it. Lilian looked around for something else she could pretend to be doing so she didn't give the impression of having done nothing for weeks but panic and wait and listen in utter agony to all the gossip. To make matters worse, Dorothy Isitt had actually been in to the sweetshop that morning, and had immediately rushed up to visit her mother, which she didn't normally do. The pair of them had, infuriatingly, sat in a corner with their heads together, whisper whisper whisper, gossip gossip gossip, every so often glancing up at her. Lilian had known they wanted her to come over and ask them about it, so of course she point-blank refused to do so and had ended up so cross she'd watched *Coronation Street* and been found doing so by the girl who changed her bed, who immediately wanted to chat about it. Lilian liked to pretend she wouldn't be caught dead watching the soaps, and now she wouldn't be able to go anywhere without discussing the Barlow family.

She heard footsteps in the hallway and tried to dampen down her excitement, but then, to her irritation, she heard a chorus of coos and the footsteps stopped. Curses! Sure enough, Ada Lumb, Millicent Miller and Carmel Smith had already gathered round, their hands stretching out towards the little bundle Rosie was carrying like three old witches trying to steal the power of youth, thought Lilian crossly. She had never had a child of her own – had only ever wanted Henry's, couldn't give a fig for the rest – but those women who had been mothers seemed, as age crept up on them and their faculties left them one by one, still to have a yearning deep inside to hold a baby, to feel the soft weight in their arms once again. It was one of the last things to leave them.

Lilian made her way slowly to the door.

'Don't crowd that child,' she barked loudly. 'You'll drown him with lavender.'

Rosie looked up, her face tired and pale but somehow soft, happy, gentle and fuzzy round the edges with an odd kind of quiet, proud joy.

'Aunt Lilian,' she said softly.

'Well bring him in,' said Lilian. 'He won't be used to that cold air out there.'

'He's getting used to it,' said Rosie.

She moved quickly and kissed Lilian's soft, powdery cheek, then gave her a hug. Lilian could smell Rosie's shampoo, but also the mild, milky fragrance of the baby. They went into the sitting room together.

'Needlepoint?' said Rosie sceptically as she looked at the arm of Lilian's chair.

'It's a great passion of mine,' said Lilian, who had grabbed it hastily once she'd seen the Land Rover pull up.

'Right,' said Rosie, smiling. 'Okay … are you ready?'

'He's only a baby, Rosie, not the second coming.'

'Says you,' said Rosie. 'And he's your second great-great-nephew!'

'Well, quite,' said Lilian. 'The novelty factor has completely worn off.'

Rosie was rolling him out of his blanket and his sling and his knitted overcoat, all the many layers she'd needed to take him out into the frosty Lipton evening. Woken up from his half-slumber, Apostil looked around, blinking, his mouth opening and shutting. He made his little mewing noise, then twisted his head round to check on his mother, who smiled at him. He smiled back, waved his good hand in the air and grabbed a handful of Rosie's hair.

Lilian gave an involuntary smile too. She couldn't help it. She hadn't known what to expect, tending to think that he would be a little mite – the kind of baby you saw on adverts for charities. But this chunky, strong-looking little fellow with the huge dark eyes and the incredibly long eyelashes ... well, he was something else altogether. He was ...

'He's beautiful,' she said, cursing her cracking voice.

'I know,' said Rosie, grinning widely. 'It is a total bonus. Do you want to hold him?'

Lilian sat down.

'He's huge. Are you feeding him too much?'

'Yes,' said Rosie. 'Cherry cola in the morning, then liquidised Mars Bars at night. Why, am I doing it wrong?'

'Don't be cheeky.'

'I'm not being cheeky, you're being cheeky. He's a baby. He drinks milk. When he's had enough milk, he throws up the rest. Don't fret.'

Lilian arranged herself carefully on the sofa, her legs looking very thin.

'Go on, then.'

Carefully Rosie propped him up on Lilian's lap, Lilian putting her arms under his back to support him. For a long moment, he and Lilian regarded each other.

'The older I get,' said Lilian crisply, 'the more surprising life becomes.'

Apostil made a grab for her pretty watch.

'Ah, you have an eye for quality,' said Lilian. Carefully she lifted the little body towards hers and gave him a cuddle. Apostil twisted his head anxiously to look for Rosie, but she shushed him gently and gave him an encouraging smile, then quickly whipped out her phone to take a photograph to add to the seventy-five million she'd already taken. Angie phoned angrily if she didn't get one every two hours.

The other old ladies were hovering anxiously around the sitting room door, Ida Delia notable by her absence.

'Come on in then, hubble, bubble, toil and trouble,' said Lilian, and Rosie went forward to thank them all for all the knitting, then Cathryn came in, her ruddy face breaking into a smile as she implored Rosie to bring him by as often as she liked, it did everybody good to have a baby around the place, and Rosie promised that she would, and left on cloud nine, Lilian again making sure to stay in the hall, watching them all the way as they went. It was why Cathryn had built up the fire.

🍬

Rosie was still floating on a happy cloud as she walked in through the front door. Even though she knew there was a long, hard winter ahead, there was still something about seeing the smoke puffing out of their little chimney that made her feel so happy and cosy.

Stephen was sitting at the little table, frowning over a huge pile of papers.

'Hello, love,' she said, planting a kiss on his handsome head. 'Too much marking?'

Stephen sighed.

'If only,' he said. 'Tea?'

He put up his hands for Apostil, who was fussing, and patted him gently into his shoulder.

'I'll make it, I need to do his lordship's bottle anyway. Oh my God, the girls at the home went NUTS for him, I swear.'

'They want to drink his blood,' said Stephen.

'They do not! They just wanted to see a young face.'

'Ha, and yours no longer counts.'

Rosie stuck her tongue out at him.

'Obviously not.'

She let the kettle boil and pulled the bottles out of the steriliser.

'What are you doing?'

'Ah,' said Stephen. 'You know we keep saying we're going to have to sit down and have a serious chat about our finances?'

Rosie's nice, happy feeling dropped out of her body immediately.

'Um, yeah?'

Stephen held up a whole sheaf of bills with his free hand.

'That time is probably now.'

'Oh bugger.'

She looked around.

'What's for tea?'

'You mean supper?'

'No, I mean TEA.'

'Well, I thought if we had the difficult conversation about money, we could have fish and chips as a reward.'

'Can we afford fish and chips?'

'We can smash Lilian's penny jar.'

Rosie sat down beside him as he went through it painstakingly. It did not make happy reading. They didn't have to pay a mortgage or rent on the house or the shop, but money that would have done that went to pay Lilian's nursing home fees. They wouldn't have told

Lilian in a thousand years, but the fees had increased massively; to keep serving good food, to keep the home warm just seemed to get more and more expensive all the time. Their joint salaries from the sweetshop – Rosie made hardly any money by the time she'd bought stock and paid Tina – and Stephen's teaching job, where he was still on the lowest rung, couldn't cover their outgoings. And now they'd have to move into a large house with all its associated running costs, even if they were lucky enough to get it rent-free from Stephen's mother, and neither of them was sure about that at all. Plus they needed to change the car, plus a million and one normal everyday expenses that Apostil had brought with him, plus paying off the credit card for Africa. And there was the debt they owed to Apostil's home town: they'd promised to help rebuild and maintain the school there. Things were cheaper in Africa, and labour was inexpensive too – though not that inexpensive, with so many of the men of the village absent or simply untrained – but the money still needed to be raised.

Mrs Baptiste, the head teacher at Stephen's school, had immediately insisted that Lipton Primary twin itself with the school in Kduli, and had launched an African project – Stephen had already sent Faustine several pictures and hellos from the children in both classes – but they couldn't rely on the kindness of the village to fund their pet project.

They stared at the spreadsheet.

'We could economise,' said Rosie, after she'd put Apostil down. He'd complained about it and shaken his little fist, then resigned himself to his lot. Mr Dog had immediately jumped up from his snooze in front of the fire; he knew this was his time. She patted him absent-mindedly and he licked her wrist.

'What on?' said Stephen. He smiled at her. 'I'd like you to have a new dress now and again.'

'You can talk,' said Rosie. 'You don't wear anything that's younger than me. We could go own-brand for Mr Dog.'

They looked at him; he'd perked up at the sound of his name. His fuzzy mop head tilted and little pink tongue panted enquiringly.

'Neh,' said Stephen.

'And thank God we didn't have to buy any clothes for Superbaby,' said Rosie fondly.

'You have to stop calling him Superbaby. You'll say it somewhere out and about and get a reputation for being conceited.'

'OR people will realise I'm right,' said Rosie dotingly.

'Anyway, the moment he realises you're dressing him entirely in lemon-coloured wool, he's going to throw a fit.'

'We have time.'

But they kept looking at the figures.

'The best thing to do,' began Stephen slowly, 'is just

to sell the cottage. In fact, I think it's the only thing to do.'

'I know, I know,' said Rosie. She had been dreading this. 'But would she agree? And how could we ask her to? She was born in this house.'

If they sold the cottage in this current, buoyant market, they would be able to cover Lilian's care for the future and take one of their burdens away.

'Can't we sell Peak House?' said Rosie. 'That would be better.'

'Not allowed under the trust,' said Stephen automatically. 'It belongs to the estate. Plus, you know, Apostil is going to need his own bedroom one day. He can't just sleep in Lilian's old room. We've outgrown this place. We need to admit it and move to the Ice Box.'

Rosie remembered her promise in Africa, never to keep anything from him again. Even though Moray had said it could keep for a bit, she wasn't going to do that any more.

'There's something else we have to consider,' she said.

'No fucking way.'

'It's just something we'll have to think about.'

'Well I have thought about it. He's perfect as he is. I'm not having some butcher chop into him. I'm not putting a *baby* under anaesthetic. I've only got three good limbs, want to chop one of mine off?'

'No,' said Rosie. 'Of course not.'

'But you'd do it to your son?'

Rosie shrugged. 'If it would be the best thing for him.'

'Bloody doctors think they know it all,' said Stephen darkly. 'And where would all this be? Because it wouldn't just be the op, would it?'

Rosie shook her head.

'It'd be rehab and appointments, and physio – for YEARS.'

'I know.'

'Whereabouts?'

'Derby,' said Rosie quietly.

'The city.'

Rosie swallowed.

'You're suggesting we go and live in the grotty city next to the hospital?'

'No,' said Rosie. 'It's just … it's just a possibility.'

Stephen blinked.

'Don't you think he's fine?'

'I don't know,' said Rosie. 'I don't know.'

Chapter Ten

The next morning dawned on a black world crackling with rime frost (including on the inside of the windows, Rosie noticed with a shudder, snuggling back under the covers with Apostil for a few more minutes of warmth. She felt a stone in the pit of her stomach and for a moment couldn't remember what it was. Then she did. It was everything. And on top of that, it was also time to visit her mother-in-law-to-be and introduce her to her new grandson. She thought wistfully of how in some families this would be a joyous occasion.

She stretched out a leg into the freezing air of the room, and swore. It was pitch dark outside still, it felt totally wrong that anyone should have to be out in this weather. Then she thought of the farmers, who'd been up for three hours already doing the milking, and felt guilty. There were many, many harder lives than hers, that was for sure.

At least they had hot water. She filled up the old claw-foot bath until the tiny bathroom was steaming and almost bearable. The sound of the water woke Stephen and he padded in blearily.

'Hey,' he said. 'There is a really disgusting nappy in that bed. With our baby in it.'

'I know,' said Rosie. She had decided before falling asleep the night before that she wasn't going to push Stephen on the arm issue. He was stubborn as a mule. She wasn't going to change his mind. And they didn't have to decide now, did they?

She smiled at him.

'I'll give you a million pounds and a striptease if you'll change it.'

'Four million,' said Stephen, throwing hot water from the bath on his face.

'I am so sleepy,' groaned Rosie. She had gone downstairs to give Apostil his bottle at four, but found it so inhospitable she had brought him upstairs to bed with her and they had all fallen asleep again, the three of them together.

'You'll be fine,' said Stephen, lathering up his face. 'It's not like we have anything really awful to do today.'

'I am looking on the bright side,' said Rosie. 'She's going to love him. Everyone loves him.'

'Yes, everyone whose house and title he's not inheriting loves him,' pointed out Stephen.

'Maybe she'll say, "Hey, here's a bunch of money for you I forgot we had, why not take it and let Lilian keep her house?"'

'No chance of that,' said Stephen. 'She's still saying I need to pay her back for boarding school, seeing as I didn't use my expensive education to the full extent of my abilities.'

'Oh,' frowned Rosie, clambering into the scalding bath and wincing.

'Was that it? Was that my striptease? It's all covered in goosebumps. And what about Ap? I'm sure it's your turn.'

'OH!' said Rosie. 'I totally forgot.'

'You forgot? You can smell him from Isitt's farm. He smells exactly *like* Isitt's farm.'

'But I'm in now,' pleaded Rosie. They only got one bathful of hot water a day from the very old boiler, and it didn't stay warm for terribly long in the frigid air.

'That was a rubbish striptease though,' grumbled Stephen, who nonetheless grabbed the box of Pampers and went and set to. Apostil was not impressed by having his bum exposed to a cold world, and made his feelings known accordingly.

'I'm bringing him in.'

Rosie reluctantly added some cold water to the bath so it wasn't too hot, then reached up for the baby.

'Hello, my sweetie.'

Apostil greeted her with his normal gummy grin, and she sat him up on her tummy and bounced him up and down till he chuckled.

'Good,' she said. 'Now today you are going to meet your EVIL GRANDMOTHER.'

Stephen popped his head back round the door.

'Are you going to call her that?'

'Maleficent?'

'Hmm. I wonder what she wants to be called.'

'How about Beelzebub, Destroyer of Worlds?'

Mr Dog as usual was beside himself with excitement as they took the familiar uphill road to Lipton Hall. The trees in the long avenue leading to the house were white, their branches heaped with early snow; the driveway was gravelly and full of icy puddles, which the Land Rover cracked with a satisfying bounce, jiggling Apostil's car seat in a faintly worrying fashion. All Mr Dog's relatives lived in the great house, and he liked nothing better than tearing about with them, even though, as the runt of an extremely suspect litter, he was about a tenth of the size of most of his pure-bred cousins. He let out a couple of happy barks as they drew closer to the house, its soft yellow sandstone and rows of glittering windows (some cracked) looking magnificent. They drove as usual round the back, where there was a large yard with several outbuildings, and always some cheerful dogs roaming about.

Rosie undid Apostil's seat belt with apprehension, as Mr Dog shot off and vanished into a furry throng. Mrs Laird, the daily, came running out with a huge grin on her face.

'Is the little master here?' she said.

'He's not a master of anything,' said Stephen affectionately. 'Not even his own bowels.'

Mrs Laird, who had worked for the great house all through Stephen's lonely, unhappy childhood, took his hands in hers and gave him a thorough inspection.

'You look well,' she concluded, and Rosie smiled to herself. Passing Mrs Laird's assessment was at least as important as passing Lady Lipton's.

'Well, come on, come on, let's see him!'

She marched over, and peered at the little bundle.

'At last!' she said cheerfully. 'Been too long since we've had a little one about the place. And the last one was terribly grumpy. Anyway, by the way, have you heard?'

'Heard what?' frowned Stephen. Their phones struggled to get a signal down in the village, and Stephen rarely bothered with his anyway, a fact, as Rosie constantly reminded him, that had once nearly split them up.

However, whatever Mrs Laird's news was was cut off as the back door opened to reveal someone who was so like Lady Lipton – except, if it was possible, with an even more imperious demeanour – that it had to be

Stephen's older sister Pamela. She was exceptionally thin, in a way Rosie had occasionally seen in London but never in Lipton, where most people tended to acquire a comfy layer to keep out the harsher winter winds. She had Stephen's strong jawline and forehead, which on her looked a little hard, and a completely smoothed-out face, her skin taut and shiny, which oddly made her appear older than her thirty-six years.

'Well,' drawled Pamela. 'What on earth have you been up to now?'

Stephen grinned.

'Hey, Pam. Wow, you're looking seriously under-weight. Well done.'

Pamela was wearing a tiny black miniskirt that Rosie could somehow tell was expensive, as were her tights – who knew tights could look expensive? – a black cashmere polo neck, fancy high leather boots with tassels and chains hanging off them in unusual ways, and a very peculiar half-leather, half-fur jacket. Her hair was tinted in varying shades of blonde, and even though nobody round here had seen the sun in a month and a half, she had Chanel sunglasses perched on top of her head.

Stephen hugged her, and Pamela gave a tentative smile.

'So, I decided to come over early, you know, pitch up and see what was happening.'

Her accent was a mixture of very posh English and American. Stephen narrowed his eyes.

'Seriously? The bank just lets you take time off like that?'

'You think I have a hidden agenda?' snapped back Pamela.

'YES!' said Stephen. 'I think you couldn't wait to see your nephew. Come and meet him.'

'My step-nephew,' said Pamela, reluctantly agreeing to be led into the kitchen along with Apostil, who was regarding the goings-on from his baby seat with interest. Rosie knew as soon as he got into the warmth of the indoors he would start wriggling and want to go free, so she started to loosen his straps.

'He's not your step-nephew,' said Stephen crossly. 'I'm your brother. This is my son. He's your NEPHEW.'

There was a short silence. Henrietta was in the kitchen, shouting at somebody on the telephone.

'Forty-five and not a penny more.' She put the phone down crossly. 'I can't believe I even have to speak to these people.'

'What people?'

'I don't know,' she said, holding up an electricity bill sadly. 'I knew an hour ago when I first got on the telephone.'

Rosie felt a sudden stab of pity for her. The world she had been born into and the world she now found herself living in were completely different places.

Stephen took the bill.

'I'll do that, Mum.'

Suddenly Henrietta looked older, a little confused. Then she shook herself out of it.

'Come on then. Let's have a look at him.'

Just as Rosie went to get him, Apostil gave a little lurch forward. Forgetting she'd already undone the straps, she almost let him topple head first on to the hard flagstone floor, before managing to catch him just in time, cursing herself to high heaven. Apostil of course let out an almighty roar.

'Well that's never happened before,' said Stephen quickly, as Lady Lipton's eyebrows went through the roof.

Desperately Rosie tried to soothe him, but Apostil obviously picked up on her slightly anxious body language, and could not be calmed, instead letting out a painful repeated wail. Lady Lipton attempted to make small talk about farming conditions, which didn't help in the slightest, as Rosie jiggled him up and down. Finally Stephen came to her rescue and plopped him over his shoulder, whereupon Rosie immediately felt conflicted between relief that he'd stopped crying and resentment that Stephen had managed what she could not, and that the other women in the room were nodding fondly at his amazing ability to do what she did every day as a matter of course. She felt a bit like growling.

'Well, he's a handsome chap, even if he does only

have one fin,' said Henrietta eventually. Rosie felt obscurely grateful that she didn't, as some people had, pretend that Apostil's disability didn't exist, or that it was hardly noticeable. Apostil, restored to his calm self, regarded his grandmother unblinkingly.

'Well then,' she coughed, 'I suppose you'll be spared those boring questions about who he looks like.'

'Do you want to hold him?' asked Stephen.

'He seems a little unpredictable,' said Henrietta.

'No, he's a sweetheart,' said Rosie, as the others gave her patronising glances.

'You know,' said Pamela, apropos of nothing, 'I had my eggs frozen when I was twenty-nine. Better safe than sorry, huh?'

'So, you're here for Christmas?' said Stephen. 'That's nice.'

Pamela frowned and looked around the kitchen. Her eyes alighted briefly on the gin bottle, then moved on.

'Yeah, well, thought it was time to check in.'

'How are things with the bank? Brought down any major economies recently?'

'How's the school? Still accountable and paid for by our taxes?'

'You're right,' said Stephen. 'Mandatory education is just a step too far.'

'Children,' said Henrietta absent-mindedly.

Rosie found it astonishing that no one was more keen

to ask about their trip, or Apostil, or what had happened to them. Her own mother had pestered her for details about every single second of everything that had happened, as had Pip's wife Desleigh, who was, Rosie was prepared to concede, a slightly nosy gossip, but even so, this family's coolness with one another was a complete mystery to her. She looked at the way Stephen was clasping Apostil to him, the baby's little bum up in the air, his legs curled round Stephen's chest, and felt a swell of reassurance. No way would Stephen be like that with his own child. Not for Apostil a cold and loveless childhood in a living mausoleum.

'So,' said Pamela, obviously wanting to get down to it, 'I wanted to talk again about primogeniture.'

Of course she did. This was Pamela's big bugbear: that even though she was older than Stephen, he would inherit after his mother died, because he was a boy. Stephen didn't care in the slightest; in fact had often spoken of how much he wished the burden would be taken away from him. Lipton Hall was crumbling and needed extraordinary amounts of money they simply would never have, and he couldn't bear the inevitable obsequiousness from total strangers. But his mother had been so insistent that it was what his father would have wanted, that it was his duty and reponsibility, that there had been Liptons in Lipton Hall for three hundred years and he had no bloody right to break that chain, etc. etc., that he had almost got used to it as a kind of hideous incoming necessity.

'Ah,' said Stephen. He glanced down at Apostil's head, which was moving from side to side; he was used to his bottle, but he still rooted around for a nipple from time to time, which made Rosie a little sad, even though she reminded herself she was being a total idiot and loads of natural mothers didn't breastfeed.

Then, as Mrs Laird brought in tea and ginger cake for everyone, Stephen gave Rosie a steady look. She looked back at him and returned it, with a slight, tiny nod, because she knew exactly what that look was and what it meant, and she needed him to know that she supported him all the way, whatever the consequences. Anyway, the sight of Henrietta trying to wrangle with the electricity department by herself on the telephone had told Rosie all she needed to know about the possibility of there being any money.

'Well,' said Stephen. He cleared his throat and glanced at Rosie again. She came across to put sugar in his tea – he couldn't manage it himself holding Apostil – and squeezed him briefly on the shoulder, to show her support. 'Well, Pamela. I don't give a tiny flying fuck. You want it, it's all yours.'

There was a long pause.

'Seriously?' said Pamela.

Stephen's jaw was set. He looked at his mother. He

knew what was running through her head, and it made him so furious he could hardly think straight. He didn't touch his tea. He knew that Henrietta, who had always been so adamant that he had to inherit, would see things differently now that he had a son – a son who was not his natural son, who was not even the same colour, but a legal son who would always be the eldest no matter what.

He paused again, waiting, just in case he had been wrong, just in case he had misjudged her. There was silence in the kitchen as the grandfather clock ticked outside in the hallway, from which the double looping staircase ascended to the long gallery lined with portraits of strong-jawed men with fixed expressions, their hairstyles and wigs resounding way back into the past. He thought about the family, their motto and coat of arms, their family pew at church, their long line of breeding, the colonels, the hunt balls and the posh schools, all of it. And as the clock ticked on, he wondered if there was room for Apostil.

Rosie quietly cleared her throat just next to him.

'Oh,' he said, unhappy to even have to ask. 'So I mean ... I mean, I'll give up my claim. To Lipton Hall. It's okay. Pam can have it. Although ... we thought ... we thought we'd move into Peak House for a bit. Now we've got the nipper and everything. I mean, we'll look after it for you whilst you're in the States.'

The silence continued.

'Actually,' drawled Pamela, 'I was thinking of taking a little leave of absence. Having some down time. Discovering my roots.'

'Staying here for a bit?' said Stephen, suddenly worried.

'Well I can't stay with *Mother*,' said Pamela, as if putting up in a fifty-room mansion was the absolute height of torture. 'So, you know. If primogeniture really isn't a problem ... I'm going to hang out in the house that's going to be mine, know what I mean?'

There was a long pause. Rosie felt uncomfortably warm and tight around the throat. Stephen's voice, when he spoke, was dangerously calm.

'Have you been fired again, sis?' he said.

Pamela ignored him.

'Mother,' said Stephen. 'Rosie and I were thinking, we could really do with the space ... '

Lady Lipton raised her hands.

'Oh, suddenly the estate means something to you, Stephen. Suddenly, finally, after all this time. After years of trying to shake it off and have nothing to do with it, and go your own way and escape our fuddy-duddy ways. But then when you need a free house ... '

Stephen had gone very white. Pamela was leaning calmly against the units. Suddenly brother and sister looked very alike.

'I think we'll take the baby home,' he said slowly.

Rosie jumped up, as happy to get away as he was. She knew she was lucky in a way – the sting was so much less for her, because she didn't care. She didn't care about the Lipton seat; she certainly had no desire to take on the responsibility of a big dusty mansion and do things the Lipton way. Henrietta reacting like this had been no more nor less than she'd expected, and as soon as she'd seen Pamela – who despite meeting her sister-in-law-to-be for the very first time had barely exchanged two words with her – she'd known she was trouble.

But oh, she felt so very awful for Stephen. And they were still going to have to move.

Chapter Eleven

'They're just HORRIBLE,' said Stephen, driving the Land Rover down the hill with such careless force that Rosie worried Apostil would be jolted up in the air. 'They're just ... like two nasty crows.'

'Everyone's family is complicated,' murmured Rosie gently, wanting to keep to platitudes and neither stoke his temper nor encourage a sulk.

'Yes, complicated. Not EVIL.'

'But this is what we wanted,' said Rosie. 'Isn't it? You didn't want all the fuss of inheritance or going to the House of Lords or any of that bollocks.'

Stephen smiled.

'I know that. I know. I didn't, I never did. I was always going to offer it to Pamela if she still gave a shit.

I've done it before. They know I don't care. But you saw what was different this time.'

There was no denying that.

There was silence in the car, as Rosie rubbed the frosted-up window.

'He's our son,' said Stephen. 'Everyone else seemed to accept it in about five seconds flat. I don't know what's wrong with her.'

Rosie didn't want to say anything, just glanced back at Apostil, who had fallen asleep as soon as the car had started moving. His grandmother could come round or not, that didn't bother her much. But the house issue was a little more pressing . . .

As they came back into town, Rosie noticed something different. There were no cars on the road. Before she had a moment to wonder why that was, a fire engine came roaring past them down the usually quiet cobbled high street, sirens and lights going.

'Bloody hell,' said Rosie. 'I wonder what that is.'

'My mother probably breathed on something,' said Stephen grumpily.

Rosie's phone buzzed. It was a text from Moray. He asked her favours from time to time, when the surgery were short-handed with medical staff, and that seemed to be the case now; *Can you come to the Hyacinth asap 999*, it said.

Rosie blinked and Stephen turned the car around immediately, wheels skidding in the dirty slush by the side of the road.

The Hyacinth was a rather ugly, chintzy hotel about ten miles south of Lipton, which served as a venue for special nights out, and was also the HQ of the apparently very good golf club. Rosie and Stephen didn't go there very often as the food was absolutely dreadful, plus you couldn't walk home. Out-of-towners stayed there, and it hosted lots of corporate away days, plus there was always a cabal of golfers (usually including Hye) holding court in the bar, which had a fake gas fire and was covered in bad watercolours of stags. It was where the local people held their big dos – Tina and Jake's wedding was scheduled there for 21 December. It was staffed during the summer by charming but slightly disorientated teenage staff from eastern Europe who came into Lipton to spend their meagre wages and were the reason Rosie had started stocking piernik.

As they drew closer, they craned their necks. The sirens were still sounding, and they could see a large column of dark grey smoke rising above the forest.

'No way,' said Stephen.

'Do you think it's them?'

'I'll drop you off and take Appy home, I don't want him breathing in smoke.'

Rosie nodded, her heart suddenly starting to beat faster. Surely not a fire.

'Shit. Shit.'

Stephen looked at her. 'And don't take any stupid risks, okay? You can't. You're a mother now.'

Rosie shook her head.

'It's all right, you know me, I'm a totally craven coward.'

'Just let the firemen do their job.'

Rosie felt her heart beat painfully fast as they sped up the gravel to the Hyacinth's front door. Sure enough, the back of the hotel was ablaze, near the kitchens. On the front lawn, standing shivering in the cold, were a bank of kitchen staff, their checked trousers and T-shirts testament to the fact that it had been a lot warmer inside than out. Also standing about – and notably not mixing with the staff – were several guests, including two in dressing gowns – an older man and a younger woman, whose face was bright red – in the middle of the day.

The fire brigade already had their hoses trained on the blaze, and several enterprising characters were taking photographs on their telephones and, presumably, sending them to the newspapers. Rosie jumped out of the car and kissed Stephen and Apostil. Stephen looked torn.

'Maybe I'll just get out and see if they need a hand . . .'

'What did you just say to me?'

'Um, no heroics.'

'Quite! No heroics! What are you going to do, teach the fire out?'

Stephen bit his lip.

'But—'

'But nothing! Look, Derbyshire's finest are all here.'

It was true, there were copious numbers of both firemen and police.

'And if they can't handle it, I promise I'll call, okay? Now get going, Apostil needs a feed. Moray can give me a lift back.'

Stephen stared at the scene for a few moments more, then sighed.

'Okay. Go. Be safe. I love you.'

Rosie ran behind the house and found Moray tending to a slightly confused-looking man.

'Did they get everyone out?' she gasped.

'I think so,' said Moray. 'I don't think there were that many people in there. The fire alarm worked well.'

His smooth, handsome face was unreadable.

'What was it?'

'A pan fire in the kitchen, I believe. Fortunately they had fewer than half their staff on rota today.'

Rosie looked at the shaking man sitting on a chair. His gaze was fixed.

'Are you all right?' she said. She recognised him from church, but she didn't think he had any children. Anyone and everyone with children Rosie knew incredibly well.

'This is Mr McIlford,' said Moray, in a toneless voice. 'He's the manager of the hotel.'

'Oh, you poor thing,' said Rosie sympathetically. 'Oh my, how awful. It's lucky there weren't many people in today.'

Mr McIlford looked at her briefly and didn't say anything.

'I think you'll be all right,' said Moray. 'One of the paramedics is bringing you a cup of tea, okay?'

The man nodded carefully. Moray led Rosie away to the side.

'Thank God,' said Rosie. 'I was terrified when I saw the smoke, really feared the worst. Have you checked out everyone else?'

'Yes,' said Moray. 'Pretty much. It seems the fire alarm went off in good time.'

He glanced back at the white-faced Mr McIlford.

'Insurance job,' he whispered.

'NO,' said Rosie. 'No way. Can't have been. Surely not. Oh my God, do people actually do that?'

'Half the kitchen staff conveniently not in today? Hotel practically empty? This place has been losing money for years.'

'He couldn't have set it on fire.'

'They're sending the police in to check, see if he used an accelerant.'

Sure enough, there was a police van there with a dog. Rosie had wondered whether the dog was to look for people in the wreckage. Clearly it wasn't.

'Oh my goodness,' she said. 'OOH, I have to ring Stephen.'

'Don't mention it to him. Don't mention it at all.'

'In case you're wrong?'

'God, no, I'm not wrong. I knew this place was up shit creek. No, in case we get called as witnesses. Seriously, you don't want to do that. It is INCREDIBLY boring.'

'Well I'm telling Stephen.'

Moray rolled his eyes.

'Oh yes, blah blah blah, we're so in love.'

'I bet you'll tell Moshe.'

Moray glanced away and didn't answer. 'How's Nemo?'

'Don't call him that. He's brilliant. Except ...'

And Rosie filled Moray in on the gossip from Lipton Hall.

'Oh my,' said Moray.

'It wouldn't matter,' said Rosie, 'but we really are skint. There are people in Africa waiting for a school we promised.'

'Nobody thinks you're skint,' said Moray. 'Everyone thinks you're minted because you're from London and Stephen's Stephen.'

'I know,' said Rosie. 'It's a problem.'

There was a skidding noise behind them, and Tina's little Ford Escort ploughed up the gravel.

'Oh GOD,' came a voice.

'Shit, I'd forgotten about Tina,' said Rosie, turning round. 'Um, who's minding the sweetshop?'

But Tina was completely distraught. Although the blaze was dying down, the fire had blown out the kitchen doors and windows and half the back wall was down. All the windows were broken and there was rubble everywhere, while the water cascading from the upper storeys was clearly making a horrible mess of the flowery wallpaper and chintzy curtains; floorboards too were splintering under the weight of the water.

'The hoses are doing more damage to this place than the COMPLETELY NATURAL AND NON-DELIBERATE fire,' said Moray loudly.

'MY WEDDING!' said Tina, bursting loudly into tears. Rosie put her arm around her.

'Oh darling,' she said. 'I am so sorry.'

'We've paid the deposit and everything,' said Tina,

sobbing and hiccuping. 'People are coming from Grimsby!!! It's all arranged.'

Rosie had listened patiently to little else but this wedding for about ten months, and couldn't help feeling desperately for Tina.

'But fortunately nobody was injured,' put in Moray, and Rosie shushed him.

'What am I going to do?' said Tina.

'Is the shop just shut then, or what?'

'Moray, I think I saw someone tripping over a paving stone,' said Rosie pointedly.

She sat Tina down on one of the ornamental benches next to a plaster urn.

'Maybe it's not as bad as it looks,' she said just as there was an enormous crash that sounded like a chandelier falling down.

Tina looked up at her.

'Oh Rosie, you know what this meant to me.'

'I know,' said Rosie. 'I've had it in the diary for a year. Circled in red!'

'What are we going to do? There's nowhere else.' She sniffed. 'Well, I mean ...'

Rosie got a sudden awful lurch in her stomach. She knew what was coming. Oh no.

'I mean, there is one other place that does weddings ...'

Lipton Hall did occasionally host weddings, but big

society weddings, with helicopters, and expensive caterers from Leeds, and three hundred guests, and Bentleys and doves and gold Portaloos and stilt-walkers and hundreds of Chinese lanterns that Stephen wanted to ban because the ducks in the pond kept eating them. It was the only way Lady Lipton could keep the lights on in the wintertime, but because she absolutely abhorred having people in the house (especially when lots of them wanted to meet 'the real lady' and cornered her to ask her stupid questions about *Downton Abbey*), she only let it happen two or three times a year, charged a frankly outrageous amount of money, and suffered it in a not very silent silence. It wasn't for the village people; nobody would ever dare hire Lady Lipton's own house for one of their gatherings. It simply wasn't done; it would be an insult. As well as a long way beyond Tina and Jake's humble means.

All of this flashed through Rosie's mind in a millisecond, as well as her own precarious position vis-à-vis her future mother-in-law. But all she said, of course, stroking Tina's hair, was 'There, there. Don't worry. We'll sort something out.'

Chapter Twelve

By the time Rosie got home, Stephen already knew the gossip. Oddly, it seemed to have cheered him up.

'Insurance job!' he announced, pulling open the door with Apostil in his left arm. Rosie thought how carefully they had handled the brand-new baby, just weeks ago, whereas now they hauled him everywhere. In fact, he loved being jiggled up and down and thrown about; he would giggle when Stephen pretended to drop him. Rosie would inwardly wince a little bit but wouldn't let it show. She knew children needed to be toughened up by their dads. And after all, she was the one who'd nearly dropped him up at Lipton Hall.

'I can't believe how quickly gossip passes through this town,' grumbled Rosie.

'Well, aren't you pleased nobody was hurt?'

'Someone was, actually,' said Rosie, explaining Tina's meltdown. Stephen's brow furrowed when he heard, and Rosie couldn't bear to mention Tina's idea, not right now. They'd had about a bellyful already. Tonight they were going to put Apostil to bed nice and early, cuddle up and do their best not to think about practicalities, or families, or anything other than the joy and warmth of being together, their baby sleeping peacefully, their own little world small, cosy and safe.

The next week passed peacefully enough – they didn't see Henrietta or Pamela at all. But the cottage was growing colder and colder every day. It simply wasn't suitable. Rosie started looking at houses online in Derby. The ones in their price range were pretty grim – long terraces on busy roads – but they had three bedrooms and central heating. She didn't dare mention it to Stephen again. They were going to have to make some very tough decisions. An estate agent came over from Carningford to have a look at the cottage, and made some very approving noises about saleability and week-enders, which Rosie did not enjoy one bit and certainly wasn't going to mention to Lilian. But he mentioned too that he could quite possibly rent it out for the summer season, which she thought might be more attractive. Not quite so devastating for her great-aunt as selling the only home she had ever known; her last remaining link to what had once been a busy little place, with her brothers thundering up and down the little steps; her father, tending the roses; Lilian herself, a funny, angular little thing, skinny and dark, running the sweetshop, looking after the house after her mother died, never marrying. Rosie didn't want to sell any more than Lilian would.

One morning in early December, the children came rushing to the school gates to meet Stephen as he walked down the hill with his cane. Mr Dog liked to accompany him about halfway, then go and have a sniff around Malik's Spar shop, in the unlikely event that Malik was throwing out any unwanted sausages. After that he would pad back home on his own.

Normally, particularly on clear sunny mornings like this one, when their breath blew cloudy on the frosty air, the children would be charging about at full pelt in the playground, cheeks pink, wrapped up in huge duvet coats that turned them into tiny Michelin men, the occasional stray mitten hung up on the climbing frame, the sound of laughter and hubbub in the air cheering the farmers passing through the village, who had already been up in the cold and the dark for several hours, and who required a steaming cup of tea, sixty-five pence from the bakery, before making their way up to Rosie's for some mint cake to see them through.

Today, however, they were lining the gates, and as soon as Stephen hove into view they yelled his name.

'Mr Lakeman! Mr Lakeman!'

Stephen looked at them enquiringly.

'We got pictures! We got pictures from our other school!!!'

Stephen walked straight into the classroom, letting the children follow for once, even though the bell hadn't rung. Sure enough, up on the wall were photographs.

Mrs Baptiste put her head round the classroom door.

'Hello!' she said. 'I hoped to get these done for you as a surprise before you came in. Unfortunately, SOME nosy parkers' – Clover Lumb, the nosiest girl in the school, looked totally unbowed – 'peered through the window and made it impossible. We got an email from your friend with the funny name ... '

'Faustine,' smiled Stephen, looking around. The photos were wonderful: pictures of the village children smiling, waving, showing off the little slates they shared one between ten. The tired-looking young, heavy female teacher, the beaten-down shed with more than sixty children crammed into it; even the scrawny pale-coffee-coloured cow who put her head through the gaps in the walls from time to time; they were all there. The contrast between the shimmering heat and arid plains of

Africa and Derbyshire's rolling fertile hills and frosted landscape filled with plenty and variety was striking. But so was the thing that didn't change at all: the smiles on the faces of the children, both there and here. There was no difference between them whatsoever.

For fifteen minutes that morning, before work could begin, Stephen took lots of pictures of the children: reading in the little library corner; playing on their climbing frame; next to the whiteboard or clustered round the vivarium with their sad lizard, Blizzard, sitting inside. The huge disparity between what these children had and what there was in Apostil's village was utterly compelling. After that, they all moved into the gym and Stephen hosted a Q&A session about his trip to Africa, about what it was like there and even, briefly, on how they had brought back Apostil.

'So,' said Emily, Tina's daughter. She was normally quiet as a mouse, so when she spoke, people tended to listen. 'So they don't have books in their school?'

'Not many,' said Stephen. 'People don't have much there.'

'So we should send them some of ours,' said Emily. Lots of agreeing noises went round the room. 'And,' she added, 'maybe we could send them some money to help them buy more books.'

Stephen nodded.

'I think maybe we should try and raise a little money for that.'

'Yay!' said the children.

Rosie, meanwhile, was not having anything like as good a morning. Apostil had been grizzly, the bathwater had got cold almost immediately and there appeared to be frost on the insides of the windows. She needed to do a shop, which meant she had to scrape the insides of the tin for Apostil's morning bottle, and he had looked at her in a very grumpy fashion as if he blamed her for that, then pooed twice in quick succession, so the entire downstairs smelled bad. She had an order list a mile long to get done with the wholesalers – frankly, if you ran out of Mars Bars, you didn't really deserve to call yourself a sweetshop – and she was conscious that even by Lipton standards her hair was becoming an absolute disaster area (although it would have surprised her to learn – and she wouldn't have believed it – that Stephen much preferred it loose and soft around her shoulders rather than lacquered and tonged into reluctant submission. He didn't really understand the concept of 'frizz', he just thought it looked nice).

So when the doorbell rang sharply and she still wasn't quite zipped into her long-sleeved dress (there had been a few jokes from Lilian about when she was going to lose the baby weight, none of which she appreciated), she cursed loudly under her breath. She did get the occasional person begging her to open early, normally on Christmas Eve or Valentine's Day, but this was a perfectly normal December Monday morning.

'Yes?' she hollered, leaving Apostil on the floor and glancing at him to make sure he didn't roll over. He couldn't, not yet, but his strong left arm was constantly flailing that way and occasionally he made it almost on to his side. He thought this was a hilarious joke whenever he managed it.

'Stay!' she said, smiling at him. His huge dark eyes crumpled up in adoration. Even your worst day, she thought, with a baby in it has its ridiculous moments of joy.

The bell rang again. Frowning, and remembering she hadn't brushed her hair, she opened the door a crack.

In front of her stood a large woman in a too-tight trouser suit, with short hair, a large pair of bright red glasses, and an iPad nestled in the crook of her elbow.

'Hello?' said Rosie. The air coming in through the door was absolutely arctic, and the fire was only embers. She didn't want to let in any more than was absolutely necessary.

'Joy Armstrong?' said the woman, without glancing up from her iPad. 'Derbyshire County Council? You're expecting us?'

Rosie's heart skipped a beat in panic. She tried to think back over all the reams of paperwork they'd read and completed, piled up and filed on the tiny kitchen table. The council had mentioned that they would be sending someone round, but did they have a meeting arranged? She absolutely couldn't remember.

'I'm so sorry, I don't have you in my ... diary,' she said lamely.

Joy let out a short laugh.

'No, we don't tell you exactly when we're coming,' she said, as if this were totally obvious. 'We need to see you in your normal environment. May I come in?'

Rosie swallowed.

'This isn't an ideal time. I'm just leaving for work ...'

'Ah,' said Joy, a concerned yet slightly pleased look stretching over her face. 'Are you finding things a struggle?'

'No,' said Rosie, and threw open the door. 'Come in.'

As Joy entered, Rosie was suddenly conscious that the smell of dirty nappies was still in the air, and that the little front room, usually so cosy and homely, was looking cold and faded: the old chintz sofa, with its footrest that they scoffed at but which Stephen found incredibly comfortable for his leg on the wet days that swept in from the mountains and got into his joints; the old

199

pictures of Lilian in her younger days, impossibly glamorous but probably in need of dusting; the nearly
gone-out stove, the baby on the—

'Is that baby on the FLOOR?' said the social worker
in horror.

Rosie dashed to where Apostil had managed to kick
off his blanket and get one of the buttons on his lemon
and purple striped mohair jumper almost into his mouth.

'Oh LORD! Normally he loves being on the floor,
don't you, Ap?'

As if in response, Apostil felt the cold draught from
the closing door, took one look at the tall, menacing
stranger and burst into tears. Rosie did her best not to
roll her eyes, knowing she was being observed. She felt
hot and funny all over, as if she was being judged. Oh,
she *was* being judged. Oh Lord.

She picked Apostil up, being very careful to support
his head properly, and gave him a cuddle. Apostil
howled steadily into her shoulder as she patted his little
back unsuccessfully.

'Babies shouldn't wear wool,' said Joy, her face arranged
into an expression of concern. 'They can choke on it and
die. Also you shouldn't leave them lying on the floor.'

She glanced at her iPad again. Rosie wanted to explain
that he liked kicking on the floor, that normally it was very
clean, that the fire had only gone down because they were
leaving the house, and by the way it was the height of

sneakiness to appear unannounced. But all she could choke out was 'Would you like a cup of tea?'

'That would be lovely,' said Joy automatically, just as Rosie realised to her horror that there wasn't a drop of milk left in the entire house.

'I'll just pop next door and get some milk,' she said before she realised the words had left her mouth. 'Taking the baby, of course,' she added as Joy raised her eyebrows.

'Do you pop out a lot?' she said, tapping hard on her iPad.

Rosie had never wished more fervently for a time machine to take her back ten minutes. Maybe twenty, so she could stoke the fire and get the milk in.

'Never,' she said.

After about a hundred years, absolutely puce in the face, Rosie managed to produce two cups of tea and sit down.

'So have you seen your health visitor?' asked Joy, bringing out a questionnaire that seemed to be about a thousand pages long.

'Um, yes,' said Rosie. In fact what had happened was that Moray had come round to dinner, played with the baby, then said, fuck the health visit, everyone was clearly fine and they ought to save the local authority the resources, it was immoral otherwise.

'Because it's not in the file.'

'Really?' said Rosie, sitting stock still. She knew

enough about NHS paperwork to suspect that she might get away with this one.

'Who was it?' said Joy.

'I can't remember,' said Rosie.

'Well, what did he or she look like?'

'It was a woman,' guessed Rosie. 'That's all I know.'

Joy stared at her for a long instant.

'Have you found yourself often suffering from memory loss since Baby arrived?'

Apostil had settled down and Rosie gave him a cuddle.

'Yes,' she confessed, honestly. 'All I think about is him. He's called Apostil, by the way.'

Joy sniffed, unimpressed.

'Can you show me where Baby sleeps?'

Rosie led her down the short passageway to Lilian's room. It was very cold, and the cot was squeezed in between the bed and the wardrobe, with no room to pass.

'Hmm,' said Joy. 'And you and your husband are where?'

'Oh, we're not married,' said Rosie. 'Yet.'

'Now I'm not here to judge,' lied Joy, 'but it's a fact that children do better from homes where the parents are married.'

'Well, one, that's a stupid fact,' said Rosie. 'My parents weren't married. And two, we are getting married. Totally. Once we get a minute.'

202

'And you sleep ...'

'Um, up in the attic.' She nodded her head towards the ceiling. The pull-down staircase that led to the attic room was up just now, it being the daytime. Joy frowned.

'You have ladders around the house?'

'No,' said Rosie. 'It's not really a ladder ...'

She tried to pull the string down whilst still holding Apostil on her hip. This was, she realised belatedly, a lot harder when she couldn't lie him on the floor like she normally did. She managed to skip out of the way of the swinging staircase just in time.

'Ta-dah!'

Joy marched up the stairs, her notable bottom blocking the way. Rosie tried to remember if she'd left anything on the bedroom floor that shouldn't be there, and hugged Apostil tightly.

'Your baby monitor isn't on,' said Joy imperiously, her voice booming from above.

'That's because I'm *with* the baby,' said Rosie. 'I normally only have it on while I'm up there. Otherwise a bird gets in and scares the life out of me.'

There was a long silence.

'One time. One time we left the window open and a bird got in.'

The large rump descended.

'We don't normally recommend having babies and birds in the same house.'

Rosie bit her lip.

'No. Me neither.'

Joy looked around pointedly.

'We're thinking of moving,' said Rosie quickly. Her fury at having her great-aunt's lovely cottage sneered at was making her pink in the cheeks.

Joy took Apostil off her without so much as asking her permission. Annoyingly for Rosie, he kicked and wriggled perfectly happily in the social worker's arms.

'Hello, Apostil,' she said, as if she was talking to another adult. Apostil gave her one of his gummy grins. She looked at his arm carefully. 'What are you thinking about this?' she said, her voice softening a touch.

'I'm not sure,' said Rosie, pleased to be on safer ground. 'Either we see how he gets on, or ...' her voice choked a little, as it usually did on this subject, 'or we amputate very early and get him used to a prothesis as he grows ...'

She turned her face away. Joy nodded.

'Well, you must choose what will be best for him.'

'Of course I will,' said Rosie, stung.

'And what will that be?'

'I ... I don't know yet.'

There was a strained silence.

'I'll need to meet your other half,' said Joy. 'What time does he get home?'

'About four thirty,' said Rosie stiffly. She did not like to think what Stephen would make of Joy.

'Good,' said Joy, handing back Apostil. Rosie breathed a sigh of relief.

'Now, were you going to work?'

'Uh, yes.'

'And who is the child's primary caregiver whilst you do so?'

'Uh, me,' said Rosie.

'You take Apostil to your workplace? Has this been checked by Health and Safety?' She glanced at the iPad again. 'You work in a shop?'

'Um, yes.'

Joy pushed up her red glasses with one finger.

'Is there any glass in it?'

Rosie thought of the rows and rows of heavy glass jars on their high shelves.

'Um, some.'

'And anything he could pick up and choke on?'

Rosie thought of all the boiled sweets and gobstoppers and hard mints.

'Well, he's not really at the picking-up stage yet ...'

They both looked at Apostil, who was making a bid for the buttons again. Joy's face, which had seemed to be lightening up, darkened again like clouds moving in over the valley.

'Well, you know,' she said, 'that will not do. That will not do at all.'

Rosie wanted to swear. She knew it wasn't ideal, but

until they got settled and knew where they were living, there was no point making arrangements or looking for childcare they couldn't afford. Appy liked being with her and she could manage him and the shop. Not for ever, but whilst he slept for half the day, she couldn't see the harm in it.

Joy made several marks on her iPad, then bid her a curt good day with an ominous 'I'll be back'-type remark. As Rosie opened the door, the vicar passed by, looking jolly and round of face as usual. He raised his hand to her.

'Hello, Rosie! When are you coming in to sort out the christening, then?'

Rosie narrowed her eyes.

'Um,' she said.

'Lady L says she's got it all arranged.'

The hackles rose on the back of Rosie's neck. They absolutely hadn't discussed this.

'Oh yes?' said Joy. 'It can be good, welcoming a baby properly into its community . . . as long as you introduce traditional elements of the child's own background, if he is differently backgrounded.'

'We're discussing it,' said Rosie. She didn't necessarily mind the idea of a big party, but Appy had already been baptised. And she did rather mind the vicar and Lady Lipton getting together to cook the entire thing up.

'Well, keep me posted,' sniffed Joy.

Then she was gone, the sound of a little white Metro puttering off down the cobbled street.

Rosie kissed Apostil fiercely.

'Oh Lord,' she said, going back inside and closing the door against the cold wind.

'Interfering old misery . . .'

Lilian was rifling through the box of Milk Tray that Rosie had brought her, flinging the ones she didn't like into the bin with a force that belied her age. Several of the old ladies had stopped by to say hello to Apostil and lingered, obviously hoping to hear the latest juicy gossip of which, Rosie had long learned to accept, she was often the focus.

'Coffee creme,' Lilian sniffed. 'Who would buy coffee creme? Why do they still make it? Quality Street don't do it any more, you know. Because it's revolting.'

'It's my favourite,' said Rosie. 'Give it to me, don't throw it in the bin.'

'I'm training your palate. What kind of a sweetshop owner are you?'

'One that's about to get done by the Health and Safety Executive, unfortunately.'

Lilian listened, puzzled.

'But you take the dog in,' she pointed out.

'Yes, but they don't know about that,' said Rosie.

'And anyway, I hide him out the back, so he doesn't count.'

'Right,' said Lilian, who pretended she didn't like Mr Dog then fed him cough drops on the sly.

She looked at Apostil, who was snoozing gently and occasionally opening a sleepy eye as he was handed round from old knee to old knee. It was strange to think that most of these women – these grandmothers, great-grand-mothers even – had once been mothers, had once held tiny bundles of their own; whispered soft words in little shell-like ears; paced floors in the early hours; fumbled with bottles and worried about colic.

Now, with their earpieces and their thin white hair, and their thick glasses, it was hard to imagine the young mothers they'd once been. Ada Lumb had raised seven, all living, as she said proudly, five boys all alike, who had had their own children who looked alike too and at hol-iday times charged round the grounds of the home like a cloned army platoon. Ada pointed out cheerfully that the children shared the cost of the home, which was why she could end her days somewhere appreciably nicer than anywhere she'd ever lived before. Rosie, right at this moment, could see the point of that.

'What about the house?'

Rosie stared at the floor and mumbled something.

'What? Speak up, girl. I haven't got a hearing aid like that deaf old post Effie McIntyre.'

'I heard that,' said Effie from across the room. 'If you're going to gossip like a washerwoman, Lilian Hopkins, at least choose your targets. Or maybe you're going doolally as well as deaf.'

'She was a terrible tart, that Effie,' went on Lilian with equanimity. 'Tried to run off with an American soldier, but he sent her straight back. NEVER MIND, EH, LOVE.'

Effie muttered something and went back to playing her internet Scrabble.

'Well,' said Rosie. 'Stephen's sister's back.'

Half the room leaned forward appreciably.

'Pamela?' said Lilian, pretending she didn't already know. 'Well well well. That rarely fails to set the cat amongst the pigeons.'

Rosie looked around.

'Can we go somewhere more private?'

'Can we keep Apostil?' said Ada. 'For ever?'

'I thought you'd have enough problems keeping up with your own grandkids,' said Rosie, smiling. She glanced at the bell pull by Ada's hand, and propped up a sleeping Apostil in the crook of her arm. Ada smiled a smile of pure happiness and whorled a curl on his warm little head.

'I'll be right outside,' said Rosie. 'Just holler or ring the bell if he gets too heavy, okay?'

'Don't worry about me,' said Ada.

They found a quiet spot in the hallway by the fire, and Rosie explained all about Pamela coming back and Stephen giving up his inheritance.

'You see,' she said, 'we were going to talk to you about ... Well, we're going to have to move. Probably. With the baby. And—'

'To pay for me?'

'We just need more space. We can rent your place out, you know, make sure we keep it for you.'

Lilian looked out the window.

'Hetty stopped by.' She looked at her niece. 'You know, Pamela probably won't stay at Peak House for ever.'

'I heard she had the builders in,' said Rosie crossly. 'Making herself the perfect home in the country. For one person to bounce around in all by themselves.'

'Now, now,' said Lilian. 'No point in being bitter about something you never had.'

'You can talk!' said Rosie, and they smiled at one another.

'I know,' said Rosie. 'I know, you're totally right, I shouldn't even think about it. And anyway, we should probably move to town.'

Lilian heaved a sigh and stared for a moment into the fire.

'Well,' she said. 'I wonder what Henry would say.'

Rosie looked at her. Henry had a useful way of knowing exactly what Lilian would like.

'Henry would say, you know, the cottage ... it's not my home any more. This is my home now.' She looked around. 'And you made it possible.'

Rosie shrugged.

'And now you need a home.' She leaned forward gently and patted Rosie on the hand. 'You can sell it, you know. You should.'

'Sell your lovely cottage?' said Rosie. 'We were only going to rent it out.'

'Well you can't live there, up a ladder. What are you going to do when Apostil starts crawling? When he needs his own room? When he starts eating my roses?' She placed her hands in her lap. 'No, it's quite decided. You must sell the cottage and get yourselves somewhere more suitable, and some of the money can cover me here, can't it? It's never had one of those ... mortgage thingies.'

'I know,' said Rosie. 'Of course we'd give all the money back to you, of course we would.'

'Nonsense,' said Lilian. 'I know you're not taking a proper salary from the shop. We'll see what it will fetch, then what I need to stay here for another—'

'Twenty years,' said Rosie stoutly.

'Year or so,' said Lilian at the same moment.

There was a pause. Lilian looked into the fire again.

'I do miss him so,' she said quietly. 'I do so want to be with him.'

211

'We will always take care of you,' said Rosie softly. 'And I thought we could do it without you having to give up your home.'

'Well, you have a family now,' said Lilian. 'Nothing but trouble, I don't know why you bother, much easier without.'

Rosie grinned.

'And that one is going to be cheeky. I can always tell. I know children. Plus you have that handful of a Stephen Lakeman to look after.'

'I like doing those things, though,' protested Rosie.

'I know,' said Lilian. 'Anyway my mind is quite made up. And Angie agrees with me.'

'What do you mean, Angie agrees with you?'

'Oh, she's on the phone all the time, blah blah, you know, Rosie's house is too small, blah blah, you should really get rid of it, give her a foot on the ladder.'

'She is AWFUL, my mother,' said Rosie.

'Oh no, she's great,' said Lilian. 'Right. Get the estate agent in.'

'But your lovely things . . .'

'What, I won't have a guest room wherever you go? You're moving to Darkest Peru?'

'No!'

'Well then. I shall see my things. And they are only things, not people.'

She waved her hands as Rosie leant in to give her a

hug. A shrill alarm went off in the sitting room and Cathryn marched past, a stern look on her face.

'Well, somebody in this room is wet,' they heard her say, as Lilian, smiling, shook her head, and Rosie leapt up to go and attend to things.

∽

'So can we go and visit our African school?'

The questions at Lipton Primary hadn't got any less relentless. Stephen had described for them the hope and the poverty and had even managed to find a video Faustine had of the children of the village singing.

The Lipton children now were completely obsessed, particularly with buying them shoes. Various events for fund-raising had been suggested, including Chloe Carr-Beckley doing a sponsored silence, and various boys volunteering to sit in a bath of baked beans for anything up to a year. Stephen managed to get them back to their quiet morning work, but at lunchtime he allowed them to stay in – it was filthy wet outside, although this didn't seem to bother most of them, country children as they were, and the playground was a sea of red and black parkas – and several of them followed him to the new music and art room, where he smiled and acquiesced and promised to teach them an African song, then, accompanying them in a clunky fashion on the piano, videoed them singing 'Jerusalem' to send back to Faustine. She might be able to show it to the village children on her phone.

So he was in a bouncy mood, despite everything, as he marched back up the cobbled street in the gloom, to be greeted by Rosie telling him about Joy.

'She said *what*?'

'Um, she said she was coming back.'

'When?'

'She wouldn't say. Just that she needs to check us all out. And Ap probably can't come to work with me.'

'Screw that, of course he can. That's what babies have been doing for thousands of years.'

'And she doesn't like the sleeping arrangements.'

'Well she can eff off and live in a hut in Kduli,' said Stephen. 'And I'll tell her that when I see her.'

Rosie winced. He would too.

'What? What's the problem? You want me to kowtow to the social worker, tell her she's right about everything and can Nazi into our lives and pass judgement on everything we say and think and do?'

'Um, kind of,' said Rosie. 'Just for a bit, till she leaves us alone.'

'What's she going to do?' said Stephen, some of his old hauteur resurfacing. 'Seriously?'

214

'Seriously, she could take the baby away,' said Rosie. 'Lilian says they do that all the time.'

'Yes, but Lilian only reads newspapers sanctioned by fascists,' said Stephen. 'It's nonsense.'

'Just in case it's not nonsense—' began Rosie, sensing she was on dangerous ground but not quite sure where to stop. Also she had to tell Stephen about the house.

Suddenly there was a sharp rapping on the door. Rosie and Stephen looked at each other.

'*Heil!*' said Stephen.

'Shut up!' hissed Rosie. The last thing she needed was Joy walking in on a domestic.

'*Jawohl, mein Führer*,' said Stephen, and Rosie gave him the feud eyes, but it didn't seem to make any difference at all. Stephen picked up Apostil defensively whilst Rosie strode over and opened the door.

To her surprise, it wasn't Joy standing there, clipboard at the ready, but Pamela, who, on seeing Rosie, immediately burst into noisy tears.

Chapter Thirteen

'What's up?' said Rosie, ushering her into the cosy sitting room.

Pamela sat down.

'Can I smoke in here?'

'No!' said Rosie.

Pamela looked straight at the fire.

'That fire is smoking.'

'Well it's not choking the baby.'

'You think?'

'You can go out the back door!' said Stephen.

'Oh, thanks. Family!'

'Would you like a drink?' said Rosie tactfully, glancing over to Lilian's drinks cupboard.

'Yes. Can I have a martini?'

'Not sure,' said Rosie. 'Is that the one with gin and stuff?'

Stephen marched over.

'I'll do it.'

Pamela nodded gratefully and took the outstretched glass, complete with maraschino cherry. Lilian was never without them.

'What's up, sis?' Stephen said, standing with his bad leg nearest the fire, Rosie noticed. The long spells of cold weather did it no good.

'Oh GOD, our FRICKING mother.'

Rosie and Stephen glanced at one another. Had Henrietta changed her mind?

'What's up now?'

'Oh GOD. Heritage tours this. Roof repairs that. She never stops banging on.'

Stephen nodded sagely.

'Quite.'

'I'm a banker, for God's sake. Why do I want to talk to some dweeb from the National Trust?' She took a large gulp of her drink. 'Oh GOD, it's just so TEDIOUS.'

Rosie covered up the pile of estate agents' listings she'd received. The brochures did their best, but there was only so much you could do with tired patterned carpets, aubergine bathrooms, and tiny scrubby back gardens pressed up against one another in long rows. She blinked and crossed her fingers. Maybe Pamela was going to go back to the US and give up on all this nonsense.

'I've made a decision,' Pamela said.

Rosie and Stephen moved imperceptibly closer together.

'I'm just going to ignore all her advice. And the so-called historical experts. I'm just going to do it my way. Make Peak House fabulous, worry about the rest of it later. It's peaceful up there. I like it.'

'So,' said Rosie, refreshing Pamela's drink. She tried to keep her tone conversational. 'Not heading back to New York?'

'You know,' said Pamela, swirling her drink, 'I am totally going to stay a while. Work online for a bit. Calm down. Get in touch with my family.'

'Fired,' said Stephen quietly. Pamela rolled her eyes.

'*Everyone* gets fired, darling,' she said. 'You're nothing if you haven't been fired. Fucking regulators.'

'Don't swear in front of the baby!' said Rosie.

'But he's a fucking baby.'

Stephen gave Pamela a filthy look until she backed down and apologised. She stayed for another half an hour, talking about how she had all these decent interior designers coming up from London to sort out 'that freezing shithole'. She seemed not to notice how quiet Rosie and

Stephen were. Rosie went off and gave Apostil his bath and put him to bed, a little fan heater – which was doing nothing for their power bill – blowing hard in his bedroom, keeping the temperature above arctic. But only just.

✦

'Well,' said Stephen, sitting down heavily in the arm-chair by the fire, as Rosie finished taking the dishes into the kitchen. 'WELL.'

Rosie came back and sat on his lap – the good side. She kissed him on the side of the head.

'What's that for?' he asked, stroking her hair, pleased.

'For not being like your sister,' she said.

'Poor old Pam,' said Stephen. 'But she always felt pushed out ... because she wasn't the boy.'

'You're the one they sent away to school.'

'Oh, they sent us both away,' said Stephen. 'I swear my parents were the kindest dog breeders you can pos-sibly imagine. And they ran the nicest, cleanest, most loving stables in three counties. I just do not know what on earth they thought they were doing when the time came for them to have children.'

Rosie shook her head.

'Well, you turned out all right.'

'And you, dear girl,' said Stephen, kissing her, 'are just about the only person on earth who thinks that.'

'Lilian likes you.'

'She does, but I wouldn't say she's blind to my flaws, or anybody else's come to that.'

'She wants us to sell the house. And keep some of the money.'

'No,' said Stephen, his eyes flying open. 'No she doesn't. Not her lovely cottage.'

'She was insistent. Said it's only stuff.'

Stephen shook his head.

'What are we going to do?'

Rosie looked down. 'Well, we could . . .'

'What?'

'Well, I mean . . . if we were going to be spending a lot of time at the hospital . . . and houses are much cheaper there. I mean, *much*.'

'Move to the city?' said Stephen, looking horrified. 'Seriously? Move into a smoky, cramped city?'

'Bits of it are lovely,' said Rosie loyally. She came from a city, she wasn't quite as anti the idea as everyone else out here.

Stephen stared straight ahead, as if imagining a different life.

'Maybe a cute little terrace?' said Rosie. 'Near the hospital.'

Stephen's jaw looked stiff.

'Oh yes, that unavoidable place where we're so desperate to shove Apostil to get chopped up.'

'We can talk about it later,' said Rosie, anxious not to

wind him up. It had been a stressful day all round. There was time to decide. They had a lot of adjustments to make; all of them, basically.

'It does slightly suck not having any money,' said Stephen.

'Mmm,' said Rosie, who had never had any, nor any expectation of having any, so didn't think the same way.

'God,' Stephen said suddenly. 'You know, Pamela's planning to spend all that money she earned – all of it, tons of it, enough to run six thousand schools in Africa, or redo Mum's roof a hundred times – on ridiculously expensive curtains she saw in a magazine. She has never offered to share a penny of it. Not that I want it, but. You know.'

Rosie nodded.

'But she doesn't seem too happy. Whereas Lilian was positively cheerful.'

'Hmm,' said Stephen. 'Are you giving a moral lecture, by any chance?'

Rosie smiled.

'Would you like to balance it up by doing something extremely immoral to me?'

'Yes,' said Stephen. 'Before that baby wakes up and we all have to move into the Land Rover, I really think I would.'

The next day in the shop passed slowly, with occasional hiccups from Tina. At three, the bell above the door jangled with unseemly force, and Lady Lipton pushed her way inside. Rosie started nervously.

'Um, hello,' she said.

'Have you seen my daughter?' demanded Henrietta without so much as a good afternoon.

'Isn't she at Peak House?'

'She isn't answering her bloody phone. She can't just go knocking down walls, she needs proper surveyors and stuff.'

'Lady Lipton?' said a quiet voice. 'Um, excuse me, Lady Lipton?'

Henrietta looked round from where she was examining the Fry's Chocolate Creams, as if she'd been summonsed by a mouse. Finally her gaze rested on Tina.

'What?' she snapped.

'Um …' Tina's face was a picture of misery as she twisted her fingers in her apron. 'Um, ma'am … I was … I was supposed to be getting married in the Hyacinth …'

Lady Lipton raised an eyebrow.

'Insurance job. Don't you think, Rosie?'

'Not a clue,' said Rosie hurriedly.

'And I was wondering …' went on Tina. 'It's … it's in two weeks and … Well, I was wondering if …'

'Spit it out, girl.'

222

'If we could maybe use your house ... I mean, just a bit of it ... I mean ...'

'Oh. No,' said Lady Lipton, handing over money for the chocolate bar.

'She was just wondering if you might be able to help with an alternative,' said Rosie, stung by her rudeness. 'She was only asking.'

'That's fine,' said Lady Lipton. 'And I'm only saying. No. She can't. Weddings are a big pain at the best of times, without half the local farming establishment getting their muddy boots on my chesterfields. I've no heating, no loos, no catering ... It's bad enough having to think about my own son's wedding.'

'Is it?' said Rosie quickly, startled.

'And of course we're having the christening on Christmas Day.'

'Are we?'

Henrietta looked at Rosie over the top of her glasses.

'It's already sorted with the church. He can wear Stephen's christening gown.'

Over my dead body, thought Rosie.

'So as you can see, I have quite enough on my plate. I would have thought you all did. Good day.'

And she swept out of the shop in her usual imperious fashion, like a galleon cutting through stormy seas.

223

Tina collapsed in tears yet again. Rosie put her arms around her.

'Hush,' she said. 'Don't worry.'

'Don't worry? I've got a hundred people turning up in two weeks' time!!! And a church service and no reception!'

Rosie gave her a cuddle.

'Look, if we have to have it round your mum's, we will.'

'It's a three-bed semi!' said Tina, still in floods.

Another thought struck Rosie.

'Oh, we could have had it at Peak House ... if Stephen still had Peak House,' she finished lamely.

'That place is cold,' said Tina.

'Hey!' said Rosie. 'Trying to help here. Can't you cancel?'

'We've paid the deposit for the photographer and the flowers and everything,' said Tina, snivelling. 'There's a juggler and mime artistes, and a lighting operator ...'

'Seriously?' said Rosie. 'A lighting operator?'

'For ambience,' sniffed Tina. 'You can't really have a wedding without it.'

'Oh,' said Rosie. 'I wasn't aware of that.'

They sat in silence for a while, punctuated by occasional sniffles from Tina. Then the bell tinged again, and Edison came in.

Rosie took a while to clock that it was him.

'Um, hello, Edison.'

He was wearing a slightly skew-whiff beret, a blue shirt with buttons done up and badges on the arm, and a tight belt. He appeared to be carrying a rolled-up flag.

'Uh, what are you doing?'

In answer, Edison clicked his heels together and saluted.

'Boys' Brigade, ma'am.'

Rosie broke into a smile.

'Seriously?'

'Yes, ma'am! Atten-HUT!'

'But isn't that . . .'

'It's quas-miltree,' nodded Edison, blinking through his glasses as if he'd anticipated the question. 'Hester is furious.'

'That's a new development,' said Rosie. 'So why are you going?'

'Dr Moray says I need the drills,' said Edison. 'Good for spinal development.'

'Does he now?' Rosie smiled to herself. It sounded exactly like Moray, trying to give Edison some kind of a normal social life outside the world of school, the social rules of which he found somewhat difficult to follow.

'And my dad thinks it's a good idea.'

'I like your dad,' said Rosie. 'Are you enjoying it?'

Edison's brow furrowed and he lowered his voice.

'Some of the mean boys at school . . . they laugh at my uniform.'

'Well don't wear it to school,' said Rosie.

'Hester says if I want to be a warmongo I need to show everyone.'

'Mmmm,' said Rosie. 'Edinburgh rock?'

Edison nodded fervently. He was unswervingly loyal to his favourite brand.

'And then can you sponsor me?'

Poor old Rosie had, of course, sponsored every child in the village. As, to be fair, had everybody else. They had all gone into fund-raising for the African school with a will. Cars were being cleaned on a daily basis, grass cut and errands run; and everyone was getting pleasantly used to mass silences, and the sight of clusters of children dressed up as bears. Rosie tried to keep it economical as she signed Edison's raggedy sheet for sponsored marching.

'Is this Boys' Brigade too? Where is it held?' she asked as she put away her purse, then fetched the glass jar of Edinburgh rock she kept within easy reach. 'Is it at the church?'

'No, that's Beavers,' said Edison. 'We hate Beavers and will shoot them with our muskets.'

Rosie looked at him.

'You know, I wonder if Hester hasn't got a point.'

'Where is it?' asked Tina, in a voice slightly brighter than before.

'At the scout hut,' said Edison, his voice muffled by

the insertion of a large stick of rock into his mouth. 'Down the other side of the village.'

The girls both fell silent.

'They still use that place?' said Tina, sounding slightly out of breath.

'Hang on, that place Lilian used to go to dances?' said Rosie. 'It must be falling down.'

'It lets in a lot of rain,' said Edison. 'Helps us pretend to be REAL soldiers on a deadly battleground. Where it is raining.'

Rosie and Tina swapped significant looks.

'I think we may be down to look at that later,' said Rosie.

'I think we may,' said Tina.

They left Jake with the twins and marched forward into the frosty Lipton night, Apostil wrapped up papoose style on Rosie's chest, his little fists clenched tightly.

They walked down the main street, their boots clicking on the cobbles, their breath steaming in the cloudy air. They waved to Malik as they passed, who waved back cheerily, still open for another few hours until everyone was home and nobody needed anything – there was almost nothing he didn't stock, and he was very generous with his change when they were in a tight spot. Past Mrs Manly's boutique, which was showing for winter a stupendously large purple quilted coat, embroidered with a picture of a wolf howling at the moon. It was hundreds of pounds and so completely a one-off that Rosie was desperate for someone to buy it, which she felt was rather cruel of her.

Past the Red Lion, where a couple of farmers were anxiously swapping tips about the cold snap, and how to stop sheep from lambing too early if they got a brief thaw; two dogs ran about having a tussle before being called to heel by their masters.

Past the market cross, and the bakery, which opened early and closed after lunch, or whenever they'd sold the last jam doughnut of the day, when perky, round-cheeked Mrs Arknop would disappear mysteriously at the same time as the milkman, Joe Longbottom. Both of them were well into their fifties, but, Rosie's doings aside, sometimes the village could be a little low on gossip.

Past the school, its Christmas paper chains hanging from every available wall space, and great sheaves of holly round the door, looking less like decoration and more like the head teacher was trying to ward off evil spirits, the jolly shining berries protection against the darkness of the very depths of the year. Sprinkled above, like fairy threads, was light, delicate mistletoe.

'Good luck to witches trying to get in there,' observed Rosie.

'It'll keep Lady Lipton out,' grumbled Tina.

Rosie craned her neck to see if she could see Stephen, his large head bent over, marking exercise books as he often did in the evening, unwilling to clutter up their little home or bring work into the cottage when he would rather be lying on his back rubbing Apostil's sturdy little shoulders and being licked by Mr Dog. He wasn't there.

Past the pretty steepled church with its kissing gate, and rainbow paintings by children in the information case, which made Lilian sniff and declare that a few more parish meetings and a few fewer rainbows might actually be a bit more useful. No lights burned in the vestry, so the vicar was probably out and about on his rounds ('Biscuit-scrounging more like,' Lilian would growl, before lauding the austere habits of the Pope once again).

They were coming to the end of the village now, past the curve of the churchyard – there was a small graveyard on the other side of the road too – then down past the farm tracks where Lilian had once whizzed on her bicycle and out on to the old road, where in amongst the woods at the top of an overgrown path stood the ramshackle wooden hut that had once hosted dances and parties, town meetings and rallies.

As people's expectations of nights out had changed somewhat and it became more acceptable for women to drink in the bar at the Red Lion, the hut had gradually fallen out of use. Tonight, however, it was lit up in the icy gloom, and from inside came the sound of small feet crashing up and down and harshly shouted orders.

Rosie and Tina swapped glances.

'It's kind of falling-down,' whispered Tina.

'Listen,' said Rosie. 'With some posh fairy lights and a couple of gas heaters and some tinsel and those funny chairs with ribbons on the back, it'll be transformed. Like when Ross married Emily on *Friends*, remember?'

'I remember that not turning out so well,' said Tina.

The noise from the old hut showed no sign of stopping.

'I wonder who runs it,' said Rosie. 'We know it's not the vicar; it involves physical exercise. Anyway, they'll know who owns the hut.'

'Do you think …' Tina's eyes were bright. 'Do you think they'd let us have our wedding here?'

'I can't imagine why not,' said Rosie. 'Who in the village could possibly not wish you and Jake every happiness and success? Except my mother-in-law-to-be, and let's assume she's got nothing to do with it.'

She walked up to the hut and knocked confidently on the door. There was silence inside, a few scuffles, then the door was thrown open, and there, looking not at all happy to be disturbed, was Roy Blaine.

Rosie could never think of Roy Blaine without reminding herself that there were loads of dentists she knew who were absolute salt-of-the-earth types: gentle, thoughtful, kind to children, and who didn't treat the occasional dental issue as a moral failing.

Roy was not like that. He was the opposite of that. He seemed to have taken his attitude towards his job from a terrifying children's book. In fact she had no idea why he was mixing with children at all. He hated the blighters.

Now he blinked at her behind his unpleasant frameless glasses, then showed his horrifically white tombstone teeth in one of his wide, insincere grins.

'Miss Hopkins,' he said. He inclined his head. 'And your new . . .'

He seemed to run out of words here and flapped his hands. Rosie gasped at his rudeness.

'This is my baby Apostil,' she said. But Roy ignored her and turned to Tina.

'And Miss Ferrers,' he said. 'Have you made a decision about young Emily's brace yet? If you don't do it soon, I'll have to dislocate her jaw or she'll be disfigured for life.'

'She's only nine,' gasped Tina. 'And it's so expensive.'

'Too expensive to avoid lifelong disfigurement? Oh well. That is a shame.'

'Why are you running the Boys' Brigade?' asked Rosie in some shock.

'Because, Miss Hopkins, thanks to you and your fellow sugar-pushers, the children of this village are WEAK. Lily-livered, pathetic mewling milquetoasts.'

Edison, still wearing his oddly tilted beret, had marched up to the door.

'Hello, Miss Rosie!' he said, beaming. Roy shot him a look and he instantly stiffened.

'They need backbone. Sinew.'

Edison nodded vigorously.

'We're weak, Miss Rosie.'

Rosie couldn't exactly argue with that, but her brow furrowed.

'But what's in it for you?'

'The satisfaction of building healthy young bodies and minds, rather than poisoning them with sugar as you do.'

He cleared his throat.

'Sixty-four more laps of the hut, please!'

Rosie narrowed her eyes at him. She didn't buy this for a second. Tina coughed, and she remembered why she was there. She tried to make her voice more conciliatory.

'The thing is, we need to borrow the hut. In two weeks.'

'There isn't a town council meeting until the new year,' said Roy. 'So no.'

'But,' said Tina desperately, 'it's for my wedding.'

'You're supposed to plan these things more than a couple of weeks in advance,' said Roy. There was a Mrs Blaine – Rosie had seen her, a pinched, terrified-looking woman called Laura, who never came into the shop –

232

but Rosie found the concept of Roy Blaine proposing marriage terrifying in the extreme.

Tina burst into noisy tears.

'Ssssh,' said Rosie. 'I'm sure Mr Blaine will do the right, kind thing and change his mind.'

'I'll do the right thing and send it through the proper council channels,' said Roy. 'Now if you don't mind, I have drill.'

He turned back into the room of slightly terrified-looking little boys and shouted, 'Atten-HUT!' and they all leapt to attention.

Rosie took Tina for a drink in the Red Lion. Les, the lugubrious landlord, didn't realise Apostil was there till he was handing over their white wines.

'No kids in 'ere,' he said, his moustache drooping into the lines that ran down from his nose.

'I haven't . . . Oh,' said Rosie, remembering. She had been so caught up in wondering what to do about Tina's wedding, she had completely forgotten the baby was there. 'Oh, dammit, he'll never sleep tonight. We'll just have to sit up and watch *I'm a Celebrity*.'

She turned round and, to her horror, caught the eye of Joy, the social worker, who was sitting at a corner table with a cup of tea, marking something up on her omnipresent iPad.

'Oh Lord,' said Rosie. 'It's just one thing after another.' She gave a weak wave. Joy got up and stalked over.

'You know you're not allowed to bring Baby to the pub?'

Well, if there was a Starbucks in Lipton we'd probably have gone there and parked our buggy right in everybody's way, like all those 'good mothers', was what Rosie wanted to say, but she didn't dare, just hung her head.

'Sorry, I just popped in ... my friend was a bit upset.'

'Now,' said Joy, in a sing-song voice that was supposed to be soothing but was actually quite the opposite, 'I realise you're a first-time mother, and that Apostil is an adopted child ...'

Mentally Rosie rolled her eyes.

'But we don't consider "the pub"' – she made air quotation marks – 'to be the safest or best environment for Baby.'

'Um. Yes. Thank you,' said Rosie, feeling rebellious inside. She was tempted to order a double whisky, even though she'd never ordered whisky in her life because she hated the taste of the stuff. 'I was just going,' she said instead.

'Don't you want your wine?' said Tina.

'No, of course not,' said Rosie, forcing herself. 'I would never drink wine in front of ... Baby.'

Joy gave her a patronising smile as Rosie, feeling absolutely red hot, slowly got up and walked across the pub, leaving behind the full glass of wine on the table.

She was watched by an agonisingly embarrassed Tina and a smug-looking Joy, as well as a full complement of locals. It would be all over the village by the next morning.

Standing up woke Apostil, who greeted the room with a hearty yell, thus alerting the last two chess-playing pensioners in the corner, who had been previously unaware of what was happening. Rosie stomped out of the pub and, crossly, into the street.

🍬

'What's up with you?' said Stephen as she threw open the door ten minutes later with a face like thunder. 'You look like my mother.'

Pamela was pacing up and down in front of the fire, shouting into her phone.

'Oh good,' said Rosie through gritted teeth. 'Pamela's back. After she threw you out of your home, she appears to be squatting at ours.'

Stephen looked uncomfortable.

'She's not been well,' he said. 'Also she says she needs miso and I don't know where to get any.'

'Halifax,' sniffed Rosie. 'Shall we go and drive her there now? There's a Force 4 coming in, but anything for Pamela.'

She unstrapped a howling Apostil and passed him over.

'What's up?' said Stephen. 'Don't tell me, is being a mum not exactly like they said it would be in all those stupid magazines you bought?'

Rosie half smiled.

'Ha, the ones with the perfect children in clean clothes doing somersaults?'

'With the skinny smiling mothers who also don't have any drool on them?'

'With their fresh-faced nine-hours-sleep faces?'

'And their high-heeled shoes?'

Rosie couldn't help laughing. It was hard to be grumpy when Stephen was teasing her.

'No. Actually, up until about ten minutes ago, he's been a total angel all day. It's not him.'

And she explained.

'I was just trying to help out, but everywhere we turn . . .'

She looked at Pamela, who was having a cigarette outside the kitchen door, even though it was absolutely freezing, and still shouting into her mobile phone. Mr Dog was jumping up and down excitedly and trying to bite the lit end; this was more entertainment than he'd seen in months.

'Who's she calling?'

'Oh, she has a full list of requirements for Peak House. You'd think it would be impossible before Christmas, but my sister can be quite persuasive when she wants to be.'

Rosie looked at her for a long moment.

'What's she even going to do up there?'

'Be a dog in a manger,' said Stephen. 'Annoy my mother. Take the pressure off us. Get bored and sell Peak House. All that good stuff.'

'Anyway,' said Rosie, and she told him the rest. To his credit, Stephen laughed heartily.

'I don't think Roy Blaine being an arsehole is going to make the papers . . . Did you really take our baby to the pub?'

Rosie switched on the kettle and allowed herself a smile.

'Oh God, I know. I promise, I absolutely wasn't thinking. I had my jacket done up and he was so quiet and keeping me warm, and Tina and I go to the Red Lion all the time, and . . . '

'Who else was there?' said Stephen, letting Apostil kick naked on a towel to give his nappy rash an airing. The layers of itchy wool had their down side sometimes.

'Oh don't,' said Rosie. 'Jeremy from Bender's Farm. Big Pete, of course. Mrs Laird. Everyone. All the worst gossips and everyone who hates me. Why was the social worker in the pub anyway?'

'Because she's a free agent?'

'No, because there's nowhere else to go in this town. I should open a café.'

'What, come and have a cup of tea and a lollipop whistle?'

'Yes,' said Rosie. 'Anyway. It was horrible.'

'They'll make allowances.'

'Plus I have an employee who can't sit up without bursting into tears. That isn't helping matters.'

'No,' said Stephen, looking grave. 'This is really getting to Tina, isn't it?'

'It would be nothing to Roy Blaine to let her use that damn scout hut,' said Rosie. 'Nothing. He's only doing it to be an arsehole.'

'I think I should introduce him to my sister.'

'No,' said Rosie. 'His teeth aren't white enough.'

Stephen made her feel a little better, but it still took her a long time to get to sleep that night, especially with Apostil making his little noises in his crib in the corner of the bedroom – they'd had to move him upstairs; it was just too cold down there. Somehow she knew he sensed they were all sleeping in the same room, and it was obvious he approved of the situation. They were going to have a heck of a job moving him back down.

Chapter Fourteen

God rest ye merry, gentlemen
Let nothing you dismay . . .
O tidings of comfort and joy, comfort and joy
O tidings of comfort and joy

It was a filthy day. Derby had a huge Christmas lights display, big ropes of sponsored adverts hanging over the streets. The traffic was awful. Rosie crawled along in the car. Some of the town centre was absolutely beautiful, and she felt her spirits rise somewhat. But as she squinted at the directions lying on the passenger seat – the car didn't run to sat nav – she found herself getting further and further away from that part and into the downtrodden rows of closed-down high-street shops, where the street cleaning wasn't as good; where mattresses and cars and blocks of flats lined the road. There were many beautiful bits of Derby, Rosie could absolutely see. But this was not one of them.

The estate agent, a nervous young chap called Lance, was waiting on the corner of Bendragon Road. It was an enormously long street of hundreds of identical terraced houses, some with dirty nets in the windows. A few of them seemed to be B&Bs. Rosie blinked.

Lance was overweight and sad-looking. His accent was from the south-west.

'Have you been here long?' Rosie asked for politeness, hoisting Appy out of his seat into the howling gale.

'Three months,' said Lance ponderously. 'I was in Cornwall. I miss Cornwall.'

'Is the weather better down there?' said Rosie.

Lance nodded.

'It's always sunny and beautiful in Cornwall.'

'Not *always*,' said Rosie, smiling.

'Always,' said Lance. He pushed open the clanking gate, which was off its hinges. A small, scrubby front garden with cracked crazy paving led to a cheap white-painted front door.

Inside, the house smelled of abandonment and loss. There was swirly carpet on the floor, in some places showing the old newspaper underneath. Obviously nobody had lived there for a long time; a huge pile of ancient mail spilled over the hall. Lance didn't bother to pick it up.

To the left was a tiny sitting room. A faded green armchair with a brown stain on the headrest stood in front of a gas fire. There was ruched wallpaper on the walls, with dirty marks where pictures had been removed. A car drove past at high speed on the street, and its beams passed through the room and across the ceiling. Apostil wriggled crossly.

'Sitting room,' sniffed Lance quickly. The house felt cold and damp.

Along the passage was a tiny kitchen with badly fitted units, an ancient and filthy oven and ripped linoleum. There was a back door leading to a patch of grasssy scrub filled with three different types of bins, and a little alley-way. Even in the cold and dark Rosie could hear the shouting and noise of children. Perhaps Apostil could make friends with them, she thought nervously.

Upstairs were three cheerless bedrooms, the master bedroom getting the full benefit of the noise from the road, with a street lamp shining through the window.

It was horrible.

'So,' said Rosie. 'Um.'

'The thing is,' said Lance, 'in your price bracket ... there's not a lot about. If you want a house ... I mean, I've got a few flats ...'

Rosie shook her head firmly.

'No,' she said. 'We need a bit of garden. We do.'

On Sunday morning Rosie sat with Lilian after Mass, drinking tea and pretending to play bezique.

The home had been decorated beautifully, as it always was at Christmas time. Residents were encouraged to bring an old decoration from home, or something that meant a lot to them, so that the place was full of exquisite treasures: a little carousel of dancing reindeer that went round and round and had hypnotised Meridian the year before; a beautiful collection of hand-painted Victorian baubles hanging high on the tree; silver and glass bells that shimmered and tinkled every time somebody opened a door; and cards hung on lines, so many cards. The generation, Rosie thought with alarm, that still wrote and sent cards at Christmas. She hadn't done any. She could do all her shopping for her family in Australia online, but there was nothing quite like getting a real card. She'd suggested to Stephen that they should dress Apostil and Mr Dog up in reindeer antlers and Santa hats, and he'd looked at her as if she'd gone stark staring mad and asked if she was kidding, and she'd immediately said yes, she was totally kidding, and hidden the antlers behind the mantelpiece.

'What we need is a bit of blackmail,' Lilian said. 'Not much. Mild. What have we got on Roy Blaine?'

'Um ... occasional overcharging?' said Rosie. 'That's not very impressive.'

'He must do something bad.'

'He does loads of things bad. Tragically, he doesn't care and he does them all in plain sight.'

Lilian wrinkled her brow.

'Maybe appeal to his softer side?'

They both gazed into the fire for a moment, then burst out laughing.

'You look tired,' observed Lilian.

'Thank you! I'm supposed to be a bride at some point!'

'I know. Probably wait until you don't look so tired.'

'I *am* tired,' said Rosie. 'And all sorts of things are going wrong. Christmas is going to be a disaster, with Pamela and Lady Lipton shouting at each other, and us with nowhere to live, and everyone else living it up in Australia, and I'm going to have an employee with a ruined wedding on her hands, being sad all over the place, not that I blame her, but she blames me a bit, I think, and—'

Lilian laid her soft old hand on Rosie's arm.

'I think it will be a wonderful Christmas,' she said. 'With all the family.' And she looked fondly at Apostil and smiled.

'Ooh,' said Rosie suddenly. 'Do you think we could come here? We'll pay for lunch.'

The catering at the home was of an exceptionally high standard. So many relatives had taken to popping in around Christmas time for a mince pie or a smoked salmon blini that Cathryn had decided to charge and allow anyone to come for Christmas lunch. It had been an enormous success. It meant no worrying for the families about taking their old – and in some cases confused and incontinent – relatives home, while for the residents themselves, the presence of noise and children's happy voices had made the entire day much jollier. Anyone who could bang a tune out of the piano or sing a song took a turn, the rooms were large enough for the children to build railway tracks, and if it wasn't wet, they could happily charge about the grounds on their new sleds and bicycles and, ill-advisedly, rollerskates.

Lilian beamed.

'Are you sure? I was rather looking forward to Hetty and Pamela throwing crockery up at the big house.'

'You can get that any day,' said Rosie.

'What about the christening?'

Rosie made a face.

'It will be a blessing, not a christening. Oh that bloody vicar. He's a pest.'

'He's a PEST,' agreed Lilian vehemently. 'That is a man who will take the last Minstrel, every time, even if you're patently only offering out of politeness.'

'Stop offering, then.'

'I never offer anyone sweets,' said Lilian peevishly. 'Sets a very bad example in business. Do you think Lord Sugar offers people free computing telephones?'

'He probably tries,' said Rosie.

'Anyway,' Lilian went on, 'that doesn't mean that you should deny the village a good party. It's the first Lipton baby in thirty years, and it would be the first one not to be welcomed in that church for three hundred.'

'I never thought of it like that,' said Rosie. 'Mind you, if Lady Lipton is anything to go by, he's probably the first bastard.'

Lilian coughed.

'I wouldn't be too sure about that.'

Rosie smiled.

'Oh, but all that fuss.' Her face grew serious. 'Will I have to put him in a dress?' Henrietta had dropped round an extraordinary cream lace christening gown, yellowing at the edges. Rosie had stared at it in disbelief. Apostil would look utterly ridiculous.

'Probably,' said Lilian serenely. 'He'll probably like it. And he looks good in white. Goes with his lovely eyes, and he might have teeth by then.'

Rosie smiled at him fondly, watching him reaching out his little arm towards the spangled heights of the Christmas tree.

'You're going to kiss that baby to death,' warned Lilian. 'He's got lipstick all over his head. So.

Christening, sorry, *blessing*, back to Hetty's for champagne and a fight, then come here,' she went on. 'That sounds about right.'

'Hmm. We'll see. It's pretty frosty between everyone at the moment. And am I going to have to stand up in front of everyone?' grumbled Rosie. 'They all know I'm a total heathen.'

'And God forgives you for that,' said Lilian. 'But he doesn't forgive you for understocking the rainbow pips.'

'I've had a lot on.'

'The rainbow pip people haven't.'

'Anyway,' said Rosie, changing the subject. 'Roy?'

'Invite him over,' said Lilian. 'Look for his soft side.'

'That's just not possible,' said Rosie. 'I loathe him.'

'Maybe that's exactly why you should do it,' said Lilian. 'Shower him with praise. What's your alternative?'

Rosie looked around.

'I don't know. Tina's mum's back garden. In December.'

'Exactly,' said Lilian. 'Exactly.'

Rosie wouldn't have given much credence to the plan if she hadn't run into Hye in the market – every second Thursday, traders turned up from miles around with sheets, blankets, livestock, cheap shoes and watches and radios, honey, home-made cheese and a general mishmash of items, and everyone flooded in from the surrounding valleys and farms, so it was always a busy day for the shop. Rosie was dashing out to grab some of the wonderful farm-made local Derby cheese when she ran slap bang into Hye buying a Victoria sponge. By the look on his face, Rosie reckoned he was planning on eating the entire thing himself.

'Hello, young Rosie,' he said. 'How are things with your little chap?'

This was unlike Hye, who tended towards the brusque. Maybe he just liked being avuncular in public.

'He's great,' said Rosie. 'Would you like to see a picture? I have two thousand.'

'I don't think ... Well, perhaps ... Have you decided on a course of treatment yet?'

'Oh,' said Rosie. 'No, not yet.'

'No rush, no rush,' he said. 'I do have a good specialist friend, Dr Murphy. Well, Mrs Pike she operates as. But she is the best there is.'

Rosie was touched. Moray had recommended exactly the same surgeon.

'Oh,' she said. 'Thank you.'

'Not at all,' said Hye. 'You don't want anything but the best for the little lad now, do you?' Then, as if regretting having spoken so kindly, he barked at the woman behind the baking counter to hurry up and wrap his cake.

'Hye,' said Rosie, now they were chatting, 'you're on the council, aren't you?'

'I am.'

'Why ... why is Roy Blaine running Boys' Brigade meetings?'

Hye laughed.

'I hope you're not implying he's trying to hang out with small boys. Roy may be many things, but—'

'NO!' said Rosie, blushing puce. She genuinely hadn't been. 'No! I wasn't, not at all. I was just wondering. It doesn't ...'

'It doesn't seem like him?'

'No, not really.'

Hye grinned.

'You're right, it's not at all like the old sod. He's bought the plot, you see. Wants to build flats on it or something. But he has to run it as a community site for now and show he'll still make it part of the community. Building regs and all that.'

'Oh!' said Rosie. 'Oh, that explains it. How many flats?'

'Between you and me,' said Hye, 'they'll be an eyesore.'

'Oh God, really?'

'Totally. They'll ruin the view of the church and he'll have to knock into half the graveyard as well. But he's getting his own way so far.'

'That's appalling,' said Rosie. 'That really is awful.'

Hye picked up his cake.

'People need places to live, Rosie. And until he starts building, or offloads the site, he's running a community centre.'

Which was how, four days later, Rosie found herself in the kitchen, chopping onions like a demon. She had been amazed that Roy had agreed immediately to the invitation when she'd popped into the surgery. In fact he seemed to see it as something totally expected, that of course she should want to have him round for dinner. Perhaps, it struck her horribly, perhaps he thought they had been getting on really well these last few years.

Stephen had looked horrified and desperately tried to pretend he was doing something else that night, but Rosie said Tina and Jake were already coming, and Stephen relaxed a little and she knew he and Jake would chat about livestock the entire evening and nobody else would get a word in edgeways. She'd invited Roy's wife Laura, the traumatised mouse of a woman who never spoke two words – in fact, Rosie realised, she hadn't seen her around for ages – but Roy had coughed and said Laura was busy that night, so it was just him. Probably just as well, Rosie caught herself thinking. He was going to be hard enough work as it was.

Tina had been speechless with gratitude, and was planning her charm offensive. She had a forty-eight-point plan on why he should let them borrow his hut.

For back-up Rosie had invited Moray, whose easy charm meant he got on well with just about everyone, plus he and Roy shared a certain professional courtesy; Pamela, who would probably have turned up anyway; and Lilian, of course, who didn't want to miss out on any of the fun. She folded out the tiny table to its full extent, pushed the furniture against the walls and borrowed chairs from all and sundry, but it was still going to be a very tight squeeze in the little sitting room.

'This is why we need to move,' she had pointed out to Stephen as they squished past one another in the hallway.

'So you can throw dinner parties for people you don't like?' said Stephen. 'Seriously? Okay, I'll tell the estate agent.'

Rosie rolled her eyes.

'I know, as if we don't have enough on.'

She was making a huge coq au vin, with lots of roast potatoes to soak up the gravy, and wilted greens, which Stephen observed was just a bunch of greens that were neither one thing nor the other and she had growled at him and he had retreated and announced he was taking Apostil for a walk.

'I'll try not to take him to the pub,' he shouted as he left.

'You probably could,' pointed out Rosie with some degree of accuracy, 'and everybody would think it was the sweetest thing ever.'

By seven she was just about ready, although she could really do with a quick shower after slaving away in the kitchen. She washed quickly, then looked at her hair – VERY frizzy after all the steam; it looked like she'd stuck her fingers in the plug socket. She pinned it up and tried to pull out a few artistic fronds, but they looked very peculiar too. Finally she just left it, and slapped on some BB cream and pinky-red lipstick.

Pamela had turned up earlier and lain about reading Italian *Vogue* in front of the fire, accompanied by Mr Dog, who, to Rosie's extreme annoyance, absolutely adored her. Then she'd announced that seeing as Rosie didn't seem to need her in the kitchen, she was going to get ready.

The doorbell rang. Vainly attempting to plaster down her hair, Rosie rushed out of the kitchen, only to be greeted by the door of Lilian's room being thrown open. She couldn't help it; she gasped. Pamela, who was tall anyway, appeared even taller in enormous spiky heels, towering nearly as high as the door frame. Her long skinny legs – that before had looked a bit spindly and sad, but now looked utterly magnificent – were encased in tight shiny leather trousers, the kind Rosie would look at in shops and wonder who on earth would ever buy such a thing. She was wearing some kind of shimmering translucent high-collared black shirt, made of a material Rosie didn't recognise, and over it a shaggy fake-fur gilet in pure black with one studded shoulder. Again, Rosie would have passed it by thinking it was hideous, but on Pamela it looked absolutely outstanding.

Her hair was a miracle: a great thick cascading bouffant of shiny blonde locks that didn't look at all as if their owner survived on a diet of cigarettes, miso and (Rosie had noticed) the odd purloined Sherbert Dip Dab. And her face looked as if it were barely made up at all, just long, innocent, shiny eyelashes, flawless creamy skin, natural lips ...

'Bloody hell,' breathed Rosie. 'You look like you've beamed in from another planet.'

Pamela tried her normal scowl, but underneath it all she was clearly pleased.

'A good planet?'

'Amazing,' said Rosie truthfully, thinking it was no use her trying to put more make-up on now; she'd only look like the hired help.

'I'll get the door,' said Pamela. Rosie looked at her. Pamela didn't normally offer to do anything.

'Cool,' she said, removing the tea towel that had somehow ended up hanging off her shoulder.

There, standing in the doorway clutching a bottle of

Malik's second cheapest wine, his face looking so bemused and startled that Rosie wished she had her camera to take a picture, was Roy Blaine.

'Uh … uh,' he stuttered. It was the first time Rosie had ever seen him speechless.

'Hi,' said Pamela coolly. This was not at all the nervy, stressy woman Rosie had got to know over the last few days. No wonder she'd been so successful at work. She held out a perfectly manicured hand. Roy held out a slightly sweaty, pudgy-looking one.

'Well, come in then,' said Rosie, smiling as warmly as she could manage. Where were Stephen and Apostil? This was going to be a long night as it was.

But Roy was still standing on the doorstep, seemingly transfixed and unable to let go of Pamela's hand.

'Yeah?' said Pamela.

Roy shook his head in disbelief.

'You,' he said. 'You have the most perfect teeth I have ever seen.'

Pamela smiled, and Roy smiled back, and between the two of them Rosie thought they might be able to abolish street lighting, so she hurried them inside, Roy still utterly transfixed.

'Hello,' she said, steeling herself to kiss him on the cheek and not make a face afterwards. 'Thanks so much for coming.'

Roy handed her his coat without looking at her,

making Rosie feel like the under scullery maid, and Pamela announced she'd make some drinks. Had Rosie not had a lot of things on her mind, she would probably have had something to say about this, but a pot was boiling over and she could see Jake and Tina marching nervously up the road, Jake looking uncomfortable in … oh my God, was that a *tie* he was wearing? Wonders would never cease … and before she knew it, she could hear Pamela's American tones going, 'I think I'll make martinis!' and Roy saying, 'I've only ever had Martini Bianco,' and Pamela laughing and saying, 'Doctor Blaine, you are so funny!' and Roy preening and saying, 'Actually, in the UK not many people know to call their dentist "Doctor", and Pamela saying, 'Really, in America, EVERYBODY does', and Rosie rolled her eyes and went and answered the door.

Tina and Jake shuffled in, looking shy, and Rosie hugged Tina and told her not to worry, her coq au vin would win him over, and if it didn't, Pamela probably would. Then Moray turned up with Lilian, a glint in his eyes. He brought two bottles of champagne and a box of toothpicks and said the only way to get through tonight was if everyone was thoroughly trollied, and she'd best feed Apostil now because she'd be asleep later, and Rosie said, don't be ridiculous, she was a sensible mother now, and Moray asked her if the social worker had installed secret CCTV and Rosie said possibly, but Lilian would serve the same function.

Lilian, comfortably installed in the best armchair, har-rumphed very loudly at this, but one second later made a cheerful noise as she took a tentative sip of the glass Pamela had offered her.

'Oh!' she said. 'Finally, SOMEBODY in Lipton who knows how to make a martini.'

Rosie gave her a sharp look. She'd tried Lilian's version; it tasted like rubbing alcohol.

'When do you drink proper martinis? Have you had a million secret trips to the Ritz that I know nothing about?'

Lilian looked at her severely.

'I've done all sorts of things you know nothing about,' she said sternly. 'Have you never heard of the sixties?'

'You were forty by then, though, weren't you?'

'I am very, very disappointed in you,' returned Lilian. 'Oh, where's your baby? Have you put him down some-where and forgotten about him again?'

'I'm just going to the kitchen,' said Rosie.

Tina sat down beside Lilian.

'I want to hear about the sixties,' she said eagerly.

'You should,' said Lilian. 'Might learn a thing or two.'

Rosie noticed that Pamela was making Roy another cocktail. That was good, hopefully. Maybe they could get him to sign something whilst incapacitated.

As she went back into the kitchen, she heard a rap-ping at the back door. It was Stephen, Mr Dog and Apostil, all jolly and pink-cheeked.

'How's it going?' said Stephen. 'Me and Apostil aren't coming in unless everyone's being nice and my sister is behaving herself.'

'What about Mr Dog?'

'He's a tart for canapés.'

This was true, he'd already wagged his way indoors. Lilian would have a thing to say about muddy footprints.

'No, it's fine, it's fine. Where *were* you?'

Stephen sighed, and his expression changed.

'God, it's nice coming home.'

'What?'

He rubbed the back of his neck as she unpinned Apostil from the sling and kissed Stephen gently on the nose.

'Don't ask.'

'That is absolutely guaranteed to get me not to ask. Yup, totally.'

She tickled Apostil, who grinned gummily.

'Tell Mummy where Daddy was! Tell me now or no milk.'

'He's a daddy's boy,' said Stephen fiercely. 'He'll never rat me in.'

In fact he didn't have to. Rosie glanced down and spotted that Stephen's trouser legs were covered in dog hairs.

'Ha!' she said. 'I am Sherlock Holmes, and I do declare you have been at your mother's!'

Stephen looked shocked for a moment, then resigned.

'Seriously,' he said. 'You're good.'

'I know,' said Rosie. 'Why?'

Stephen shrugged. His handsome face looked suddenly sad.

'I just . . . I just wanted to ask her if she'd reconsider. About Peak House.'

'You're kidding,' said Rosie, shocked. 'You went behind Pamela's back?'

'I know, because she just stabbed me in the front.'

'And you didn't consult me first?'

Stephen looked disgruntled.

'I thought it would be a nice surprise.'

'What, to know we ran begging to your mother?'

Instantly Rosie could have bitten off her tongue. That sounded awful, and so unfair. Stephen just looked at her.

'Well, what did she say?' said Rosie. She already knew the answer, of course.

'I'm going to go and get a drink,' said Stephen, in a steely voice.

'What's up, you two having a domestic?' said Pamela cheerily, entering the kitchen. 'Have you guys got any more ice? I never understand this deep belief in England that ice is, like, rationed.'

They both fell silent. Rosie was fuming inside, and couldn't believe she'd stoked the matter up again. It didn't help anything.

257

'Here's the ice!' she said, pasting a bright smile on her face. 'Everyone seems to be loving your martinis.'

'Could you pass some canapés around?' said Pamela. 'I think people are hungry.'

'Hi, Pamela,' said Stephen. 'You look ridiculous. Can I have a drink?'

Rosie let pass the fact that she was still being treated as staff and took the little sausage rolls out of the oven. Stephen took Apostil into the sitting room, where he was greeted with coos and general approval. It would be nice, Rosie thought crossly, if she got a welcome like that. Then she cursed herself for making such a big fuss. Dinner was under control. It was time to go and get a drink.

The cosy sitting room made a pretty sight, with the tree tucked away carefully to the side, bent over with the weight of the old wooden designs from Stephen's childhood; holly, of course, over the fireplace, candles burning everywhere, and people chatting away. Lilian and Tina were cooing over the baby; Stephen was taking long slugs of his drink, then making a face at how strong it was, and had immediately launched into a long conversation about dairy yields with Jake, whose lazy grin and laid-back style belied his deep knowledge and understanding of the land. Moray was pretending to be interested in how the dental trade was going – and Roy was explaining it in some detail – but really, Rosie could tell, he was sniffing around for gossip. Pamela was playing with her glass and laughing, showing those truly stunning teeth, looking as if she hadn't a care in the world. In fact, thought Rosie, anyone glancing through the window would think what a happy, blessed lot they were, not at all a couple rowing and about to be turfed out on the street, an old lady still recovering from the loss of the love of her life, a sacked banker and an anxious Bridezilla. Maybe, she wondered briefly, all parties were like this, everyone wearing a facade.

Then she looked out into the night, where a hailstorm had come up and was throwing handfuls of what sounded like gravel against the little window panes of their cosy home, and heard Tina give a genuine shout of laughter at something Lilian had said. 'I saw Three Ships' came on the iPod and she thought, well, at this, the closing-down of the year, it didn't matter. Guests in their home, for however long – old friends and new, people coming to be warm with one another in the deepest, darkest time of the year, to light candles, share the Yule log, make merry – actually, it was lovely. And she was lucky. She picked up one of Pamela's cocktails – the gin bottle, she noticed, was emptying extremely quickly – and took a slug.

'Bloody hell,' she said, spluttering. 'I hope that's medicinal.'

Roy put his arm around her.

'Of course it is, my dear,' he said. 'Now come and grace us with your lovely presence.'

'How many of these has he had?' said Rosie, as everyone descended on the sausage rolls.

'Three,' said Pamela, smiling.

'Cor,' said Rosie. 'Mind you, I suppose he's used to it with all that mouthwash around.'

Roy grinned his terrifying Simon Cowell grin and raised his glass, and Pamela smiled back at him. Rosie made a mental note to get him to sign something before he actually passed out.

Apostil was in absolutely no mood for going to bed with all the noise and excitement about, so eventually they decided just to pretend to be European and let him stay up, even though Rosie knew that the person feeling the effects tomorrow would undoubtedly be her. She got everyone seated finally, although they seemed a little tight, and Pamela ended up practically on Roy's lap, which was making him very pink in the face.

'So, dentists earn good money, yeah?'

'I've got a swimming pool,' boasted Roy. 'With all those, like, Grecian statues. Except they're not Grecians. They're of me! I do triathlons, you know.'

Pamela squeezed his biceps.

'I see that,' she said.

'Oh my God,' said Rosie, forgetting she was cross with Stephen. 'This is disgusting.'

'Hush,' said Lilian. 'You're spoiling the fun.'

'Plus, what about his wife?'

'There's a theory about his wife,' said Lilian, but infuriatingly she refused to be drawn.

Rosie brought in the huge steaming enamel pot that had been in Lilian's family for goodness knew how long, plus a large bowl of local roast potatoes, good hearty fresh bread from the bakery, Isitt's butter from the farm down the road, and the greens from Jake's allotment. Everyone sighed happily and dug in, even Pamela taking a large pile of vegetables and a tiny bit of sauce, and for a few seconds there was an appreciative silence as they regarded their loaded plates. Then Lilian said the Selkirk Grace, pointing out that the new vicar didn't believe in grace.

'He's not that new,' said Stephen. 'He's been here for five years.'

'Oh, five years!' said Lilian. 'That's right, that is an awfully long time, particularly compared to, I don't know, eighty-four years.'

'You can't just trump everything by being old,' said Stephen.

'I certainly can,' said Lilian. 'There are precious few up sides to being my age, you know. You take them where you can. Thank you for the breast meat, Rosie.'

'That's all right,' said Rosie, who had made sure her great-aunt got something so tender she could eat it with a spoon.

Stephen poured everyone a glass of very expensive-looking dusty old wine. Pamela eyed it beadily.

'Where did you get that? Did you take it from Dad's cellar? That belongs to the estate.'

'Well you'd better drink as much of it as you can, then,' said Stephen crossly, filling her glass to the brim.

'I shall,' said Pamela, equally crossly, throwing some back and filling Roy's glass.

Roy was now attempting to focus on his plate, one of his eyes wandering slightly. Rosie nudged Tina.

'You know, I think we should probably ask this sooner rather than later.'

Moray glanced over and frowned.

'Oh Lord, amateur night.' He looked at his own glass. 'Well thank God Hye's on call. Tally ho! This is a fabulous Bordeaux, Stephen, just amazing.'

'I know,' said Stephen, emptying the bottle into Moray's glass and going into the kitchen to open another.

'You should be—' began Pamela.

Lilian leant over.

'Excuse me, dear, I am a trifle deaf, but would I be right in thinking that you've donated these lovely bottles tonight? Almost like rent, isn't it?'

Pamela looked at her, startled.

'Oh yes,' said Lilian. 'This is my house. For now. Of course you're making my great-niece homeless with her baby, but I shan't hold that against you.'

Pamela stuck out her jaw.

'I'm only claiming what's rightfully mine,' she said. 'I'm the eldest. I was born first.'

'Oh no, quite,' said Lilian, patting her gently on the arm and giving the impression of being the loveliest, sweetest old lady in the world. 'Of course. You do what's right.'

Tina put down her fork and cleared her throat.

'So, we're really glad you're all able to come to the wedding next Saturday,' she said. (She and Rosie had hurriedly made an invitation for Roy and dropped it in to his surgery. It had said 'Venue tbc'.) 'Of course, we're just putting the final touches—'

All of a sudden Roy stood up. He made quite a lot of noise doing so.

'Oh it's nice to be getting out and about again. After, you know. That business.'

'With the scout hut?' said Rosie. Roy looked confused.

'No.'

'With trying to knock down the sweetshop to build a car park?'

'No.'

'With trying to close the village school?'

'No,' said Roy, swaying slightly. 'I can't imagine why anyone would have had a problem with any of those things.'

He took another gulp of wine. Rosie was aware of Stephen wincing as the beautiful vintage, thick and dense and full of flavour, and so rich she herself could only sip at it, was swilled down Roy's shiny gullet.

'NO!' said Roy, suddenly loud. 'I mean things that have happened to ME. Like that old witch.'

'Who, me?' said Lilian.

'No, not you,' said Roy. 'No, the WITCH. Laura.'

'Laura? Your wife Laura?' said Rosie.

Roy brought his fist down hard on the table.

'My EX-wife Laura. My soon-to-be-EX-wife. She bloody left me! ME! With my swimming pool. I do triathlons, you know.'

'We do know,' said Tina.

'And I think that's amazing,' said Pamela.

'I'm sorry,' said Rosie. She was. He looked so miserable. 'I didn't know she'd left you.'

'Nobody knows,' said Roy. Then, as if realising he'd just told half the village, he looked round the table balefully. 'So don't tell them, right? I'm going to say I chucked her out. Like she deserved! Witch.'

'I cannot imagine why she left him,' whispered Stephen in Rosie's ear. She kicked him.

'I did her teeth for free! For free!'

Pamela patted him on the shoulder.

'Sssh,' she said comfortingly. 'Don't worry about it.'

'But she's going to take all my money!'

'We'll find you a good lawyer,' said Pamela. 'Trust me, I've dated hundreds of them, and they were all completely evil sharks. Perfect for you.'

Roy nodded.

'She says I've ruined her life.'

'Well, maybe you'll feel better if you make her a nice fair settlement,' suggested Rosie.

Roy looked at her.

'Don't be ridiculous. She's made me totally miserable by leaving me, so I will give her nothing.'

'I'm glad they've made it so easy to get divorced,' said Lilian. 'Makes everyone so much happier.'

Rosie gave her a look. Then something occurred to her.

'Do you know what would be great?' she said suddenly, pouring Roy some more wine. 'You should have a big party. Celebrate with all your friends. A divorce party.'

Roy looked bemused.

'What, like you guys?'

'Um, YES,' said Rosie.

'And me,' said Pamela, stroking his arm. Roy looked befuddled but extremely pleased.

'That'll show her, won't it?' said Rosie. 'Plenty of drink, plenty of food, dancing, everyone having a wonderful time, all in honour of you. Hmm, if only I knew where we could do it. Hmm.'

There was a short silence.

'Well,' said Tina, 'we'll be having a lot of food and drink for, you know, our wedding party.' She swallowed hard. 'I wouldn't mind sharing it at all. But, oh, we don't really have anywhere to have it.'

'Yes we do!' said Roy, banging down his glass. 'Yes we bloody do! I've got a hut we can use, you know! It's mine, I own it! Plenty of space! We'll show that stupid cow! We'll make a fine noise! Yeah, then they'll all know about it!'

He frowned.

'I don't know who to ask,' he said. 'I don't get to see many of my dentist friends these days.'

'I know at least ... a hundred people who'd love to come,' said Rosie boldly. 'And it will hardly cost you a penny.' She thought about it briefly. 'Well, unless you want people to have champagne, of course.'

Tina gasped. Rosie glanced at her. She was actually shaking.

'Of course I want champagne!' said Roy. 'We must have champagne! It will be the best "sod off, bitch" party of all time!'

He took out his phone.

'When are we having it?'

'On Saturday!' said Rosie. 'Better to have it soon! Really Christmassy, too.'

'RIGHT!' slurred Roy, and dialled a number in his address book.

'Yes. Hi. Right, I need to order ... six cases of your best champagne. No. Wait. Your cheapest champagne.'

There was a pause. Then he said, 'Yup. Yup, on the account. Deliver it to the sweetshop in Lipton. Good stuff. Bye.'

He hung up the phone, smiled beatifically around the table, then sat back in his chair and immediately fell asleep with his mouth wide open, snoring loudly.

Stephen took Roy home, whilst Moray took Lilian. Rosie, incredibly tired, tidied up as Tina and Jake stumbled over themselves with excitement and planning in the tiny kitchen, both quite tiddly.

'You know we'll probably have to let him make a speech,' said Rosie. 'People will think he's your dad.'

'I don't care,' said Tina. 'I don't care. Oh my God, champagne!!! Lots of it, not just a little glass!'

'I know! And free space!'

Pamela stumbled in elegantly from the sitting room.

'Great job helping us with Roy,' said Rosie. 'Seriously, we'd never have managed it without you.'

'Managed what?' said Pamela, whose eyes looked sleepy, but still magnificent.

'To get him to give us the venue for the wedding, of course! You pretending to flirt with him was a master-stroke. Well, that and whatever that terrifying drink was.'

Pamela still looked puzzled.

'I don't know what you're talking about,' she said. 'I like him. Can I stay, Rosie? My house is full of builders. Right, I'm going to bed. Oh, and by the way, there's lots of glasses still round the windowsill.'

Rosie managed not to growl, as Stephen came through the back door again.

'Okay, off you go, everyone,' he said cheerily. 'You've got what you wanted. And you have totally knackered out my—'

It must have been the lateness of the hour, the tone of the discussion, the alcohol consumed that made him do it. But he knew – and Rosie knew, and they swapped significant looks as he stopped himself – that he had been about to say 'my wife'.

Chapter Fifteen

Two nights later, the snow that had been threatening for weeks began in earnest; proper heavy-flaked settling snow. It was freezing up in the little attic, even when Rosie let Apostil in to cuddle up after his early-morning feed. He was nearly eight weeks now; she couldn't believe how fast he was growing.

Rosie looked at Stephen and he looked at her. Then they both looked at the gigantic green down-lined waxed jacket hanging on the back of the bedroom door. It had been a birthday gift from Stephen and Moray together. Rosie hadn't even pretended to be pleased.

'You have to,' he said.

'I don't,' she said. 'I swore I never would.'

'There are a lot of things you never thought would happen,' pointed out Stephen, with some justification.

'Yes, but . . .'

'Do you still think you're a swinging London Town girl hopping up and down Carnaby Street in a miniskirt?'

'I was never like that,' protested Rosie. 'But . . .'

They both looked at the jacket again. It was Thursday, two days before the wedding and a week before Christmas. The last few days had been a blur of activity. Everyone had texted Roy the morning after the dinner party, assuring him he had been completely splendid and what a brilliant guy he was. The champagne had arrived that same afternoon, and was crammed into the tiny storage room at the shop. It made Rosie's heart leap with joy every time she saw it, and Tina was beside herself. Although the payout from the wedding insurance didn't really help when it came to hiring new catering rather than taking what the hotel arranged as a package, Rosie had had the brilliant idea – and she was very proud of this – of asking Stan from the chippy to bring his van down, along with the pizza van that swung past occasionally. Even if everyone there ate a cod supper *and* a pizza, it would still be substantially cheaper than what they'd planned before. A few of the local teenagers would be serving drinks, and the cake could double as pudding.

'I didn't really care for the salmon anyway,' pointed

out Jake. 'We were only having it because she saw it in a magazine.'

'I did see it in a magazine,' said Tina. 'I thought that's what you had to have. I don't like it either.'

Rosie smiled.

'You're not too fussed?' she said. 'About it not being like those wedding mags you like?' She knew what a shopaholic Tina was, and how long she'd dreamed about having the perfect wedding.

'Not at all!' said Tina, beaming. 'Look!'

And she showed Rosie the latest edition of a glossy weddings magazine (which Rosie couldn't help being at least slightly interested in). Emblazoned across the cover was the strapline 'THE YEAR'S MOST FASHIONABLE CHOICE – SHABBY CHIC AND FISH AND CHIPS!!!'

'It's the newest thing!' beamed Tina. 'Apparently hotel weddings with salmon and place setting are really old hat! Now you need old-fashioned surroundings, lots of bunting . . . look!'

She flicked to a piece that explained how you could hire an authentic-style old-fashioned fish and chip van for 'only a few thousand pounds'. Rosie burst out laughing. 'I think Stan's a bit cheaper than that.'

'Exactly,' said Tina, her face pink with happiness. 'It's going to be the coolest wedding ever. Look, they've even got bales of straw in to sit on!'

'Well, Jake can get a few of those!'

'Exactly!' Tina said again.

Her joy was infectious. Rosie hugged her.

'Are you sure—' began Tina.

'No!' said Rosie. 'For the last time, Apostil is not being the ring-bearer. He'll eat it or spew on it. That's what he does!'

Tina sighed.

'But he was going to be my something borrowed!'

Rosie gave her a look. At least one thing was falling into place. She couldn't bear to think of what had happened yesterday.

'No. No no no NO. Dammit.'

Rosie had stared miserably at the floor.

'I don't know what other choice we have.'

'Here's the choice we have. I don't leave my job, which I love; you don't leave your job, which you love; we don't leave this village, which we love, and we work it out.'

Rosie blinked.

'I've thought and thought and thought, and I just don't know how. Go live with your mother?'

Stephen swore copiously.

'We need to be near the hospital,' said Rosie. She'd spoken to the consultant that Hye and Moray had both recommended and she seemed excellent. She had walked past the school one day and seen the children hanging off the monkey bars and screaming and running and throwing balls. Apostil would be able to do all of those things with a prosthesis. But they had to put the effort in, she knew. It wasn't a simple procedure, and it was a long and complicated rehab. But with all her nurse's soul she knew it was worth it, and she couldn't work out why Stephen was being so stubborn about admitting it.

'In some grotty, cramped little house?'

'It's a house,' said Rosie. 'You're just being a snob.'

'Fine,' Stephen had snarled. 'Call me a snob if that solves everything. Tear us away from our entire lives so you can chop his hand off. Go for it.'

'It's not like that!'

The doorbell had rung, and Rosie had opened it without thinking. Standing there fiddling with her red spectacles was Joy. It took everything Rosie had not to swear.

'Ah, the father, I presume,' twittered Joy. Rosie looked at her. She wasn't normally this friendly.

Stephen looked at her in a hostile fashion.

'Who are you?'

'I'm from social services. Just checking up on Baby!'

'Oh for Christ's sake,' said Stephen, turning away. 'Great. Just what we need. You'll be pleased, Rosie, she'll probably be on your side.'

'It's not about sides,' protested Rosie. 'We're all on the same side. Doing what's best for our son.'

'Yes, except what you think is best for our son is growing up in a dump and chopping off his fucking hand.'

'STEPHEN!'

Rosie had literally never been so cross with him. She could have thrown something at him. Apostil started to wail.

'Don't mind me,' said Joy, in a voice that was meant to be calming. 'But babies often pick up on tension in the household.'

'Well I shall leave the household then,' said Stephen, picking up his satchel. 'Let the coven get on with it.'

'AND HE'S NOT WEARING THAT DRESS!' shouted Rosie after him, still incoherent with rage. All she got in response was a slammed door.

There was a long pause. Rosie tried to soothe Apostil. Great tears plopped from her eyes on to his soft curly head. Joy made no effort to comfort her, simply made more notes on her iPad.

'Um, tea?' said Rosie eventually.

'No thank you,' said Joy, pressing a button emphatically.

'Are you ... I mean, what are you doing? Are you making a report?'

'We always make reports,' said Joy.

She glanced at her watch.

'Right, I must get on. Do you think you can keep things calm for Baby? I can send a team in if needs be.'

'NO!' said Rosie. 'No, we're fine! We're fine, just ... I mean, we're fine.'

'Is he coming back?'

'What do you mean? Of course he's coming back.'

_

Stephen leant heavily on his stick as he walked crossly down the main street. People hailed him as he went, but one look at his lowered brow and they quickly marched on. Old habits died hard round Lipton. He took a sharp right and headed up the hill.

Even though he couldn't bear to admit it, he knew deep down that Rosie was right; that trying to pretend that everything would be okay with Appy's arm was not going to get them anywhere. The idea of uprooting their lovely life, away from the fresh air and the outdoors and home, and moving to somewhere noisy and hemmed in and full of stress and pressure ... Stephen squeezed his eyes tight shut. Well, if they had to do that, at least he ought to get paid.

He came back an hour later. Joy, thank God, had gone, but Rosie was still cross with him. He knew this because she told him straight out.

'I'm still very cross with you.'

'Isn't that what you say when you want to kiss and make up and then have sex so that everything's all right again?' he attempted.

Rosie shook her head.

'No! And I can't believe you think that being

high-handed with someone who can take away our son and put him in a home is some kind of a joke.'

Stephen kissed Apostil fiercely.

'But she's a horrible old boot.'

'She could be Adolf fucking Hitler, you still have to impress her!'

Rosie never, ever swore. Stephen looked at her.

'I have an idea,' he said.

'Does it involve you sucking up to the social worker?'

Stephen shook his head.

'No. But it might help. I'll need to go away for a couple of days.'

She looked at him mistrustfully.

'Where?'

'London.'

'Seriously?'

He shrugged.

'Can't hurt.'

'Well, see that lovesick psychologist of yours while you're down there. Tell her what you said when Joy was here and see if she agrees with me or you. And if she says you, that's because she's lust-fuddled and you're STILL WRONG.'

'Are you still cross with me and Apostil?' said Stephen, nuzzling the baby under the chin.

'I'm not cross with him,' said Rosie.

'Oh well, I'm halfway there,' said Stephen.

Rosie bit her tongue. She wasn't happy about Stephen going to London, not a bit. But the fact that he was looking for a solution rather than sticking his fingers in his ears and pretending this wasn't happening was a big step forward.

Stephen took the first train to London. His old friend Piers came to meet him, as instructed, at St Pancras. They sat in a flashy champagne bar full of people shouting at waiters or into their phones or anything other than talking to each other.

Piers was as round and pink-faced as ever. Stephen had known him since school; he was an amiable bumbler, who had nonetheless managed to make an absolute fortune. His new lifestyle of extremely beautiful girls and eyewatering tabs at nightclubs where he didn't even know who he was paying for didn't look like much fun to Stephen, and it was starting to show on his girth and the broken veins across his nose.

'So, crawling back to forget your principles?' said Piers in a jolly fashion, ordering a bottle of the best champagne on the menu, even though Stephen was drinking coffee.

Stephen didn't smile.

'It's all got a little more complicated.'

'Thought as much,' said Piers. 'Women, huh, they're

all the same. Did she pretend to be all sweet and innocent till she had you and now it's oh buy me some shoes,
let's go to this restaurant, let's fly to the Maldives?
They're all the same, grasping minxes.'

Stephen tried to think of the last time Rosie had
asked him for something. He couldn't. She never bought
herself anything either. The only time she spent money
was on Lilian, whose thin skin only responded well to
cashmere, or M&S at a push, and who loved beautiful
clothes.

'Not quite,' said Stephen.

'Got her pregnant then? If they can't get you one way,
they'll always get you another.'

Stephen screwed up his face and decided not to go
into it.

'I'm just ... I was just wondering ... I mean, if I was
to start in banking ... I mean, would it be too late?'

'Let's see,' said Piers, draining and refilling his glass
in a satisfied manner. 'I could start you off, but you'd be
up against the eighteen-year-old barrow boys and the
weird maths quant geeks. It's fifteen-hour days on the
computer now. You'd start cold-calling, though.
Fourteen, fifteen hours of cold-calling a day, to offload
our absolute shit. Bonds and big bundles of crap we
couldn't possibly sell to anyone with a brain in their head
who can read our small print or understand what we're
selling, which they can't, because it's also our job to

make it as obscure and confusing as possible. If you get good at selling toxic shit on some thick-ass pension funds in the north – no offence – we'll put you on to better stuff. Defence firms, fags, all the slash-and-burn accounts nobody wants. Take it from there. '

There was a long pause. Stephen stared at his empty coffee cup. He wondered if Rosie had known that this was what would happen, and figured that she had. No wonder she'd been happy to let him come.

'It was good to see you, Piers.'

'Seriously, you're going back to bury yourself in the country?' said Piers, amazed.

'I'd do anything to help my family,' said Stephen. 'But I cannot think of a quicker way to blow us apart than working like you guys.'

'Great!' said Piers, unperturbed. 'Then we'll be single men on the town again. You are ace at pulling. Even your limp seems to help.'

'Thanks, Piers.'

'What are you going to do, take a night shift at a chicken factory?'

Stephen sighed.

'I don't know,' he said. 'And PLEASE don't invest my pension fund.'

'Wouldn't dream of it, my old mucker. I'm sticking all mine under the bed.'

Diane, Stephen's therapist, put her fingers to her lips, then crossly put them down on her notepad again. Outside it was freezing; London was heavily weighted down with Christmas lights, swaying gently in the breeze. There was a massive tree in the lobby of the smart Harley Street offices, where the beautiful receptionist who spoke four languages had tidily ticked Stephen's name off the list, and sent him straight up to the elegant room with its antique desk, expensive roped curtains and striped wallpaper. There was a couch, but Stephen preferred to sit in the heavy leather armchair, stretching his long legs out in front of him, stick by the side of the fire. Diane was trying not to look at his legs.

'Do you think you're subconsciously trying to sabotage this?' she asked calmly. 'So you don't have to move?'

Stephen looked horrified, and ran his fingers through his thick hair.

'Oh God, what kind of a monster am I? Do you think I'd mess with my wife and child just so I didn't have to move *house*?'

'That's one possibility,' said Diane. 'Or perhaps you're trying to delay making a decision of another kind . . . '

She left the statement open-ended. Stephen stared out into the frosty morning.

'I . . .' He swallowed hard, then took a quick intake of breath as he realised something. 'I don't want Apostil to be in hospital.'

Diane nodded, pleased.

'And why not?'

'Because . . . because *I* can't bear to be in hospital.'

She made a mark on a piece of paper.

'Because?'

'Because . . .'

Stephen knew it was important to go through it, to say it; that every time he relived the accident, the hideous stench and horrors of the field hospital, the lives blown apart, every time he could confront it head on, the monsters of his imagination grew a little smaller.

'Because I was there. I was blown up. I lost his uncles. I can't lose him. I CAN'T lose him.'

There was a long pause in the consulting room. Diane looked at him levelly. He looked back, a slight twitch around his mouth.

'Thank you, Doctor,' he said.

'Does Rosie think you'll lose him? What about Moray?'

Stephen shook his head.

'God, no, of course not. It's a relatively straightforward operation.'

'Hospitals will never be that straightforward to you,' said Diane, glancing at her watch. 'But I rather think you can deal with it, don't you?'

Stephen nodded.

'Yes,' he said quietly.

'You're ...' Diane never talked on a personal level to her clients, but she couldn't stop herself as he hauled himself out of the chair to go. Two tiny spots of pink appeared on her high cheekbones, but you would have had to be very close to her to see them. 'You're doing well,' she said, then cursed herself for it.

'Thank you,' said Stephen, an unexpected smile lighting up his face. He felt better already. 'Merry Christmas.'

Chapter Sixteen

Rosie, on the other hand, had lain awake half the night, alternately furious, and paranoid that Joy was going to activate something terrifying at social services and come and take Apostil away.

After kissing Apostil a lingering goodbye and handing him over to Mrs Laird to look after, she marched down the street, her boots crunching through the snow. She could tell from the cutting wind on her cheeks that it was freezing, but although she hated to admit it, inside her despised waxed jacket she was warm as toast. She sighed. Oh well. At least *she* knew, even if her shadow on the snow looked uncomfortably like a yeti.

'Hey there,' she said, falling into step with Edison and his family.

'Hello, Rosie!' said Edison, slipping a mittened hand in hers. She squeezed it.

'Hey, you,' she said. 'Where are you off to?'

'To school!' he said cheerfully. 'We're doing a Great Big Secret Thing! I can't tell you what it is.'

Rosie looked at him.

'That's not very secret.'

'Secrecy is tyrny,' said Edison.

Hester glanced over.

'Where's your baby?' she enquired.

'I sent him to the amusement arcade with a cupful of two pees,' said Rosie. 'Is that wrong?'

Hester frowned.

'I thought you were doing attachment parenting.'

The gigantic Marie, who was nearly one, was wriggling and squirming in her tight sling, grabbing handfuls of her mother's hair and kicking her in the stomach to indicate her fervent desire to escape.

'Um, no, just regular.'

Rosie tickled Marie, who instantly raised her pudgy little fists in a gesture that unambiguously meant 'GET ME OUT OF HERE.'

'She looks lively,' said Rosie, smiling and caressing Marie's round rosy cheeks.

'She's very calm and centred, actually,' said Hester. 'We use baby massage and baby sign.'

Marie bit Rosie's finger.

'Ooh, what's that the sign for?'

'"Don't invade my personal space",' said Hester. 'I don't know anyone who likes getting fingers pointed in their face, do you?'

'No,' said Rosie.

Edison squeezed her hand.

'I really do want to tell you my most big and exciting surprise.'

'Really?' said Rosie. 'Am I in it?'

'Yes!' said Edison. 'And the other woman who—'

Rosie hushed him and crouched down in the snow. Her new jacket really was amazing.

'It would be,' she said, 'a real gift to me and a real delight if you would consider not spoiling the surprise, Edison.'

He blinked behind his glasses.

'Only if we have secrets, is bad.'

'For some things,' said Rosie. 'Do you think you could possibly make an exception just for me?'

Edison was nothing if not kind.

'Of course for you,' he said.

Hester gave a big sigh.

'I'm trying to teach him about WikiLeaks,' she said. 'So thanks for setting that back.'

'I didn't know that,' said Rosie as they reached the school gates. 'Have a good day, you guys!'

Edison waved and walked in to join his great friend

and acolyte Kent, and Rosie said hello to the mums milling around and felt a little cheered. Most of them asked her about the wedding – it seemed Tina and Jake had invited pretty much the entire village, and Rosie felt nearly as nervous and excited as her friend.

At the scout hut, there was a large truck backed up in front of the door, big black track marks through the pristine white snow. All around, the branches of the trees were piled high; every so often, with a splash, some would fall off. Rosie looked up with trepidation.

'Is that going to fall on the bride?'

'You want me to personally polish all the snow off the branches?' said Jake, emerging from behind the truck and smiling.

'No,' said Rosie, giving him a hug. 'What's the lorry for? Stephen's bringing the champagne down later.'

'Tina's cousin worked at the hotel. She managed to save all their Christmas decorations from the basement and got them sent over, along with some extra chairs. They've been really helpful, considering their boss is going to prison for arson and they've all lost their jobs.'

'Wow,' said Rosie. 'That really is amazing.'

Sure enough, from out of the lorry two men were bringing rows and rows of fairy lights, great big tough, industrial ropes of them. There was power in the hut, but they'd also rented a spare generator to provide for the heating and extra lighting, and everyone went to it with a will.

Inside, even though it was early, Mrs Arknop from the bakery had sent down jam doughnuts, and there was a large tea urn dispensing steaming drinks for everyone, but it wasn't that which caught Rosie's attention. The large hut, with its plain plank walls and rough wooden floor, had been transformed. What felt like miles of thick holly had been hung in great luxuriant arches around the walls, and the fairy lights were already going up and being tested, creating great walls of shimmering white. Each corner contained a Christmas tree; they were being lavishly decorated – no wonder the hotel had been losing money, thought Rosie – with little rocking horses, silver bells, red ribbons and hanging gingerbread men for the children. Rosie would add her own supply of chocolate Santas.

Little clusters of seats and tables were being laid out, and a PA system was being set up on the raised area for speeches and the band. And there were, indeed, straw bales being dragged into a corner, Rosie was delighted to see, covered with tartan blankets. They were going to make an unbelievable mess, but they could worry about that after the festivities.

Tina wasn't there – Rosie had sent her packing to Carningford to get her hair and nails done in anticipation – but her mother, Jan, was overseeing, very cheerfully. She rushed up to Rosie.

'Thanks for all this,' she said excitedly.

'Oh, I didn't do anything,' said Rosie. 'It was just lucky something came together.'

'It's marvellous,' she said. 'I like it better than the hotel.'

'You know,' said Rosie, 'so do I.'

Jan, who had the same petite, pretty features as her daughter, leant over.

'Now, about this ring-bearing business ...'

'It's not going to happen,' said Rosie. 'I'm sorry. He's just so young, he'll swallow them or cry and just ruin everything. I am sorry.'

Jan nodded, then brought out a parcel.

'Well, even if he's not doing it, we bought him a present.' She handed it over, beaming. 'You've done such a lot. We'd love him to wear this tomorrow.'

'Oh no, I haven't ...' said Rosie, opening up the parcel with a slightly sinking feeling; she had rather been hoping that his nicest babygro – the unbelievably expensive Tartine et Chocolat one Pamela had bought him – would do. Inside was a babygro in black and white, made up to look like a dinner suit, complete with black trousers, black jacket, patterned waistcoat, carnation in the buttonhole and bow tie.

Jan grinned.

'Isn't it just totally and utterly perfect?'

Rosie couldn't say she didn't like it; that it was even

worse than the christening gown he still wasn't going to wear. Instead she smiled and hugged Tina's mum.

'It's perfect,' she said. 'If I manage to get him out the door without throwing up all over it, he'll definitely be wearing it.'

Rosie spent the day happily making paper chains, decorating trees, and bringing things in from the lorry. Small snifters of whisky were passed around after lunch to help with the cold, even though the heaters were gradually warming the place through. Rosie had had ample reason to be glad of her new coat, albeit grudgingly. Moray managed to turn up magically at the exact moment whisky was being handed out, and grinned to see her wearing it.

'At last!' he said, leading her out into the winter sunshine, as they clinked glasses. 'Finally we've done it! We've turned the town mouse into the country mouse!'

Rosie smiled sadly.

'For now,' she said, and told him about the Derby house she was going to see again, despite Stephen's objections. He could shout and swear all he wanted, but it was going to happen.

'Seriously?' said Moray.

'Seriously,' said Rosie. 'If . . . if, you know, we have to go through this with Apostil . . . then it makes sense to be near the hospital, even if we could find a place round here we could afford, which we can't.'

'I know,' said Moray. 'It's almost like people enjoy living in beautiful, unspoiled country villages.'

'That don't even have Starbucks or proper broadband,' said Rosie, looking at the sun prickling the frosted surface of the snow. Just a little way into the forest behind the hut, a robin hopped on to a twig, grabbed it in his little talons and flew away again. There was barely a sound in the air except the cheerful noises from inside the hut – Christmas carols were playing on the stereo – and the rustling of the wind through the snow-heavy trees.

'I'll miss this place,' said Rosie suddenly. 'All of it.'

'You're definitely going?'

'We have to,' said Rosie. 'Stephen doesn't see it yet, but he will. He's just struggling against having to come round to what he knows is right.'

'We'll miss you,' said Moray. 'I can't believe you've only been here three years. Feels like you're really a part of the place. Most incomers it takes about ... um, a hundred and fifty.'

Rosie swallowed.

'Well, we'll be back to visit. We'll have to, we don't know anybody else. '

'Oh, life moves on,' said Moray. 'And the snow will close the road, and you'll be so busy with Apostil growing up, you'll forget all about us.'

Rosie shook her head.

'No, I don't think we will. Anyway, we'll always be back for Lilian.'

'That's true,' said Moray.

'So I don't suppose you're bringing anyone to the wedding?' said Rosie, returning to a lighter, more teasing voice.

'Actually . . . ' said Moray, grinning.

'No way? You're bringing Moshe?'

Moray's boyfriend only lived in Carningford, but Moray very rarely went out with him in public.

'Well I had a think about it,' said Moray. 'And I thought, what better way to really, really annoy Roy?'

Just as he said this, Roy's horrible oversized Porsche appeared, its bodywork flashing against the snow. Moray and Rosie went quiet, watching as Roy parked up to look at the hut.

'He's not getting out!' said Moray. Given their vantage point, sitting on a tree stump round the side of the building, Roy was unlikely to see them. 'He's checking everyone is working really hard, but he isn't getting out.'

'That's because he's a nobber,' said Rosie. 'Hardly a news flash.'

"No, no, LOOK!' hissed Moray, collapsing into giggles. Sure enough, through the side window they could just glimpse somebody else; somebody with long, expensively highlighted blonde hair. Pamela.

'No way,' said Rosie, clasping her hand over her mouth. The next moment, the two heads had moved together; they were patently snogging. 'Oh. My. GOD.'

Moray was puce in the face trying not to explode with laughter.

'But their teeth might clash and start a fire,' he choked.

'Watch out in case they reflect the sun and kill you like a laser,' Rosie said back.

There was nothing to be done that wouldn't give away their location. Rosie buried her head in Moray's jacket to hide her eyes, but otherwise they just had to sit there and not move whilst sloppy kissing sounds reached them from the lowered car window.

'Arrrgh,' said Rosie. 'I'll never be clean again.'

Finally, thankfully, someone came out of the hut to collect something, whereupon the Porsche immediately burst into action with a puff of exhaust, and, with a waved hand from Roy, sped off. Rosie and Moray burst out into loud laughter.

'This is already a Really Good Wedding,' said Rosie.

'It is,' said Moray. 'Whilst you were hiding your face I took some pics on my phone.'

Moray left for his afternoon calls and Rosie went back inside to help with the finishing touches. Strung out on the floor was a banner they had been making for the front of the hut. Rosie couldn't help smiling. Huge cut-out letters, painstakingly stitched on by the church ladies, spelled out 'CONGRATULATIONS TINA AND JAKE', to which had been hastily added 'AND ROY'.

Halfway through the afternoon, another large car drew up, honking loudly. Rosie went out to see what the commotion was. Lady Lipton was sitting in her battered old Land Rover. Rosie went over nervously.

'Hello.'

'Have you seen Pamela?' asked Lady Lipton, looking distracted. 'I can't find her anywhere.'

Rosie plumped for discretion being the greater part of valour, and shook her head sadly.

'Um, I don't think so.'

Lady Lipton examined the hut more closely, peering in through the open door.

'What on earth is going on here?' She indicated the walls, which were now so festooned with banners and lights it was hard to see the wooden panelling. 'It looks like a tart's boudoir. Are you opening a brothel?'

She looked at Rosie with a look that suggested she would have absolutely no problem believing this.

'Of course I'm not opening a brothel,' said Rosie crossly. 'It's for Tina's wedding.'

'Who?'

Rosie rolled her eyes.

'My colleague and friend Tina. She's getting married tomorrow.'

'Is she? I don't recall being invited.'

'She asked if she could hold the wedding in your house, and you said no.'

'Did I?' said Henrietta distractedly. She looked at the hut for a little longer, and Rosie thought she seemed slightly wistful.

'Well,' she said eventually. Are we all sorted for the christening?'

'Yes,' said Rosie. She had been thinking about this since the first time Henrietta had met Apostil, remembering how she had behaved. She didn't want the gown, the fuss, the Lipton family burden. She would bless Apostil for his town and his community, but not for Henrietta. 'But it's going to be a blessing because he was baptised in Africa. We're doing it at the wedding. Quickly and quietly.'

'Indeed,' said Henrietta. 'And afterwards?'

'We'll go to the wedding party,' said Rosie. 'At the scout hut.'

Lady Lipton looked at her aghast.

'But Lipton babies always have a drinks party at Lipton Hall. It's tradition. It's always been that way.'

Rosie found herself uncharacteristically outspoken for once. She had had enough of biting her tongue with half the town; enough of the sideways looks, enough of the remarks.

'Well you can do it with Pamela's children then,' she shot back. 'The ones you really want.'

And she turned round and stormed back into the hut, her hands shaking.

🍬

'Sorry,' he said, before she'd even walked in. 'I'm sorry. I talked it out with Diane, and—'

Rosie turned to him.

'Do you know,' she said, as calmly as she was able, 'do you know they can reverse what we signed in Africa? Take the baby away?'

'They're a bunch of interfering busybodies.'

'With the full support of the law behind them.'

Stephen nodded. 'I know, I understand.'

'Did you see your mates in London?' asked Rosie.

'Don't ask,' grimaced Stephen. 'Was just a thought. Anyway, Mother called about the blessing . . .'

'No. Don't start with me,' said Rosie. 'I know she's your mum, but this is the limit. They've basically made us homeless and now they want us to play happy families? No. I'll do the christening for Lilian, but we'll do it tomorrow. Without that fricking dress thing.'

'It was my sister who made us homeless,' said Stephen, his face pained.

'Yeah, backed up by Witchiepoo.'

Stephen still looked sad.

'I know,' said Rosie. 'I'm sorry. But I have tried and tried with that woman.'

'I know you have,' said Stephen. 'But Rosie, you've got a whole family that is just going to dote on Apostil – I can't get your bloody mother off Skype. He's going to have everyone from your side, all his life. And nobody from mine.'

'Well tell them to come and visit us in the little Derby terrace,' said Rosie. 'See how often that happens.'

'Can you stop?' said Stephen, suddenly riled. 'You've won, okay? We're moving. We're going to the hospital. We're living in a city. I'm changing my job.'

'How have I won, Stephen?' shouted Rosie, at the end of her tether. 'HOW HAVE I WON? Do you think I want my mother-in-law to hate my guts because I've only got one surname? Do you think I want to leave Lipton and end up in some sooty tenement, going back to stitching up drunks on a Saturday night? Do you think I want to spend the next two years sitting by our son's hospital bed, praying that he'll be all right? Or watching you come home to a shitty little house, exhausted from marking thirty-six kids' exercise books every night? HOW have I won?'

She sat down in exhaustion.

'You don't have to do this, you know. You didn't know

what you were getting yourself into last year. Some barren old cow with nowhere to live. It's not too late, you know. You're still your mother's golden boy. You can crawl back. Live in the freaking east wing or something.'

The colour drained from Stephen's face.

'You'd keep me from my son?'

Rosie shook her head, shocked at her own outburst.

'No. No. Of course not.' She looked up at him. 'But Stephen, it won't just be you sacrificing everything for Apostil. It'll be me too.'

Chapter Seventeen

After a sleepless night for both of them, Rosie opened the shop by herself on Saturday morning. She had completely forgotten – although Tina, typically, had not and had ordered up the stock well in advance – that there would be something of a run on sugared almonds to exchange as gifts, as well as the little wrapped jelly sweets that would be thrown out of the car. Although in her excitement at changing her by-the-book hotel wedding into a more down-home one, Tina had also cancelled the Rolls-Royce, so Rosie supposed she was just walking to the church now.

It was a perfect winter's day. The sun was shining but the snow still lay – deep and crisp and even, Rosie liked to think – across the fields, each melting drop shining like a diamond. The roads, though, had been cleared, so people coming from further afield wouldn't have to worry about getting snowed in. With a heavy heart she had left the black-tie babygro out where Stephen could see it, hoping he'd know to get Appy dressed in it. He was an usher, so he'd have to be down at the church early.

The shop was busy, which was a useful distraction, with mothers buying sweets for the little ones to keep them quiet in church, and boxes of chocolates being bought for the happy couple, as people decided that the vouchers that had been on their wedding list looked a little bit sad on their own. Rosie happily offered to wrap them in Christmas paper, thinking how pretty they would look under the surfeit of overdecorated Christmas trees. The vicar came in for his mints, of course, wearing his best dog collar and smiling cheerfully.

'Is it true there's going to be free fish and chips?' he asked.

'There is.'

He beamed.

'God does love a wedding.'

Anton, formerly the village's fattest man, came in. He was wearing a suit that was at least nine sizes too big for him.

'Okay,' he said. 'Look at this! Don't I look like an advert?' He started to unbuckle his belt.

299

'What are you doing?' Rosie said, alarmed.

'LOOK!'

He pulled the waistband of his suit trousers slowly outwards. There was enough free space there to fit another person inside.

'Look at you!' said Rosie, pleased.

'I thought you would like it! This is the first time I've worn my suit in three years. It was for the funeral of an old pizza buddy,' he added sadly.

'Oh, I'm sorry about that.'

'Well, he'd had his time.'

'Really? How old was he?'

'Fifty-two,' said Anton sorrowfully.

'Well look at you!' said Rosie cheerfully. 'You've done so brilliantly!'

'I know,' said Anton, buckling his belt again. 'So. Can I have a pound of fudge?'

'No,' said Rosie.

'Please?'

'No. You can have one small packet of Parma violets,' Rosie said sternly.

A last-minute rush meant there were just minutes to spare when she finally shut up shop and slipped next door. Stephen and Apostil had already left, but Moray and Lilian were there. Lilian was making up her face in the mirror. She was wearing a beautiful lavender dress, and a matching coat with a huge fur collar.

'Is that real fur?' asked Rosie.

Lilian looked at Moray.

'No-ooo,' she said. 'It's completely imaginary. You're actually looking at a raincoat. Are you coming like that?'

'Like this? In a black skirt and white shirt?'

'You can never tell with your sartorial choices.'

'Seriously? No, of course I'm not.'

She disappeared crossly and got into the pretty black and white flowered dress she'd bought specially. Annoyingly, she couldn't zip it up the side and had to get Moray in to do it.

'Breathe in, Podge,' he said.

'Shut up!' said Rosie. 'For goodness' sake, has no one got a good word to say about me round here?'

Moray patted her on the shoulder.

'You look beautiful. Like a goddess.'

'Yeah, all right, all right.'

She turned to face the mirror and started applying make-up.

'You do look nice,' said Moray, musing. 'Pretty. Softer. Motherhood suits you.'

'I don't want to be soft!' said Rosie. 'I need to be tough!'

Moray smiled and leaned forward, his face concerned.

'Rosie, I got an email from the surgical team at Derby General. They need to start scheduling consultations. Darling, I hate to do this today of all days, but ... it's decision time. It really is. The longer you leave it, the harder it's going to be for Appy to adjust as he starts to hit his milestones.'

Rosie swallowed hugely.

'I know,' she said. 'It's just ... with so much going on ...'

'I understand,' said Moray. 'But there's never a good time for any of this shit, I promise.'

'I realise that.'

She closed her eyes.

'I'm so sorry you have to move,' said Moray.

'Oh well, fair's fair. It's Pamela's house and so on.'

'Hmm,' said Moray. 'Spoiled brat.'

'They're both spoiled brats, those children,' smiled Rosie. 'It's just I really fancy one of them.'

Moray stroked her hair.

'Honestly,' said Rosie. 'Tell me honestly. If Apostil were your son, what would you do?'

'I would want him to have every possible advantage in life,' said Moray, gently. 'Like I would for any child.'

Rosie nodded.

'And Stephen's not happy about it?'

It was kind of Moray to let her cry all down the front of his morning suit.

Lilian helped her clean herself up, wisely without asking too many questions, and put on her mascara for her.

'Everyone cries at weddings,' she said. 'Can't bear the damn things myself. Can't believe you're getting me to this one.'

'You and Henry should have got married,' sniffed Rosie.

'Oh, we were, my love,' said Lilian. 'In our hearts, I think. Now, how long do you think that fat vicar is going to go on for today? Let's get the fish and chip van to drive past after twenty minutes. He'll follow the smell right out the door.'

'You *are* awful,' said Rosie, but it did the trick. She felt a little better, and not as if she'd be sobbing over everyone all through the service. She twisted her own engagement ring anxiously.

'Stop that,' said Moray. 'You'll look weird.'

'Okay, okay!'

They were driving the short distance to the church, the icy cobbles being deemed absolutely far too hazardous for Lilian's delicate bones

'That's true, you know,' Lilian had said. 'One fall and it's all over. Everyone knows. Nelly Quivox tripped down the stairs. Only broke her ankle but was dead in a week. I think she did it on purpose.'

'You are a GHOUL,' said Rosie. 'Stop it.'

'I can't stop it,' said Lilian. 'I'm at the opposite bit to you. Everyone you know is having babies, not dying. So you sit around and bore everyone to tears about people who have just arrived, whereas I tell stories about people who have just left. It's precisely the same thing, except my stories are interesting and not all blah blah blah milk oh look he did a burp call the Marconi office.'

'That's . . . Well. That's a bit true,' said Rosie, taking her great-aunt's bird-like arm in hers as they stepped out of the cottage and towards the car. Most of Lipton was heading down the main street in their Sunday best. Even those who were not invited were going to see Tina and Jake off; a wedding in the village was, after all, a wedding, and there was a merry Christmas feel to the air as people hailed their neighbours, the women in fancy hats, the farmer's wives who spent all year in practical, warm clothes pink and nervous-looking, clopping across the cobbles in unaccustomed heels.

The church had white ribbons and holly draped over the lychgate, and great bunches of white flowers at the end of every pew with mistletoe and big white bows everywhere. Stephen – Apostil having been borne off by some of the other mothers – was standing at the door handing out orders of service, his stick leaning against the old arched doorway. For a second, he took Rosie's breath away.

He was so handsome in his old morning suit, his top hat by his stick, the smart waistcoat with its white buttonhole. He looked exactly, in fact, like the man she'd dreamed of marrying, of being with, for so long. Her heart softened and she wanted to run to him. As if sensing her, he glanced up; she smiled at him, nervously, apologetically, and he raised his hand a little bit, and again she wanted to run and beg forgiveness, and make everything all right again.

But how *could* it be all right when she was tearing him away from his job and his life and his family and everything he loved?

If she had been different, would his mother have liked her more? Accepted her? Invited her to stay with them, be a part of his family? If she'd been like his other girlfriends: posh, blonde *Made in Chelsea* types with plenty of money, who could have bought somewhere nice on their own, none of the boring problems that belonged to little people, who ran sweetshops and had no inheritance. And of course if she had a working set of Fallopian tubes, that would probably have helped things too . . .

She swallowed heavily and checked on Apostil, who was being doted on by some of Jake's rugby chums. Apostil was giggling and laughing his head off. She went a little closer, conscious now – all the time – of the possibility that the damn social worker might pop up at any moment and that she should probably not be letting him out of her sight.

Apostil's face lit up when he saw her. There was no other way to describe it. His smile, already wide from the fuss being made of him, suddenly became even wider, his eyes sparkled with excitement, his little hand stretched out towards her. He was the sun coming out; she and Stephen were everything to him, and that was all that mattered.

'Here's Mam,' said one of the boys cheerfully, handing him over. 'Hey there, our Rosie. Can your lad come and play prop forward? He's going to be a big 'un.'

'Maybe not this Saturday,' said Rosie, smiling, and thinking how, after his op, he'd be able to do all that stuff – all the throwing, and sport, and joining in things. She thought Apostil was the most amazing thing in the world; the operation would give him all the tools to show everybody else that too.

Eventually they were all sitting down. Rosie saw Jake, anxious and sweaty, with a terrible new haircut, and the vicar, in special celebration robes, beaming pinkly and casting ominous glances towards his acoustic guitar. Tina had been pretty adamant about that, though, and someone was playing the organ.

Just as everyone was getting fidgety, the good old

wedding march started up, and everyone rose, Rosie realising two things at the same time: firstly, that Lady Lipton and Pamela were there, both looking furious (and extremely similar) at the fact that, of course, their normal pew, the front one, was taken by the families of the bride and groom; and secondly, that she had completely forgotten to check whether Apostil was wearing his special wedding babygro, and she could tell under his jumper that he wasn't.

First the twins, Kent and Emily, came forward, holding hands, Emily in a beautiful white dress with a big red bow and a soft white cardigan; Kent in white shorts and shirt and a red tie. The entire church sighed with happiness at what a lovely picture they made as they walked slowly and incredibly seriously to the front, the nervous looks on their faces being replaced with relief as they got to within two steps of Jake, their stepdad-to-be, at which point they broke ranks and ran into his arms. He hugged them tightly, tears already streaming down his cheeks.

'This is emotional,' said Lilian sarcastically, and Rosie nudged her, whilst sniffing.

Then Jake's brother and best man came on the arm of Tina's sister, then the three ushers, including Stephen, with three other bridesmaids, school friends of Tina's. And trotting next to Stephen, to Rosie's utter surprise – and the delight of the many children in the church, chivvied in rows for the school choir – was Mr

Dog, wearing Apostil's bow tie babygro with the feet chopped off, and carrying a knotted box, obviously containing the rings, in his mouth.

Then the laughter and the delighted noises stopped, as Tina appeared on her father's arm at the far end of the nave.

Her dress was plain and long, with a red bow just like Emily's tight around her tiny waist, matching her lipstick exactly. Her hair was soft and tousled, and she wore a thin gold circlet around her head, with a little medieval-style tuft of a veil coming off the back of it. Long strands of ivy were threaded in and out of her plaits (which were thicker, Rosie thought suspiciously, than Tina's normal hair). She had a little fake fur shrug round her shoulders, and the sleeves of the satin dress hung long, nearly to the floor. The effect was beautiful, like a carved tomb come to life. She held a bouquet of holly and mistletoe interlaced with ivy. From up and down the church there were gasps. Jake was now extremely red in the face, his mouth hanging open. Rosie beamed. It was, she knew, exactly the effect Tina had dreamed of for a long time, had worked on so hard. For her, it was all worthwhile.

The choir of children began to sing, though it wasn't 'Jesu, Joy of Man's Desiring' or one of the more usual wedding songs. Stephen had quietly gone and taken up his place in front of them as default choirmaster. Very softly they started up the old Advent hymn, their pure voices echoing in the high vaults of the church ceiling.

O come, O come, Emmanuel
And ransom captive Israel
That mourns in lonely exile here
Until the Son of God appear
Rejoice! Rejoice! Emmanuel
Shall come to thee, O Israel.

When Tina had told Rosie that that was what they were going to sing, she had been rather taken aback.

'Isn't it about the baby Jesus?'

'It's church, Rosie. You're a heathen. They're all about Jesus.'

'Yes, I know, but it doesn't sound very weddingy.'

But Tina had been right and Rosie wrong. The gentle beseeching tone of the hymn, with its celebratory final cadences, was cathartic and beautiful, the children's voices joined by the congregation for 'Rejoice! Rejoice!'

The vicar welcomed everyone and made a lame joke about broadband internet, which most of the congregation didn't get, then invited Emily up to the front.

She stood, as white as her dress, almost hidden behind the mike stand until Stephen moved over and lowered it for her, clasping her briefly on the shoulder and smiling at her as he did so. She smiled tentatively back, her look of terror replaced by something more relaxed, and the audience relaxed too as Stephen signalled to the organist.

Quietly at first, then with growing confidence, Emily sang as sweetly as a bird:

O Little Town of Bethlehem
How still we see thee lie
Above thy deep and dreamless sleep
The silent stars go by
Yet in thy dark streets shineth
The everlasting light
The hopes and fears of all the years
Are met in thee tonight

'Oh MAN,' said Rosie quietly, digging in her handbag for a tissue. 'This is totally unfair. Who can compete with that?'

The high, clear voice rang through the church, a celebration of all that was fresh and new, and there was barely an eye left dry.

As the marriage service got under way, and the old words were spoken, Rosie thought about the bundle in her bag. She would have time; nobody was looking at them, and she was right next to the loo, entirely deliberately.

'*To have, and to hold . . .*'.

She glanced up and saw with a start that Stephen was staring straight at her, with such a naked look of pain and doubt, she couldn't tear her eyes away.

'*For better, for worse . . .*'

She blinked away the tears. It was she who had brought all these doubts; questioned Stephen's ability to change, to do what needed to be done; blamed him for the tough times of the past, failed to trust him in the hard times coming.

'*For richer, for poorer . . .*'

The rest of the church faded away. The music, the bride, the flowers, the fancy hats (the village boutique had been completely emptied in the preceding weeks), the fuss, the squabbles all disappeared and suddenly there was nobody there but the three of them, in the ancient space where those same words had been said for hundreds of years.

'*In sickness and in health . . .*'

Rosie held their son tight to her chest, so tightly he looked at her enquiringly, plucking at the little silk buttons on her collar, but she did not glance down.

'*Till death us do part . . .*'

Stephen strode across the church, leaving the children behind, barely noticed by most of the congregation, who were transfixed by Tina and Jake, equally in a world of their own. Not taking his eyes off Rosie for a second, he grabbed her, and Apostil, and her bag, and without a word pulled her into the back of the church, surrounded by flowers and a disgruntled-looking video technician, and grabbed her to him and kissed her again and again, the tears running down her face.

'*I now pronounce you man and wife.*'

They held each other close, and Stephen promised his family with all his heart that he would never leave them, that he didn't care where they were or how they lived, as long as Apostil had every chance to get better, and Rosie could only say, 'I know, I know, I know.'

The choir started up (rather raggedly without Stephen to guide them, but the organist tipped them the wink) with a lusty and thrilling version of 'Torches', involving much full-hearted singing and some bellowing, as Stephen and Rosie drew apart. They hadn't much time: the blessing was to take place after the signing of the register.

'Quick,' said Stephen. 'Go on. Let's get him changed.'

'No way,' said Rosie, not betraying it was in her bag.

'Way. Come on. This one thing.'

She looked at his face, smiling at her.

'Argh,' she said, grinning. 'He will NEVER FORGIVE US.'

'He will never forgive us for a lot of things,' said Stephen. 'I reckon this will come pretty far down the list by the time we're finished with him.'

With a few squawks from the normally obliging Apostil, they wrestled him into the ridiculous lacy white christening gown, which he promptly dribbled down. Rosie cleaned him up as best she could with a wipe, which he did not enjoy, and there was a clearing of throats from the altar.

'And now,' said the vicar, 'we are pleased to be welcoming a baby into the family of our church.'

'I don't want to give the vicar my baby,' squeaked Rosie, her face turning pink.

'Ssssh,' said Stephen, squeezing her tight. 'You can cross your fingers.'

'If I can ask Stephen Lakeman and Rosie ...' the vicar coughed, making it entirely clear he was making a point about their different surnames, and glanced at the front pew, 'Hopkins to step forward.'

'Oh crap,' said Rosie. 'He thinks we're down there.'

'You know what that means,' said Stephen, as the congregation started to twist around looking for them. 'We are actually going to have to walk down the aisle.'

Rosie went bright pink.

'Oh bloody hell.'

Helpfully, the organist sprang into action, playing 'Paiste Am Betlehem', the ancient Manx carol, that sounded so unearthly it made Rosie shiver.

'Seriously?' she said.

'Seriously,' said Stephen, proffering his arm. And desperately trying not to laugh, particularly under the disapproving eye of Stephen's mother and Lilian, both of whom clearly thought they were showing off, they proceeded down the aisle, in Stephen's case for the second time that morning.

'Well that was unorthodox,' said the vicar as they arrived at the front, blushing.

'You should know,' murmured Stephen under his breath.

'Can I also have the godparents?' said the vicar into the microphone.

Rosie looked round nervously. Moray had disappeared when they'd arrived at the church; she'd expected him to sit with them, but he wasn't there. Finally she saw him, right at the back, easing out of the end of the pew, followed by a slim, handsome, dark-eyed man.

A gasp of shock went through the congregation as the two men walked up the aisle hand in hand. The vicar was beside himself. Rosie handed Apostil to Stephen and went and met them at the top of the aisle, throwing her arms around them both.

'Moshe!' she said. 'I can't believe you came! Oh my God, Moray, you've really done it this time.'

'I do hope so,' said Moray into her ear. 'Bloody hell.'

Rosie laughed. She'd never seen him without his sangfroid.

Stephen came forward to shake both their hands.

'The vicar is calling up his agent as we speak to try and get on television. Welcome.'

314

'We come as a job lot,' said Moray. 'Is that okay?'

'Totally!' said Rosie. 'Do you have a clue what you're doing?'

'Nope,' said Moshe. 'But I haven't been burned up in a fiery pit yet.'

'There's time,' said Rosie. 'Just nod a lot.'

She turned on Moray's smartphone, which was somehow patching in to Angie in Australia. All the children whooped to see their auntie Rosie, and were rapidly silenced by Angie and Pip.

Tina and Jake, the other godparents, emerged shyly from signing the register, and there were hugs and kisses all round. Rosie, glancing up, caught sight of Henrietta, standing proud and cold at the end of her pew, staring straight ahead as if at a funeral, and felt, in the midst of all her joy, a clutch of pity. Then she thought again of all her empty rooms, and how she still could not open her arms to her own son, and looked away.

'If we could just get started,' said the vicar, who was still peeved at not being allowed to perform his original baptism song on his guitar.

He gabbled through the introductory words. Apostil was thoroughly entranced by the lights and the candles and the being handed about, and seemed to be enjoying himself hugely. Then, just as the vicar put his arms out to take him, there was a sudden eruption of giggles and fidgeting from the children's choir, and

Stephen glanced over at them, smiled, and held up his hand.

'Um,' he said. 'We have just one thing.'

'What?' said Rosie, feeling that this service had turned into enough of a carnival already.

'Well,' said Stephen, clearing his throat. 'What with the sponsored bean sitting, and the sponsored swim and the sponsored silence, and everyone in the village who kept a tin on their shop counter ... we managed to do this ...'

He grinned, and turned towards the little choir at the side, who turned on several laptop computers Rosie hadn't noticed before. After some inevitable fidgeting, they all got fixed and lined up, and Rosie gasped. To her amazement, there it was, right in front of them – the school, the little school in Kduli. But it had a fresh coat of paint, and a large solar-powered fan, and in the corner, a massive selection of books; and every child had a new slate.

A huge group of laughing children were hogging the camera, waving, showing off their new toy, making faces in front of it. A loud 'CHUT,' could be heard off camera, from Faustine, and all the children settled down, except one little girl with tight braids, who came forward very slowly and said, with a heavy French accent, 'We would like to send our love to our brother Apostil and all our brothers and sisters in Lipton.'

Then Stephen raised his arm, and suddenly, from

Africa, and from the chilly, snow-covered church, all the children's voices rose as one.

Sama raka modou, sama raka modou
Yéwougham, Yéwougham
Gnoundé yayou diné gnoundé yayou diné
Ding dang dong, ding dang dong

Frère Jacques, Frère Jacques,
Dormez vous? Dormez Vous?
Sonnez le matin, sonnez le matin
Ding dang dong, ding dang dong.

Then the music changed to something slower, and the voices raised.

Douce nuit, sainte nuit!
Dans les cieux ! L'astre luit.
Le mystère annoncé s'accomplit.
Cet enfant sur la paille endormit,
C'est l'amour infini,
C'est l'amour infini!

Silent night, holy night
All is calm all is bright
Round yon virgin mother and child
Holy infant so tender and mild

317

Sleep in heavenly peace
Sleep in heavenly peace.

The sound was glorious, filling the entire nave. The children sang the lilting African lullaby first in Swahili, then in French, then the last time round in a charming, halting English, Stephen conducting madly the entire time.

Rosie held Apostil very tight, the tears rolling off her chin and dripping on his head. Tina whispered how she was going to kill Stephen for ruining her mascara. The church sat rapt, then, when the final voices had died away, erupted in a massive storm of clapping and cheering. It took a while to calm everybody down, and they were in the process of saying goodbye to the children in Kduli when the line collapsed and froze, and contact was lost.

'That was our surprise, Miss Rosie.' Edison's voice rang out from the choristers.

'Well it certainly was,' said Rosie through her tears. 'It was a very good one.'

'*If* we can finally get on,' said the vicar peevishly. 'I welcome thee, in the name of the Father, the Son and the Holy Ghost, Apostil Akibo Edward Lakeman.'

Then it was Lilian's turn to gasp.

🍬

It was freezing outside the church, but nobody noticed, and nobody minded. People kept coming over to congratulate Tina and Jake, and cuddle Apostil, and hug everyone else, and the photographer grew increasingly exasperated and warned them that they'd have no formal pics at all, and Tina – Tina, the devotee of the perfect wedding, Tina who had planned everything down to the nth degree, Tina with her magazines and colour-coded folders and Post-its – tossed her head and said those pictures were absolutely crap anyway, and superboring, and please, just to take pictures of their day as it actually was.

The sun shone on the icicles lining the church walls, and followed them as they all crunched their way on foot up towards the hut – everyone except Tina, who was borne away triumphantly by her new husband on a shiny tractor lent to them by Peter Isitt, which had been decorated with flowers and holly and lined with blankets. They threw sweets as they went, to Lilian's horror, and the schoolchildren, already hyped up from the massive success of their concert, and the pressure of having to stay incredibly well-behaved for over an hour, went completely crazy for them. Holes were made in the knees of new trousers; icy mud was spattered across pretty dresses and smocks; shoes were trampled into oblivion. But today, nobody seemed to mind too much. Tina's ushers, in another surprise for Rosie, were all shaking buckets for the African fund, and people were donating with a will.

Amid all the excitement, a rather shell-shocked

Moshe announced that if it was always like this, he thought he might convert. Lilian told him to come and talk to her first. She had adopted him without a second thought, and he was pleased to be invited to take her free arm; the other one of course was being held by Moray.

'You are SUCH a coquette,' said Rosie.

'Always,' returned Lilian serenely.

To give credit to Henrietta, she did come over, with a slight stiffness in her gait and a set to her shoulders, to where the little family was standing.

'Quaint,' she said, peering at Apostil, who was democratically beaming at everyone while also desperately trying to pull off his lace robe, which was scratching at his neck. 'Hello,' she said formally. 'I'm your grandmother, remember?'

Apostil stared at her with his big round eyes and blew a spit bubble.

'Have you seen Pamela?' Henrietta asked. Rosie suspected she'd already gone ahead to the scout hut – the party to which Hetty was not invited – but didn't say. Stephen stood, stony-faced.

Rosie couldn't help it.

'Would you like to come on? To the party? I mean, everybody else is …'

Hetty sniffed.

'I dislike doing things everybody else is doing.'

'We know that,' said Stephen.

Hetty pulled herself up.

'No. I want to check the gardener has spliced up the winter garden properly. There's always plenty to be getting on with in the house.'

'If you *have* a house,' said Stephen sotto voce as she turned and walked away, the sole figure heading back up towards town, where her Land Rover was parked. Rosie clasped his arm.

'Don't you dare start to say anything about us being better off,' said Stephen, tightly.

'I shan't,' said Rosie, then reached up and kissed him lightly on the ear. 'But we—'

'Ssssh! I don't want to hear it!'

'But—'

'I've just agreed to spend the rest of my life waiting at bus stops and shopping at Poundingtons.'

'You can get amazing stuff at Poundingtons!'

'I'm going to have to go through a metal detector to get to work every day!'

'I'll fancy you even more for your extraordinary bravery.'

He squeezed her hand.

'You'd better,' he said.

Chapter Eighteen

They were nearly the last to arrive at the hut. Outside, a huge bonfire had been set up in a great circle of stones in the forest clearing, and the children were running around it, shouting and hollering like wild things. Awkward teenagers were handing out champagne in plastic glasses, while Roy was eyeing it carefully. Many people had brought bottles too, which were cheerfully added to the makeshift bar inside. Outside, Tina and Jake, Kent and Emily and Roy and Pamela made up a slightly peculiar receiving line, and, with good grace, Rosie and Stephen joined it too, so everyone could have a cuddle of Apostil, who was showing signs of getting hungry. Rosie sipped from a glass of champagne, and found time to say hello to everyone who was there; from

Hye right down to Edison, who shook hands very gravely and seriously.

Pamela was all over Roy, who people were nodding at pleasantly enough.

'So that's going well?' said Rosie politely, trying not to betray her vast sense of surprise. They were as unlikely a couple as could be imagined.

Pamela downed her drink as they all politely shook hands with Mrs Pettigrew who lived in the old row of cottages that had only got electricity in the nineties, and the Johnson family, six enormous boys who ran the vast dairy farm on the other side of the peaks, all of them looking identical, pink-faced and very cheerful in ill-fitting suits and slip-on shoes. They were some of Rosie's best customers, but she couldn't tell them apart any more than anyone else could, since they worked, ate, lived, played rugby and socialised together. Two of them were apparently married, but nobody knew which two. Moray also insisted that one of them was gay, but could never remember which one either.

'You have to realise,' Pamela said, nudging Roy to get her a refill. 'The men in New York, they're all totally unavailable. They'd never show vulnerability like he has, they never open up.'

'Hmm,' said Rosie.

'And you know, I'm ready to settle down. Nobody in New York is; they're all trying to make another million.

I mean, I've got my house here now, my roots are here, Roy's made his money.'

'He certainly has,' said Rosie.

'Maybe this is my time to get out of the rat race, you know? Slow it down a bit. Stop being the incredibly successful and popular party girl. You know what that's like.'

Rosie thought it best to keep staring straight ahead at this point.

'I can settle down ... make jam.'

'You don't eat sugar.'

Pamela ignored this.

'Keep chickens.'

'You're vegetarian.'

'Get my home photographed for *Vogue Living*. I can see the profile now ... "After years at the sharp end of the hurly-burly, the Right Honourable Dr Mrs Pamela Blaine-Lipton has formed an exquisite haven for herself and her dental surgeon husband ..."'

'You certainly have this worked out well for someone you've only known for five days,' said Rosie, smiling stiffly at Tina's nice out-of-town cousins.

'Yes, but I'm done looking,' said Pamela. 'I'm done dating broke screenwriters who are actually rubbish, evil bankers who would kill someone for three bucks forty, commitment-phobes and guys who steal from you. I'm done, Rosie. I'm ready. I want what you have ... except I want my own baby, obviously.'

Rosie summoned up all her reserves of cheer to greet Jake's Irish grandmother, who was being helped along the line.

'Obviously,' she said through gritted teeth.

Pamela turned to Roy and ran her carefully manicured hand up his jacket.

'Sweetie, you are looking so good,' she murmured, and Roy went pink to the tips of his ears. Rosie shook her head.

When they finally got inside the hut, the noise levels were unbelievable. Even Stephen was impressed by the decor; the massive layering of decorations and the endless fairy lights had turned the place into a magical grotto. The band had started playing by the strawbales at one end. They had banjos and fiddles and were making a fabulous traditional racket that involved lots of yelling and banging of clogs on the floor. Several children had already started dancing. The old folks who'd come from the home in a minibus were seated at tables, watching cheerfully with great brimming pints of cider in front of them. The farmers and Rodge the vet were lined up against the makeshift bar, drinking pints – no champagne for them – and discussing livestock as if they were in the bar at the Red Lion, which, Rosie was pleased to note, they practically were, because the pub's droopy-moustached barman was serving here too.

'I thought you'd been invited,' she said to him cheerily.

'I was,' he said, his usual lugubrious, unsmiling manner not faltering. 'I just thought this would make a nice wedding gift.'

Rosie looked at him, blinking.

'You know, it does,' she said. 'It really does.'

The band were magnificent, and had the effect of turning what was supposed to be a formal wedding breakfast (in Tina's original, sophisticated dreams) into what already felt more like a night-time affair. Nonetheless, Apostil absolutely could not keep his eyes open – he'd been up very early, as had Rosie, and had had a lot of wriggling and excitement since then. He was visibly drooping. Rosie found a spot near the musicians – they were making quite a lot of noise, but there were no amps or wires, and behind the great strawbales it was actually quite quiet – and sat down and fed him with the bottle she'd been carrying in her jacket to keep it warm.

She picked up the car seat Stephen had brought in and put it in the cosy straw, then she slipped Apostil out of his scratchy christening dress and into a comfy fleece-lined sleepsuit covered in little blue fish, and wrapped him in his favourite blanket with the spots on. He was so sleepy he obediently closed his eyes as soon as he saw it, and she laid him down gently in his seat, buckled loosely. Then, because it was funny, she plumped up the hay so it covered the plastic of the seat and made him look like they actually had laid him down in a barn.

His little hand that had been gripping the bottle fell, and he tumbled elegantly into sleep, the way babies do, taking a little step from one state of consciousness to another.

Rosie sat watching him for a long time, engrossed, as ever, in the rise and fall of his tiny chest; the long eyelashes shaded on the roundness of his plump cheeks; the way his eyes flickered under his eyelids, looking at those things only dreaming babies can see. Then, smiling at a nearby table of older people, she asked them to keep an eye on him, and they were happy to oblige. Cathryn, busying around too much to even get herself a glass of champagne, nodded at Rosie and told her she'd add him to her rounds, and Rosie went back to the party.

There were piles of gifts everywhere. Although they had tried not to infringe too much on Tina and Jake's big day, and although they'd already received so many things, for some reason people had once again been incredibly generous, and heaps of small pale blue parcels had been added beneath the tree to those for the happy couple, who were rushing about the wedding in a whirl of happiness. Every so often they would pass each other in the room, and kiss and hold one another in a way that made the old folk sigh, the middle-aged roll their eyes and Rosie grin to herself about how nice it was to see her friend so happy.

After a while the scent of fish and chips got too much

for her and she realised she'd been up for hours and was absolutely starving. She went to see if Lilian wanted to eat too.

'Go away,' said Lilian, with her mouth full. 'You're not having any of my chips.'

She was holding court at a large table full of other residents of the home. Ida Delia was stoically ploughing through what was clearly a second or third helping. Her startlingly blonde hair was tied up with a bright red ribbon like Emily's. Rosie rather liked it.

'Mam, you're to stop that, you're getting fat,' the similarly well-upholstered Dorothy Isitt was scolding her from the next table.

'Shut up,' said Ida Delia. 'Don't tell me what to do.'

'Hello, Ida Delia,' said Rosie. 'You look nice.'

'Tarty, more like,' said Lilian. 'And have you seen how much she eats?'

'Stop with the torture,' said Rosie severely. 'I've told you before.'

'I'm just trying to be ladylike,' said Lilian serenely. 'And stay away from my chips!'

'And I was just trying to be helpful,' said Rosie.

'If you want to be helpful,' said Lilian, 'you can bring us more champagne. Matron keeps making remarks about peeing the bed, and we think just for one night and one big celebration we should all be allowed to wet our beds.'

'Hear hear!' chorused the table, raising their glasses in unison.

'I'll just go and see to it,' said Rosie hurriedly, backing away.

Outside, the light was already failing, even though it was only early afternoon. December the twenty-first, Rosie thought, the shortest day of the year. After this, everything would get lighter again. It would. This festival, with the great bonfire crackling, its heat so intense that snow was melting off the branches all around, was fighting off the powers of darkness; the forces that had, at times, threatened to close over her head, so hard had this year seemed. She found Stephen, who was idly chatting with Moshe, drinking cider and leaning on his stick; she took his hand and rested her head on his shoulder. Without missing a beat, he moved his arm around her, held her close, kissed the top of her head, as if he could tell what she was thinking without her having to mention it. He leaned over to whisper something in her ear.

'Have you lost that baby again?'

Oh well, maybe he wasn't quite that psychic.

'No! He's fine, he's asleep in the straw.'

'You Christians are amazing,' said Moshe, shaking his head.

'And you came out to fill your face?' said Stephen.

'Actually,' said Rosie, 'I was being all romantic and contemplative.'

Stephen smiled.

'Can't you be those things and fill your face at the same time?'

'Yes!'

'Want me to get you some?'

'No. If I go, I get the crispy bits.'

'Now you see why she's my girl,' said Stephen to Moshe, with pride.

The fish and chip van was proving the more popular of the two, and Rosie queued happily for the silken-fleshed haddock and the extra-crispy chips, golden and steaming, wrapped in specially printed paper that said 'Tina & Jake, 21 December 2014'. Rosie smiled. Tina always did think of everything.

She got some Fanta too and went back to stand with Stephen and Moshe, smiling cheerfully at even the twelfth person who passed and said, 'You two next.'

Everyone was rather well oiled and jolly by the time they got to the speeches.

Jake's had been so sincere and nice about Tina – and short; he obviously couldn't bear public speaking, and had turned brick red – and he was patently relieved when the attention turned to Rosie and Stephen. Even the children, who had been running wild building snowmen in the woods and hurling themselves about the dance floor, sat up to watch with expectant faces. Jake held the microphone out to them insistently.

'Oh Lord,' said Stephen.

'You spend ALL DAY standing up and talking to people,' said Rosie.

'Small people,' said Stephen.

'Everyone's small to you.'

Finally, realising that he had no choice, Stephen got up, reluctantly, to good-humoured applause.

'Um,' he said. As he stood up, he realised he was a bit drunk. Actually, really quite drunk. He hadn't been paying attention out round the bonfire with everyone in such a good mood, instead letting his glass be refilled by a teenager with a crush on him.

'Thanks for coming ... um, and big thanks to Tina and Jake for letting us gatecrash their simply fabulous wedding. There were times this past year when ...' he turned to look at Rosie, 'when thinking about this wedding has been one of the very few things that's cheered us up.'

Rosie nodded madly, slightly worried as she noticed him swaying.

'Hear hear,' shouted someone, and there was a general toast. Stephen cracked a big lopsided grin at everyone.

'And I wanted to say as well how sorry we are to be leaving, and how much we're going to miss all of this and all of you, and hopefully we'll be back and forth a bit ...'

His voice trailed off as he realised everyone had gone silent.

'Stephen!' hissed Rosie loudly. She caught sight of Mrs Baptiste, the headmistress of the school, whose jaw had dropped open. Tina was looking at her in absolute horror. All the children had gasped.

'What?' the old people were saying on their table.

'Ah,' said Stephen, realising belatedly that he'd said rather too much. 'Anyway, the happy couple.' He raised his glass quickly and collapsed back into his seat.

'Well,' he said, to Rosie's white face, 'at least we're spared the trouble of telling everyone.'

There was hubbub in the hall. Tina was coming up to Rosie with a shocked look on her face.

'Don't worry,' Rosie reassured her. 'The sweetshop will continue, I promise. But ... yes. I think we're going to have to leave.'

Lilian was looking awkward, and Rosie wanted to go over to her and reassure her that they weren't sad, that it wasn't her fault, but she kept being waylaid. One of Stephen's pupils, Rosie noticed, was in tears. Then she turned round to find Edison standing quiet and pale by her chair.

'Are you moving to Switzerland?' he asked.

'No,' said Rosie, puzzled. 'Why?'

'I just think people go to Switzerland,' said Edison, pushing up his glasses.

'Are you reading those Second World War books again?'

'You'll be safe in Switzerland.'

'We're not going to Switzerland! We're going to Derby! We'll be thirty miles down the road!'

'That's pretty far.'

'It's not far! We'll be back all the time!'

'How far's a mile?'

'Not very far.'

Edison stared at the ground.

'But you're my friend,' he said quietly.

Rosie put her arms around him.

'I will always be your friend,' she said. 'I promise.'

'That won't help me when you're in Switzerland,' grumbled Edison, as she cuddled his thin body.

Stephen meanwhile had been shocked sober and was talking to Mrs Baptiste, who was, justifiably, absolutely furious with him for announcing his de facto resignation at a wedding ceremony. Stephen tried to explain that he'd commute until he found something else, but that cut no ice with Mrs Baptiste, who pointed out quite rightly that there was a huge teacher shortage in central Derby and he'd get offered something very senior in five minutes, and he'd better be wearing his lion tamer's outfit. Pamela stared at them both completely stony-faced, as person after person asked loudly why they were moving away.

Even though the hall was still buzzing with gossip, suddenly Roy Blaine himself stood and cleared his throat. Pamela banged her glass loudly to get everyone to stop talking, and people did finally turn round.

'Welcome to my party,' he started. There was scattered and quite puzzled-sounding applause. 'And make sure you floss after all that cake, it can really get in the spaces between your teeth and cause abscesses if left untreated.'

There was a long pause. Rosie wasn't sure if he thought this was a joke or not. He didn't really do jokes. Pamela was looking up at him with the fervour of a political wife at a party conference.

'So, now that I've finally managed to escape the coils of that witch . . . '

He paused for longer this time, and Rosie realised to her horror that he did actually think that was a joke and they were all meant to laugh, though thankfully nobody did.

' . . . I can celebrate my freedom . . . with you, my dear friends.'

There was a kind of embarrassed murmur round the hall. Pamela ran her hand lightly up and down Roy's arm. Across the hall, Rosie heard Lilian cough, loudly and clearly, on purpose.

'So let's all raise a glass . . . ' said Roy, which everyone, by now getting quite confused, was happy to do as the champagne kept on flowing.

As they did so, there was a noise at the end of the hut, and the door crashed open. Standing there, her cheeks very pink, both from the cold and from every eye in the room being on her, was Laura, Roy's absent wife.

Roy's face drained of all colour. Without even turning round, he shook Pamela's hand off his arm, and swallowed, hard. There was a deathly silence in the room. Laura looked around, and several of her friends, slightly in their cups, raised their glasses and said hello.

Slowly, watched by everyone, her face pinker by the minute, she marched up to the top table and stood right in front of Roy, who was gripping his glass so hard it looked like it might shatter. Rosie glanced across at Lilian and was delighted to see she had lost her uncomfortable expression from earlier, and was looking increasingly perked up with all the lovely gossip. Tina clutched Rosie's hand, eyebrows raised.

'So,' Laura said quietly. 'You never take me out. You never socialise with me. You never host parties. You are no fun. You never buy champagne. You never do anything nice. And the SECOND I leave . . . ' She put out her hand to indicate the happy, heaving room, and shook her head. 'You're a cruel and despicable man, Roy Blaine.'

Roy seemed struck dumb. Laura looked him up and

down, nodded quietly, then slowly turned to go.

'Wait,' croaked Roy as she began making her way across the hall. 'LAURA! I LOVE YOU! I'VE BEEN AN IDIOT! I CAN CHANGE!'

There was a long, long pause. Rosie glanced at Pamela's face. It was white and taut with anger.

Laura froze, and closed her eyes.

'I mean it. I MEAN IT!'

Roy held up one of the bottles of champagne.

'I won't make you clean the swimming pool any more!'

'He really needs to shut up about that damn swimming pool,' whispered Stephen.

'This is not the time for you to comment on things people don't know to shut up about,' whispered Rosie back. She was grateful to Laura for taking the spotlight off them, but she was still going to have a lot of mopping up to do.

'Laura . . .'

Roy's voice was cracking. Then, amazingly, he started to sing.

'*Tell Laura I love her . . .*'

It was such an unlikely, pretty little song he sang, and, to Rosie's amazement, he had a lovely voice: a deep baritone that rang out through the hall. A tear gradually stole its way down Laura's cheek. Tina went and put her arms around her, then gently turned her round.

Roy stood there, two glasses in his hands.

'I've been such a shit husband.'

'And such a shit,' some wag piped up from the tables.

Laura nodded dumbly.

'I miss you so much,' Roy said.

'So much you threw a party?'

'I hoped you'd hear about it.'

'You know, I always did love champagne. But with you it was like waiting for a special occasion that never, ever came.'

Roy held out a glass.

'Can I change that?'

Laura took a step forward.

'I don't know.'

Roy's hand was shaking.

'I will try.'

Laura stepped forward once more and tentatively reached out and took the glass. Everyone clapped and roared as she clinked it against Roy's and they both took a sip. Then Roy, amazingly, jumped over the table – knocking over Pamela's glass as he went, and not even noticing – took Laura into his arms and kissed her, their teeth clanging together.

'Well,' said Rosie, stunned.

'Fuck this,' said Pamela, and, largely unnoticed, she marched out of the hall, her stilettos clattering on the wooden floor. The band immediately struck up a happy reel, and finally Jake and Tina got to take to the floor for their first dance.

Much later – she had taken to dancing to avoid the many awkward questions that would doubtless take up much of her time over the next few days – Rosie found herself picking up Apostil, who had been sitting watching the dancers absolutely fascinated, swaying his head to the music and being bounced and jiggled by everyone who came by. She decided it was time to get him home for his bath and bed, before he got overtired. She asked Stephen – who had decided to deal with the situation by drinking rather more – if he'd like to stay, but seeing everyone dancing arm in arm, and Cathryn rounding up the old folk, who were complaining mightily (except for Ida Delia, who had fallen noisily asleep at the table and was snoring loudly with her mouth open, despite Dorothy prodding her and telling her to stop), he decided to come too.

It took them about forty minutes to get round everyone to say goodbye, and Rosie found herself overwhelmed by the levels of love, drunkenness, community and consideration in the warm room; such an outpouring of happiness for the newly-weds, concern for themselves, and extraordinary, jolly bonhomie. It was how, she told herself, she would always remember Lipton.

'Best wedding ever,' she whispered in Tina's hair, which had come completely undone from its posh do and was flying wildly about her shoulders. Her immaculate make-up was also running down her cheeks, and Emily and her friends were taking turns wearing the headpiece and the veil. Of her bouquet there was no sign.

'It was, wasn't it?' said Tina. The joy beaming from her made her still the loveliest bride. 'But you can't go.'

'We must,' said Rosie, as Apostil grabbed on to Tina's finger and tried to put her new rings in his mouth. 'We'll still see you, though.'

'What, out here in the middle of nowhere, when it's snowing up to our waists and pitch dark?' joked Tina.

'This isn't the middle of nowhere,' said Rosie, sincerely. 'It's the middle of my everywhere.'

Rosie carried Apostil in the sling and half carried Stephen as he wobbled back up the main street. A well-fed Mr Dog was running cheerfully behind them.

'Ha, that was ace,' said Stephen. 'Oh God, the look on those old fuckers' faces when I told them we were leaving.'

'It was nice,' said Rosie. 'That they were sad. You shouldn't have done that. Especially not to Mrs Baptiste.'

339

She glanced across the road. The village was utterly deserted, everyone still at the party. But was that a figure stepping out of the shadows?

'I know,' said Stephen, still talking loudly. 'But still. Nice to be appreciated for a change. Funny, when I was younger, I couldn't wait to get out of this FUCKING SHITHOLE!' He burst out laughing.

'You are a really daft drunk,' Rosie complained.

'It's true! I used to think it was a FUCKING SHIT-HOLE!' he yelled again. Then his face turned glum. 'Now I can't believe we have to leave it,' he added quietly, but it was too late. The figure had turned round and was waving.

'No way,' said Rosie. It was Joy. 'Does that cow never sleep?'

Joy approached them, iPad welded to her bosom.

'I was just coming to see you, but you weren't there,' she said. She glanced at her watch.

Rosie glanced down. Apostil had pulled off his hat and it was nowhere to be seen. She pulled her jacket over him protectively. The wind was biting.

'Why are you hanging round this FUCKING SHIT-HOLE?' said Stephen, giggling to himself. Rosie felt like kicking his stick away.

Joy pushed a button on her iPad.

'Do you have many problems with substance abuse?' she asked.

'It's late,' said Rosie. 'I need to get the baby home.'

'Yes, this is an absurd time to have a baby out,' said Joy. 'There's really a lot you need to learn about parenting, you know.'

Stephen was still laughing, and suddenly, all the emotion of the day welled up in Rosie, everything she'd done and was trying to do, and she couldn't hold it in any more. Knowing as she did it that it was terribly dangerous, she turned on Joy.

'There's a lot EVERYONE has to learn about parenting,' she said loudly. 'That's the whole point. It's a LEARNING PROCESS. If it wasn't, nobody would bother having the damn things, they'd know it all. But I'll tell you one thing I've learned. This baby is adored, beloved, spoiled rotten by everyone he's ever met, and that includes his mum, which is me, and his dad, which is that man over there who works like a Trojan every bloody day of his life, and if he isn't allowed to get a bit pissed at a wedding and his own fricking baby's christening, well then it's you who's got the problem.

'If you think we're not good enough for Apostil, you tell your bosses, and we will fight you for our son until there is no fight left in us and we are both lying dead in a ditch. Otherwise, you can just shut the fuck up and get out of our lives. Good night. There's a party on at the scout hut you could go to, if you ever let your hair down, which I doubt, though it could certainly do with a wash.'

And exhilarated and shocked at herself, she turned round without another word and stomped off with Apostil, Stephen wobbling along as fast as he could on his stick at her side.

'I have NEVER fancied you more,' he said as they made their way up past the darkened door of the sweet-shop.

Chapter Nineteen

'Oh God ...'

'Sssssh.'

Downstairs, Apostil was crying, a long, thin wail that sounded like he was absolutely furious at the world and wasn't afraid to show it. Rosie felt like she'd been punched in the head repeatedly. Stephen was lying behind her, his eyes tight shut, making a thick, groaning noise.

'Oh God ...'

'Jesus,' said Rosie. She'd kept a close eye on her consumption and was sure she'd only had a few glasses of champagne ... well, and some cider, she supposed. And a bit of beer to wash down the fish and chips. And obviously more champagne for all the toasts ...

'Oh crap,' she said, as Apostil became more demanding. 'I did that thing where I was drunkenly utterly convinced I was sober.'

'Rrrrrrr,' said Stephen, still refusing to open his eyes. His dark stubble stood out on his pale chin.

With great difficulty Rosie managed to roll herself over to the side of the bed.

'Oh GOD,' she said. 'Oh God, what did I say to Joy?'

Stephen put a pillow over his head.

'She caught you driving a baby whilst drunk,' he muttered.

Rosie put her head in her hands.

'Oh God oh God oh God. It's all right, baby boy, I'm coming.'

She rolled off the bed and resisted the temptation to crawl down the stairs. Her thoughts were churning in her head. What had she done? What had she said? Icy water plummeted into her stomach. Oh God. They'd take Apostil away. They'd done too much, been too rude. Social services would speak to Stephen's mother and conclude he didn't have a stable family background. They'd see the house was up for sale and judge them financially incompetent. And what if they'd dropped him? What if something had happened whilst she'd been a bit squiffy?

By the time she got downstairs she was in full-blown tears, and it took her a second or two to realise what she was seeing. Firstly, it was eight o'clock – it was light!

Apostil had slept right through! And secondly, he had manoeuvred himself somehow out of his sleeping bag, and was, wonder of wonders, over on his tummy. When he saw her, he stretched up his arm and beamed a proud gummy smile so enormous that Rosie felt worse than ever.

'Look at you!' she said. 'Are you rolling? Don't roll on your tummy, that's bad! Ha, the first thing you have ever done and I'm telling you not to do it.'

'Gah,' said Apostil.

Rosie picked him up and covered him in kisses.

'Sorry,' she said. 'I probably smell awful.'

'Bu,' said Apostil.

Three cups of tea and four Nurofen later, Rosie was trying to put things in perspective. Apostil had rolled over four times. This was better than everything else.

'Woah,' she said. 'Stephen! You're missing, like, all the milestones! If you don't get down here soon, he'll be off to university.'

'Grraaaah,' came a voice from upstairs.

'Hangovers are much worse when you're a parent,' confided Rosie to Apostil. 'That is why you mustn't drink.' She looked around the kitchen dolefully. 'In fact, almost anything you see your mum and dad do in life, just do the opposite and you'll be all right.'

Apostil batted her arm until she gave him some more of his bottle. Maybe, thought Rosie. Maybe she hadn't been too bad with Joy last night. Then she remembered something about lying dead in a ditch and closed her eyes. Oh Lord.

She also remembered Stephen announcing to everyone that they were leaving. Oh God, no wonder he didn't want to get up. She checked her phone, as usual having to hang her arm out of the window to get a signal. It started bleeping with messages. She glanced at one from Tina announcing what a fabulous day she'd had, and remembered that they would have to go up there at some point this afternoon and help clear up so the hut could revert to the Boys' Brigade. She couldn't help smiling when she remembered Roy and Laura, though. Except, God, poor Pamela.

Eventually she couldn't take it any longer and went out to get the Sunday papers and some Lucozade for Stephen. Malik looked absolutely fine and cheerful behind the shop counter, even though he'd still been there when they'd left last night.

'Don't worry,' he said when he saw her. 'Everyone is suffering this morning.'

'Seriously?' said Rosie. 'I look that bad?'

'No,' said Malik quickly.

Rosie bought fizzy drinks, papers and some bacon to make sandwiches.

'So,' said Malik, 'you are leaving us.'

'It's only a few miles,' said Rosie. 'We'll come back and visit.'

Even as she said it, it sounded hollow to her own ears.

'We need to do what's best for this little man,' she said.

As he always did, Malik tried to give Apostil a lollipop, and Apostil tried to grab it, and Rosie politely returned it.

'I never know why you think I have a lollipop shortage.' She smiled at Malik, who smiled back.

'We'll miss him,' he said. 'The village, it needs children.'

'I know,' said Rosie. 'But, you know ... life ...'

Malik nodded.

'Life,' he said.

Rosie sat on the edge of the bed and prodded Stephen until he eventually woke up. His eyes focused on Apostil, who was lying on his tummy.

'No way,' he said. Apostil let out the same proud grin and showed off how good he was at rolling. The motion, though, demonstrated how useless his right hand was.

'Look at you, my boy!' Stephen said, picking him up in his strong arms. 'See. Your parents going out and getting pissed is obviously really, really good for you.'

'That's a shame, because it's NEVER happening again,' said Rosie. 'Oh God, I can't even think what Joy's going to do. Do you think they knock on your door at four o'clock in the morning?'

'Ssssh,' said Stephen, downing half his Lucozade. 'Come here, both of you.'

He pointed out of the window.

'Look, it's started snowing again. It's nearly Christmas. Today is a day to cuddle up in front of the fire and make Apostil watch *The Great Escape*. Followed, if he's good, by *Goldfinger*. Then we'll wrap presents and eat toast and drink tea, and we won't think about social workers, or moving house, or operations, or families, or anything. Okay?'

Rosie rested her head on his shoulder, Apostil in between them, and watched the snow fall softly on the quiet Sunday-morning village.

'Okay,' she whispered.

'On the other hand, I wouldn't mind nipping down to church to see how the vicar manages. Last thing I remember last night, he was dancing the Macarena.'

They did curl up on the sofa together, the room cosy and flickering in the firelight, and Rosie watched the film, but also the tree, with its shining bells and little lights all over it, trying to brand on to her memory how it felt: the three of them together, all cuddled up and happy and cosy, with Mr Dog at Stephen's feet, snorting little doggy dreams, and Christmas upon them and everything quiet and peaceful in the world. She vowed that whatever happened next, whatever lay ahead on the hard road they had to take, away from everything they knew and loved, it wouldn't come between them; wouldn't take away this deep peace and happiness, the strong bond of their little family, however unconventional, however hard-won.

'What are you looking so pensive about?' said Stephen, glancing over at her face, made pink by the fire, her hair falling softly down her back. She hadn't had time to get it cut. He was glad.

'God rest ye merry, gentlemen,' murmured Rosie softly.

'And so say all of us,' said Stephen, kissing her lightly on the head.

Just as it was starting to get dark, after three, and every-one was snoozing comfortably, the phone jangled furiously, breaking into their calm. Stephen started, and Apostil let out a disgruntled noise.

'What?' said Rosie. 'Oh God, what now?' All her happy cosiness fell away with a start and she leapt up. 'The phone. That is never good news. I hate phones.'

They both looked at it as it jangled again.

'Joy?' said Rosie.

Stephen's eyes narrowed.

'It's probably my bloody mother, wanting a full run-down on everything whilst pretending she doesn't. Don't answer it.'

Rosie gave him a look.

'What if it's Lilian?'

Stephen picked it up and passed it to her.

'I'm going to change Ap,' he said, leaving the room.

'Hello?' said Rosie with trepidation.

'FUCKING HELL,' came the well-bred mid-Atlantic voice. Rosie could have collapsed with relief.

'Oh. Hello, Pamela,' she said. 'Um, what's up?'

'What's UP? The love of my life fucks off and you ask me what's up?'

'Seriously?' said Rosie. 'Was he really the love of your life?'

She wanted to bite her tongue; that had come out harsher than she'd intended.

'He's such an asshole,' said Pamela.

'I'm really, really sorry,' said Rosie. 'I really am. But you're right, he *is* an arsehole. I think you're probably well out of it.'

'They're all assholes,' said Pamela. 'Well, I don't need to tell *you*.'

Rosie just looked at the phone and didn't answer.

'Anyway, what are you guys doing? I'm bored up here. Are you making Sunday lunch? Are you doing those local carrot things?'

Rosie didn't want to say they were eating bacon sandwiches and crisps on the sofa.

'Um ...' she said.

'I could bring down some margarita mix, we could have Sunday-night margaritas?'

Rosie could not think of anything worse.

Stephen came back into the room.

'It's your sister,' said Rosie, as brightly as she could. 'She's coming over.'

Stephen took the phone off her.

'Don't come over. We're busy,' he said. 'Why don't you have a dinner party in one of your ninety-two rooms?'

He hung up.

'Woah,' said Rosie.

'You're far too nice to her,' said Stephen. 'You're far too nice to everyone.'

'Including you,' Rosie pointed out.

'Yes, including me,' said Stephen. 'But that's different.'

As the snow had stopped, they took an unimpressed Mr Dog out for a walk in the fading light, everyone in wellingtons. Rosie had bought Mr Dog snow shoes but he point-blank refused to wear them, which she understood.

Up at the scout hut, she was astonished to see an immaculate bare room. It was like the massive overdecoration had been a dream, had vanished like fairy food,

351

leaving only the bones of the stage set that had been there before.

'Wow,' said Rosie. 'What happened here? Did we dream yesterday?'

'It would be very useful if we did,' said Stephen, who was already worrying about going back to school in the morning and facing the music.

But instead, there was Roy Blaine, Laura by his side, standing by with a shovel. He hailed Rosie when he saw her.

'How did you manage all this?' she asked.

'Got the Boys' Brigade to do it,' said Roy. 'Good for them; bit of energy and discipline. Sort 'em out.'

Laura beamed proudly.

'That was a brilliant idea,' said Rosie. She looked at Laura. 'Is he a changed man?' she asked.

'He's giving it a shot,' said Laura.

'I'll believe it when you invite us round for a swim,' said Rosie teasingly, as he grimaced.

'Merry Christmas,' she said, meaning it. 'Merry Christmas to you both.'

'I suppose we should start packing up too,' said Stephen, as they made their way back down the icy street. Lipton looked like a Christmas card, snowy fog softening the street lights and casting a gentle golden glow on the little town.

Rosie nodded.

'I spoke to the estate agent,' she said. 'He said it'll sell in two minutes. Lipton's much sought after, apparently.'

'That's because nobody ever leaves,' said Stephen sadly.

'We'll come back,' Rosie said. 'We'll be up to see Lilian . . . and Moray.'

'Moray won't stay. He'll go to Carningford with Moshe, mark my words.'

'You think?'

'They'll get married before we do.'

Rosie looked around.

'So it's all ending,' she said.

'Don't, be daft,' said Stephen. 'It never really ends, not old places like this. The heart of the country. Pamela will chloroform some hapless sperm donor and carry on up there. Mother will always be here, of course. Tina and Jake will have about nine sets of twins, you'll see. It'll all go on.'

'I know. I just didn't think it would go on without us.'

Rosie woke early the next morning, her heart sinking in her chest. It took a moment for her to realise why. Joy. God. Oh God. Going back to make her report . . . drunk in the street . . . shouting at the social worker, who was only trying to help, only doing her best . . . oh God.

She was up even before Apostil. She went to the door of Lilian's bedroom and stared at him, taking in every inch of him: his long, long eyelashes casting shadows on his round brown cheeks; his right hand tucked away carefully, skinny and flat and grey, unlike his left, which was always on the move, chubby little fingers that waved and grabbed and clung and tugged hair and pulled telephone wires. His soft curled hair, tight on his scalp, and the curve of his solid back underneath his bedclothes. She gazed at him, leaning her head on the door frame of the little room, the sills heavy with snow. They wouldn't. They couldn't take her baby away.

At nine, after they had dressed and breakfasted in near silence, quite different from the usual busy hubbub that started their days, both of them nervous and keyed up, Stephen had kissed her, gently but firmly, saying more with that kiss than any conversation could have done. Then he'd sighed and pulled open the door, and, stick in front of him, set off towards the school for a meeting, and the explanations, and the recriminations, and the awful finality of knowing that this was really it; it was really happening.

Rosie decided to open up late, not quite feeling up to the many, many questions that would undoubtedly come through the shop door from the second she turned over the old-fashioned 'Closed' sign. Instead she cleaned the little house, looked at the presents piled up under the tree; even ignored a phone call from Angie, who wanted every single last detail of the wedding and the party she would have enjoyed so much. Apostil, sensing something was wrong, was fussy and wanted to be picked up. She hoisted him into her arms – he was getting heavy – and nuzzled him quickly before, with her heart beating so hard she felt she could hear it, she finally picked up the heavy rotary-dial phone.

Her hands were shaking so much she could barely hold the receiver, and it took her three goes, swearing all the while, to get the digits dialled. Finally the extension rang, and rang, and rang. Rosie was feeling torn between being desperate to get this over with and relief at putting it off for a while when the phone was finally picked up, and a different, younger voice said, 'Hello?'

'Um, hello,' said Rosie, discombobulated. 'Is, uh, is Joy there?'

'Nooo,' came the voice. 'No. She's on sick leave. She's been signed off. I'm the replacement.'

'What's wrong with her?' said Rosie, horrified. 'Is she okay?'

'Stress?' said the voice, still sounding very chipper. 'Yeah, she was finding it too stressful. People do, you know.'

'I bet,' said Rosie, a tiny pilot light of hope suddenly

leaping into flame in her chest as well as some astonishment at the leakiness of social service departments. 'Um, we're the Lakeman family. I wondered if ... I mean, are you going to be looking after us?'

'I guess so?' said the voice, still in that youthful questioning register. 'The thing is, Joy dropped her iPad, and she hadn't backed up all the notes, so it's a bit of a mess this end.'

'Oh,' said Rosie, blinking hard and letting out a breath she hadn't even known she was holding.

'Hang on,' said the girl. 'I can call you up on the computer ... L-a-k-e-m-a-n?'

'Yes,' said Rosie. There was a long pause, and lots of clicking.

'Okay, all it says is you've adopted a baby from overseas?'

'Seriously?'

'Yup, I know, she didn't back a thing up.'

'Wow.'

'So, how are you getting on?'

'We're GREAT,' said Rosie. 'Really terrific.'

As if on cue, Apostil gurgled cheerfully into the telephone.

'Sounds like it,' said the girl on the other end. 'Okay, well, listen, I don't think you're on our priority list for now ... Can I put you on the end of my very long list, and pop round to see you in a month or so?'

'We're moving,' said Rosie.

'Oh, no problem. Just send us your new address when you get settled. And call if there are any problems, okay?'

'Okay.'

'How are you finding it?' said the voice, in a friendly way. 'My first baby, I was a bit all over the place.'

'Us too,' said Rosie, fervently. 'But do you know, we just about seem to be pulling it together.'

'That's the spirit!' said the woman, and gave Rosie her details, which Rosie pretended to write down before hanging up the phone.

Then she collapsed on to the sofa and burst into tears.

There was an envelope waiting in the sweetshop. Rosie, still slightly tear-stained, opened it. It was a copy of a referral letter from Moray to Derby General. He'd attached a Post-it: 'Stephen told me. Good luck.'

There was also a letter from the nursing agency that she needed to use to re-register herself so she could get a job. So much paperwork. But oh my goodness, this was nothing compared with the relief – and slight guilt – she felt at slipping down the social worker's files. She wondered if it had been her that had caused Joy's stress. But weren't social workers used to people shouting at them?

She wished she could send Joy a card or something to cheer her up, but was wary of bringing herself to her attention in any way.

She looked up as Hester clanged the bell loudly. Marie was, as usual, wriggling like crazy. When she saw Apostil, her face lit up. He also struggled forward.

'They're like two dogs sniffing each other's bottoms,' said Rosie, then wished she hadn't. Even though it was against about a million Health and Safety regulations, she plopped Apostil on top of the glass cabinet that housed the chocolate bars, nose to nose with Marie, still in the ethnic sling, who stuck out a pudgy hand and patted Apostil hard on the head.

'HEH,' she said.

'That's right,' said Hester. 'That is his head. She's a very early speaker,' she said to Rosie. 'I have to struggle to keep up with her! Ha ha!'

'Ha ha,' smiled Rosie.

Marie reached out and batted Apostil in the nose.

'NEH!'

Apostil burst into tears.

'Oh, does he cry a lot?' said Hester, putting her head on one side. 'Sometimes children do that when they don't feel securely connected to their mothers.'

'What can I get you?' said Rosie, comforting Apostil and moving him backwards out of Marie's reach.

'Barley sugar, please. Arthur needs them for his

throat.' This was Hester's long-suffering husband. 'He's giving a paper at a major conference in Geneva. No surprise Marie is so verbal really.'

'That's nice,' said Rosie blandly, fetching down the glass jar. 'Small bag or large?'

'Large, please … How's Apostil coping in the cold weather?'

Rosie gave her a sharp look.

'What's that supposed to mean?'

'Well, you know. He won't be used to the cold.'

'He's lived here for over half his life. He's more used to it than I bloody am.'

Hester smiled beatifically.

'Now don't be so touchy, Rosie. I think it's part of your duty to keep Apostil in touch with his heritage, that's all.'

'By turning up the thermostat?'

'It's all right for him to be different, Rosie,' said Hester in her most infuriatingly gentle voice. 'You must never force a child to fit in.'

'I shall force him to fit in his duvet jacket,' muttered Rosie, handing over the bag with bad grace.

'Sorry to hear you're leaving us,' said Hester. 'It was nice to have a bit of colour in the village.'

Rosie wanted to hit Hester quite badly now, so she turned away and forced herself to concentrate on the morning's good news.

'Although I suppose in Derby it's a lot more … mixed.'

(Stephen said to Rosie later that you had to realise that Hester was probably only saying what other people were thinking, and Rosie had snapped back, yes, other RACIST people, and Stephen had shrugged and said, okay, she was evil, and Rosie had said, yes, she was and that was the end of that conversation. Rosie was already cross with him because he had been so delighted that Joy was ill, and didn't have a word of sympathy for her. 'She hounded us,' he said.

'She was doing her job,' said Rosie. 'Probably pretty well.'

'Well go and call her, tell her to get up out of her sickbed and take our baby away,' said Stephen, and Rosie silently fumed at him.)

Rosie stared so long at Hester that even Hester's normally redoubtable self-confidence seemed to shrink a little, and she paid for her sweets and left, leaving Rosie furious and shaking and absolutely not in the mood for her next customer of the morning, as she heard spiky heels clopping up the street and looked with weariness at the skin-tight jeans and the tiny cropped furry coat and the huge pair of sunglasses even though there was no sun in the sky today and no prospect of any for quite some time.

'Pamela.'

The door tinging was less of a welcoming ring and more of a clanging doom chime.

'My brother is a prick,' said Pamela, without bothering with any of the niceties. Old Mrs Brown, who was browsing for humbugs, scurried to one side.

'Um, yes, sorry about yesterday, we had a lot going on,' said Rosie. 'Do you want to see Apostil?'

'Yeah, great. Well done. Et cetera,' said Pamela.

'What are you up to?' said Rosie politely. 'Are your builders still in?'

'Oh no, I told them if they weren't clear by the weekend they'd not be getting paid. Triple shifts. You've got to be firm with these people.'

'Okay,' said Rosie.

'No, I'm on my way to have it out with him once and for all,' said Pamela.

'Who?' said Rosie.

'Roy, of course.'

'Uh, of course,' said Rosie. She had rather thought that Roy snogging his ex-wife and getting back together with her in front of everyone in the entire town might have settled the matter pretty conclusively, but she wasn't going to step in front of Pamela's wrath.

'Give me some chewing gum.'

'We don't stock it,' said Rosie apologetically. 'Lilian thinks it's common.'

Pamela rolled her eyes.

'How can it be when *I* want some?'

Rosie didn't have an answer to that, so brought out the sugar-free mints instead.

'What are you going to say to him?'

'Apart from the fact that he's a cock-sucking son of a bitch ... sorry, Appy.'

Apostil beamed cheerfully. It slightly tickled Rosie that he seemed to love his aunt Pamela so completely. It was a combination of her making a lot of noise and wearing masses of sparkly, shiny things that attracted his attention, plus the fact that she didn't coo or fuss over him. It reminded Rosie of those people who didn't like cats, who would instantly have the nearest cat drape itself over them.

'No, I just need to hear it from him. For closure, you know what I mean?'

Close up, Pamela didn't look as tremendous as usual. Her skin had lost that buffed-up American sheen, and underneath the heavy make-up she was wearing she looked pale and wan, with dark shadows underneath her eyes. Her highlights had started to grow out at the roots, with little wiry grey hairs showing here and there, and she had lipstick on one of her teeth.

'Um, are you sure that him getting back with Laura wasn't closure?'

'Not for me!' shouted Pamela, popping two mints into her mouth. 'And as soon as he sees me, I totally reckon he'll reconsider.'

'Do you really want him that much?' said Rosie.

Pamela tilted her head.

'Well. You know,' she said. 'There's not a lot of men in this town.'

'There's nothing *but* men in this town,' said Rosie, exasperated.

'Yeah, if you want to marry a farmer. Or a primary school teacher.'

'I would like that,' said Rosie. 'Come on, Pamela, you've been here for ten minutes. I'm sure there's loads of other guys around here.'

'Roy and I had a connection.'

'Yeah, as long as you were debating brands of toothpaste,' said Rosie. 'Be sensible, Pamela.'

Pamela looked at her.

'Well it's all right for you, isn't it, Miss Goody Two-shoes? With the man and the baby and the oh-so-sweetie sweetshop. Your life is totally sorted. So please don't tell me how I should run mine.'

Rosie was completely taken aback by this. The idea that she could inspire jealousy in someone like Pamela had never crossed her mind.

'All right then,' she said. 'Do you want me to call ahead to the surgery, see if he's free?'

'No,' said Pamela, turning to leave without paying. 'I want the element of surprise.'

'How's your morning been?' Stephen had run up at lunchtime; he didn't normally, but it wasn't a full school day.

'Surprising,' said Rosie.

'Oh,' said Stephen, after she'd explained. 'Ah.'

'What?'

'I heard shouting. On my way.'

'Was it possibly dentist's surgery shouting?'

'I think I might have heard a drill going.'

'Oh God, we should probably alert Moray.'

A thought struck her.

'Laura isn't back being his receptionist, is she?'

Stephen nodded slowly.

'Oh my good Lord.'

With Tina off on honeymoon to Disneyland, Rosie was having to work harder than ever dealing with the Christmas rush, and they still had to go into Derby to look at the house. The longer they put the process off, the worse it would get. So on Christmas Eve, with Stephen complaining mightily, they all got into the Land Rover.

Being down in the lowlands, Derby wasn't covered in snow at all, but instead was being lashed by heavy driving rain, which got in through the flaps along the side. Rosie sat in the back with Apostil in his car seat, keeping him cosy and occasionally shouting directions to Stephen, who was swearing mightily at the traffic. Everything was blurry: traffic lights and headlights, and tired-looking people anxious to get home, and huge trucks making great waves as they smashed through puddles, and huddled pedestrians with their heads down against the driving rain, waiting to cross roads that seemed to be lined with pound shops.

'There's a new Westfield,' said Rosie brightly.

'I don't know what that is,' said Stephen, who didn't understand the concept of shopping.

'You will.'

Finally, late, tired and absolutely starving, they arrived in the long road of identical houses. Even the dark and the rain couldn't disguise the burnt-out cars; the washing machines and old mattresses littering the front gardens; a noisy party taking place at an upstairs window. There were plenty of beautiful streets in Derby, and some lovely houses. This wasn't one, and that was that. Rosie sighed. Maybe it would be better than she remembered.

Lance was waiting for them under a large golf umbrella. He was wearing a huge puffa jacket over his suit, which made him look a little like a jovial bear.

'Weather a bit different from Cornwall, then?' said

Rosie, and Lance got a rather faraway look in his eye and fumbled with his keys and said, let's go in if we're going, then, which Rosie didn't think he'd have said if they were going to see somewhere really lovely.

It was worse than Rosie remembered. She didn't know how it could be, but it was. The living room, with its dangerous-looking gas fire, and cars passing in front of the window, mere inches away, it seemed, every two seconds. The horrible kitchen, with its stained and ripped linoleum and empty unit spaces like gaping teeth; the dark stains on the peeling wallpaper; the weird, musty smell; the sagging ceilings.

'So you know it's very hard to find a house in your budget,' said Lance quickly. 'And this is an extremely vibrant area.'

As if in answer, a siren went off so loudly it sounded as if it were in the front room. Apostil woke up with a start and started grumping. Rosie ferreted in her bag for a bottle.

Upstairs was even worse. The solitary bathroom was peach in colour and deeply stained. A cracked window looked out over a tiny patch of brambles and bins that was officially their new back garden. Rosie tried not to think about the view from the dormer windows in Lipton: Lilian's beautiful garden, with its neat rows of vegetables and stunning tumbling roses; the great rolling hills beyond their back door; barely a person to be seen;

sheep occasionally straying close to town; snowdrops that would be appearing any day now, followed by daffodils carpeting the hills as spring arrived again . . .

Rosie blinked.

'And the internet speeds round here are very reasonable,' Lance was saying, obviously somewhat at a loss as to how to continue. 'As a starter property . . .' He ran out of inspiration. 'It's . . . it's definitely a starter property.'

They were standing in a horrible, tiny bedroom at the front of the house. An old, highly suspicious mattress was lying on the floor. A bare wire came down from the ceiling; there was not even a light bulb. But the curtainless room was bright with a street light directly outside it and car headlamps shining across the pockmarked ceiling, illuminating cobwebs in every corner.

Stephen turned to Lance.

'Can you . . . can you give us a minute?'

'Sure,' said Lance, who looked slightly nervous about going downstairs all by himself, but retreated nonetheless. Rosie could feel a familiar lump in her throat. No. She wasn't going to cry.

Without saying a word, Stephen pulled them both into his arms.

'We'll make it okay,' he said, his voice low. 'I'm sorry . . . I'm so sorry I was such a dick about this. I was sticking my head in the sand, I really was. I'm so sorry. I didn't . . . I didn't realise quite how bad it was.'

Rosie swallowed.

'There's nothing … you know there's nothing we can do.'

'I know,' said Stephen, rocking her. 'But it'll be all right. We'll make it all right, won't we?'

Another siren split the night.

'We'll have a roof over our heads. So many people have it much worse.'

'But so far away from our friends, and everyone we know.'

'So we'll make new friends. Well, you will. I'm rubbish at it.'

'You are,' agreed Rosie, half laughing.

'Come on, you'll make it nice. It will be fine. Bit of paint …' There was some shouting down the road. 'Few extra burglar alarms.'

Rosie chose not to tell him that the home insurance was going to cost almost as much as the mortgage.

'All that matters is us. Not the money, not my ridiculous family, not anybody else's opinion. You, me and Apostil. And Lilian. Who'd better get us a REALLY good housewarming present.'

'Lilian,' said Rosie softly, 'already gave me everything.'

They stood together for a while, until suddenly Rosie's phone buzzed.

'See. Good phone connection,' said Stephen, trying to cheer her up.

It was a message from Pamela.

'Fuck it,' Rosie read. 'My boss has had a heart attack. Old job back. Fuck yeah! Back to NYC, baby! Fuck you losers! At the airport now. Tell that brother of mine to break it to the old bat. Am sure she'll be pleased. Oh, and you can stay in that fucking house if it means so much to you. Sayonara.'

Blinking, Stephen and Rosie walked slowly together down the rickety stairs.

'Um,' said Stephen, clearing his throat. 'Lancelot.'

'Just Lance,' said Lance.

'Lance. Anyway. We've changed our minds. For now. I don't think we're going to take the house.'

'Quite right,' said Lance instantly. 'It's a shithole. The survey is unbelievable. I can't believe it's still standing. There's been two murders in this street in eight months.'

Rosie coughed.

'We're going to DISCUSS it,' she said, looking at Stephen, horrified. 'We're going to TALK IT OVER.'

'Oh. Sorry,' said Stephen.

Apostil slept all the way home in the Land Rover, as the rain gradually turned to hail, then snow. At last they

369

turned in to sleepy Lipton, the lights of the houses and farms shining brightly, Christmas trees lit in every window, with the town's tree up at the market cross, its lights sparkling against the snow. In unspoken agreement they drove straight past the sweetshop, its little Christmas train in the window, then turned left, taking the steep, unlit road up through the hills that Rosie had cycled in inclement weather; where they had walked Mr Dog and picnicked and chatted and where they would teach Apostil to walk, to identify trees, to find conkers and snail shells, and worms; where he and Mr Dog could roam together, have adventures, grow up together. One hand in his father's, the other – however it turned out – safely tucked in his mother's, they would swing him, then later he would run, his dark eyes sparkling in the wind or the rain; his strong body filling out, raised on Isitt's cream, and local butter and milk, and strawberries in the summer, and cabbages and carrots from their own patch, and lemon drops when he was good.

In the huge wooded garden of Peak House, he could run with his friends from the little school; Stephen could build him a tree house, where he could camp in the summer, and tell horror stories round the fire until they all got too scared and came tearing back indoors, where Rosie would make them hot chocolate and put them to bed. He would wake here every day to fresh air, and a view across the beautiful Derbyshire landscape, and he would be the luckiest boy in the world, with everything Rosie had ever dreamed of for him, for her, for them . . .

Still neither of them could speak as they alighted from the car, Apostil fast asleep still. There was a little lamp burning outside, and lights still on inside; obviously in her haste, Pamela had just made a dash for it. Stephen felt under the rock where the spare key was kept and glanced at Rosie, whose heart was in her mouth. He put out a hand to her, and together they pushed open the door.

Inside, as Rosie's eyes adjusted to the light, she realised that something was different. The old flagstone floor in the hallway was exactly the same, but that was about it. The lights overhead, for starters, were inlaid spotlights in the ceiling rather than fringed hanging shades. The walls, once a dark red that had made the place gloomy and a little sinister, were now a pale grey-beige colour, in a stripe that looked cosy and expensive. Instead of the spooky old pictures, a beautiful big mirror hung on the wall, reflecting the light. The house was warm. Rosie put her foot on the floor.

'Oh my God,' she whispered. 'Underfloor heating!!! No way!!!!'

Stephen was shaking his head.

'This can't be right. She can't mean for us to stay here.'

As they moved from room to room, their astonishment grew. In a month, Pamela had effected the most astonishing transformation. The front sitting room was now a harmonious palette of pale tartans and cream and grey, with a smart marble surround on the original fireplace. The walls had been toned down from their harsh, cold colours into something softer, fresher and warmer. The best parts of the kitchen – which had always been the nicest part of the house, with its big old scrubbed table and huge windows – had been kept the same, but with brand-new appliances and units.

'She'll be back in three days when she's fallen out with her new boss,' said Stephen, examining everything in wonder. 'Christ, how rich IS she?'

Rosie's mouth was hanging open. She'd texted back about three times asking if Pamela really meant it about the house, but she must have been on the flight, because she hadn't replied.

'It's a mistake,' she said, as they went up the staircase with its beautiful new striped carpet. 'There's been some kind of mistake. She can't really have meant it. Maybe she meant, keep an eye on it for me until I get back.'

'That must be it,' said Stephen. 'She must want us to become unpaid housekeepers, popping up here on top of everything else we have to do.'

'She has done such a beautiful job,' said Rosie sadly.

The large bedrooms had been done out in a beautiful tongue and groove that made them look like a New England beach house, but somehow it still suited the wonderful old Georgian windows, now with gorgeous shabby-chic curtains. Everything had huge plump pillows and expensively heavy linen, and when Stephen turned on the taps in the new all-stone bathroom that looked like something out of a very expensive hotel, hot water gushed out.

'New boiler,' he said, whistling. 'Amazing. God, she doesn't mess about, my sister. She must be poshing it up to sell.'

'Oh yes,' said Rosie, her disappointment reasserting itself. 'She must. Of course. This will make a fortune, look at it.'

Stephen nodded.

'I know.'

They glanced in the last bedroom at the back. Rosie paused.

'Hang on,' she said.

There was a dark shape on the other side of this room, and no bed. She switched on the light; instead of the overhead light, lovely warm side lights came on, in pale blue sea shades. They both gasped. The shape, next to the window, overlooking the back garden, was a huge cot bed in white, with soft blue striped linen. There was a large trunk – Stephen's own, from boarding school – filled with toys at the bottom of the bed. The walls were painted blue and white, and had beautiful old toy posters framed and hung on them. And on the side wall, just above an expensive changing table filled with nappies, E45 cream, nappy bags and a nappy bin – all things Rosie had dismissed as unnecessary expense – large cloth letters, blue with white dots, spelled out A-P-O-S-T-I-L.

◦

They both looked at it for a while, unable to speak. Then Stephen turned to Rosie.

'I think maybe she did mean for us to have it.'

'Fuck a duck,' said Rosie, taking out her phone. There was no answer, so she sent another message.

Downstairs, there was a fully stocked fridge, full of tasty treats from Marks & Spencer, and a bottle of champagne, which they opened after putting Apostil down to sleep in his new bed, taking picture after picture and sending them to Pamela. Everyone else could have one tomorrow, when they would explain.

Stephen lit the little fire, but the house was so cosy already it was barely required. Then they sat in front of it, just looking at each other. They toasted Pamela, then they toasted themselves – 'the luckiest sons of bitches,' as Stephen pointed out, 'in the history of the world'.

'Your family is totally amazing,' added Rosie. 'I've always said so.'

And then they burst out laughing, and held each other incredibly tight, side by side, staring into the fire, heads together, tears intermingled, waiting for Christmas morning.

Chapter Twenty

Because they had always planned to have Christmas dinner at Lilian's home, they didn't have to worry about much, except for telling everyone that they weren't moving after all. There would be regular commutes to Derby, particularly for Rosie, for Apostil's appointments, but it would be worth it. Plus it was about time Tina was made a full partner in the business anyway.

Pamela refused to discuss the house or the succession in any way, so they didn't press her on it. Not for now. But they sent her lots of pictures of Apostil and she didn't seem to object to those.

It was going to be a lovely day. Rosie and Stephen loaded up the car with gifts. They would go to church first, then on to the home, where the local catering college always did the residents proud. They were looking forward to seeing everyone, and showing off Apostil, who was wearing a red and green outfit and looked extraordinarily smart. The old ladies would be cooing over him even more than usual.

'You know she's going to be at church,' said Rosie, as they sat eating breakfast.

Stephen looked at her.

'I know.'

'Is she spending the day by herself?'

'She is pleasing herself, as she always does.'

Rosie gave him The Look. Stephen sighed.

'Okay,' he said, picking up the phone. 'Okay. Just to give her the pleasure of telling me to piss off. As a gift.'

'Ah, the true spirit of Christmas,' said Rosie. She took out the dishes while Stephen reluctantly dialled his mother.

'Hey,' he said awkwardly. There was a long silence; Henrietta was obviously talking. Rosie pretended not to be earwigging.

'I think,' Stephen said eventually, 'I think there's probably a spare space ... you know, at Lilian's ... Yes ...'

Another long silence.

'Yes. We are thrilled. The letters on the wall ... those were your idea?'

Stupefied, Rosie moved closer to the phone so she

377

could hear. Henrietta's voice was still imperious, but it sounded frailer, too.

'Yes,' she said. 'I wanted ... I wanted to make sure he felt part of the family.'

There was a pause.

'Merry Christmas ... Mum.'

Cathryn had excelled herself this year. Great garlands of holly and ivy had been gathered by the gardeners and hung all around the home, and the old ladies had been busy crocheting silver stars, which they had managed so successfully they now covered every available wall space, along with the hundreds of cards, from a generation whose handwriting grew increasingly faint and wobbly.

Relatives arrived with piles of gifts; surly teenagers fiddled with their phones; exuberant little ones, suddenly anxious at the sight of all the old people, caught sight of the huge tree in the corner, lit up and brilliant, and were struck dumb.

Lilian had bagsied the best table, between the windows looking out on to the snow-covered gardens and the crackling fire, simply by putting a cardigan on the back of each chair and giving a deep snarl to anyone who came over and considered complaining. Cathryn had managed to source a high chair from somewhere, so

Apostil, who was only just beginning to sit up, could enjoy watching over the proceedings.

The young, nervous teens from the local Prince of Wales scheme, which trained them up in catering, came round with the first delicious canapés of the day, and aperitifs were served. Lilian asked loudly for a gin fizz, but was ignored and made do with a port and lemon.

Rosie and Stephen came bustling in, brimming over with laughter and gifts, Apostil beaming, Mr Dog sneaking in behind. Cathryn saw the dog but turned a blind eye as he sniffed around appreciatively for chipolatas. Moray and Moshe weren't far behind.

'No ailments!' Moray was shouting. 'I am NOT on call today, so nobody choke on a turkey bone. Or do if you like; I shall stand by whilst you wake Hye out of his underground lair. Someone give me a Campari and soda.'

Frank Sinatra was singing Christmas carols in the background as gifts were exchanged. To Rosie's growing embarrassment, all anyone seemed to have bought was a plethora of toys and ridiculous outfits for Apostil, who ignored all of them in favour of trying to eat some bubble wrap. Across the large dining room, similar scenes were taking place in every family group; even Maud Winton, who had nobody left in all the world, had been co-opted by Ada Lumb's family for the duration. Ida Delia was grumpily examining a necklace Dorothy had bought her and asking if she'd kept the receipt.

Outside, the snow was falling – as it would fall now until March – but Rosie didn't mind, thinking with a shiver of pleasure of their new carpets, their cosy windows, all the ridiculous luxury of Peak House. She still couldn't quite get her head around it. She squeezed Stephen's hand very tightly, and without turning away from flirting with Lilian, he squeezed hers back in a way that showed her he understood; that he would always understand; that he would always be there, hand in hand, side by side, for the good and the bad.

At 12.30, everyone who could manage it stood up, as Cathryn said the grace.

I heard the bells on Christmas Day,
Their old familiar carols play
And wild and sweet
The words repeat
Of peace on earth, goodwill to men!

Suddenly the door opened, letting in a bitter icy draught. Everyone turned to stare. Standing in the doorway, as proud and formidable-looking as ever – possibly more so in her red greatcoat – was Henrietta. For a few moments everyone was silent. Then Lilian's voice rang out.

'Oh, *there* you are.'

She indicated an empty place at the end of the table

that Rosie had thought she was keeping free for Henry, and Rosie dropped Stephen's hand and urged him forward to greet his mother. He extended his arm to take hers, and kissed her gently on the cheek – at which she coloured, which was unlike her – then led her to the top of the table.

'I have,' she said, caressing Apostil's head, 'I have a gift for . . . for my grandchild.'

'You are his gift,' said Stephen gently. 'His grandma.'

And there, gentle reader, we are going to leave them. Eating a wonderful meal – nobody did choke on a turkey bone – in a room full of love and warmth and fellowship, which for my money is just about the best we can get in this world.

Moray will tell a terribly off-colour joke, which Lilian will absolutely love, and Apostil will hit a toy drum someone bought him until they take it away, and Ida Delia will be persuaded to lead the charades (she always was a show-off, Lilian will remark, and refuse to guess), and they will toast their beloved Henry Carr, and the spirit of Célestine, never forgetting that Apostil has two mothers. The weak daylight will soften into early dark, but no one will pay the least bit of attention, and the carers will dance with their elderly clients, even when they pretend they don't want to, and Lilian will wear her paper hat at a jaunty angle and make it look rather chic, whereas Rosie will get a bit overheated and pink, and her hat will stick to her forehead. And Apostil will try and put anything from the crackers into his mouth and have to be rescued from choking about four times, and he will think this is a tremendous game, and crack up laughing each time. And in about ten minutes, Rosie will go to the bathroom and throw up for the fourth time that day, then run downstairs and whisper to Stephen what has just happened, and he will say, 'Just like you did yesterday morning?'

And she will nod, terrified, and Stephen will smile, his paper hat falling off the side of his head in surprise, and say, 'Well I will say one thing about life with you, Rosie Hopkins: there is never a dull moment.'

But that is quite another story.

So hush: let us leave them, draw back above the beautiful house with its lovingly tended gardens; above the valley, with Lipton nestled in it, cosy in its blanket of snow, the lights blinking their Christmas message of hope and fraternity and love; over the gently rolling land, and higher still, across the world, its freezing mountains, its boiling deserts, its great seas, and over all, Polaris, blinking out its message to everyone, in hut and mansion alike: peace on earth, goodwill, goodwill.

Acknowledgements

As you can see from the dedication in this book, this year I lost my wonderful agent and great friend Ali Gunn. We have all been heartbroken; she dug me out of the slush pile many years ago and we had so many wonderful adventures together. So she is still upfront in the acknowledgements, where she belongs. Wholehearted thanks also to Douglas Kean and Sarah McFadden.

Also: Rebecca Saunders, Manpreet Grewal, Thalia Proctor, David Shelley, Ursula Mackenzie, Emma Williams, Charlie King, Jen and the phenomenal sales team, Victoria Gilder, Jo Wickham . . . actually, the whole of Little, Brown is just amazing and I know how unbelievably lucky I am. Thanks also and welcome to Jo Unwin whose unflappability and sensitivity were so helpful at a difficult time. And a huge thanks to Jane Selley and Elizabeth Dobson for their excellent copyediting and proofreading skills.

Karen Murphy MRCS, Christian Aid, for showing me Africa; Deborah Schneider and Mallors; Faustine Reynaud, the board, and of course and for always, Mr B and the wee bees.

Life is sweet with

Jenny
COLGAN

CHRISTMAS TREE COOKIES

This feels a bit of a cheat because you need to buy the moulds. But they do look so lovely on the tree! And of course the smell.

300g plain flour
40g soft butter
100g brown sugar
150g golden syrup
1 tbspn ground ginger
1 tbspn ground cinnamon
1 tspn bicarbonate of soda
Icing – I buy the coloured stuff that comes in the little tubes that you can squeeze into nice whirly shapes, but any will do for decoration.

Preheat oven to 180 degrees. Mix together the butter and sugar, and then add the syrup.

Sift in the dry ingredients and knead together to form first crumbs, then a dough. Refrigerate for half an hour or so – go on Facebook, have some tea.

Roll out the dough under cling film so it doesn't get dry and cracky. Then go nuts with the moulds. Make sure to leave little holes at the top so you can thread them with cotton/ribbon for hanging.

Bake the cookies for 15-20 minutes. Keep an eye on them – they should be lovely golden biscuits. Leave them to cool then let your imagination go wild with the icing!

SALT DOUGH DECORATIONS

Of course, sometimes you want your Christmas tree decorations to last a little longer, which is why we love salt dough decorations for the tree. They are so easy but they last for YEARS. You can't eat them, obviously, which you might see as something of a downside, but this is such a lovely thing to do with children on a chilly December afternoon. Also I like the measurements for this.

100g plain flour
100g salt
100g water

Preheat the oven to 100 degrees. Combine all the ingredients to form a dough. If it's too wet or dry, adjust.

Roll out the dough and cut out shapes – angels, stars, Christmas trees and hearts all work well. Remember to make a hanging hole.

Bake for 3 hours.

When they're dry, the decorations can be painted (gold spray paint is fab), you can stick on glitter or sequins or anything. Thread with gold ribbon, then hang. And if you are a sentimental sort, keep them from year to year so you can remember your three year old's misshapen angel, and have a bit of a wobble every December.

FIGGY PUDDING

Every year at Christmas time somebody says, 'What's figgy pudding?' when we sing the song (even my computer thinks it's called 'foggy pudding') so I am telling you now: it is Christmas pudding except with MORE FIGS and it is yummy and here it is.

Tip: start the day before, but it takes just five minutes the day before and five minutes on the day so FEAR NOT.

75g dried figs
50g raisins
35g sultanas
15g chopped glade cherries (if you like them, which I do. If you
    don't, up the sultanas)
25g chopped cored apple
Brandy
40g plain flour
30g ground almonds
60g brown sugar
1 egg
1/4 tspn mixed spice
1/4 tspn cinnamon
1 clove
40g butter
1/2 lemon squeezed, plus grate the rind in
1 tspn golden syrup
1/2 cup of milk

The day before, combine the figs, raisins, sultanas, cherries and apple and pour in a slosh of brandy (a slosh being the scientific term for a measure of 'how much brandy you like'). Cover with a cloth and leave overnight to soak.

The following day, add the remaining ingredients and mix well. Pour into a greaseproof paper lined pudding basin. Now you can either steam the pudding, which involves bain mairies and boiling water and so on, or you can do the BAD THING I do (complaining letters to the usual address) which is microwave it for 5 minutes and turn it out until it cooks through.

Serve with custard or brandy butter. But, you know. CUSTARD.

GALETTE DES ROIS

Where we live in France, the big thing to eat at Christmas is yule log (coming next) and, after Christmas, *galette des rois* up to the feast of the Ephiphany, or Twelfth Night. There are little ceramic creatures, called *fèves*, or favours, hidden in each cake. They can be angels or religious figures, but these days you can also get Scooby Doo. Whoever finds it is crowned the *Roi* with the gold paper crown that traditionally goes around the outside. Then it is their turn to host the next *galette des rois*. We have found through trial and error it is usually prudent to push the *fève* piece towards the youngest person in the room. If you can't lay your hand on some *fèves*, a coin wrapped in greaseproof paper should have the same cheerful effect in warding off the post-chrimbo blues.

1 roll ready-made puff pastry, unless you are a fantastic pastry nut (I worship you)
1 egg, beaten
2 tbspn jam

100g soft butter
100g caster sugar
100g ground almonds
1 tbspn brandy

Preheat the oven to 190 degrees. Divide the ready-made puff pastry in half, roll out each piece into two circles. Put one of the circles on a baking sheet and spread with the jam.

Whisk the butter and sugar until fluffy. Beat in most of the egg. Stir in the almonds, brandy, and add the *fève*.

Spread the mix on top of the jam, then cover with the second piece of pastry. Seal up with a pinch. You can decorate the top of the *galette* with a fork if you like.

Bake for 25 minutes or until crisp and golden. Serve warm or cold.

YULE LOG

This is called *Büche de Noël* in France, which I like because I like writing letters with dots on them. Swiss roll is what it is *really*.

    50ml double cream
    50g icing sugar
    50g cocoa powder
    1 teaspoon vanilla extract
    6 egg yolks
    125g caster sugar
    5 tbspn cocoa powder
    1 1/2 tspn vanilla extract
    1/8 tspn salt
    6 egg whites
    25g sugar

Preheat the oven to 190 degrees. Line a tin – loaf is fine – with greaseproof paper.

Whip the cream, icing sugar, cocoa powder and vanilla extract until it thickens, then bung in the fridge.

Probably use a mixer for this bit: beat the egg yolks with the caster sugar until thick. Add the second lot of cocoa powder and vanilla extract, and a pinch of salt.

Separately (obviously. Sorry) whip the egg whites to soft peaks. Add the sugar, slowly, until the mixture gets stiffer. Fold the two mixes together and pour into the tin.

Put in oven for 12 to 15 minutes – the cake should 'spring back' when gently prodded.

Dust a clean tea towel with icing sugar.

Run a knife around the edge of the tin, and upend the cake onto the tea towel. Get rid of the baking paper. Carefully, carefully, CAREFULLY, roll the cake up with the tea towel. Start at the shorter edge. Then let it cool for half an hour.

Take the filling out of the fridge. Unroll the cake and spread the filling on it but not right to the edge. Then carefully roll it up again, put on a plate and stick in the fridge (put the edge side down on the plate). You probably want to make icing powder snow before serving. Also if you don't decorate it with holly, it doesn't count.

TURN THE PAGE TO SEE HOW ROSIE'S
ADVENTURES BEGAN

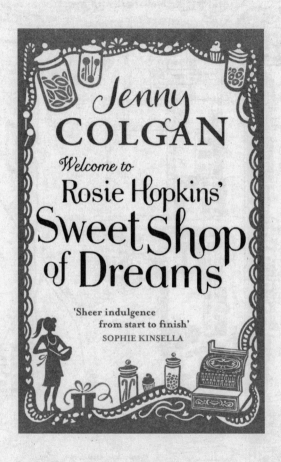

A sweetshop where all your dreams come true –
filled with treats, laughter and love.
Available now

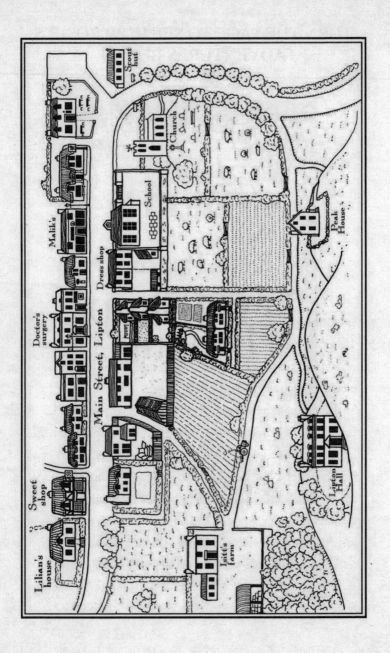

Spout
hut

Church

School

Dress shop

Malik's

Doctor's
surgery

Main Street, Lipton

Sweet
shop

Lilian's
house

Isitt's
farm

Lipton
Hall

Peak
House

Chapter One

Soor Plooms

This is a Scots term that translates as sour plums, but in its original language imitates exactly the contortions of your mouth as soon as you pop one in.

More of an endurance exercise than a treat, this is a hard candy of exquisite, roof-of-the-mouth-stripping bitter intensity; the occasional rush of sweetness comes as a blessed relief. Near-impossible to bite and still maintain an entire set of teeth, they are therefore the ideal purchase for the pocket-money-strapped child as, number one, they last for ever, and number two they are something of a rarefied taste and therefore require less sharing than other sweets.

Downsides include being a choking hazard; their bright green colour which renders them very visible to teachers, and their density – a correctly projected soor ploom can knock out a dog from forty feet.

Rosie put the very peculiar book down. She was in any case sitting near the front of the bus, hopping up every now and again, anxiously; trying to peer through the grimy windows. The little single-decker green-painted bus with ripped, ancient leather seats looked like it should have been retired years ago. Why was the countryside so *dark*? Every time they left a tiny village with a few streetlights, it felt like they hit a great sea of blackness, a vast wall of nothingness surrounding a few scattered remnants of civilisation.

Rosie, a city girl born and bred, wasn't used to it at all. It was sinister up there. How could anyone live amid so much dark? The few people who had joined the bus in Derby, old ladies mostly, and a couple of foreign-speaking young men whom Rosie took to be farm workers, had all got off ages ago. She'd asked the driver, who had an enormous beard, to tell her when they got to Lipton, but he'd grunted at her in a non-committal way, which meant that now she was hopping up and down nervously every time they entered a village, trying to figure out from his head movements whether it was this one or not.

Rosie stared at her reflection in the dark window of the bus. Her dark curly bob was held back with hair clips above a button nose full of freckles. Her large soft-grey eyes were probably her best feature, but now they looked worried, lost and anxious. A sturdy suitcase sat above her in the ancient luggage rack, feeling irrevocably heavy; reminding her that there was no easy route back. People's lives, she thought to herself, were meant to be full of excitement, lightness and freedom. Hers was just baggage. She checked her phone to ring Gerard, but there was no signal.

The bus chuffed and coughed up another endless hill into nothingness. Rosie had thought England was a small country, but she had never ever felt so far away from everything she had known. She glanced anxiously at the driver, hoping he had remembered she was still there.

That last day at work, though. Really, when you thought about it, her mother couldn't have chosen to ring at a better time.

'Where the *hell* is that sodding bedpan? What the *hell* is going on here? What do you think you're doing?'

The young doctor didn't look more than twenty years old, and absolutely terrified to boot. He was covering his terror by being aggressive; Rosie had seen it a million times before. She rushed to his side; every other nurse had disappeared from view and he was trying to help an old lady who appeared to be reacting to the lancing of a particularly unpleasant boil by peeing the bed at the same time. Which would have been fine, but Rosie had only been on the ward ten minutes, and no one had bothered to give her even the most cursory tour – she didn't blame the staff nurses, they were up to their eyeballs, and there were different agency nurses in every day.

So she had tried unobtrusively to change sheets, bring water to those who needed it and take lunch orders, and do the tea round and empty the bedpans and the sharps boxes and generally help as much as she could without getting in anyone's way, even though she'd worked a twelve-hour day in a different hospital across town the day before and was still absolutely exhausted, but was terrified that the agency would take her off their roster if she ever turned a job down.

Meanwhile the very young, rather posh-looking doc was getting positively hosed with pee and pus, which might, Rosie tried not to think, have been funny under different circumstances. As it was, she managed to dart to another elderly patient and grab a large cardboard bedpan, pushing it in front of the doc to catch the remainder like a doubles tennis player.

'God,' said the doctor, rudely.

The old woman, in pain and upset, started to cry. Rosie knew the young doctor's type. Straight out of medical school, he'd have barely met a real patient before. Had spent years in nice lecture theatres, being treated like the crème de la crème by his friends and family for being a student doctor, and now getting his first unpleasant wake-up call in the real world; discovering that much medicine was looking after the old, and the poor, and very little was performing dramatic life-saving operations on fashion models.

'There, there,' said Rosie, sitting on the bed and comforting the old lady, who was a shapeless bulk beneath her humiliatingly open hospital robe. It was a mixed ward, and the young doc hadn't even pulled the curtains properly. Rosie did so now. As she did, she heard the shrill tones of someone she could identify even at this distance as the Grade 2.

'Where's that bloody agency G grade? They turn up, hide

out drinking coffee all day and make twice the wage of every-one else.'

'I'm here,' said Rosie, poking her head out. 'I'll be right with you.'

'Now, please,' said the Grade 2. 'There's a mess in the men's loos you'll need to sort out. I'd plastic up if I were you.'

It had been a long, long day, not helped by getting home three hours after Gerard to find that the breakfast dishes were still on the table, next to the huge pile of post, and he barely turned round from grunting with a mouthful of pepperoni pizza and Grand Theft Auto. Their little flat needed a window open. And, Rosie thought with a sigh, probably the sheets changed. The chances of her changing another pair of sheets today were, frankly, very small indeed.

So dark, Rosie thought, trying to make out shapes behind the streaky glass of the bus window. It never really got that dark in East London, where she'd grown up. The streetlights, and the cars, and the hum of the traffic and the people and the police helicopter . . . Then, when Mum had left for Australia, she'd moved to St Mary's, the hospital in Paddington, where you were never far away from sirens and people shouting, and thronged streets. She thrived on living in the city, had always adored London; its shiny side, and the dark side she stitched up on a regular basis when it came in through Accident and Emergency, or post-surgery. She'd even liked the grotty nurses' lodgings she'd lived in, although buying her own place with Gerard had been . . .

Well, it was grown-up, she supposed. It wasn't quite what she'd expected – she hadn't remembered the meeting where she'd volunteered to do all the housework, but he did earn more money. And the fact that it was so tiny, with no prospect of a move on the horizon.

Still, that was adult life, wasn't it? And she and Gerard were settled now. A bit too settled. But settled. She could, it was true, do without all her girlfriends eyeing her deliberately when that Beyoncé song played. They'd been telling her for ages that if he didn't put a ring on her finger by their second anniversary, he wasn't serious and in it for the long term. She had closed her ears and chosen not to believe them – Gerard was cautious, and safe, and didn't make big decisions lightly, and that was one of the reasons why she liked him.

But still, at the end of that long, long day, when her mother had called, she couldn't deny that she was annoyed, cross, feeling hard done by, backed into a corner and emotionally blackmailed – and a teeny tiny part curious.

Their last night had been sweet and sad all at once.

'It's only six weeks or so,' she'd reminded Gerard.

'Yes, so you say,' he said. 'You'll be round-the-clock caring from now till the end of time. And I shall stay in London and waste away.'

Gerard rarely looked like he was going to waste away. Round of head and tummy, he had a cheery countenance, like he was always on the verge of a laugh or a joke. Or a sulk, but only Rosie got to see those.

Rosie sighed. 'I wish you'd come. Just for a bit. A long weekend?'

'We'll see, we'll see,' said Gerard. He hated any change to his routine.

Rosie looked at him. They'd been together so long now she could barely remember when they first met. He'd been at her very first hospital, when she was just out of a nearly all-female nursing college and dizzy with excitement at having a little money and a job. She'd hardly noticed the small, jolly pharmacist, who turned up occasionally when drugs were late, or rare, or urgent, and always had a quip, although she saw he was kind to the patients. He'd make silly remarks to her and she dismissed them as standard banter, until one night he'd joined them on a work night out and made it clear that he was actually a bit more serious than that.

The other, more experienced nurses had giggled and nudged each other, but Rosie hadn't minded about that. She was young, she'd had some pink wine and she was open to new people, and at the end of the night, when he offered to walk her to her tube stop, then tentatively took her hand, she suddenly felt alive with possibility, excited that someone could be so clear about fancying her. She'd often found that kind of thing confusing before; crushing helplessly on men who were out of her league, ignoring chaps with whom she later realised she might have had a chance.

Rosie often felt that she'd missed a meeting every other girl in the world had had, when they were about fourteen, in which they'd learned how the boyfriend-and-girlfriend thing actually worked. Maybe the PE teacher had taken everyone aside, like she did with the period-and-BO talk, and briefed them all thoroughly. This is how to tell who fancies you. This is how to talk to a guy you like without making a complete idiot of yourself. This is how to politely leave a one-night stand and find your way home. It was all a bit of a mystery to Rosie, and everyone else seemed to find it so easy.

Meeting Gerard at twenty-three seemed like the answer to her prayers – a real, proper boyfriend with a good job. At least it would get her mum off her back for once. And right from the start he'd been keen. She was a bit taken aback to learn he was twenty-eight and still lived with his mother, but hey, everyone knew how expensive London was. And she enjoyed, at least to begin with, having someone to look after; it made her feel grown-up to buy him shirts, and to cook. When, after two years, he suggested they get a place together, she'd been absolutely delighted.

That had been six years ago. They'd bought a tiny grotty flat that they both felt too tired to do up. And since then, nothing. They were, if she was totally honest, in something of a rut, and perhaps a little separation might just . . . She felt disloyal for even thinking it. Even if her best friend Mike was always rolling his eyes. But still. It might just shake them up a little bit.

The bus driver grunted. Rosie jumped up, reaching for her bag, and followed his beard, which he'd nodded in the direction of a tiny pinpoint of light, far away. Rosie realised this must be the village, and that they must be at the top of a big hill. Cripes, where were they, the Alps?

Spring 2016

The second children's book
from Jenny Colgan.

Perfect for bedtime stories
and early readers.

Features Neil
the Puffin from
the Beach Street
Bakery books

'The boat masts jangled louder and louder.
Above their heads, black clouds gathered. Polly shivered,
and then the rain started to fall: plop, plop, plop.'

Polly is waiting for something important to happen.
But waiting is hard. It's even harder when it's raining
and you can't go outside…Can Polly find enough to do
to keep busy ALL day? And what will happen when her
puffin friend, Neil, decides to fly off into the storm?

Also contains recipes, activities and rhymes.

To find out more visit **www.jennycolgan.com**

'A fun, warm-hearted read'
WOMAN & HOME

Can baking mend a broken heart?

Polly Waterford is recovering from a toxic relationship. Unable to afford their flat, she has to move to a quiet seaside resort in Cornwall, where she lives alone. And so Polly takes out her frustrations on her favourite hobby: making bread. With nuts and seeds, olives and chorizo, and with reserves of determination Polly never knew she had, she bakes and bakes and bakes. And people start to hear about it ...

Jenny Colgan's debut novel for young readers!

When Polly discovers an injured puffin, she and her mummy look after him in their cottage by the sea. Slowly, Neil's wing heals and Polly must prepare herself to say goodbye to her new friend. Will she ever see him again?

Keep in touch with
Jenny COLGAN

Chat with Jenny and meet her other readers:

 /JennyColganBooks /@jennycolgan

Check out Jenny's website and sign up
to her newsletter for all the latest book news
plus mouth-watering recipes.

www.jennycolgan.com

LOVE TO READ?

Join **The Little Book Café** for competitions,
sneak peeks and more.

 /TheLittleBookCafe
 /@littlebookcafe

How does an It Girl survive when she loses everything?

Sophie Chesterton is a girl about town, but deep down she suspects that her superficial lifestyle doesn't amount to very much. Her father is desperate for her to make her own way in the world, and when after one shocking evening her life is turned upside down, she suddenly has no choice. Barely scraping by, living in a hovel with four smelly boys, eating baked beans from the can, Sophie is desperate to get her life back. But does a girl really need diamonds to be happy?

A feisty, flirty tale of one woman's quest to cure her disastrous love life

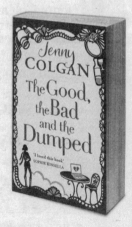

Posy is delighted when Matt proposes, but a few days later disaster strikes: he backs out of the engagement. Crushed and humiliated, Posy wonders why her love life has always ended in disaster. Determined to discover how she got to this point, Posy resolves to get online and track down her exes. Can she learn from past mistakes? And what if she has let Mr Right slip through her fingers on the way?